Maximilian and Carlotta Are Dead

A Novel

Scott R. Larson

BEST WISHES,
PABLO !

Scott

To

Eric and Mañuco

*who taught me everything I know about friendship
and male bonding*

and to

Teresa and Maggie

*who taught me everything I know
about love*

Many thanks to Dayle Moss and Michael Morrow,
who generously offered feedback, improvements,
corrections and encouragement when they were most sorely
needed and appreciated. Also thanks to Stacy Waters
for long ago giving this book a title.

Contents

1
Escaping the Valley

RIGHT AFTER we graduated from high school, Lonnie McKay and I took off in his '65 Chevy and drove down to Mexico.

Well, it wasn't *right* after graduation. First Lonnie had to get out of the hospital. Before he had a Chevy, Lonnie had a Ford Mustang, and on graduation night he drove it up Porterville Highway and sideswiped a station wagon full of Mexicans. That was all she wrote for the Mustang, and it was almost all she wrote for Lonnie. He was drunk as a skunk, of course, and when he woke up, he didn't even remember the accident. He had skipped the graduation ceremony and decided instead he would go out and get totally smashed—in more ways than one.

I heard about it at the dance after they handed out the diplomas. His girlfriend Linda came running into the gym and made her way through the crowd until she found me. Her words made my heart miss a whole beat.

"Lonnie's been in an accident!" From the sound of her voice, I was sure that he was dead. I had already been kind of preparing myself for quite a while that Lonnie was going to get himself killed one day. Our last day in high school seemed as good a day as any.

"Tell me what happened, Linda," I said, trying to stay calm and to act like my father would. "Where is he?"

"Mercy Hospital," she sobbed. Then, after a pause, "Dallas, I'm scared. I think he might have gone and really done it this time."

I put my arm around her and took her out of the gym to the parking lot. It took me a minute to remember where I had parked my VW bug. I was scared shitless, but there was no way that I was going to lose my cool now that Linda needed me. I drove us to the hospital. My mind was racing and I didn't know exactly what to say. Not saying anything was bad because my silence seemed to make Linda crazy.

"This is it," she squealed. "I just know it. He's going to be dead!"

"You don't know that," I said. "Don't go making it any worse than it is. We'll find out how he is when we get to the fucking hospital. And then we'll deal with it."

The truth was that I was feeling pretty guilty because part of me wouldn't have been completely sorry if Lonnie actually died. My black secret was that for most of senior year I couldn't think about anything besides Linda. Part of me hated Lonnie because she was his girl. Being around Lonnie was hard in any case because of all the drinking he did and because of all the crazy things he did. Being around him and Linda together was even harder because I kept wishing that it was me that she was with instead of him.

When we got to the hospital, we found Lonnie laying flat on his back. There were cuts on his face. He was wearing a sheepish grin, like he'd been caught somewhere he shouldn't have been.

"Hi," he said simply. He was like a little boy who knew he was in trouble but who also knew that he was charming enough to get away with it. "I guess I went and did it this time, huh? The cop told me the Mustang's totaled."

"Lonnie, baby," cried Linda as she rushed to his side. "Are you all right?"

At that precise moment I was royally pissed with him for not being dead. But I also knew that if he had been dead it would have been like a part of me had been cut away with a knife. We had known each other our whole lives and, for better or worse, we were part of each other and always would be.

"How you doing, man?" I asked as nonchalantly as I could manage.

With obvious effort, he raised his arm and clasped my palm. "I'm going to be okay, man," he said earnestly, as though his life had reached some sort of turning point.

"You scared the shit out of me!" scolded Linda, her panic now turning to anger. "I don't know what I would have done if you had gotten yourself killed, you son of a bitch."

Lonnie was quiet. That wasn't like him, even if he was in a hospital bed and had just been in an accident. Finally, he looked into Linda's eyes and spoke.

"This is it, babe. I'm not going to drink anymore. I damn near died tonight, and it was all because of booze. I almost threw it all away for a fifth of Jack Daniels. I'm finally going to clean up my act."

It was a bit melodramatic, and I had heard Lonnie say he was quitting drinking before. But this time it seemed different. For one thing, he was laying there in a white nightgown in a hospital. For another, the tone in his voice was dead serious in a way I hadn't heard before. Like he had finally grown up after all those years of fucking up and getting himself into trouble. I wanted to believe that this time was different, but I wanted to believe it all those other times too. Still, this was the first time he had come this close to really dying.

"I know I've been a fuck-up," continued Lonnie, "but it's going to be different from now on. I know what I have to do now. It's been in the back of my mind all along, but I was too fucked up to see it until now."

This was the most serious I had seen Lonnie in a long time. My mind raced as I tried to figure out what he was leading up to. Was he going to get a job? Was he going to propose to Linda? Join the army? I didn't have a clue.

"I'm going to find Tommy Dowd."

That may not have been the last thing I expected to hear him say, but it definitely would have made the top ten. It had been a long time since I had even thought about Tommy Dowd.

"Tommy Dowd?" echoed a totally perplexed Linda. The blank look on her face confirmed that Lonnie's announcement wasn't something that a normal, rational person would be expecting to hear.

"Yeah," said Lonnie, as if he was talking about the most logical thing in the whole world. "He's my friend. He's in trouble. And I haven't done one thing to help him."

The silence seemed awkward to me. Finally, I said, "I didn't know you and he were that close. He's five years older than us."

Still using a serious tone that I hadn't heard very often before, Lonnie said, "Tommy Dowd is the smartest person I have ever known. I learned a shitload of stuff from him. He was different than most people around here. He was on a whole different level than everyone else."

I didn't say anything and tried to make some kind of sense out of what Lonnie was saying. I hadn't even thought about Tommy Dowd in a year. I guess I really hadn't known him all that well. I was surprised when Linda suddenly broke the silence.

"Years ago, when we were kids, Tommy Dowd tied a bunch of candy bars on a bush. He told me that it was a candy bar tree. I totally believed it. For years after that, I really believed that candy bars could grow on trees."

Lonnie and I didn't quite know what to say, so we just kept on sitting there, kind of quiet. Tommy Dowd was a strange one, that was for sure. I guess he was a lot smarter than the other kids we knew, but I never thought he had all that much common sense. He liked to hang out with Mexicans and he could even talk with them. We all had to take Spanish in school, but he was the only white guy I ever knew who actually learned enough of it to talk to a Mexican. I didn't know who his friends were. It didn't seem like he did any normal things that a guy does. He never got drunk or went cruising down Chester Avenue. As far as I know, he never had a girlfriend.

After he graduated from high school, he went to work for a newspaper somewhere up north. Last I heard, he quit that job and took off for Central America. There was something political going on down there, and he was going to write about it and then try to sell his stories to a big newspaper or magazine. But there was some kind of civil war or something and a bunch of people got killed. Tommy disappeared, and nobody ever found out what happened to him. His old man tried going down there, but he didn't find any trace of him. That was a year or so ago, and since there was no more news about him, most people sort of forgot about him. Except Lonnie, I guess.

Lonnie and Tommy hung out together sometimes. Tommy would talk to him about books he'd read or places he wanted to go, and I guess Lonnie liked that this older kid would talk to him like they were friends and make him think about things he didn't usually think about. They were kind of a strange pair, but I guess they had something in common. They both liked to talk about getting out of the San Joaquin Valley and seeing the world. Everyone always figured that Tommy would actually do it. Everyone knew he was smart. I don't think anybody figured that Lonnie would ever leave. It never occurred to me that Lonnie's talk about going to find Tommy Dowd was anything more than that—just talk. It was the kind of thing Lonnie did, especially when he was feeling down. He would talk about getting away and starting over somewhere else.

After a couple days, Lonnie got out of the hospital, and I didn't hear him talk about Tommy Dowd any more. He hung around home for a week and then got a job down at Bob Hanson's garage. Meanwhile, my dad's cousin Walt Newman gave me a job on his farm driving a tractor. I was figuring to save up some money and maybe go to junior college in the fall. I didn't particularly care for going to school, but I didn't really like farm work either. If you ever spent a summer in the San Joaquin Valley, you know it's fucking hot. The first week I got the worst sun burn I ever got on my wrist. I thought I was tanned enough not to burn, but I took my watch off while I was driving the tractor and I got a hell of a sunburn where that watch had been. It was so fucking hot, that when I got to the end of a row, I would put my head and shoulders under the water that was coming out of the irrigation well and get totally drenched. By the time I got to the other end of the row, I would be bone dry again. Pretty fucking hot.

After work I'd go home and eat dinner and watch TV and try to keep cool until it was time for bed. Even with all the windows open and the swamp cooler going, it was damn hot at night. But I was so tired that I almost never had trouble sleeping. I got up at five in the morning and my mom would fix me and my dad a big breakfast. At that hour, the temperature was almost tolerable. But by the time I would get to work at six it was already getting hot again.

On Friday night, Lonnie and I would usually go somewhere and shoot some pool. Sometimes he and Linda and I would go to the drive-in and see a movie. It was always hard for me to go out with the two of them. The truth is that I was jealous as hell, and sometimes late at night I would lay in bed, wide awake and sweating because of the heat, and I'd think about Linda and get really pissed off that I was in love with her and that she was in love with my best friend. The whole situation pretty much sucked.

That's how most of the summer went. Lonnie seemed to forget about his idea of going to find Tommy Dowd. He also seemed to forget about his idea of not drinking any more. He pretty much got drunk every weekend and sometimes even during the week.

Then, part way through the summer, things kind of changed. They held a lottery to see who was going to get drafted and who wasn't.

I couldn't really remember a time when there wasn't a Vietnam War, and I always figured that I would do like my brother and go to school and get a student deferment. 'Course my brother finally got fed up with college and decided to enlist in the Navy. I thought just maybe, if I could go to school another year or two, the fucking war would be over and I could skip the sucker. But Dick Nixon changed all that. He did away with student deferments and he started this lottery. Some bald-headed guy on TV picked out the balls with the numbers on them, and that decided if you were going to 'Nam or if you were going to get off the hook.

If Lonnie and I had been born just a few weeks later than we were, we would have had a whole year after high school before going into the lottery. Of all the guys in our class, it was just Lonnie and me and maybe one or two other ones who got their draft lottery numbers so soon after graduation. That's because we were born in a different year than almost all the other guys in our class. That's what we got for being born in December.

I took a long lunch that day and went home to watch. Mom made me a sandwich and sat there quietly watching with me. Lonnie's birthday came up really quick. He got number 5.

"Damn!" I said. "They're going to get him for sure. He isn't going to like the army one little bit."

My birthday came up about halfway through. I got 181. According to what the reporters on TV were saying, that meant that it could go either way. I might get called up. Then again I might not. The only thing that was certain was uncertainty.

"Fuck this shit!" I said as I walked out the door and went back to work.

That night Lonnie and I went out driving. He brought a bottle of Jack Daniels that he swiped from his stepfather Don, and we got royally fucked up. Lonnie was used to drinking whiskey, but I wasn't. It wasn't long before I was pretty much out of things. When Lonnie wasn't laying rubber, he was cranking up his stereo and treating anyone within earshot to his collection of heavy metal. The next day I barely remembered getting home. Lonnie always scared the shit out of me when he drove, and it was even worse when he was drunk. He always insisted that he actually drove better when he was drunk than when he was sober, and I think it actually might have been true. It certainly couldn't have made him drive any worse. The truth is, Lonnie was basically a good driver, but he always drove way too fast. And he did stupid things. Like when he would go racing down Highway 99 at a hundred miles an hour in the middle of the night and then make a sound with his lips like he was blowing out a match and then suddenly turn off the headlights. That kind of shit scared the crap out of me.

Lonnie was really upset that he got such a low draft number. He did not want to go into the army at all. I wasn't sure that the army wouldn't actually do him some good. The army was supposed to make you more mature and more disciplined. God knows that Lonnie could have used some of that. But in those days, going into the army meant going to 'Nam. And a lot of those boys didn't come back.

This draft business had me really bothered too. But after a few days, I didn't really think about it much anymore. I was too tired from working ten hours a day and from the heat to do too much thinking about much of anything. As for Lonnie, if it was bothering him, he wasn't talking about it. The summer continued to drag on forever, and just when you thought it couldn't get any hotter, it did.

It was getting pretty close to the end of August when all hell broke loose. I was eating a TV dinner in front of the television when Lonnie drove up. I knew that Lonnie was outside the house because I could hear the wheels of his Chevy squealing in the street. As soon as he had gotten out of the hospital, he managed to get someone to loan him the money to buy a Chevrolet Impala to replace the Mustang he totaled on Porterville Highway. He didn't kill the engine. He just sat out there revving it up. He knew that I would hear it and go on out there. I pulled on a tee-shirt and went out. It was almost ten o'clock and time that I should be getting to bed. I was kind of pissed at him for showing up this late when he knew I had to work in the morning.

"Get in," he said grimly, like it was some kind of order.

When he was like that, I always figured it was easiest to just do what he said and find out what was up. As soon as I was in the car, he floored the accelerator and laid rubber on the street in front of my house. I slid down in the seat, knowing that all the neighbors were going to be pissed. He drove us around for several minutes without saying anything.

Finally, I said, "What the fuck's going on? I got to go to work in the morning, you know."

"I'm going to kill that fucking asshole," he announced. "I ain't fucking going to take this shit anymore."

I knew immediately who he was talking about. Lonnie hated his stepfather.

"You think it's time you and Don worked this out?" I asked.

"It's different this time," he said. "That son of a bitch has pushed me too far. I'm going to fucking kill him."

I hadn't seen Lonnie this mad before, and I was getting just a little bit nervous. I figured that I better do something to calm him down.

"Look, man," I said, "it's not worth getting so worked up about. Hell, you're out of high school now. Why don't you get your own place? There's no way you and Don are going to get along together. Why don't you just get the fuck out of there?"

"Hell, I don't want to give the asshole the satisfaction."

It was clear that he wasn't going to be reasonable. At least not for a while. He continued to drive around like a maniac and finally took us up to College Heights. He sped to the edge of the bluff and then jerked the car to a stop just before the edge. He killed the engine.

We sat there in silence for quite a few minutes, watching the lights below. Lonnie pulled out a bottle of Jack Daniels and took a couple of gulps. Finally, in his most dramatic tone, Lonnie made his announcement.

"I'm going to do what I said I was going to do," he said.

Oh, shit, I thought to myself. He's really going to do it. He's going to shoot Don. I was totally caught by surprise when he explained what he was really talking about.

"I'm going down to Central America to find Tommy Dowd."

I had totally forgotten about what he had talked about when he was in the hospital. I figured he had too. I guess I was wrong. Anyway, I was relieved that he had stopped talking about killing Don.

"How are you going to get down there?" I asked, trying to bring a little common sense to a fucking weird conversation.

"Drive," he said, like I'd asked a pretty stupid question.

"Drive?" I asked. "How are you going to drive from here down there?"

"You can drive there," he lectured me. "You go down through Mexico."

"You're just going to drive all the way down through Mexico. Where are you going to stay? What are you going to use for money? How are you going to get by? You speak any Spanish?"

Lonnie acted like I was the one who was crazy.

"Lots of people down there speak English. My cousin Randy has been to Mexico lots of times. He says they all speak English down there."

"Hell," I said. "Half the fucking Mexicans around *here* don't speak English. What makes you think that Mexicans in their own country are going to speak it?"

There was no arguing with him.

"Randy says everything is cheap down there. I won't need much money. I'll sleep in the fucking car."

"This is crazy," I said. It was starting to get through to me that I wasn't dealing with a rational person. "You've never been outside of California before. And now you're going to drive all the way down through Mexico?"

"I owe it to Tommy," he said very seriously. "I should have gone down there before this. I let him down."

We didn't say anything else for a while, and then I said what was on my mind. "This is about the draft, isn't it? You want to get out of the country before they call you up." I was trying to be careful. After all, I was more or less calling him a chicken shit.

"No, it isn't that," he said convincingly. "Hell, when I've done what I've got to do, they can have me. I'll go to 'Nam if I have to. If my Uncle Sam wants me to kill a few gooks, hell, I'll go do it. It's just that I got to find Tommy and bring him back first. Or at least find out what happened to him."

I was finally getting convinced that he really meant it. It was really important for him to find Tommy. I never thought of Lonnie as the type to do something for someone else. Hell, he was always needing someone else to do something for *him*. But for whatever reason, he really felt the need to find his friend. That didn't mean that it wasn't a basically stupid idea and that I wasn't going to do my best to talk him out of it.

"What about Linda?" I asked. This was playing kind of dirty. "What's she going to think when you just take off like that?"

"She'll just have to understand," he said simply.

I finally conceded. "Well, if you're really going to do it, have a good trip." I felt bad about it, but there was a part of me that actually wanted to see him go. Maybe if he took off, he wouldn't want to come back. Maybe he would forget about Linda. Or maybe she would forget about him.

But Lonnie wasn't content with just answering all of my arguments against him going. After a minute or two, he got that sly grin on his face when he knew he was going to tempt me into doing something I knew I really shouldn't do.

"Come with me, Dallas."

"What?" I knew he was crazy. I just hadn't realized that he was fucking insane.

"You're so fucking worried about me, come with me and keep me out of trouble. It'll be great. We'll have a blast!"

Now it was starting to seem like conversations we used to have when we were kids. Making plans that there was no way in hell we were actually going to follow through on.

"Yeah, right," I said. "When are we leaving?"

"Tonight," he said excitedly. "Why not?"

"Tonight? You *are* crazy. I got a job. I have to be at work in the morning."

"You'd rather drive that tractor than go on an adventure south of the border? Hell, we aren't in school any more. We can do what we want now. We're fucking free. If we don't do this now, we never will."

"I'm supposed to be in Bobby Herring's wedding next week." There were just too many reasons why this whole idea of Lonnie's was bad.

"Shit, is that peckerhead really getting married?"

"Yes, he's really getting married. I'm supposed to be one of his groomsmen."

"He's marrying Pam?"

"Yeah, he's marrying Pam. Who else?"

Tommy chuckled evilly. "He knocked her up, didn't he?"

"Well, yeah, but they were going to get married anyway. They just had to do it a little sooner than they planned is all."

"Yeah, how long before you have to get married, Dallas. Then you'll be stuck. Working for a living to support your wife. Before you know it, you'll have kids and your whole life will be over. When will you get a chance to do something like this again?"

"This is crazy," I said. "I'm not even going with anyone. I'm not getting married."

"Hell, that could change in a minute. The point is, this is the time in our lives we have to go for it. If we don't do this now, we never will."

As crazy as Lonnie was, when it came down to it, he was actually right about this. What was the point of being 18 if you were just going to drive a tractor for ten hours a day? Lonnie passed me the bottle of Jack Daniels. I took a swig. It burned my throat.

"Okay, you win, asshole. Let's do it."

Lonnie dropped me off at my house. I threw some clothes and my razor and a toothbrush into my backpack, got together what cash I had and grabbed my sleeping bag. My parents were asleep. I left them a note telling them that I was going to be gone for a while. I asked them to apologize to Walt for me. I knew Walt was going to be pissed. So was my dad. Just as well I wasn't going to be around to see it.

About an hour later, Lonnie came back. He was as high as a kite.

"Look what I got," he said, like a little kid, as I got in the car. He pulled out a wad of money. "This should get us by for a little while."

"Where the fuck did you get that?" I asked.

"I borrowed it from Don. I figure he owes it to me. I'll pay him back when we get back. Look what else I borrowed from him."

Lonnie opened the glove compartment. Mixed up with a bunch of papers and Kleenex and two half-full packs of Kool cigarettes was a Smith & Wesson .44 Magnum.

"Shit, man, what do you want that for?"

"We're going to be going through some pretty rough country," he explained matter of factly. "We might need it."

I didn't have an entirely good feeling about the gun. In fact, I didn't have an entirely good feeling about the whole damn thing. But that was actually the point. Doing something I didn't feel entirely good about. Lonnie cranked up his stereo and put his foot to the accelerator and in the middle of the night we headed south down Highway 99.

2
A Night in the Canyon

AS LONNIE'S Impala strained its engine climbing the Ridge Route toward Tejon Pass, I turned to look back at the lights on the San Joaquin Valley floor. When it came down to it, I hated the valley. I always had a feeling of escape when I drove up out of it. Even hell isn't as hot as the San Joaquin Valley in the summer. And it's flat. It has to be the most boring place on the face of the earth. As we got higher into the mountains, things felt different. We were headed to places that weren't boring and hot. We were headed to places that people had actually heard of. We were less than two hours from Los Angeles. I had only been there a few times, and that was only straight to my uncle Jack's and back with my parents. Now it was just me and Lonnie heading down there, and anything was possible.

We drove through the night without talking too much. Mostly we listened to the radio. Our favorite Bakersfield station crapped out on us around Tejon Pass. Lonnie fiddled around with the dial. He found an L.A. station that was playing The Who, and he left it there. I thought about how pissed my parents were going to be when they found me gone. And how pissed Walt was going to be when I didn't show up for work. It was easier to think about L.A. and Mexico. Before we knew it, we saw the lights of the San Fernando Valley.

"You hungry?" Lonnie asked.

"Yeah," I said.

Lonnie pulled off the freeway and stopped at a Denny's. The place was pretty much empty except for a couple of truckers.

We walked in like we owned the place and sat down in a booth that had a nice view of the Impala. An old waitress who looked like she had the most boring job in the whole world wandered over.

"Coffee?"

"Double bourbon," shot back Lonnie without a moment's reflection.

"Bar's closed, fellas," she informed us.

"Steak and eggs and black coffee," said Lonnie.

"I'll have the same," I said.

Lonnie immediately jumped up and announced, "I got to make a phone call."

"Who you gonna call?" I wanted to know.

"Linda," he said. "I gotta get some info from her."

"It's kinda early to be calling her, don't you think?" I said, looking at my watch.

"I need to talk to her," he said, and that pretty much settled the issue. The waitress brought our coffees, and I took a sip. I never thought I liked coffee, but lately Lonnie had started me drinking it in the morning. As I held the hot cup in my hand, I figured that one word from Linda would end this whole thing, and our big adventure would be over before it began. She would have him heading back home, and I would have to explain to Walt why I was late for work.

Lonnie cradled the receiver on his shoulder as he leaned against the wall next to the men's restroom. I could hear him talking. He could turn downright disgusting when he talked to Linda on the phone. His voice would change, sort of like a parent talking to a sick child. "Hi, babe. Did I wake you, babe? ... I'm sorry, babe.... Dallas and I are in L.A. We're heading down to look for Tommy. I need Michael's address... Hey, babe. Don't worry, babe... It'll be okay. I love you, babe."

I tried to ignore the conversation and took another gulp of coffee, turning my head to admire the Impala. After a while he came back to the booth.

"She really misses me," he said. I thought to myself, this is it.

Lonnie continued. "We can't waste a lot of time on this trip. We got to find Tommy and head right back." Lonnie took a swig of his coffee. "She's a good woman. A good woman." So we weren't turning around just yet.

"I got her brother Michael's address down in L.A. We can crash there for a night or two. I need to talk to him. He and Tommy were good friends."

The waitress brought our steak and eggs. It was a great breakfast. I was starving. I got more excited about the whole trip because I was finally starting to believe that we were actually going to do it. Up until this point, I half figured that Lonnie would turn around before we got past L.A.

We saw the first traces of daylight as we got to the Santa Monica Mountains. Lonnie said, "It's too early to go to Michael's. What do you want to do?"

Without a moment's hesitation, I said "Let's go somewhere where we can see the ocean."

"All right," said Lonnie.

He then proceeded to get us lost. After several wrong turns we found ourselves heading west on the Santa Monica Freeway. When we got to the Pacific Coast Highway, we decided to head north toward Zuma Beach and Malibu. As we came around a turn, we saw the sun rising behind the hills and reflecting against the ocean. Lonnie pulled over into a turnout. We sat there watching the sunrise and how the color of the ocean changed. Lonnie pulled out a pack of cigarettes, and we lit up.

"Sure is pretty," Lonnie said, as he took a drag.

"Yeah," I said, in total agreement.

"I wish Linda was here to see this."

It always made me feel like a piece of shit when he talked about Linda like that. It made me feel guilty. Being in love with your best friend's girl is fucking hell.

I would have been happy to sit there for hours watching the sun come up and see the color of the ocean change as it got lighter. But Lonnie could never sit still for very long. Pretty soon he finished his cigarette and crushed it in the ashtray. "Let's book," he said as he spun out in reverse and pulled out onto the road, making me wonder for a second if we were going over the edge of the bluff.

Lonnie headed north like he knew where he was going. I kept quiet, waiting to see where he was taking us. Because the ocean was on our left, I knew we were heading up the coast and leaving L.A. When he didn't say anything for a long time, I finally spoke up.

"So, have you decided to go to San Francisco?"

"Huh?"

It was like he had been in a trance. I honestly don't know if he knew which way he was heading or just didn't care.

"I just thought as long as we were here, we should see some of the coast. I never been on this road before."

And so he kept on going. We were nearly at Oxnard before he finally turned around and headed back south. I still don't know if he really meant to do that or if he just kept going because he didn't want to admit that he didn't know where he was. Anyway, I actually enjoyed the drive. I had never been on that road either.

We stayed on Pacific Coast Highway until we were nearly in Santa Monica. Lonnie saw a left turn and took it. Darned if it didn't turn out to be Sunset Boulevard. That was a name that was famous. I think there was even a movie called that.

The road snaked around in the hills, and somehow we managed to get off on some side street and then we really didn't know where we were. Lonnie drove around pretty aimlessly for a while, sometimes doubling back down a street where we had already been. We seemed to be getting higher and higher into the hills. The houses were really nice. Some of them had really great views. I had thought that there were some nice houses back home, including some with big yards and swimming pools. But nobody had houses like these. These people really had it made. And best of all, it wasn't a hundred fucking degrees in the shade.

Lonnie pulled over and parked one house down from where we saw a guy about our age playing basketball in the driveway. He had his shirt off and he had a nice even tan all over his body. Lonnie pulled out a cigarette and lit up, as he watched the guy do lay-ups. I knew what Lonnie was thinking. This guy didn't have tan lines on his upper arms like me and most of the guys I knew who worked on a farm. He had gotten his tan on the beach. Even though he was playing by himself, he was working hard at it, like someone else was playing against him.

"Fucking candy ass," said Lonnie with contempt. "I bet he hasn't had anything to do all summer except lay on the beach and go to parties."

Lonnie didn't hear me snicker. I thought Lonnie had it pretty easy in the garage where he worked. He wouldn't have lasted one day out on the farm. But there was no way I would tell him that. I kept watching the guy play basketball in his driveway, driving for lay-ups on top of the garage door. Even though it was still morning and the air was cool, he had managed to work up a sweat. Out of nowhere I heard a girl's voice. The gate to the backyard opened, and I heard her call, "Kevin?"

I sat up and looked closer. First I saw the arm that was pushing the gate open. Then I saw her. She was as tanned as Kevin, but her white shorts and top made her look even darker. I couldn't believe how good she looked.

"Hey, not bad," said Lonnie appreciatively.

"Hey! You're practically married, remember?" I said. The only thing that pissed me off more than the fact that Lonnie was Linda's boyfriend was the fact that he could so easily forget about her.

"That doesn't mean I'm dead," he said in self-defense as he ogled the lovely creature before us.

Kevin took a break from his game long enough to talk to her a few minutes while he balanced the basketball on his hip. From the way they were talking, I figured that she was his sister.

"I'm going to talk to her," I announced.

Lonnie was skeptical. "What are you going to say to her?"

"I'm going to get directions from her."

I got out of the car and walked over to them. They both looked at me with suspicion.

"Hi," I said. "Can you tell me how to get to Benedict Canyon?"

Kevin looked at me with distaste. He turned his head and gave Lonnie's car the same look.

She, on the other hand, seemed to be trying not to laugh. "You're in Brentwood," she said. "Benedict Canyon is way over there." She pointed off in the distance with her lovely arm.

"You aren't even close to Benedict Canyon," said Kevin uneasily. "Follow that street down the hill and cross the freeway. It turns into Wilshire. Follow that until you make a left on Rodeo Drive."

"How far is it to Ro-day-oh?" I asked.

"Kevin, they're totally lost," she said. "Maybe one of us should go with them to show them how to get there."

Kevin looked at Lonnie's car with alarm. "Are you crazy? We don't even know them. They'll find it on their own just fine."

I ignored Kevin and just talked to the girl. "If you showed us how to get there, we'd bring you right back. My friend and I aren't from around here. We've never been to Benedict Canyon before."

Kevin was quickly losing patience. "She's not going with you, okay? I told you how to get there. Now just go."

I totally ignored Kevin and continued to address the girl. "I'd really like it if you could show us how to get there."

"Well, okay," she said, "but you have to promise to bring me right back."

Kevin completely lost his patience. "Kathy, no way are you going with them. You don't even know them."

"It'll be okay, Kevin. Really," I said, leading Kathy toward Lonnie's car. "We'll have her back in two shakes. We just need her to show us the way to Benedict Canyon."

Kevin dropped his basketball and started toward me. His lip curled like an animal's.

"She's not going with you."

He stepped close enough for me to smell the sweat on his body. I put my hand against his shoulder to stop him from walking into me. As soon as I touched him, I could feel the tension in his body, and I could tell how really pissed he was. He slapped my hand down. It was then that I realized that we were actually going to have a fight. I took a breath and braced myself for the first blow. Kevin shifted the weight of his body, and I sensed that he was about to make a move against me. Suddenly, however, I could see him hold back. I glanced to my side and saw Lonnie there.

"Get in the car, man. We're getting out of here," he said. And for once I was glad to have that asshole around.

Kathy stood by the car. I opened the passenger door and motioned for her to get in. I don't know why I did that because I didn't think there was any chance she would actually do it. To my amazement, however, she slid into the car. I jumped in and shut the door. Lonnie slipped into the driver's seat and started the engine. Kevin's face twisted in disbelief. He watched simply as Lonnie laid rubber on the street and sped down the hill.

As Lonnie leaned into each curve of the street for dramatic effect, the force pushed Kathy's body against mine. I was still having trouble believing that she had gotten into the car.

"Your brother's pretty pissed," I said.

"He'll get over it." She then continued to bite her lip.

"So how the hell do we get to Benedict Canyon?" asked Lonnie, being the practical one for once. He didn't seem particularly thrilled that Kathy had gotten in the car.

Kathy directed him to Wilshire Boulevard and then to the left turn on Rodeo Drive that we needed to take.

"So why are you going to Benedict," she asked. "Are you going to see the Tate house?"

"Who the fuck are the Tates?" Lonnie wanted to know. "We're going to see a guy we know named Michael."

"Oh," she said. "I just thought, since you are obviously not from around here, you were going to see where the murders happened. For a while, after it happened, a lot of people were going up there to gawk."

That's when it hit me what she was talking about. Up to then I hadn't realized that the neighborhood where Michael lived was the same one where Charles Manson killed all those people a couple of years before. An actress named Sharon Tate was butchered in her house along with several other people. At the time it happened, it was huge news, but it seemed like something that happened a million miles away. Now it dawned on me that it happened a lot closer to me than I realized. And now we were actually going to be somewhere close to it. It made me feel kind of creepy.

Lonnie, on the other hand, didn't seem too bothered by the coincidence. He simply reached into the pocket of his jeans, pulled out Michael's address, and gave it to Kathy.

"Here," he said. "This is where we're going."

With no trouble she was able to get us to the road that led us up the canyon where Michael lived.

It was around lunch time when we pulled into Michael's driveway. His house wasn't big, but it looked really cool to us. One side had a view down a gulley. Lonnie walked up to the door and knocked. It opened, and there was Michael. I hadn't seen him in years. I don't think I would have known it was him if I had passed him on the street. He was a lot thinner than I remembered, and his hair was longer. His face was rougher too, like he had had a skin problem.

I watched Kathy out of the corner of my eye while Lonnie and Michael talked. I wondered what was going through her mind. Pretty soon Lonnie walked back to the car and leaned through the window. "Get your stuff, man. We're crashing here for a while."

I pulled the keys out of the ignition and pushed open the car door. Kathy didn't move.

"If you want to go home," I told her, "just say so and we can take you back anytime."

"I don't want to go home," she said.

I got my backpack out of the trunk and held the car door open until she got out. We walked into Michael's house. He had all kinds of posters on the walls of his living room like I'd never seen before, including one with Mickey Mouse, Donald Duck, and Goofy all smoking dope. I smelled incense burning. I thought it was the neatest place I had ever been in. Kathy stood in the doorway. She was fucking beautiful. I couldn't believe how good this trip was turning out.

Lonnie came out of another room. He held up his hand and I knew instinctively to throw him the car keys. "There's going to be a party here tonight, and we're invited. Michael says that people from Hollywood will be coming." Lonnie was talking like he hung out with people from Hollywood all the time.

Michael appeared right after Lonnie. He put his arm around me and said, "Hello, Dallas. It's been a long time. How are you? I wish I could stop and chat, but I have to get things ready for the party tonight. We'll talk later." And with that he disappeared into another part of the house.

Lonnie followed Michael around, talking to him as he cleaned up and fixed appetizers. I asked Kathy if she wanted to go for a walk, and she said yes. We walked down the canyon road a ways.

"This feels nice," I said as I looked up at the sun. "It's probably over a hundred degrees at home."

22

"Where are you from?" she asked.

"The valley."

"San Fernando?"

"No, the San Joaquin Valley."

"You mean like up around Bakersfield? Sounds pretty boring to me."

"Yeah, I guess it is. This is a lot nicer. What do you do for fun around here?"

"I don't know. Go to the beach. Go shopping. Go to movies. What kind of a name is Dallas?"

"It was my uncle's name. He got killed in Korea. Why? Don't you like it?"

"It's just that I never knew anyone named Dallas before."

"You got a boyfriend?"

"There's this guy I'm dating, but we're just friends really."

"I think you're the prettiest girl I've seen in my whole life."

Hearing that brought a smile to her face. I leaned over to kiss her, but she pulled away.

"No, I shouldn't..."

I was confused. Why had she gotten in the car if she didn't like me? Maybe it was Lonnie she really liked. Women. Who could figure them out? We walked back to Michael's house. I glanced over at Lonnie's Chevy and noticed that the skinniest Mexican kid I had ever seen was sticking his head in the driver's window.

"Something I can do for you?" I asked him loud enough to give him a start.

The kid pulled his head out of the window. He was wearing blue jeans and a white tee-shirt and looked to be about 14. His brown face flashed a big white toothy smile. "Nice car," he said. "Yours?"

"It's my friend's," I said. "He might not appreciate you poking your head in there like that."

He didn't seem the least bit intimidated. "You visiting Michael?" he asked.

"Yeah," I said. "You know Michael?"

"I work for him. Is this a '65?"

"Yeah," I said. "What do you do for Michael?"

"Stuff around the house. And I do his yard. I'm helping out with the party. How's she run? Can we go for a ride?"

"Lonnie's got the keys," I said. "He's inside. What's your name?"

"Antonio," he replied. "Where you from?"

"The San Joaquin Valley."

"Oh yeah, I have cousins up there. It's pretty nice up there, isn't it?"

"Right now it's hot as hell up there. I think it's better here."

"So what are you doing down here?"

This kid sure asked a lot of questions. "We're visiting. What does it look like we're doing?"

"Ask your friend for the keys. Let's go for a ride."

"I don't think so," I said. "I got stuff to do."

"Okay, maybe later," he said, cheerful and undaunted as ever. With that he wandered off around the back of the house.

Kathy and I went in the house and killed the time as best we could. We spent a lot of time reading Michael's magazines. He sure had a lot of them. He had *Time* and *The New Yorker* and several I hadn't heard of before.

The party didn't get started until around eight o'clock. Michael had lots of booze—whiskey, gin, vodka, and tequila—and he told Lonnie and me to help ourselves to whatever we wanted. This was the first time someone had openly offered me liquor like I was an adult. Lonnie and I started doing shots of Wild Turkey. People kept arriving, and before we knew it, the house had gotten pretty full. Michael sure knew a lot of people. They all seemed really neat too. They were older than us, but they didn't treat us any different for it. When Lonnie said people from Hollywood were coming, I thought maybe I would see someone I knew from TV or movies. But I didn't. However, some of the people worked for studios and knew people that were famous. I figured that was about as close as I was going to get anyway.

There was a lot of drinking going on as well as a lot of dope smoking. Lonnie was doing both rather excessively. I stuck to alcohol myself. Kathy was drinking some fizzy white wine. I kept filling her glass, hoping that it would put her in the most agreeable mood possible. It wasn't too long before I was feeling pretty silly. Since Kathy and I didn't really know anyone else except for Lonnie and Michael, we pretty much kept to ourselves. We drank and we danced and we talked. She seemed to be having a good time. As the evening wore on, things got noisier and noisier and it was harder for us to hear each other. Not that it much mattered. We were both pretty much laughing at anything by that point. I couldn't remember when I had had such a good time before.

Lonnie seemed to be having an even better time. He was laughing at the top of his lungs almost constantly. He danced with just about every woman there, and in between dances he and Michael would sneak off to another room like they had some secret they were sharing. After a while, they both seemed to have disappeared completely. Kathy seemed a bit worried and wanted to go find Lonnie. I said okay, and we started down a hallway. All of a sudden I saw a camera sitting on a bookshelf.

"Hey, look at this," I said as I grabbed it. "This looks like a really nice one. I've been wanting a nice camera for a long time."

"Cool," said Kathy. "Take my picture."

"Let me see if I can figure it out," I said. "Wow, it's got a flash and everything!"

"Is it one of those where you get to see the picture right away?" Kathy asked.

"'Fraid not. We'll have to take the film to get it developed."

25

"A lot of good that does us," she complained. "We won't be around long enough to see it."

"Let me take some of you anyway."

"Dallas, that isn't even your camera or your film. Should you be doing that?"

"I don't think Michael will mind. Let's go in here where we can have some privacy."

I led her into a bedroom. I wasn't sure if I convinced her that it was a good idea, but she went anyway. I closed the door and started shooting her.

"You really act like you know what you're doing with that thing," she said. "Are you into photography?"

"I always wanted to be. I just never had a decent camera. This one seems pretty nice."

As I kept clicking the shutter, an interesting thing began to happen. Kathy laid down on the bed and began striking some pretty interesting poses.

"You really act like you know what you're doing," I said. "Are you sure you haven't done professional modeling before?"

She laughed. "I wish. I'm way too ugly to be a model."

"No you're not," I said with total honesty. "You look incredible."

I don't know if it was the alcohol or my flattery or what. But she gave me a look that seemed to say that she wasn't going to fight it anymore. I put down the camera and laid down on the bed next to her.

"You really think so?" she asked.

"I really think so," I said. With that I put my mouth on hers. Her hand worked its way up and down my body and wound up on my crotch. God, I thought to myself. This is really going to happen!

I unbuttoned her blouse while she pulled off my shirt. As we both got more excited, I fumbled madly with the clasp on her

26

bra. She tugged roughly at my zipper. Before I knew it, we were both buck naked. I couldn't believe my luck.

And then the bedroom door burst open.

I couldn't fucking believe it. I glanced over and saw Lonnie standing there. He was the last person I expected to see at that point. I couldn't figure out why he didn't excuse himself and close the door. One of the few absolute rules that were understood between us was that nothing takes precedence over being alone with a woman. Especially when one of us was clearly getting lucky. Of course, Lonnie had up to this point been the main beneficiary of this unwritten rule, but I always reasonably assumed that its benefits extended to me as well.

"Close the door, asshole," I gasped.

"Get dressed," Lonnie said grimly. "We're getting out of here."

Now I *really* couldn't fucking believe it. I was there on the bed with the most beautiful woman I had ever met and Lonnie was standing there telling me to stop everything and just leave.

"Are you out of your fucking mind?" I demanded.

"I mean it, Dallas," he barked. "This is no joke."

The tone of his voice told me that something was terribly wrong. It also told me that, as pissed as I was, I had better do as he said. I sat up and got dressed. Kathy pulled the bedspread around her and curled into a ball. She didn't say a word. I had absolutely no idea of what must have been going through her mind.

"Better get dressed, Kathy," I said quietly.

She didn't make a move.

Lonnie shouted at me. "We can't wait for her! Get your fucking ass in gear!"

"I'll be back," I said as I pulled on my boots and stood up. For some reason I grabbed the camera as I walked out of the room.

"No, you won't," Lonnie corrected me as I followed him through the crowd in the living and out the front door.

"What the fuck is going on?" I demanded to know.

"I'll explain on the road," he said. "Get in the car."

Antonio was sitting on the hood of the Chevy. I knew that wasn't going to go over well.

"Get your ass off the car, you little prick!" yelled Lonnie.

Antonio obediently leapt to the ground. "We going for a ride now, guys?"

"You're not going anywhere, piss-for-brains," said Lonnie as he slid into the driver's seat and turned the engine over.

I expected Antonio to take a step back, but instead he made a move so fast that I didn't see it coming. In a split second he opened the car door and slipped into the back seat. "Where we going, guys?"

Lonnie turned around and yelled, "I mean it, you little prick! Get out of the car!"

"We might not be coming back," I tried to explain to him more reasonably. "We might not be able to bring you back here."

"That's okay," said Antonio undeterred. "I need to get away from here anyway."

"Forget it," I said. "What about your parents? Shouldn't you be at home anyway?"

"My mom's in Mexico. I don't know where my dad is."

Lonnie was rapidly losing patience. "Get in the car, Dallas. If the little prick wants to go with us, that's his problem. He'll have to find his own ride home."

I got in the car, and Lonnie laid his customary stretch of rubber on the driveway as he took off down the canyon road.

"This is great!" exclaimed Antonio. "What a cool car!"

I kept waiting for Lonnie to explain why we had to leave so suddenly, but for now he was intent on his driving and not saying a word. He promptly got us lost in the canyons. I could tell that he had no idea where he was, but I didn't say a word. Finally, he asked, "Kid, how do I get to the freeway from here?"

Antonio cheerfully guided him to the San Diego Freeway. Soon we were among the army of headlights heading south.

After about a half-hour, I asked, "So are you going to tell me what this is all about?"

Lonnie paused for dramatic effect. "I fuckin' killed Michael," he said.

3
Crashing with Steve

"SHIT," I said.

"I fuckin' killed him, man. I fuckin' killed him."

Lonnie had a look on his face like he was going crazy.

"What happened, man?" I asked. "You're joking, right?"

"I fuckin' killed him," Lonnie repeated.

"Yeah, I got that part." I was starting to get impatient with him. "Tell me what happened for Christ's sake."

"He touched me," said Lonnie defensively.

"You killed Michael because he touched you?"

"He didn't just touch me. He... he felt me up."

Lonnie was clearly uncomfortable.

"I don't understand," I said unhelpfully but truthfully.

"I never knew it," said Lonnie shaking his head. "Michael's queer. He likes guys. He wanted to... do it... with me."

"Are you sure?"

I had never known anyone who was homosexual before. I had heard gossip about one of the teachers in grade school who had to move to another town. But queers were always something to joke about. It had never occurred to me that someone I knew might actually be one. Certainly not Michael. "It was probably a misunderstanding. Tell me exactly what happened."

"He and I were getting high. We were having a great time. We were in his bedroom. He put his hand on my leg. I didn't think anything about it. I thought he was just being friendly. I mean, he was being friendly. But I didn't think he was being that kind of friendly. Hell, you know what I mean. I told him about going down to Central America to find Tommy. He got in a real strange mood when I mentioned Tommy's name. He thought it was great that I wanted to find him. Then he took a shot of bourbon and told me that when we were kids he had always liked me. I told him that I had liked him too. Hell, but I didn't mean it that way. Anyway, he got, well, kind of sad and started running his hand up and down my leg. I thought it was kind of strange, but I figured, hell, he was drunk. I was drunk. You get kind of carried away sometimes when you're drunk. You know? Then he put his hand on my crotch, and I thought, okay, this is a little too weird for me. Before I could say anything, he leans over and, real sad like, says, 'Lonnie, do you want to spend the night with me tonight?' Then he kissed me! Right on the lips!"

I felt a shiver. Knowing Lonnie, I was aware that he had to be embarrassed as hell to be talking about this. Even to me. (He had pretty much forgotten about Antonio by this point.) But he seemed to need to talk about it.

"What did you do?" I asked, full of morbid curiosity.

"I guess I panicked. He had a statue thing on his night table. I grabbed it and clobbered him with it. He fell onto the floor, and he wasn't moving. His head was covered in blood, man."

I digested this information for a moment. "So how do you know you actually killed him? Maybe you just knocked him out."

"I hit him hard, man. I really clobbered him."

"Yeah, but how do you know he's dead? Did you check his pulse or anything?"

"Hell, no. I wasn't about to stick around. He wasn't moving and his head was all bloody. I just had to get out of there. The last thing I need is to be talking to the police. Hell. For all I know Don reported this car stolen. His name's on the registration. And the money. And the gun. No, I'm not talking to no cops. The sooner we get to Mexico, the better."

"We going to Mexico?" The question came from the back seat.

"Shit!" said Lonnie. "I forgot about you, peckerhead. The next exit that comes up, you're getting out."

"Hey, man," said Antonio. "I need to go back to Mexico anyway. I need to see my mama. She's in Hermosillo."

"You been listening to anything I been saying?" shouted Lonnie. "We may have the law after us already. The last thing we need is some kid tagging along. Hell, they'd probably toss in a kidnapping charge on top of everything else."

"There must be someone who's going to be missing you," I said.

"No. Just Michael. And it sounds like your friend killed him."

"Do you live with Michael?" I asked.

"Sometimes. Sometimes I live other places. Sometimes I live downtown."

I got a weird feeling about Antonio.

"Antonio, did Michael ever make you do... stuff?"

"Michael was my friend," said Antonio. "We helped each other out. He gave me money, and I did things for him."

"Are you queer, Antonio?" Lonnie demanded to know.

"*Yo soy un hombre*," said Antonio somewhat defensively. "But sometimes a man has to do certain things to get by."

"That does it," said Lonnie. "I'm not having some pervert Mexican kid in this car."

"You're going to need someone to help you find your way through Mexico," said Antonio reasonably. "You're going to need someone who speaks Spanish."

"He's got a point there," I said. I had been worried about the language problem for some time.

"Okay," Lonnie conceded. "But if he lays a finger on me, I'll bash his head in too."

"Don't worry, *gringo*," said Antonio. "I'm not interested in your ugly body."

We drove on down Interstate 5 in silence for a while. Finally, I was the one to break the silence.

"Say, Lon," I said. "Michael and Tommy were awfully good friends. You don't think that Tommy..."

"I knew Tommy Dowd," said Lonnie, "and he wasn't no queer. That's all there is to it."

We didn't talk anymore for a long time after that.

When we started getting close to San Diego, Lonnie pulled off the freeway and parked the car. "Man, I got to get some sleep," he said.

I was feeling pretty out of it myself. The alcohol and two nights without sleep were taking their toll.

"You want me to drive for a while?" volunteered Antonio.

"Forget it, peckerhead," Lonnie shot back. "You ain't driving this car. Period."

I started to doze off, sitting there in the passenger seat. Lonnie looked like he was about to nod off, but he kept wanting to talk.

"Shit, man," he said. "I can't even call her now. I can't even call Linda. I killed her brother. She'll never forgive me for this one. I really fucked up. I really fucked up this time."

Guiltily, I thought maybe now I would have a chance with Linda. It was an awful thing to think. Michael probably wasn't even dead. Even if he was, I didn't want to take Lonnie's girl away from him because Michael was dead. But, boy, if he was dead, she would be needing someone to comfort her, probably for a long time. Shit. Got to get thoughts like that out of my head. Besides, maybe I was in love with Kathy now. She sure was pretty. I'd like to go back and find her again. But, hell, she definitely had to be pissed about us leaving her at Michael's house like that. That one was probably a lost cause. I wonder what she told the police, assuming that the police were called after someone found Michael. Did we tell her our last names? What else did she know about us? Right about then I was figuring that I really wasn't cut out to be an outlaw. There was a lot of shit going through my head. But before long I was out like a light.

The next thing I knew, something woke me up. I looked around and tried to remember where I was. Then I saw the cop. He was staring at me through the car window. He was tapping on the glass.

"Fuck!" I sat up straight. I looked over at Lonnie. He was fast asleep.

"You boys can't sleep here," said the cop gruffly. "You're going to have to move along."

"Yes, sir," I said. "No problem."

I started pushing on Lonnie's shoulder.

"Leave me the fuck alone, asshole," he mumbled.

"Time to go, Lon," I said as I kept pushing. I was trying to sound calm, like we weren't on the run from a crime or something.

"Get your fucking hands off me..." His next epithet was cut short when he saw the cop.

"Yeah, we were just leaving," explained Lonnie as he turned over the engine. We were back on the freeway in short order.

"That was fucking close," said Lonnie. "We're not fucking stopping again until we're in fucking Mexico."

Meeting that cop had given us a shot of adrenaline, but we were still dead tired. Not only were Lonnie and I still short on sleep, but we were both still a bit drunk or hung over or both. Even

Lonnie, who normally never seemed to get tired, admitted that he had to get some more sleep.

"We need to find a place where we can get some shuteye and not get hassled," said Lonnie. Do we know anyone who lives in San Diego? Someone we can trust?"

With effort, I forced my increasingly sore head to think. Then it came to me. "Steve Barton," I said. "He's going to San Diego State. He's already moved down and got an apartment."

"Cool," said Lonnie. "Where the fuck is it?"

I went back to forcing my head to think. Obviously, he wouldn't be in the phone book. There was no way we were going to find him unless we called someone back home to get his address or phone number. I said as much to Lonnie. He looked grim. He knew what I was getting at.

"I can't call Linda," he said painfully. "There is no way I can talk to her after what I did to her brother. I wouldn't be able to keep it together, man. I can't do it. She'd know right away that something was wrong, and she would get it out of me. I can't do it, man."

We sat in silence for a few minutes. Something worked its way out of my gut and up into my mouth. I was actually afraid of how it would sound when it came out as words. "I could call her," I said. "I could say you were busy, and I could ask her to find out Steve's phone number. I wouldn't tip her off that anything was wrong. I didn't see what happened to Michael. I don't think I even believe he's dead. She wouldn't hear anything wrong in my voice."

"Yeah, but she knows we were going to see Michael," responded Lonnie, being infuriatingly logical for once in his life. "She's going to ask you how he is and how we got on at his house. How are you going to handle that? Hell, if he's dead, she probably already knows, and she knows that I killed him. If you told her where we are, she'd probably go straight to the police."

I hoped Lonnie was just talking crazy, but I had to admit that he had a point. The problem was that we just didn't know how much trouble we were in. I did some more thinking.

35

"Okay. This is what I'll do," I said finally. "When it gets later, I'll call Chuck Simms. I'll tell him to call Steve's mother and get his phone number or address and then wait for me to call him back. He won't tell Steve's mom or anybody else that it was me who wanted the info if I tell him not to."

Lonnie was okay with that plan. So we found a place by the beach where we could park and use a pay phone. We hung around the beach to give Chuck enough time to get the info before I called him back. I loved being on the beach. It was like being on vacation. Most summers, my family only got a few days of vacation, usually in August. Mostly, we went to Pismo, and it was great. The weather was cool, and there were plenty of things to do. There were arcades and a movie theater and lots of restaurants. And there was the beach. The vacation was always over too fast. I'd give anything to live in a place like that all the time.

I looked over at Lonnie. He was laying on his back on the sand, like he didn't have a care in the world. The fucker. He always had a knack for getting me in trouble. And while I'd be worrying about it, he would always act like it had nothing at all to do with him. I often thought that I would be better off without him. On the other hand, I couldn't really imagine life without him. We had been best friends too long. I couldn't remember a time when we didn't know each other. The fact was, I was closer to him than I was to my own brother. If not for him, I would never have met a girl as neat as Kathy. On the other hand, because of him, there was no chance I would ever see her again. I didn't even get her phone number. Heck, I never even found out her last name. But my night with her hadn't been a total waste. For the first time, I realized that I could actually be in love with someone besides Linda.

I looked at my watch. Time to call Chuck back. I dialed his number and put the coins in the slot. He picked up right away.

"Hey, where are you, Dallas?" Chuck wanted to know. "Why didn't you want me to tell anyone you wanted Steve's address?"

"It's a long story, Chuck," I said, making it clear I had absolutely no intention of getting into it. "What do you have for me?"

"His mom says he doesn't have a phone yet, but I got his address. You got something to write with?"

"I'm good to go," I said. "Shoot."

Armed with a scribbled address on a bit of paper, we piled into the Chevy.

"Hurry up, Tony!" Lonnie barked. I took note of the fact that Lonnie had given the kid a nickname. Despite the gruff way he kept talking to him, that meant that Lonnie was actually starting to take a liking to him. Antonio had more or less become part of our outlaw gang.

We headed into the city. San Diego wasn't nearly as big as Los Angeles, but it was still way bigger than anything we were used to. Even Bakersfield seemed pretty small next to places like this. It took ages to locate Steve's apartment. We found the college with no problem by following the road signs, but once we got there we had to stop and ask a few times to find the right neighborhood and then the right street. Finally, we pulled up in front of the apartment building. I walked up to his door and knocked. No answer.

"He's not home," I said.

"Let's go find something to do for a while," said Lonnie. "We'll come back later."

We found a McDonald's and got some burgers at the drive-thru. Lonnie and I agreed that the Big Macs were nowhere near as good as the burgers at our local Fosters Freeze.

"But at least they're fast," grinned Lonnie. "You go in, you get your shit, and you go out again."

"Yeah, you get your shit all right," I said, motioning to my Big Mac. We had a good laugh over that.

After we had eaten, we needed something else to do to kill some time.

"Let's go to a movie!" said Antonio.

Lonnie and I looked at each other. "Sounds good to me," I said. Lonnie shrugged.

We found a movie theater near the college that was open during the day. It was a funky student kind of place that showed older movies instead of the latest ones. They were showing *Butch Cassidy and the Sundance Kid*, which had come out a year or two before but which I never got the chance to see.

"It's great," said Antonio enthusiastically. "You got to see it." Clearly, Antonio had seen a lot of movies. And he wanted to see this one again.

It was a good movie all right. It had Paul Newman and Robert Redford and that song about raindrops falling on my head. And it seemed extremely appropriate, given our situation. It was like Lonnie and I were Butch and Sundance, on the run from the law in the Old West. All we were missing was Linda to be our Katharine Ross. Darned if Butch and Sundance didn't wind up going down to Latin America, just like we were planning to do. I could only hope that it turned out better for us than it did for them and that we didn't end up trying to shoot our way out against the whole fucking Bolivian army.

After the movie, we went back to Steve's apartment. I knocked on the door. This time it opened. There was Steve, skinny as ever and his straight blond hair all down to his shoulders. His eyes were glassy and he smelled of pot.

"Dallas! Lonnie! What are you guys doing here?" he exclaimed with a big shit-eating grin.

"We're on the lam from the law," I said, as if I was joking. "Can you put us up for a night? We really need to get caught up on our sleep."

"Sure," said Steve, in a laid-back way that signaled that nothing was going to faze him. "I've got a surprise for you."

I wasn't sure if I was ready for any more surprises on this trip, but I followed him into his apartment. His girlfriend Tina was there.

"Guess what," said Steve. "We're living together. And we're married!" He held up his left hand to show us a ring on his finger. Somehow I didn't expect to be this surprised.

"When did this happen?" I asked. My face was surely radiating shock.

"A week ago," said Steve, still grinning widely. "Nobody knows. You guys are the first to know about it. We decided to live together, and we just figured, what the fuck, we might as well be married. We knew it was eventually going to happen anyway. Why wait?"

Tina was smiling but quiet. She was a pretty girl. She was Italian and had dark hair. I couldn't really read exactly what she was thinking about all this. Steve and Tina had been going steady since he was a junior and she was a sophomore. I tried to think of something appropriate to say, but Lonnie had no problem with that.

"This calls for a celebration!" he shouted. "I've got a bottle of Chivas Regal in the car. Let's have a drink!"

On the way to the movie theater, Lonnie had popped into a liquor store to buy that bottle. Even though he was underage, he never seemed to have any trouble getting a liquor store to take his money.

And the money he took from Don was clearly burning a hole in his pocket because he bought the good stuff. I was thinking that the last thing we needed was another night of drinking, but I also knew enough to realize that it was going to happen whether I said anything or not.

For the next couple of hours, the scotch was passed around and we all got pretty buzzed. I had been afraid that Steve would want to know what we were up to and why we were there and would start asking questions that we shouldn't answer but might anyway because we were so relaxed from drinking the whiskey. Fortunately, he had absolutely no interest in any of that. He only wanted to talk about what a great place San Diego was and how much he was looking forward to starting school.

Tina kept on being quiet. I kind of felt sorry for her. It was a small apartment and now it was overrun with guys drinking and laughing. She was kind of being ignored, so I tried to get her to talk.

"So you didn't want a big wedding?" I asked her.

"I'm pregnant," she said quietly. "It seemed like a good idea not to wait."

"Cool!" I said, trying to sound as positive as I could. What I was thinking, though, was how her father was going to kill her—and Steve—when he found out. Now it finally made sense to me why they had gotten married so suddenly and quietly. Despite how relaxed—actually tired—I felt and how good a time we were having, I started feeling like we were imposing. Steve always struck me as the kind of guy who was never going to grow up. Now I realized that, despite the partying he was into, he was already starting to grow up, faster than I was. His life was changing fast, and it was never going to be the same again.

I looked over at Antonio and noticed that he was drinking the scotch as well.

"You're a bit young to be drinking, aren't you, Tony?" I said, surprising myself at how much I sounded like my father.

"It's all right, man," he replied casually, slurring his words a bit. "Michael always used to let me drink with him. I'm used to it."

I bet he did, I thought to myself, feeling a bit disgusted at what Michael had been doing to this kid. He wasn't a bad kid at all. He was bright and friendly and had been no trouble at all since he had been tagging along with us. I didn't know his whole story, but I knew he deserved better than he had been getting so far. Next thing I knew, Antonio's brown face turned a sickly green color and he got a panicked look on his face. He jumped up and ran to a window, opened it and shoved his head through it. The sound he made brought back unpleasant memories of times when I had gotten sick. Steve's apartment was on the second floor, and I hoped there was no one standing below the window.

Lonnie went over to him quickly. "You okay, Tony?" he said gently. Lonnie actually had a sensitive side, although you didn't see it all that often. Antonio just kept making a sickening sound like he was drowning. "It's okay, kid," Lonnie reassured him. "You'll be all right. But I think your partying is over for the night."

The party was over for all of us. We were all too wasted to go out to the car for our sleeping bags, so Tina made places for us on the living room floor with whatever blankets and pillows she could find. We let Antonio have the couch. Tina found a bucket to put beside him—just in case.

As I dozed off, I thought to myself, that's probably enough resting before we go. If we do any more resting before we head into Mexico, it just might kill us.

4
A Night in Tijuana

I WOKE up with one of the worst headaches I ever had in my whole life. I glanced at the coffee table and saw the empty Chivas Regal bottle.

Damn, I thought, We finished the whole bottle. Probably not a good idea.

Lonnie and Antonio were sprawled out in the same places I had last seen them. They could both be dead for all I could tell. I stood up and went to the window and raised the blinds. The sun was low on the horizon and the light burnt my eyes. I looked down and saw a bit of Antonio's vomit on the window ledge. For some reason it made me need to take a piss as quick as possible. I stumbled toward the bathroom, trying not to step on Lonnie. The bathroom was cleaner than the bathrooms of most guys I knew living on their own. The shelves were loaded with lots of skin and hair and feminine hygiene products. I made a mental note to myself that life is apparently very different when you live with a woman.

I went back out to the living room and saw no more signs of life than before. I quietly undid the deadbolt on the door and went out for a walk. It was early and there weren't many people stirring yet. I couldn't help but think how cool the early morning air was and how it was probably already up to ninety degrees back home. It could be kind of cool to live in a place like this and go to school and learn all kinds of crap and maybe eventually get a job where you didn't have to drive a tractor for twelve hours a day. I glanced at the back seat of Lonnie's car through the window and noticed something. He hadn't even locked the car yesterday. I opened the door and grabbed Michael's camera. I had completely forgotten about it. Pretty darned lucky that someone hadn't swiped it. I walked down the street and took a few pictures. I wondered whether they would tack on a charge of theft for the camera on top of murder and leaving the scene of a crime. Hell, they might even go after us for kidnapping a child, like Lonnie said. Never mind what trouble Lonnie was in back home for the way he went off with Don's money and gun. Normally, in the cold light of morning this whole Mexico thing would look like the crazy idea that it was. But there was a whole bunch of accumulating problems that made hightailing it to Mexico seem more and more prudent. Yep, Butch and Sundance hitting the trail and keeping ahead of the posse. We'll be sleeping by the campfire with one eye open and our finger on the trigger. This here is injun country, pardner.

You would think that all I would be able to think about was all the trouble we were in or at least we thought we were in. But it all seemed so far away there in San Diego. It was easy to pretend that none of it had even happened. Instead, as I kept walking, I started playing a strange game in my head. I tried to figure out, if I could have my choice of either Linda or Kathy—I mean if one wasn't my best friend's girl and the other didn't hate my guts about now—which one I would choose. God, I'd be thrilled to have either. And the truth was that I was never going to have either of them. And after getting a load of Steve's situation, maybe it wasn't a bad thing to be single a while longer anyway.

I eventually wound up back at the apartment and went in. Steve was standing there in his boxer shorts.

"So there you are," he said with the same grin as usual. The guy never seemed to have a down moment. "I haven't been able to get a stir out of these other two. Hungry?"

Food hadn't even crossed my mind since I woke up, but now that he mentioned it, I was starving. "Yeah!" I said.

He stepped into his bedroom and addressed his bride, who apparently was still in bed. "Honey? We got three hurt cowboys out here. Think you could rustle us up some grub?" I heard a quiet moan in response.

"Hey, man," I said in a sudden fit of common sense, "why don't you get dressed and we'll take you out for breakfast. We could go to Denny's or someplace. Lonnie's loaded with cash."

"That's all right," said Steve, his grin still intact. "Tina doesn't mind. C'mon, honey, everybody's hungry."

Tina's quiet response was meant for Steve alone, but I could hear it as well. "Stevie, I'm feeling a bit sicky this morning. Maybe you could go out for breakfast, like Dallas said."

"C'mon, honey, they're our guests. We should at least make them breakfast."

Steve wasn't going to let it go, and I was feeling uncomfortable. I leaned down and roused Lonnie. "Hey, man, I think we should get on the road."

Sounding more than a bit like Tina, Lonnie made a pitiful moan. "C'mon, man, I'm wrecked. Jeez, I can't believe how much we drank last night."

I leaned down closer and whispered, "Listen, Tina's pregnant and she's not feeling well. I think we should get out of their hair."

Not exactly picking up on my attempt at discretion, Lonnie sat up with sudden interest and announced loudly and with a devilish laugh, "So, you knocked her up! What a stud! Congratulations, man!"

"That's it," I said with the last of my patience gone. "We're going *now!* Put your pants on and let's go."

"What's your hurry, Dallas? Jeez, I didn't know we were celebrating a baby as well as a marriage last night. I have to congratulate Tina." He stood up, his briefs barely clinging to his hips, and walked into the bedroom.

"Congratulations, you two!" he boomed. "That's great news."

"Could you go now, Lonnie?" Tina pleaded tiredly. "Steve and I need to have a talk."

"Sorry," said Lonnie, confused. "I just wanted to congratulate you on everything."

I stepped into the bedroom and grabbed him by the arm. "Grab your stuff. Tony, get up! We're hitting the road."

As we dragged ourselves out the door and down the stairs, Steve looked dejected. "Sorry, guys. I guess she's just not feeling well. You could come back later."

"That's all right, Steve," I called back to him. "Thanks for letting us crash. We're heading south of the border today. We might stop by on our way back."

"Wow! Mexico! Hey, maybe I could come with you? Sounds like a blast!"

"Uh, I think you might want to stay and look after your wife, man. Maybe another time."

"Hey, I never even asked you what you were doing here and why you came down."

"You'll read about it in the papers," interjected Lonnie. "Later, man."

We piled into the Chevy and headed down the street.

"Man, he's got it great," said Lonnie, summing up his impression of our visit with Steve. "He's got a beautiful wife, a baby on the way, and he's living in a great place. Man, that's the life. Makes me want to go back to Linda."

Me, I had a different take on it. He had barely gotten away from his mother and now he had another woman telling him what to do. And if driving tractor six days a week seemed like being a slave, just imagine what it was going to be like when the baby came. He was never going to have any free time for himself ever again. An adventure like the one we were on was out of the question for him. On the other hand, he probably didn't need to be worrying that the police might be out looking for him.

We found a Denny's and had breakfast. Antonio was much quieter than usual, apparently still suffering the effects of the night before.

"How are you doing, kid?" asked Lonnie. "You going to live?"

"I don't think scotch is my drink," said Antonio, trying to sound grown up.

"I think maybe you should stick to Coke or Pepsi for a few more years," I counseled. "There'll be plenty time for drinking later on. I was two or three years older than you before I had my first drink."

"Hell, I was drinking younger than him," said Lonnie, putting himself forth as an even better role model. "It didn't do me any harm."

I glared at him. "Well, that's your opinion. Most people might not agree. His mother probably wouldn't like him out drinking like that at his age."

"She don't care," said Antonio, a bit sadly.

"Where is your mom anyway?" asked Lonnie. "How come you aren't with her?"

"She's in Mexico. She met a new man a couple of years ago, and we moved in with him. But he got picked up by the INS and they sent him home to Hermosillo. She left to go be with him. She told me to wait until she got back. But I got tired of waiting and I ran out of money to pay the rent anyway. But you can take me down there now, and I can go stay with them in Hermosillo."

He was an amazing little kid. He was four years younger than me, and he had already had to do a lot more looking after himself than I ever had to. I might get mad at my parents sometimes, but at least they were always there and I always had a roof over my head and food to eat.

"Sure," I said, "we'll take you to Hermosillo. You'll be better off with your mom than with the likes of us. I'm not even sure that we won't wind up in jail before it's all over."

I was trying to sound positive, but inside I was hoping that his mother would actually want to see him. Frankly, she didn't really sound like much of a mother.

46

"Okay," said Lonnie, making an effort to be practical. "So how do we get to Mexico?"

"That's easy," replied Antonio, brightening up. "You just take Interstate 5 all the way to the border. You can't miss it." He flashed his toothy grin. He seemed to be getting over his hangover. The ham and eggs and black coffee must have done him good.

After breakfast, we all got back in the car and got on the freeway heading south.

Still being practical, Lonnie asked, "Do we need passports or anything?"

"No," answered Antonio, our international authority. "Just tell them that you are going to Tijuana for the day. Americans don't need passports or visas if they're not going far past the border. It's coming the other way that's tricky, but you'll be all right if you have your driver's licenses."

It was hardly any time before we came to the end of the interstate. Cars were lined up at the border at the various checkpoints. When we finally got to the head of our line, the American border guard stuck his head in the window and had a good look at the inside of the car. He asked for our driver's licenses and took a quick look at them.

"Where you boys headed?" he asked, sounding more curious than official.

"We're just going to visit Tijuana for a few hours and then come back," explained Lonnie, lying like a natural.

"Stay out of trouble," he said, kind of in a fatherly way, as he stepped back and started focusing on the next car.

A bit further ahead was the Mexican border guard. He looked totally bored. He gave us a good and tired look and then waved us through. Apparently, Mexico wasn't too fussy about who they let into the country.

Spontaneously, we all let out a yell. We did it! We were in Mexico! This crazy, weird, totally loco idea of ours had actually happened. We were in a foreign country. We really had left our old lives behind. The adventure was now truly underway.

I was kind of surprised how easy it was for us to cross the border into Mexico. Of course, we hadn't told them that we were really going to fucking Central America.

Now I had considered the fact that it might get a bit complicated when it was time to leave Mexico and cross the border to the next country. But that seemed a far piece down the road and, frankly, I wasn't even convinced that we would get that far. I kept figuring it was only a matter of time before Lonnie came to his senses and turned around and went home to face the music and be comforted in Linda's arms. Damn, I wish I hadn't thought of Linda's arms.

I mentioned to Lonnie and Antonio how surprised I was that we could cross the border so easy. Antonio responded with the weariness of someone who had done this a few times before.

"Going into Mexico is easy. It's coming back the other way that's hard. At least for us."

I understood that "us" meant anyone who was Mexican or who looked Mexican. I wondered why so many of them went to so much trouble to go north into our country, especially when so many of them had to do it illegally. But I knew the answer. There was work in California. The farms needed people to chop cotton or pick grapes or any other kind of hard work. Forty years ago it was my grandparents, along with my parents and my aunts and uncles, who would have been coming from Oklahoma to do that work. Now they had made something of themselves and they didn't do that work anymore 'cause they didn't have to. And they didn't want their kids to do it either. Well, not too much of it anyway. Just enough to learn to hate it, which is what my dad said. He wanted me to go to college and get a degree and get a good job in an office.

So California needed Mexicans to do the work. And they wanted to do the work because it was more money than they ever saw in their own country. It was kind of a crazy system, but it seemed to work okay. But I wondered what was going to happen when the Mexicans starting saving up a bit of money and they didn't want to do the work anymore. Who would the farmers get then? I supposed they would get more Mexicans. From Mexico, I mean. There always seemed to be plenty more.

I wondered how hard it really was for Mexicans to come into the U.S.? Illegally, I mean. Every year during cotton season, Walt would hire a labor contractor who'd bring a bunch of Mexicans in to work the fields. Every once in a while the INS would show up and round up a bunch of them and take them away. They'd put them on a bus for Mexico and off they'd go. Then, a week or two later, most of the same Mexicans would be back at work in the same fields again. They were basically just getting a free ride for a visit home.

Of course now there was a group trying to put the labor contractors out of business. A guy by the name of Cesar Chavez was organizing farm workers so that the farmers would have to deal with his union instead of going through the labor contractors. Walt wasn't one bit happy about that. He said he couldn't afford to pay any more for farm workers than he was already paying.

"You know, Dallas," he always said to me, "farming is the only job where your costs are fixed but you never know what your income is going to be. If you have a bad year, you might not make anything. But you still have to pay your bills. And now these damn union guys want us to pay more for workers and tell us how to run our farms. I don't know why anybody bothers farming anyway."

And yet, despite all the complaining, he and all the other farmers keep at it. The fact is, a lot of them make good money at it. Some do end up going bust all right. Like Walt says, it's really a crap shoot.

Lonnie was still making whooping noises, and that brought me back to reality. This was the first time Lonnie and I had ever crossed a border, and it was exciting. For Antonio, however, it was apparently old hat. It was like now that we were in his country, we were the kids and he was the adult. He pointed over to a collection of rundown buildings over to one side.

"You want to get insurance for your car," he said matter-of-factly.

"The car's insured," said Lonnie.

"Not in Mexico it ain't," corrected Antonio. "Pick one of these guys and buy some Mexican car insurance. It doesn't cost very much, but you'll be in real trouble without it if you have an accident. You'll want to buy some pesos too. Most places will take dollars, especially near the border, but you'll get better prices if you pay in pesos. And if you let me do the talking."

I was starting to realize that there was way more to Antonio than I had realized.

After we had taken care of the various transactions, Lonnie announced that he wanted to stop in Tijuana.

"Why?" I asked. For some reason, I had just assumed that he would be in a hurry to make as much time going south as he could.

"Tijuana is a blast," he answered, suddenly trying to be the expert. "Randy says it's like a nonstop party. Lots of bars and whorehouses and everything's cheap. Nothing there is illegal. You can do what you want. Hell, if you want to pay for it, you can even see a woman get fucked by a donkey."

I'd been hearing the story about the woman and the donkey in Tijuana for years. Now that we were actually there, I was starting to wonder if it was really true. But right now more practical things were on my mind.

"Uh, didn't Randy come back from there with gonorrhea one time?" I asked.

"Yeah, but a little penicillin fixed him up just fine," replied Lonnie, unfazed. "You just have to be careful about which places you give your business to."

"And you know which whorehouses are the high-class whorehouses?" I asked skeptically.

"When did you become such a schoolmarm?" he shot back, trying to shame me out of being responsible.

"I just don't want the clap," I said reasonably. "It's not like we'll be going straight back home where we know where to find a doctor we trust."

"Jeez," exclaimed my best friend, fed up with logic. "I might as well have brought my mom along. Let's look for someplace to eat. I'm ready for some real Mexican food. We're going to TEE-A-WANA!"

"Hey," interjected Antonio, deciding he was our tutor now. "It's not TEE-A-WANA. It's TEE-HUANA! Tía Juana is your Aunt Jane."

"Okay," responded Lonnie. "Let's fucking go to TEE-HUANA!"

We walked along the streets of Tijuana, and it was indeed like a party. There were people everywhere. There were shops and stalls of every kind and description. It took a while to get used to prices in pesos. At first everything seemed really expensive because the Mexicans used dollar signs for their prices, even though the prices were in pesos. But once we got a handle on that, we realized that the prices on everything were really dirt cheap.

Short little men kept accosting us and trying to get us to buy whatever they had. Little kids kept coming up to us yelling "*¡Chicle! ¡Chicle!*" trying to get us to buy chewing gum. Lonnie was inclined to yell "Scram!" at them ferociously, but Antonio was more effective at protectively shooing them away from us.

"Wow, there're sure a lot of poor people in this country," judged Lonnie.

We eventually came to a big restaurant called Caesar's. It seemed like a popular place that was nice and clean. Some of the smaller places we had passed had frankly not looked very sanitary. Lonnie's cousin Randy had told him to eat at Caesar's and that, in fact, it was famous. Sure enough, the menus said that this is where the Caesar salad was invented.

"Is that right?" I asked. "Somehow I always thought Caesar salad was invented in Italy. Wasn't Caesar a Roman?"

They brought us huge plates of enchiladas and tacos with Spanish rice and refried beans. It tasted great. Lonnie decided that, now that we were a few miles into Mexican territory, we really needed to get into the Mexican culture. That consisted of ordering a series of tequila shots with salt and lime. I didn't have an entirely good feeling about this, but I was so glad to have gotten this far and not to have been arrested or anything that I didn't worry about the fact that I hadn't managed to get completely sober for about three days now. The shots kept on coming. And they were dirt cheap, compared to what we would be paying at home. Not that anyone would even be serving us tequila shots at home since we weren't even twenty-one yet. The amazing thing was that the tequila didn't even seem to be affecting me.

And then I stood up. The room started spinning, and it took me a moment to get my balance. I was starting to have second thoughts about the last shot or two. Fortunately, Antonio had wisely taken my earlier advice to heart and had stuck to Pepsi during the meal. He had apparently decided that he was going to be our chaperone while we were in his country. Lonnie, on the other hand, was going to be the tour director.

"Let's go get laid!" he announced to one and all as he led us out of the restaurant.

It had gotten dark while we were in the restaurant. With no plan of my own, I followed Lonnie as he marched forward in whatever direction he took a notion to. It wasn't too long before a pleasant man in a suit spotted us and, approaching us like old friends, invited us into his establishment for a drink. My first reaction was to keep moving, but Lonnie was clearly open for anything. Without pausing to consult with me or anyone else, he ducked inside.

It was a cheap little dive. It was dingy and dark and more than a little musty. Before we knew it, he had us seated on rickety little chairs next to a tiny table. Like magic, someone appeared and put four drinks on the table.

"Who are all those for?" I wondered, but I didn't have to wonder long. Suddenly Lonnie and I each had a woman on our lap. They were small and dark and wearing a ton of makeup and wore tiny little miniskirts.

"*Eres muy guapo*," said mine. "You are very handsome. What is your name?" She began running her hand through my hair. And we'd only just met.

"Dallas," I answered obediently.

"*¡Que lindo nombre!*" she exclaimed, as if she had never heard such a beautiful name before. "Do you like me, Dallas?"

Now I know that I should have been totally thrilled to have such a willing and anxious woman sitting there on my lap and telling me how good-looking I was and how beautiful my name was. And she wasn't even that old or bad looking. In fact, she looked like she was actually kind of pretty under all that makeup. And if I ever was going to be uninhibited, all those tequila shots should have taken care of that. But the weird thing was that, in that moment, all I could think of was Linda. Which was silly because Linda wasn't even my girlfriend and there was absolutely no reason for me to feel faithful to her. Hell, if she knew what was going on, she would probably be happy for me. How she would feel about her actual boyfriend on the chair next to me with his own whore, well...

I glanced over at Lonnie, expecting to see him already going at it with his woman. After all, this is what he had been looking forward to, and he wasn't the type to be thinking about his girlfriend hundreds of miles away. His philosophy had always been like the song said, when you're not with the one you love, then love the one you're with. But Lonnie had stood up and looked as though he was going to get into a fight with the gentleman who had invited us in. I was having trouble focusing on what it was about, thanks to all the tequila, but it seemed to have something to do with the price of the drinks.

"Look, peckerhead," Lonnie was explaining, "I was drinking shots all evening for five pesos apiece down the street, and you want to charge me five dollars a drink? And no way am I paying for the woman's drinks. I didn't order those."

I couldn't quite believe it. Lonnie had been determined to get laid, and now he was haggling over the price of drinks? In a way, I was kind of proud of him. For years I had been lecturing him on being more responsible with money. And finally, tonight of all nights, the message had finally broken through. My woman tried to get my attention again. She turned my head back in her direction and asked, "Don't you like me?"

"You're very nice," I responded politely, but I had a strong feeling that I should keep tabs on what was happening next to me.

The gentleman who had been so friendly before was turning angry. "Those drinks have to be paid for, *señor*! If you do not pay your bill, I will have to call the *policía*."

Those words went a good way toward sobering me up. I realized that he wasn't talking about the friendly local cops we knew in our hometown. I had heard stories of Americans getting arrested in Mexico and being locked up and not let out until they had arranged to have big bribes paid. As fucked up as I was at that moment, I knew there was no way in hell I could call my parents and ask them to come to Mexico to get me out of jail. After the way I had left with no warning, they might not even come.

I gently as possible lifted the woman off my lap, stood up, put my hand on Lonnie's shoulder and calmly told him to pay the man so we could leave.

"I know when I'm fucking being hustled!" shouted Lonnie, with no sign that he could be reasoned with. The owner was looking more and more threatening.

I started to panic. I got out my wallet and pulled out a twenty-dollar bill and threw it on the table. I then grabbed Lonnie and forced him toward the door.

"Come on, jerk-off," I insisted. "We're leaving now. Unless you want to spend the rest of your life in a Mexican jail."

"This is not acceptable!" shouted the owner. "This is no way to do business! I am calling the police!"

By this time, reason was finally starting to get through to Lonnie. I think it was the word jail. The owner started following us, giving no indication that he considered the matter settled. As we cleared the door, I shouted, "Run!"

I don't know if he tried to follow us or if he really called the cops. But we weren't taking any chances. We ran for what seemed like a mile until we were sure that no one was following us. We stopped and looked at each other and then burst out laughing. We laughed so hard that I think we both wet our pants. We fell back against a wall, still laughing, and sank to the ground.

"Fuck," Lonnie exclaimed. "I suppose we're on wanted posters in two countries now. Not bad for three days' work." And we both started laughing all over again.

I don't know how long we sat there, laughing for a while until we were exhausted and then laughing about it all over again. At some point it occurred to me to wonder where we were exactly and where the car was and where—or if—we were going to sleep that night. And then something else occurred to me.

"Where the fuck is Tony?"

Somehow we had both forgotten about him.

"He was with us up until we went into that dive," recalled Lonnie. "He didn't come in with us."

"Well, he was smarter than we were. But where did he go?"

Now I was starting to feel like shit. I had actually started to feel responsible for the kid and then we went and lost him without ever giving him a thought. Damn tequila anyway.

"He knows where the car is parked," said Lonnie reasonably. "He probably went there."

"Yeah, you're probably right. He has more sense than we do. Now if only *we* can find where the car is parked."

And then we both started laughing again.

Finally, we stood up and staggered down the streets of Tijuana. Every so often we came across other young Americans also staggering down the streets. We were all walking like Frankenstein or something. When our paths crossed, we would sort of acknowledge each other and then keep going. Just a bunch of young American Frankensteins trudging the empty streets south of the border. We had no idea where we were or where we were heading, so we just kept walking.

It seemed like we had been walking for hours and we were never going to find the car. Finally, we turned down a street that seemed familiar. "It's this way," motioned Lonnie, like he had known the right way to go all along. But even I could have found the parking place at that point. We worked our way back to the parking lot and, after a few wrong turns among the rows of cars, we finally found the Impala.

I found myself hoping that we would see Antonio spread out on the hood of the car and that Lonnie would yell at him to get his puny ass off his car. But there was no sign of the kid. I started to get really worried about him. Sure, this was his country, but I figured Tijuana at night couldn't be the safest place in the world for a kid his age. Hell, I wasn't even sure it was that safe for a guy my age. On the other hand, in some ways Antonio really had more experience and more sense than either Lonnie or I had. But he was still just a kid. I hoped he was all right.

"I got dibs on the back seat!" yelled Lonnie as he unlocked the doors.

"Fuck you," I answered, as I resolved to try to get comfortable in the front. It wasn't the first time that Lonnie and I had slept in that car, and it never did my back any favors. I was dead tired, though, and being a little uncomfortable wasn't going to keep me from drifting off to sleep within minutes. My last thoughts as I conked out were of Antonio and wondering where the hell he was.

5
Looking for Tony

I WOKE up in a world of hurt. My head was throbbing, and my back felt like it had a bruise up one side and down the other. Damn, I thought to myself, I really need to cut back on my drinking. And I really need to stop sleeping in Lonnie's fucking car.

I opened the car door and forced my body out onto the ground, kind of like toothpaste being squeezed out of a toothpaste tube. I stood up straight—or at least as straight as I could manage—and blinked in the direction of the distant rising sun. There was a foggy smell of vehicle exhaust in the cool morning air. I tried to gather my thoughts, but the only thought I could gather right at that moment was of hot black coffee.

"Wake up, asshole!" I shouted at the still form in the back seat. If I was going to stand there feeling hung over, I sure as hell was going to have some company. An angry grunt answered me.

"Hey, get up," I continued. "Let's you and me go get some huevos rancheros."

Another grunt answered me, but this time it was more pathetic than angry.

"Come on," I insisted. "I'm starving, and I need coffee. And we need to find Tony."

The next grunt was more conflicted. I'd say the coffee sounded right to him, but he was having none of the rest of it. I opened the door next to his head and gave his shoulder a shove.

"C'mon. I'm not staying here, and I'm not leaving you on your own. Get up, asshole."

I knew I had broken through when he reached into his shirt pocket and pulled out his pack of cigarettes. He sucked one out into his lips while he reached into his jeans pocket and pulled out his lighter and lit his coffin nail. I couldn't be completely sure that he had actually woken up, since I had seen him make this same exact move millions of times, sometimes awake, sometimes still in a deep sleep. By this time it was pretty much an automatic move that didn't really require his brain to get involved in. But I knew enough to know that there was no point pressing him any more until he had had a few good drags.

While I waited for Lonnie to get his bearings, I had a good look around at the sea of cars surrounding us. The sun was a bit higher in the sky now. I rubbed my chin and thought maybe this was the time to try growing a beard. It wasn't like life on the road was particularly conducive to shaving every morning.

Finally, Lonnie dragged himself out of the car. I laughed to myself because it kind of looked like the Impala was giving birth to him. He stood up and looked every bit as miserable as I had felt a few minutes earlier. The fun thing about getting up first was being a few minutes ahead of him and watching him go through what I had just gone through. Misery might love company, but it especially loves even more miserable company.

"Okay, peckerhead," volunteered my esteemed partner in crime, "where are you taking me for breakfast?"

Needless to say, I didn't have a clue where to go. But I acted like I did and motioned in a particular direction. I figured we had to run into something if we kept walking. And I was hoping that we would somehow run into Antonio. Now that I was thinking a bit straighter than I was the night before, I was starting to get really worried about him. I was imagining all kinds of horrible things happening to him and how guilty I would feel if any of it had actually happened. But the thing that scared me the most was this. What if we never saw him again? What if Lonnie and I went the whole rest of our lives wondering what happened to him? We would never know if he was okay and grown up and having a great life or if his fourteen-year-old body was lying dead somewhere in Tijuana just out of our sight.

Get a grip, I told myself, feeling a bit stupid. You're starting to turn into a girl, for God's sake. The kid's fine. We'll probably catch up with him in no time. And if we don't, he'll be fine. After all, he's been looking after himself for a long time now. He's already got more street smarts at his age than I'll ever have.

There wasn't much happening at that time of the morning in Tijuana, but we finally found a hotel that had a restaurant and was serving breakfast. Lonnie couldn't face a plate of huevos rancheros, but I sure could. I was liking Mexico. Lonnie had his usual restaurant breakfast, which consisted of steak and eggs and a shot of scotch. No matter how much I worried that my drinking was getting out of control, at least I wasn't having whiskey instead of orange juice with breakfast. An extra bonus was the sick look on Lonnie's face every time he looked in the direction of my runny egg yolks mixing with the refried beans. I was feeling pretty good, and the pains I had woke up with were already forgotten.

As we were sipping on our third or fourth cups of black coffee, I asked Lonnie what we were going to do. The plan at this point would have been to get back on the road and keep heading south.

"Maybe we should walk around and see if we can find Antonio," I suggested.

"What if we don't find him?" asked Lonnie matter-of-factly. "He knows where to find us. We don't have a clue where to find him, do we?"

"Do you remember him saying anything to us before we went into that bar?"

"Shit, I don't even really remember going into the bar. I sure as hell don't remember if he was saying anything or not. He should have gone back to the car and waited for us there. He had to know that."

"That's what makes me think something must have happened. Something that made him go somewhere else."

"Well, that kid's been living on his own for a long time. I guess he can make his own decisions about whether he wants to travel with us or go off on his own. I mean, this is his country. Maybe he prefers traveling on his own from here on."

"Yeah." I thought Lonnie wasn't nearly concerned enough, but I couldn't really argue with what he was saying. "I'd just feel better if he had said something or at least said goodbye. I mean, I know he's been living by his wits, but he's still a pretty young kid. And this town doesn't exactly strike me as the safest place. I'd just like to know that he's all right."

"Jesus," teased Lonnie. "You've turned into a real girl. You're worrying about that kid way more than even his own mother is."

I gave him a dirty look while I thought for a moment. "Okay, just humor me. Let's take a half-hour walk around and see if we run into him. And if we don't run into him or find him waiting back at the car, then we'll keep going. I guess that's fair."

Lonnie looked doubtful, but I think he was kind of touched by my concern for the kid. A half-hour wasn't going to make much of a difference, and it wasn't like we even knew where we were going or how far we wanted to get anyway.

"Besides," I continued, "it would really be handy having him along the rest of the trip. He speaks Spanish. He knows the country. He could really help us avoid getting into problems."

Lonnie thought about this. Even he knew that I had a real point. Say we got pulled over by the police somewhere, for example, it could be a real help to have someone with us who could talk to the cops in their own language. Hell, we didn't even have a road map. How did we know which roads to take anyway? The more I thought about it, the less hurry I had about getting back in the car. On the other hand, I was already more than ready to put distance between us and Tijuana.

We walked the streets more or less aimlessly. It was still early and there wasn't much happening. For some reason, that song "The Streets of Laredo" popped into my head, and I couldn't get rid of it.

It became clear fairly quickly that it would be some kind of miracle if we just happened to run into Antonio. But we kept walking anyway. I think we were really walking for the exercise. Stretching the legs felt good after all the time we'd spent in the car and all the drinking. As the morning wore on, there were more people on the streets. And more little kids started tagging after us, yelling at us to give them money or buy *chicle*. That kind of made me feel uncomfortable. We had traveled barely any distance at all across the border, and here there were so many more poor people than we had back home. We really didn't know how good we had it in the good old U.S. of A.

If Lonnie was bothered by the poverty level, it didn't show. "Fuck off, you damn little midgets!" he roared at them.

One little kid was especially persistent. No amount of abuse from Lonnie discouraged him in the slightest. Lonnie's solution was to walk faster, but I got an idea.

"You speak English?" I asked him.

"Yes. English. I speak English!" he replied. "You buy gum?"

"We're looking for a kid. He's about this tall and he's wearing a blue tee-shirt and blue jeans. He's got hair that looks like yours. His name's Antonio. Have you seen him?"

The kid thought for a moment and then smiled. "Yes. I know Antonio. Will I take you to Antonio?"

I was thinking we were pretty lucky to run into this kid, but Lonnie wasn't buying it. "The hell he knows Tony. He's just going to take you off somewhere so his older brother can mug you."

Yeah, it was just a little too lucky. "How do you know Antonio?"

"Antonio's a good friend of mine. I see him all the time. *Vengan conmigo*. I take you to him."

"When was the last time you saw him?" asked Lonnie suspiciously.

"Today. I see him today."

"Did you see him yesterday?" asked Lonnie.

"Yes, I see him yesterday."

"How about two days ago?"

"Yes, I see him then too. I see him all the time. Every day."

"He's shitting us," said Lonnie to me. "He doesn't know Tony. He's just telling you what you want to hear."

We started walking away, but the kid kept following us.

"No. Really. I can take you to Antonio. Come with me. I show you."

"Look," I said, getting ticked off. "If you know where he is, just tell me. Where is he?"

"I can't tell you, *señor*. It's easier if you follow me. It's not far. Just come with me. *Vengan conmigo.*"

Lonnie shot me a look that said, not on your life. I had to agree that the kid was almost certainly full of shit, but I hated not to at least check it out anyway.

"Okay," I said. "I'll come with you, but if I don't like where you're taking me, I'm outta here. Got it?"

"Yeah, yeah, no problem. Come. Come."

Lonnie's face made it clear that he thought I was making a huge mistake. And that's why he would be coming along.

We followed the kid, and he immediately led us away from the center of the town. The buildings quickly became a lot more rundown looking. My suspicions were fast changing into a real sense of alarm. There were a lot fewer people on the street, and the ones that were there were pretty scruffy looking and looked at us with suspicion.

Lonnie stopped short and announced, "Okay, this is far enough. I'm turning around."

"No. No. We're almost there. I promise. Just a little farther. Really."

I must be the biggest sucker in the world because all I could think about was how, if I turned around at that point, I would always be wondering if I was really that close to Antonio and should have kept going.

"How much further exactly? You said he was really close."

"Around the corner. Just around the corner. Really, *señor*. Really!"

"We've come this far," I said to Lonnie. "We might as well go around the corner."

Lonnie's face told me that he didn't agree, but I didn't give him a choice. We kept following the kid. We turned the corner, and the kid kept on going. We stopped again and had the same conversation about the next corner.

"He's just going to keep us going until he's got us lost," said Lonnie. "We've wasted enough time with him."

I addressed the kid very seriously. "We'll go around this corner with you, but if he isn't there, we're turning around. We won't go any further. Got that? Is there any point in us going around this corner?"

"Yes. Yes," he insisted. "Just around this corner. Really. Come."

But once we were around that corner, we were told that there was one more corner.

"That's it," said Lonnie. "We're done. We're going back."

This time he meant it. I knew he was going back, with or without me. And there was no way I was going any further without him. We turned around and began retracing our steps. The kid followed after us, yelling, "No. Really. Just a little farther. Come back."

We picked up our pace, and went around the last corner. I noticed that the kid wasn't following us. I guessed he had given up. Maybe his wild goose chase was just his way of amusing himself. Who knew?

As we approached the next corner, a couple of hefty guys with black mustaches were walking in our direction. I didn't think anything about it at first, but Lonnie picked up on the fact that they were keeping an eye on us while trying to look like they weren't paying any attention. Under his breath, he said, "Get ready to run."

In just a second my heart was thumping so hard in my chest, I thought it was going to explode. In perfect sync, the two guys reached in their pockets. Meeting them was definitely no coincidence. "Go!" shouted Lonnie, and we took off across the street in order to go around them. The two of them began running to intercept us. The problem was that Lonnie and I were tourists, while this was those guys' job. They came better prepared. I could tell that we weren't going to outrun them. Lonnie dropped back, but I tried to speed up, in the hope that I might slip by. It was a brief hope because suddenly I was jerked to a stop by one of them grabbing my shirt. Before I could do anything, he had me pushed up against a wall and had knife at my throat. With no hesitation his hand had reached around me and was pulling my wallet out of my back pocket. Please, God, I thought to myself, let him only be after the wallet.

Only seconds had passed while I waited to have my throat slit when I heard Lonnie yelling louder and more ferocious than I had ever heard him before. "Drop the knife, motherfucker!"

Still feeling the steel of the blade against my throat, I shifted my eyeballs in Lonnie's direction. I saw something I never expected to see. Lonnie was standing there in the street with his legs spread and he was pointing the Smith & Wesson at the guy with the knife. At the same time he was keeping an eye on the other guy who had been running for him but who had stopped in his tracks. I don't know which had me more scared: the thought of having my throat slit or of Lonnie firing that gun.

Time froze. Aside from thinking I was going to die any second, there was something absurdly funny about Lonnie standing there with the gun. First, it was so unexpected. Second, it was just Lonnie trying to look like he was in a cop movie. I just stood there, my upper body pressed against the wall, waiting to see what would happen. After what seemed like an eternity, the guy stepped back and held his hands up so we could all see them.

"*Con calma, hombre. No seas tonto.*"

I had no idea what he was saying, but he sounded perfectly reasonable—for a guy that had just had a knife at my throat. The other guy, who was closer to Lonnie, looked less reasonable. I could tell he was sizing Lonnie up, trying to figure out if he had the balls to fire. But he seemed to be taking his cue from my guy. Pretty soon the second guy lifted his hands up, although he wasn't a bit happy about it.

"*Hombre. Váyanse. No queremos que nadie haga una tontería.*"

It would have been helpful to know what he was saying, but the fact that they were both backing slowly away from us gave us a pretty good idea that they were taking us seriously. Lonnie and I slowly began walking sideways away from them until we lost sight of them. Then we turned and ran like hell.

"Shit! Fuck!" yelled Lonnie. "I am more than ready to get the hell out of Tijuana!"

"Amen," I muttered under my breath.

We kept running as fast as we possibly could. I don't think we even turned around to see if those guys were following us. We didn't slow down until we got to the entrance of the parking lot. Then we stopped and bent over and started breathing in big, heaving gulps. It felt like I was never going to get enough air into my lungs. Once I felt like I had enough air in me to not pass out, I found myself laughing like a crazy man. Lonnie was laughing the same way. We couldn't believe we had gotten out of that situation alive.

"I clean forgot you even brought that gun," I panted. "I thought it was a stupid idea, but I'm sure fucking glad you brought it."

Lonnie started laughing even harder. "Hell, you don't know the half of it."

"What d'ya mean?"

"The sucker wasn't even loaded." He had the biggest shit-eating grin I'd ever seen.

"What?"

"I'd been carrying that thing in my pants ever since we got to Tijuana. Made me feel safer. But I got paranoid that it was gonna go off and shoot my balls off. The cartridges are here in my pocket."

Whatever rush I was getting from having just dodged death suddenly got even bigger, if that was possible.

"You mean you were bluffing with an unloaded gun?"

"That's the size of it," he laughed, enjoying the fact that, once again, he could scare the shit out of me.

"Christ," I said. "We're two crazy motherfuckers. Let's get in the car and get the hell out of Tijuana."

"Amen, brother."

We walked quickly toward the Impala. But just when we got within sight of it, Lonnie stopped short.

"Shit," he said.

"What the hell is it?" Now that we were this close to getting on the road, I didn't feel like delaying.

"There's someone in the car. It's one of them Mexican fuckers, sitting there, waiting for us."

"Fuck." Just when we thought we were home free, we weren't. "Did they manage to get back here before us? Or are we just on every mugger's list today?"

"Well, I sure as hell won't be bluffing this time." Lonnie pulled out the gun and the cartridges and began loading them in.

"Shit, Lonnie." I was really starting to get nervous. "What if that guy has a gun too?"

"Well, then he better be fast on the trigger," replied Lonnie, switching into macho movie mode.

Part of me wanted to run off in another direction, but that didn't make any sense. Where would I go? For better or worse, Lonnie's and my best chance was to deal with whatever was in the car and try to get on the road as fast as possible. We stepped cautiously toward the Impala, doing our best not to be noticed by the guy in the car. Lonnie held the gun with two hands and the barrel pointed up—just like we'd seen in a lot of movies and TV shows. He might be scaring the shit out of me, but I had to admit that he had an eerie sense of confidence in these situations.

We worked our way around so that we were approaching the car from behind. We could see the back of the guy's head through the rear window. The black hair was kind of swaying, sort of like that guy was humming or singing to himself. For a moment I was worried that Lonnie was actually going to shoot the window. But he kept edging closer to the car and slipped along the side. It was clear that he was going to try to get the drop on the guy, and that really had me worried. I imagined the guy sitting there with a shotgun, ready to blow Lonnie away.

Very cautiously, Lonnie reached a place where he could touch the door handle. I held my breath. I really expected this to go badly. Very quickly, he flung the door open and swung around with the gun, held in his two hands, pointing at the Mexican.

"Freeze, motherfucker!"

I stood there frozen, waiting to see what was going to happen. I expected to hear one or more guns go off. What I didn't expect was for Lonnie to lower the gun and slap himself on the head.

"Fuck me sideways! You little cunt. Do you know you almost got yourself killed?"

I ran up to Lonnie's side, and it was true. It was Antonio sitting in the car. I was so relieved to see him, in so many ways, that I felt like grabbing him and giving him a big hug. But that would have been weird. So I didn't.

"Where have you been?" I asked him. "We've been looking all over for you. We thought you'd been killed or kidnapped or something."

The kid was shook up from the surprise of what had happened and from realizing how close he had come to getting shot. "Sheesh, guys. What are you so uptight for? You didn't seem too concerned about me last night when you went into that whorehouse, did you? What do you care if or when I come back?"

At this Lonnie completely lost it. He began yelling at the kid. "You goddamn fucker! We nearly got ourselves killed trying to find you! Hell, I was happy to take off without you, but this guy insisted we try to find you. I won't make that mistake again. If you're going to be traveling with us, there are going to have to be some rules around here! Understand?"

I had to laugh. Lonnie didn't realize it, of course, but he sounded exactly like the stepfather that he hated so much. Antonio, on the other hand, didn't seem the least bit impressed. "Hey, if you don't want me along, that's fine. I can find my own way from here. Can you?"

"Calm down, both of you," I said, trying to be the voice of reason. "Look, Antonio, we're sorry. We didn't mean to go off without you. We weren't thinking straight." Memories of my hangover earlier in the morning came flooding back to me. "We *seriously* weren't thinking straight. But we were really worried about you. We're glad you're back, and we're ready to get back on the road. Okay?"

The kid gave a sheepish grin. "Okay. Let's go. But I think you guys need to stop drinking so much. It doesn't suit you."

Lonnie and I gave each other a look. It was kind of like having our mother along with us. But that wasn't the worst thing in the world. I had actually been wishing that I was back home with my mother. But now everything seemed okay again, and I was ready to get on with it.

We climbed into the car, and Lonnie started it up. There was never any question of anyone but Lonnie being the driver. He couldn't stand being in any car where he wasn't driving.

"Tell me something, peckerhead," he said. "This car was locked. How did you get into it?"

"I know a few tricks," laughed Antonio with a sly smile. "You learn a lot of useful tricks when you live on the streets." One thing was for sure. If we were now living a life of crime, Antonio wasn't the worst partner to have in our gang.

"So where do we go from here?" asked Lonnie, since he didn't have a clue as to where he was going.

"We want to go to Hermosillo. You need to take the road to Tecate. From there you head to Mexicali."

"How far is it to Air Moe See Yo?" asked Lonnie.

"It's a long way. It will take more than a day. Especially starting out late like this."

"How much further past Hermosillo is it until we get to the southern border?"

Antonio laughed. "Hermosillo is in the far north of Mexico. You will be driving many hours a day for weeks to get to Guatemala. Mexico is a huge country. Not as huge as the United States, but it's still huge. I hope this old car is up to it." He laughed again.

I hoped so too. This idea of Lonnie's seemed crazy from the beginning, but it was just starting to dawn on me exactly how crazy. At some point, I thought, Lonnie will see sense and turn around and head home. He'll realize that this makes no sense.

In the meantime, as we drove down Highway 2, or *Carretera Dos*, as Antonio called it, I felt uneasy at the idea of getting further and further away from the U.S.A. Actually, as it turned out, we weren't really getting further away. The fact was we were pretty much hugging the border until we got to Mexicali. Then we turned south. And that's when we started getting further and further away from what Lonnie and I thought of as civilization.

6
Meeting Mary Loneliness

I HAVE to say that I was not all that impressed with Mexico during that drive.

Even though we were just across the border from California, it was an entirely different world. Hell, we might as well have been on an entirely different planet. There are parts of California that are really dry, but I never saw any place as dry as northern Mexico. It was like being on the moon or Mars or someplace. Except for cactuses, there didn't seem to be any plants. And the roads were shit. We were on one of the major roads in the country and we still had to be really careful we didn't wreck the car by running over huge potholes or hitting gigantic rocks that no one had bothered to clear off the road.

Also, it was hard to figure out how far we were from anywhere. Road signs, when and where they existed, had exaggerated distances for places. At least that's what I thought until Antonio explained that they were in kilometers instead of miles. No wonder Mexico is such a backward country, I thought. They don't even know how to use miles.

It was awful hot, and we found we were the most comfortable with all the windows rolled down. Lonnie called it four-sixty air conditioning: four windows down, sixty miles per hour. The heat kept making us parched, and we made regular stops to pick up drinks—when we could find places to buy them. Antonio drank a soda pop called Jarritos. Lonnie and I developed a real liking for Tecate beer. If we could locate a place that sold it in cold bottles, that was a real find—even though the stores charged more for cold bottles than for warm bottles.

Antonio was anxious to get to Hermosillo as fast as possible, and that suited Lonnie. He didn't care much for the area around the border or the desolate desert we were driving through. He couldn't wait to get to a more civilized place. I suppose he was thinking about what would happen if the car broke down in the middle of nowhere. There were long stretches where we hardly met any other cars. We could be waiting an awful long time to get help if we broke down in the wrong place.

We drove late into the night until we were all feeling pretty sleepy. Lonnie pulled over to the side of the road and we slept for a while. The sun was already pretty high in the sky when we woke up the next morning.

"We're making good time, guys," announced Antonio. We should be there by this afternoon."

I could have used a cup of black coffee, but that would have to wait. We didn't have far to go before our road joined up with the main highway that was coming south from Nogales. It was now a straight shot due south to Hermosillo.

The three of us had now spent enough time together that we really didn't have that much to talk about anymore. And we couldn't really hear each other anyway with the wind blowing through the open windows. During the rest of that drive I was mostly rolling the same thoughts over and over in my head. Wondering what was going on back home. How pissed off my parents must be. Wondering if Kathy got home okay and what she thought about our evening together. And what happened to Michael? Was he dead or not? And how long were Steve and Tina going to last? And was the war in Vietnam ever going to end? I was starting to think that the hardest part about being an outlaw on the road was dealing with all your own crazy thoughts.

It seemed like no time whatsoever before we rolled into Hermosillo. It turned out to be a really nice place. I think, after all the hours of driving through the desert, I was starting to think that all of Mexico was barren and desolate. Hermosillo was like finding an oasis. I guess I got so caught up in taking in this new place that I was in my own world. Lonnie jolted me out of it.

"Okay, Tony. Where do you find your mom so we can drop you off?"

I had more or less forgotten that this is where we were taking Antonio and that we would be leaving him here. It did not make me happy. Not only had I gotten used to him, but he was awful handy to have when we went into shops. A lot of people spoke enough English to sell us stuff, but it was handy to have someone speaking for us. And he knew which roads we were supposed to be taking. Things were definitely going to be a lot more challenging without him.

If I wasn't too excited about leaving Antonio here, he didn't seem that excited to finally reach his destination. He shrugged at Lonnie's question. "I don't know where she lives. I just know this is where she was going to live with her new man."

Lonnie raised his eyebrows at this. "So how were you planning to find her once you got here?"

Antonio shrugged again. "You can just let me out. I'll find her."

Lonnie pulled the car over. This plan seemed fine to him.

"Wait a minute," I said. "What if she's not here? What if she moved again? Do you know anybody else in Hermosillo?"

Another shrug followed. "Don't worry. I'll find her. Thanks for the ride, guys." He reached to open the door.

"Look," I said. "After all this time, another day won't matter. Why don't we have one last day together before we leave you?"

Lonnie looked at me sideways, but Antonio broke out with a big smile. "Okay. You want to go to the beach?"

"Is there a beach here?" asked Lonnie, looking around.

"It's only a couple of hours to Guaymas," said Antonio. "There's a great beach there. Let's go!"

Lonnie and I looked at each other. "Well," I said, "it's not like we have a deadline or anything. I wouldn't mind an afternoon on the beach. After all the driving and our little adventure in

Tijuana, it'd be nice to kick back and relax by the ocean for a while. Recharge our batteries and then get back on the road. We might as well enjoy ourselves a little bit."

Lonnie couldn't really argue with this, and so we got back on the road and continued south to the Gulf of California.

It hardly seemed like any time before we arrived, especially compared to how long it took to drive down from Tijuana. Just like Antonio had said, it was only a couple of hours.

Guaymas was even better than Hermosillo. It was smaller, but it was on the coast. The water in the Gulf of California was the strangest color I had ever seen in an ocean. It was kind of a bright aqua green color. The whole place seemed very relaxed and the beaches looked great. Lonnie and I decided that this would be a great place to hang out for a while. In fact, Lonnie said he was tired of sleeping in the car and wanted to live it up for a few days. Antonio directed us to a place called Miramar, and Lonnie used some of the cash he had taken from his stepfather to book us into a really nice hotel that was right on the beach.

The next thing we did was find a shop that sold bathing suits, and we each got one as well as some beach towels. I also bought some film for Michael's camera. I still felt kind of guilty about having that camera, but it was a really good one, and I figured I should be taking more pictures with it. Who knew when, if ever, I would get down to Mexico again? Antonio had us buy a roadmap of Mexico, and he also insisted that I buy a little Spanish dictionary that he found in the shop. He said I needed to start learning some Spanish. I went ahead and got it. It might come in handy, I thought.

We spent the rest of the day laying out on the beach at the hotel, swimming in the surf and just generally relaxing and living the good life. Our escape from Los Angeles and our near-tragic adventure in Tijuana seemed very far away.

In the evening we ate in the hotel restaurant. I had cheese enchiladas and Lonnie had *carne asada*. Antonio scarfed a whole plate of tacos. The best part was that the bar served margaritas in the most humungous glasses I had ever seen. They were like punch bowls with stems. And they only cost eight pesos apiece. That worked out to about 64 cents U.S. per drink. At those prices, we couldn't afford *not* to drink. As Lonnie said, what choice did we have? We had always been told not to drink the water in Mexico.

The problem with margaritas is that they taste so darned good. They're like lemonade with a hell of a kick. Before you know it, you've had several and, while you think they aren't affecting you that much, suddenly you find that you can't think straight. That's what happened to Lonnie and me. Antonio, as usual, was downing Coca-Colas and was fine. It was dark outside, and Lonnie and I decided to go for a walk. We walked along the beach. There was a full moon low over the horizon, and it looked huge. The tequila in the margaritas had us talking nonsense as we walked along, having no idea where we were heading.

"This is fucking great!" said Lonnie. "It's so warm. You could wander around all night with no fucking clothes on, if you wanted."

"This is the life all right," I chimed in. "It doesn't get better than this. Sure beats driving a tractor in hundred-degree heat."

The beach at night was so beautiful and my head was so dizzy, it started to get me a little sad. I thought about Linda and how great it would be if it was her and me here, just the two of us. But that made no sense. It was Lonnie she loved, not me. It was always Lonnie. No, I thought, if I'm going to fantasize a romantic night, better to fantasize about Kathy. I think she actually liked me. But that didn't really make sense either. Like I kept telling myself, I was never going to see Kathy again. Hell, I don't think I could even find Brentwood again.

Lonnie must have started thinking about Linda too because, right at that moment, he said, "I got to find a phone. I need to call Linda."

"Let's go back to the hotel. You can use the phone there," I said, being sensible.

But Lonnie had an idea in his head and, once he had an idea in his head, he wasn't able to change it.

"Let's go up to the road," he said. "There's bound to be a phone booth up there somewhere." And then he added something that actually sounded pretty sensible—at least in Lonnie's paranoid world. "If they trace the call, it's better I'm calling from a public phone instead of a hotel."

That's something I hadn't really thought about. I hadn't even thought about calling my parents or anyone else back home because I didn't want to hear how mad they were at me. Besides, I figured it would cost a fortune to make an international phone call. But Lonnie had obviously considered the possibility that there was actually a manhunt out for us and maybe our nearest and dearest had their phones tapped by the FBI to try to track us down. In my margarita-induced delirium, I considered whether it was a good idea for either of us to be making any phone calls at all.

"Come on," he said, as he walked up to where the road was. He was a man with a purpose, and I had to hurry to keep up with him.

There wasn't much along the road. It was pretty deserted. But Lonnie kept walking, apparently certain that there had to be a phone booth just a bit further ahead. By this time, I was really starting to feel the margaritas. Everything around us seemed like some sort of dream. Everything felt so strange and foreign, and the moonlight made everything feel like some other world. I became aware that I was not exactly walking in a straight line. My head was a bit dizzy. Without noticing exactly, I gradually became aware of things moving along the ground. Such was the state of my mind that this did not register with me for a good long while. But at some point my mind clicked and I said to Lonnie, "Hey, Lon, do you see something crawling on the road?"

Lonnie did not want to be distracted from his search for the phone booth. He glanced grudgingly at the ground, clearly determined that there was going to be nothing there. He did not slow his pace, but I could see the wheels turning inside his head and that his brain was getting around to telling him that, yes, there were things crawling along the road. He stopped short. So did I.

"What the hell are those things?" he said, finally convinced to pay attention. In the dark, they looked like clumps of grass on the pavement, but they were definitely moving. They could be some kind of bug, but they were bigger than my hand.

"Shit," whispered Lonnie. "You know what those are? They're tarantulas."

"Fuck me. You can't be serious." It made no sense. I had seen a tarantula once, in a jar at school. But there aren't any around where we live. You only see them in other countries. Like… Mexico. "Oh shit."

I took a good look at the little critters. And they were definitely hairy, eight-legged spiders. I stood there, thinking I was probably going to shit in my drawers. Years ago I had seen a James Bond movie called *Dr. No*. In the movie Bond is on an assignment in Jamaica and, while he is in bed in a hotel sleeping, a big hairy tarantula started crawling up on top of him. The scene freaked me out, and now here I was in the middle of a whole bunch of the little monsters.

Lonnie could see that I was starting to freak out. "Take it easy. They won't bite us if we don't bother them. Let's just start walking back the way we came. And be careful not to step on them."

That made sense. In the most fucking carefully way we could, we retraced our steps back to the place where we had left the beach. The spiders didn't seem to mind us at all. But I felt better when we had gotten off the road. I also took some comfort in remembering that the teacher who had showed us the tarantula in school had said something about them not being poisonous. At least not enough to kill a person.

"Well, that was fucking weird," said Lonnie. He seemed to have forgotten about calling Linda. Or maybe it had seeped through his tequila-and-lime-juice-drenched brain that he didn't really want to find out what happened to Michael and how mad Linda was about it. "Let's go back to the hotel and hit the hay."

And that's what we did.

The next morning I woke up before Lonnie and Antonio did. This seemed like a good chance to spend some time alone. Despite all of the annoying things he did, Lonnie was actually good company. But sometimes it was nice to get a break from him. I pulled on my swim suit and, on an impulse, I grabbed the camera. I thought I might take some pictures. The scenery was actually nice around here. Dry and rocky with cactus and other plants here and there. But the sea was what made it beautiful. I couldn't get over the color of the water.

I wandered down to the beach. There was hardly anyone else out at this hour. The sand felt really good under my feet, and the sun felt good on my face. Yeah, this was the life. I shot a few pics looking out to the sea and of some of the rocks along the shore. And I shot a few looking back toward the hotel. It was a cool looking hotel. It was old-fashioned, with a red-tile roof. It looked just like you'd imagine an old Spanish hacienda would look. It had a nice swimming pool, but who would want to use it when you had a nice beach so close?

When I had taken all the obvious pictures, I just started pointing the camera around the beach zooming in on things that might be interesting. I was zooming in on a palm tree when I realized that there was someone sitting against it. I zoomed in closer. And I actually gasped. It was a girl. But not just any girl, but the most beautiful girl I had ever seen in my whole life.

I lowered the camera, and started walking in the general direction of the palm tree, trying to look as natural as I could. As I got closer, I was amazed at how beautiful she was. She had dark brown skin and jet black hair, not quite down to her shoulders. She was wearing a very short dress that showed off her legs. And what legs they were! They were smooth and brown and perfectly shaped. How, I wondered, could a girl look so perfect?

She didn't even notice I was there. She was reading a book and laughing at whatever it was she was reading. She had a beautiful laugh. I walked closer until she finally noticed me. I lifted the camera with one hand and pointed to it with the other and made an expression with my face to let her know I'd like to take her picture. She smiled but looked at me like she didn't have a clue what I wanted. I pointed at the camera with my finger more energetically. She gave a little shrug and a bit of a laugh. Was it really so hard to figure out what I wanted?

Then an idea hit me. I remembered that I still had that little Spanish dictionary in my pocket. I pulled it out and looked through its pages. The palm tree girl was getting even more amused.

"*¿Toma fotografía?*" I said, no doubt butchering the language something awful.

"*¿Qué?*"

"*Fotografía. Toma fotografía.*"

"*¿Quieres sacar una foto? ¿De mí?*"

I nodded my head energetically. "*¡Sí! ¡Sí!* Photo!"

She set the book down on her lap and gave a smug little smile. "*Yo te doy permiso. Saca tu foto.*"

I didn't know exactly what she was saying for sure, but it seemed pretty clear that she was letting me take a picture. I took some time focusing and checking other settings, trying to give the impression that I actually knew what I was doing. I had it all ready and then an idea hit me. She sat there patiently while I dug out the dictionary again and looked up a word. "*¡Sonrisa!*"

With that, her face broke out in the most gorgeous smile I had ever seen. I lifted the camera and quickly shot her. And again. And again. I changed my position and shot her from a different angle. She put her hands behind her head and lifted her elbows, looking like a fashion model. God, she was beautiful. Before I knew it, I had shot all the film in the camera. I pretended to take a few more shots and then reluctantly stopped altogether.

I pulled out the dictionary again. "*Bonito.*"

She laughed. "*¡Bonita! Menos que tú hablas de ti mismo.*"

She was so friendly that I decided it was okay to sit down near her. I thumbed through the dictionary some more.

"*Español malo.*" I shrugged my shoulders and gave her a look that was meant to say that I really, really wished I could talk to her so that she could understand.

"*Y ¿quién es este español malo de quien tú hablas?*"

I may not have known exactly what she was saying to me, but it was easy enough to tell that she was teasing me. Damn, I wish I had paid more attention in Spanish class. This was one time when I really would have liked to understand and speak this lingo. It made me think of that Beatles song "Michelle" about the guy trying to make his feelings known to the French woman. Now I knew just how he felt.

I just wanted to sit there next to her as long as I could. I kept trying to think of things to say, but it wasn't easy, given the language barrier.

"*Me llamo Dallas.*" Well, at least there was one phrase I could remember clearly from Spanish class. I put my hand out.

She took my hand and shook it lightly. "*Un placer. Yo soy María Soledad.*"

"María Soledad?" I thumbed through the little dictionary. Trying to sound clever, I said, "In English your name would be Mary Loneliness."

She had a good laugh over that one. "Mary Loneliness," she chuckled. "I like that."

I shook my head. "You speak English!"

"I'm sorry, Dallas," she laughed. She didn't even speak with an accent. At least not with a Mexican one. Her English was perfect. Better than mine, in fact. "You were so cute, trying to speak Spanish. I couldn't help it. I wanted to hear you keep trying."

I looked down at the book folded open on her lap. It was *Love Story* by Erich Fucking Segal. In English.

"Good one," I said. "You really had me going there. What part of the States are you from?"

"I'm not from the States. I'm Mexican. I live in Monterrey. *Yo soy regia.*"

"Cool. Wait. Monterey *is* in the States. It's in California. I was even there once."

She laughed again. She was clearly finding me pretty fucking amusing. "That's a different Monterrey." She said the name with Spanish pronunciation (moan tay ray) with that rolling "r" sound that I could never do good enough to make my Spanish teacher happy. When Miss Daniels made that sound, it was dorky. When this girl made it, it was damn sexy.

"You mean there's a Monterey in Mexico too?"

This time she was actually making a real effort not to laugh. "Yes, there is. Have you not noticed that most of the names of places in California are Spanish names?"

"Bakersfield isn't."

Ha! At least I got her that time. But then she began a list of names that *were* Spanish. And she pronounced each one with a definite Mexican accent. "Loas On Hay Less. Sahn Frahn Cease Co. Sahn Dee Eggo."

"Okay, okay, you made your point."

"You do know that California used to be part of Mexico, don't you?"

"Yeah, yeah, but that was a long time ago."

"It doesn't seem so long ago to us."

"Yeah, well, we stole it fair and square."

She had been getting a bit worked up about us white people stealing California, but that last comeback made her laugh again.

"What's your family name, Dallas?"

"Green. Dallas Green."

"That's a perfect name for you. You have such lovely green eyes."

I was pretty sure I had lovely red cheeks by this time. I never had a girl as pretty as her give me a compliment like that before.

"Oh, you're blushing." She said it like she was talking to a small child, with tenderness in her voice. Boy, my cheeks were *really* burning now. And she wasn't through. "I like your freckles. And your blond hair."

"Huh? My hair isn't blond. It's brown." Lonnie was the one with the blond hair that girls seemed to like so much.

"No, it's blond. And it's beautiful." She teasingly reached just above my forehead twisted a few locks with her fingers. I wondered if, with just that little bit of contact, she could feel my heart racing a mile a minute. Blond, eh? I guessed that when you're in a country where everybody's hair is coal black, then brown kind of looks like blond.

"I like the way you wear your hair long. It's very sexy."

That was the first time I heard that. Usually, Lonnie and I got nothing but grief for wearing our hair long—from our parents and from the jocks at school, who were always calling us fags or hippies.

"But you're too skinny," she said. "You need some muscles. My name for you is going to be *flaco*. That means skinny."

I didn't really like the way this conversation was going. If she thought I was too skinny, she'd probably like Lonnie better. He had a pretty muscular build. That was another reason girls always seemed to like him better than me. He could have played football if he wanted. But he never wanted to. He always said it was a waste of time.

I decided it was time to change the conversation.

"So, what's *your* last name?"

"Carvajal. María Soledad Carvajal."

"That's quite a mouthful."

"Everyone just calls me Marisol. That's a lot shorter, isn't it?"

"And what are you doing here in Guaymas if you live in Monterrey?" I did my best job of rolling the r's, like she did, but I'm sure it came out sounding like I was choking on something.

"My family is here for a wedding. A cousin of mine will be married tomorrow in Empalme."

"And how come you speak English so good?"

"We study it in school. And I have been to the States lots of times. My father takes us to New York at least one time a year for shopping."

I was starting to get the distinct impression that Marisol came from a pretty darn rich family. Maybe she even had her own English tutor.

"I have to go back to my room now, *flaco*. Maybe I will see you later?"

"When will you be coming back to the beach?"

She smiled slyly. "Oh, I suppose I could arrange to come back to this place around seven this evening. After *la merienda*."

"After the what?"

"*La merienda*. It's what we call tea time. Oh, *flaco*, I have so much to teach you."

And with that she walked off back toward the hotel. I felt like I was in a dream. My heart was still racing. I really couldn't believe this had happened to me. Not only did I meet the most beautiful girl I had ever seen in my life, but she seemed really interested in me. She really seemed to like me. I couldn't figure out in the name of God why. But she did. And I was going to see her again in a few hours. For the first time in quite a while, I absolutely couldn't bear to wait for time to pass.

I thought I had been in love before, but now I realized I never knew the first thing about being in love. In that moment, Linda meant absolutely nothing to me. It's like those years of being jealous of her and Lonnie had never happened. If I never saw her again, it wouldn't make one bit of difference. As for Kathy, it was like she never existed. From now on, there was only Marisol. I couldn't imagine not being in love with her for the entire rest of my life.

7
A Night in Heaven

I WANDERED back to the hotel room, my head still buzzing. I decided I wasn't going to say anything to Lonnie. I knew what would happen if I did. There would be one hell of a lot of teasing. And he would want to get a look at her, maybe even talk to her. Just so he could do or say something to embarrass me. No, I needed to play this cool.

As soon as I walked into the room, Lonnie said, "What the fuck happened to you?"

"Huh? What d'you mean?"

"You got a shit-eatin' grin on your face. Like the cat that swallowed the canary. What have you been up to?"

I should have known that Lonnie knew me too well. We had known each other so long that there was no way either of us could keep a secret from the other. Come to think of it, it was a miracle that he never copped on to the fact that I was in love with his girlfriend. Or did he? Anyway, he was like a dog with a rag. He wasn't going to let go now until he got everything out of me.

"It's no big deal," I said. "I met a girl on the beach."

And that was all it took for Lonnie to break out in that leering grin that usually meant trouble for me. "Do tell. Was she a fox? C'mon. I need details."

At this point Antonio, who was reading a comic book on the bed, started to take an interest.

"Did you talk to her, man? What was she like? I bet she was a fox."

"She was just a Mexican girl. She barely spoke any English. She let me take a few pictures of her. That's all."

"What was her name?" asked Antonio.

"María Soledad Carvajal," I answered before I had time to think about it.

"Well, her English couldn't have been too bad if you got a name like that out of her." Lonnie was grinning like some kind of pervert.

"Is she from here?" asked Antonio, who was getting more and more interested.

"No," I said. "She's from Monterrey." Without meaning it, I had rolled the r's in my own awkward way. Antonio chuckled. "Not the one in California," I clarified. "The one in Mexico."

"Fuck, you got a lot of information out of her for a girl that barely speaks English. You must have been paying attention in Spanish class after all."

"Look, forget it," I said. "She was nice and we just talked a little bit. That's all. End of story."

"Then why do you have such a big boner?"

Before I even had a chance to think, I was looking down at my crotch. Lonnie started laughing, "Ha! Made you look!"

"Jesus, you are such a pain. You know that?"

"So are you going to see her again? Sounds like she likes you. You're going to try to score, aren't you?"

"I'm not going to score, asshole. She's here with her family. They're here for a wedding. It's not like we're going to be going out on a date or anything."

"I think I need to see this chick. When are you seeing her again?"

Jesus, just what I needed. Lonnie trying to embarrass me in front of Marisol. Worse, though I didn't want to admit it, I was kind of scared that, if she met Lonnie, she might like him better than me. Despite him being such a jerk most of the time, women always seemed to like him. When he was around, they never seemed to give me a look.

"It's not like that, jerk. She's a nice girl. That's all. She's not like…"

"Like who? What were you going to say?"

"Hell, I don't know. It's just that she's not like the girls we know back home. She's different. She's got class. And style."

"You saying that Linda doesn't have class or style?"

"No, no. You know I think the world of Linda. It's just that Marisol's… different. I don't know how else to say it."

"Fuck, man. If I didn't know better, I would say you're in love. Is that possible, Tony? Could he just go out on the beach one morning and fall in love, just like that?"

"I don't know much about falling in love," said Antonio, actually giving it some serious thought. "But why not?"

"Look," I said, trying to put my foot down. "She said she might be back out on the beach this evening. I'm going to go out there and see if she shows up. And I'm going by myself. I don't need a fucking audience or a cheering section. Understand?"

I didn't really expect Lonnie to give up. But he let it drop. "Whatever, man." Then, after a pause, "But don't show your sorry face back here tonight unless you fuck her."

We wasted the day wandering around and exploring the local area and drinking more than a bit of Tecate—or Jarritos, in Antonio's case. We had an early dinner in the hotel restaurant, and then I asked, "So, what are you guys going to do for the evening?"

"I might have a few tequila shots in the bar and check out the talent. If even you can get lucky here, I should be getting laid all night."

I looked at Antonio. Hanging out in the bar watching Lonnie get drunk didn't seem like the best plan for him. "I'm going to the room and watching TV. Tell Marisol that I send her *saludos*."

"Okay," I smiled. The thought came into my head that Marisol would like Antonio. To look at them, I thought they could practically be brother and sister.

As I walked out of the hotel, I kept looking over my shoulder. I was half expecting Lonnie and maybe Antonio too to try to follow me, just to get a look at Marisol. I wondered if she would even show up. I had to figure that, with the way she looked and everything, her father must be very protective of her. I wondered what kind of business he was in that he would be so well off. Was he a gangster or something? Maybe he was the type who had henchmen who make gringos disappear if they tried to make time with his daughter. Okay, now I was starting to get a bit crazy.

It was still light out, although it wouldn't be that long until sunset. The beach was mostly deserted, and the light made the beach and the sea beautiful. I looked around for Marisol. I was disappointed when I didn't see her right away. I kept on walking. After ten minutes, I decided that she wasn't going to come. Her father probably had her locked up in her hotel room. Heck, maybe she had a boyfriend and was just playing around with me. What would a girl like her want to do with a hick like me anyhow?

"*¡Hola flaco!*"

It was her. She came. And she was alone. There was no boyfriend or father with her. It was definitely my lucky day.

"*Hola Marisol,*" I said. It wasn't much, but I wanted to make some effort to let her know I'd actually like to learn to speak more of her language. She smiled.

"Shall we go for a walk?"

"Sure," I said. "Just as long as we keep an eye out for tarantulas." She gave me a curious look.

It was a beautiful evening. Everything was perfect. The beach was perfect. The sea was perfect. And she was perfect. How did I manage to get so lucky? Especially after the way things had gone so wrong in L.A. and Tijuana. This was definitely turning into the best trip I had ever been on. Marisol wanted to know lots of stuff about me. About my family, my brother, what my life was like in California. She wanted to know what I thought about everything. What music I liked. What movies I liked. I wasn't used to talking about myself so much. She must have thought I wasn't very smart.

After we got tired of walking and it started to get dark, we sat down in the sand.

"Are you cold?" I asked.

"A little."

This was the moment I was looking forward to and was afraid of. As nonchalantly as I could manage, I lifted my arm and put it around her. She didn't act like she minded at all.

"I really like you, Marisol."

"I like you too, *flaco*. I bet you have a girlfriend back home."

I was never so happy to be single as I was in that moment. "No. There's no one. There was a girl that I used to like, but she was with another guy."

"Mexican boys don't know how to treat a girl. They aren't thoughtful like American boys. I can tell you are very thoughtful, Dallas."

"If I had a girlfriend like you, I'd treat her so good she'd get sick of it."

"Do you really like me, Dallas?"

What a question. I was completely in love with her. But it was crazy to actually say that to her. "I like you a lot, Marisol."

"I like you too. *Tú eres muy simpático.*"

When it came to women, I was pretty dense. Lonnie never had any trouble kissing a girl when he wanted, but I was always worrying that I was misreading the signals and going to cause a big awkward thing. But in that moment even I could tell that Marisol wanted me to kiss her. Hell, she probably wanted me to kiss her an hour ago. But she definitely wanted me to kiss her now. I leaned in. And nothing ever felt so right before. We massaged our lips together like we could go for hours without breathing. She was so different from the girls I knew back home. She was really into the kissing. She moaned like it was the best thing that had ever happened to her in her whole life. And she did it with an urgency like she was going to be overcome with emotion.

I don't know how long we were there in that spot on the beach, making out for what seemed like hours. I ran my hand up and down her beautiful leg. It was so smooth and it felt so good to touch it that it made me ache. Her mouth tasted so good and warm that I didn't want to pull away from it. Even the scent of her perfume had me turned on. I had kissed girls before, but I never came close to realizing how good it could actually be.

She guided my hand up and down one leg and then the other. She ran her fingers though my hair with such force that I thought she might pull some of it out. She seemed like she was going to explode.

Finally, she pulled her mouth away from mine and gasped, "I want to be with you, Dallas. But I cannot here, like this. You understand?"

I nodded my head, even though my brain was barely taking in what she was saying. Mostly, what I got out of what she was saying was that I wasn't going to get laid on the beach. At least not tonight.

"Will you come to me tomorrow night?"

"Huh? Wha'? Tomorrow night? Don't you have a wedding to go to?"

"I'm going to tell my parents I can't go. At the last minute, I will tell them I have... *una migraña, dolor de cabeza*. I will tell them to go without me. I will stay in the room. Will you come to me tomorrow night?"

"God yes, Marisol. I'll be there. Just try to keep me away."

"*Yo te quiero*, Dallas." I don't know if it was a half-remembered lesson from Spanish class or just the way she said it, but I pretty much knew that she was telling me she loved me.

"Me too," I said.

"Can you say it to me, Dallas? Can you say it like I did?"

"Yo tay..."

"*Yo te quiero.*"

"Yo tay key arrow."

With that, her mouth was hard against mine again and her tongue was down my throat. I couldn't help thinking that, if Miss Daniels had used incentive like this, I would have probably gotten an A+ in Spanish instead of a C.

When we finally disengaged again, Marisol said she had better get back to the hotel because her parents would be out looking for her. She told me that her room number was 217 and what time I should come to her the next night. I wondered if it would really happen. Would her parents believe that she had a headache? Would they make her go to the wedding anyway? Would her mother insist on staying in the room with her? One way or another, I was going to find out. Either I would have the best night of my life or I would go back to my own room with the worst disappointment of my life. Worst case: I would get shot by her protective gangster father. No, scratch that. Thinking back to the disaster that happened to me in L.A., this was the ultimate worst case: right in the middle of us making love, Lonnie barrels into the room and says we gotta go right now because he's killed somebody (again).

I watched Marisol disappear through the door of the hotel. I was so worked up that I couldn't stand still. I had to be moving. I went for a long walk up and down the beach to let off some steam. My head was racing. I still couldn't quite believe any of this was really happening. Finally, I wandered back to the hotel. I was dreading Lonnie's questions, but I figured I might as well get it over with. I walked into the bar, and sure enough Lonnie was there. He was heavily involved in a conversation with an American couple.

"Yeah, I have a friend whose dad has a car dealership in Bakersfield," Lonnie was saying as he lit a cigarette with his Bic lighter. "He said he can get me a job there no problem. That's my plan. But I got a few things I'm doing first."

The American couple, who were wearing bright-colored Hawaiian-style shirts and looked old enough to be our parents, looked pretty bored.

"Hey, man," I said to Lonnie. "How you getting on?"

Lonnie gave me a sly look. "The question is, how did *you* get on?" Turning to the couple, he said, "Dallas, this is Mert and Opal. They're from Fresno."

"Nice to meet you," said Opal unenthusiastically. "Mert and I were just heading back to our room. It's past our bedtime. Good night."

Mert quickly finished his screwdriver and obediently followed Opal out of the room. Lonnie caught the eye of the waitress and gestured for another scotch on the rocks.

"So? Tell me, tell me. Did you get laid?"

"We just talked," I lied. "She's not that kind of girl."

"So, you struck out. No biggie. It happens. So you ready to get back on the road tomorrow?"

That caught me by surprise, and I felt something that felt kind of like panic. Of course, it made sense to be leaving. We had been here for a couple of days already. But there was no way I was going anywhere. At least not before tomorrow night.

"Uh, I need some more time here. I can't leave tomorrow."

Lonnie's sly smile returned. "Aha! So something did happen! Going back for more nooky tomorrow night?"

"Maybe. I don't know. Anyway, she wants to see me tomorrow night, and I'm going to be there. Sorry if that doesn't fit in with your plans."

"Hey, pal, nothing's more important than nooky. Sure, we'll hang around another day so you can get your rocks off. Why don't you ask her if she has a friend for me? Say, I've got to see this chick. I bet she's a real dog."

"She's no dog," I said quietly.

"Says you. I'll be the judge. Man, I think you're in love. I don't think I've ever seen you like this before."

"Drop it, will ya? What were you talking to that couple about?"

"Those old fogies? Just a boring couple from Fresno. But it was nice to have someone to talk English to. I mean besides you and Tony. I get tired of everyone around me talking Mexican all the time."

I had successfully gotten Lonnie off the topic of Marisol. And I had put him off leaving Guaymas for one more night. Potentially the most important night of my life. We spent the rest of the evening talking the usual bullshit and then went to bed.

For most of the next day we were basically cooling our heels. Antonio was happy to be hanging around Guaymas for another day. He didn't seem in any hurry to get back to Hermosillo. Lonnie, on the other hand, was clearly getting antsy. He was getting bored just hanging around and was more than ready to get back on the road again. We swam in the surf, had lunch and went for a drive, exploring the surrounding area.

When evening came, I did my best to slip away without making too much of a fuss. Antonio didn't seem to mind too much that, for the second night in a row, I wasn't going to be around. He was always happy reading a comic book or watching TV. But Lonnie looked like he was getting bored with being left on his own. Anyway, I mumbled something like "Don't wait up" and slipped away.

I'd be lying if I said I wasn't scared shitless walking down the hall to Marisol's hotel room. My heart was thumping and my head was starting to imagine all kinds of things I might find behind the door. Maybe her father would be there with a machete. Maybe she had been lying to me all along, leading me on. Maybe she was working with banditos and they would be lying in wait to kidnap me for ransom. (Good luck getting any money out of *my* parents.) But maybe the thing that had me most scared was the thought that it would just be Marisol there and that by the end of the night she'd be disappointed.

I knocked quietly on the door to room 217 and held my breath. I heard nothing. I stood there very still and waited. Finally, I knocked again, this time a bit louder. I continued standing there, working out in my head how much longer I should stay there before giving up. Then the door opened a crack. There was no light coming from the other side.

"*¿Flaco?*"

"*¡Sí!*" I nearly choked on that one word. My heart pounded even faster until my chest hurt.

"*Pasa. Rápido.*"

I quickly slipped into the room, and she immediately closed the door behind me. The room was like something magic. The electric lights were all off, but she had placed something like a million little candles on top of every table, dresser and desk. Marisol was wearing a small nighty that stopped just short of her hips, and she looked stunning in the soft flickering light. I felt like pinching myself to make sure I wasn't dreaming.

"I was afraid you wouldn't come," she whispered. Did she really think I would have missed this? "My father was very angry with me. He was very upset that I didn't go to the wedding."

"I hope you don't get into too much trouble over this." I was amazed at how big a chance she taking in order to be with me.

She sat down on the bed. On the night table was a bottle of red wine and two large round wine glasses. She filled each one halfway and handed me one. She lifted the other one in her hand.

"*Salud, flaco. A nosotros.*"

We drank to her toast, and then she looked at me with eyes like a little girl, like she felt helpless and at my mercy. She unclasped a chain that was around her neck and took it off. A small cross was hanging on the end of it. She put the cross to her lips, kissed it tenderly and then laid it gently on the night table next to the bed. Then she turned to me.

"Please be gentle with me. You must have had lots of women before. I do not have anything at all like your experience."

Was she kidding? She was the one who seemed to know all the right moves, while I felt like I was in way over my head. But she seemed to need to feel like I was the one who was in charge and that all this was something I did all the time. I moved in next to her and gave her a kiss. That was all it took.

She laid back onto the bed and gave me that look like she would be in pain until I made love to her. I started to take off my shirt, but she stopped me with a touch of her hand.

"Let me do that, *flaco.*" Slowly and deliberately, she removed everything I was wearing, pausing after each item of clothing for a passionate kiss. My nose was filled with the wonderful smell of her perfume. It was the most wonderful thing I had ever smelled. Marisol was doing everything perfect. At times, I thought, it was all nearly too perfect. Like she was trying to pretend that we were in a movie. But I wasn't about to complain. I was more than ready to be the star of my own movie.

Once she had me completely naked, I figured it was her turn. I lifted her nighty over her head. Her brown body was exquisite and there was no sign of a tan line anywhere. I leaned down and kissed her breast. I was so excited, I was seriously afraid I would finish before she got started.

And then I remembered something. I reached to the floor and pulled my wallet out of my jeans. From the place where normally a credit card would be, I removed a wrinkled thin square package.

"Hold on a sec," I told her. "I've got a rubber."

I had been carrying it around with me for a good year or two. One night when Lonnie was buying a box of them at a drugstore on Chester Avenue, he ripped the box open and tossed me one. "Here," he said, "put this in your wallet. You never know when you'll need it." I never needed it until now. I didn't know if it would even still work since it had been crammed in my wallet forever and it looked pretty crumpled up.

Marisol gave me that look with her eyes again. It was a kind of pleading look. The kind of look you can't possibly say no to.

"Please don't put that on, *flaco*," she said. "I don't want there to be anything between us. I want to feel you inside me."

I knew there were all kinds of reasons why the rubber was a good idea, but strangely I couldn't think of any of them right at that moment. In fact, at that moment her suggestion seemed like a pretty darn good one. Besides, I was kind of nervous about putting it on in front of her. I wasn't sure I could even get it on right, and fumbling around for ten minutes while she laid there waiting seemed like a real good way to kill the mood. So I tossed the rubber away and got back to business.

She opened her legs, and I made my approach. I had a moment of panic when I didn't think I was going to be able to find where I was supposed to go. But she took ahold of me gently and guided me in. I was barely in before it was all over.

"Sorry," I apologized. "I didn't mean for that to happen so quick."

I thought she might be disappointed or even angry. But she just smiled her beautiful sly smile and said, "Don't worry, *flaco*, you're just getting started."

And she was right. That first misfire on the launching pad was just the first of many launches that night. Each one took a bit longer than the one before, which was good because I really needed to go slower to give her a chance to keep up with me. At first I felt a little guilty because it seemed like I was having all the fun. But when her turn finally came, she made up for it. She actually screamed. She screamed with such emotion that it scared me. Could it really feel that good for her? It nearly didn't seem possible. Was it partly play-acting, part of making the night the perfect romantic scene in the perfect movie? I couldn't tell, and in the end I didn't care. All I knew was that she made me feel like I was the greatest lover in the whole history of making love. And it was a great feeling.

It was definitely the best way ever to finally lose my virginity.

Marisol seemed so experienced in so many ways that I found it hard to believe that she couldn't tell that that night was my first time. But she kept talking about me like she knew I had had lots of women before and she made me feel like I was the best lover ever. Did she really think that, or was that her way of making the night great for both of us?

The fact is, I felt like I was way behind every other guy I knew when it came to having sex. It seemed like everyone I knew was having sex all the time. Or at least that was the impression they gave. Maybe some of it—or even most of it—was bullshit, just to impress everyone else. Who knows. Lonnie and I always talked like we were both experienced sexually, but he had to know that I hadn't had much opportunity to "become a man." Lonnie, on the other hand, had lost his virginity at the age of 12, at least according to him. That was thanks to the 14-year-old girl that lived next door to him. From the time he reached 15, I was hearing about one sexual exploit after another. It was interesting, though, he never talked about having sex with Linda. I sometimes wondered if they had ever actually done it. But there was no point thinking about it too much because it always ended up making me feel depressed. At least now I didn't have to pretend I knew what sex was all about. Now I could speak from experience. And what an experience! I felt like I had gotten two years' worth of experience all in that one night.

At one point during the night, Marisol cuddled up to me and said, "Thank you, Dallas, for being so gentle with me."

"Yo tay key arrow," I said.

"You know…" she said.

"Hmmm…"

"This was very special," she said. "You know, it was my first time."

"Huh?" Somehow I was sure she had done this lots of times. I mean, she did everything so perfect. Was she shitting me?

"You were very good," I said. "Uh, Marisol. I forgot to ask. How old are you?"

"How old do you think?"

"Nineteen? Twenty?"

She smiled that sly smile. "I'm sixteen since last week. *¿Tú lo crees?*"

No, I didn't believe it. Could this really be true? She was so self-assured, so mature, so sophisticated. Could she really be two years younger than me? Thinking about it made my head hurt. I took another sip of *vino tinto* and decided to pretend I hadn't heard her say it.

While we laid there, we could hear music coming through wall from one of the other rooms. It must have been a radio or a television. A song was playing. I never heard it before. But it would stick in my mind forever. The guy who was singing it was a bit over-dramatic for my taste. But Marisol became very sentimental.

"You know, *flaco*, I always hated this song. It is so corny. But now, whenever I hear it, I will always think of you. Now it is our song."

"What's it about?"

"It's called '*Bésame Mucho*.' That means, kiss me. Kiss me a lot."

"Well, then," I said, trying to be clever. "I guess that's what I better do."

"It's true, *flaco*. I will never hear this song again without thinking of you."

And I knew that, whenever I heard it, I would think of her too. Always. I kissed her and whispered, "I love you, Mary Loneliness."

I lost count of how many times Marisol and I made love that night. I just felt sorry for the maid who was going to have to take the sheets off the bed! I didn't want that wonderful night to ever end. Even when we weren't making love, lying there in her arms was the most comfortable place I ever was. I didn't ever want to leave. The longer the night went on, the more it all seemed like a dream. I don't even remember falling asleep.

I do remember, though, after what seemed like many hours later, the sound of the door being unlocked and then being opened. It took me several seconds to remember where I was. The candles had all burned down, and the room was dark. The only other sound was Marisol's breathing. I had no idea what time it was, but it was clearly the middle of the night.

As the door opened, the light that came in hurt my eyes. I shaded them with my hand and squinted in the direction of the door. A fat man in an expensive suit stood there. He was bald and had a black moustache. He looked and smelled like he was coming off a long evening of brandy and cigars. I detected a huge amount of anger in his voice. Maybe even violence.

"*¡Qué diablos!*"

My mind was working in slow motion. But I can remember finally thinking to myself, oh, this must be Marisol's father.

8
Escaping Guaymas

I DIDN'T have a lot of time to think about what an awkward situation I was in. To the extent that I had come to this room with a plan, it hadn't involved falling asleep and then being woke up by the furious father of the sixteen-year-old I had just fucked—twenty-seven times. I guess I had sort of planned to slip out of the room sometime before her parents came back, but that's just not the way it worked out. Now I was meeting daddy. And daddy, to put it mildly, was not one bit happy.

Before I could say or do anything, I was lifted up out of the bed by two arms that were a lot stronger than I would have expected an old fat guy to have. Mr. Carvajal had a strong smell of smoke and what was probably a pretty pricy aftershave. He pressed me up hard against the wall of the room and growled at me—just an inch or two away from my face. His breath reeked of alcohol and cigars. My shoulder blades hurt something terrible. And the fact that he wasn't letting me move was scaring me shitless. Me being as naked as a jaybird was only making it worse.

"*¡Qué coño te crees que estás haciendo, cabrón!*"

Marisol quickly sat up and pulled the sheet up to her neck.

"*¡Papi!*" she cried. "*¡No le hagas daño! ¡Por favor!*"

I hoped he would listen to her. But he didn't. So fast I didn't even see it coming, he punched me right in the gut. I don't know if it's possible, but he hit me so hard it felt like he actually managed to bruise a kidney. I would have doubled over in pain if he wasn't pressing me so hard against the wall. I thought I might pass out. In desperation and still groggy from sleeping and drinking wine, I thought for some reason that, if I could just explain to him how much I loved his daughter, he might cool down. I gave it my best shot.

"Yo tay key arrow," I gasped, immediately feeling like an idiot.

I can't imagine what he and Marisol were thinking at this point. Clearly, he was not impressed. The way he was holding me against the wall and pressing harder and harder made it clear that he was mad as hell, like a raging bull. I was seriously afraid that I was going to be beaten to death.

"*¡Hi' de puta!*" he snarled.

He punched me again, this time even harder. Things started going black. Only the feeling that I was going to throw up seemed to be keeping me conscious.

At this point, a woman walked into the room. I figured it was Marisol's mother. She was dressed to the nines with a ton of jewelry. She took one look at her husband and me up against the wall, and she screamed. That was all it took for him to relax the pressure against my aching body—just for a second. Somehow my survival instinct kicked in and I slipped out of his grip.

Unfortunately, there was no way I could get past him to the door, so I moved as fast as I could toward the only other means of escape, the sliding door to the balcony. I rushed over to that sucker and had it open in seconds. Without a moment's hesitation, I ran out and threw myself over the railing.

I landed with a thud on the hard red tiles below. I was afraid I had broken a leg or an arm. As I struggled to stand, all of the pain seemed to be coming only from where I was punched and where I had hit the ground—not from any broken bones. I was sure that he would be coming after me as soon as he could get to an outside door, so I ran (hobbled, actually) back to my own room. I only paused long enough to throw up on the side of a wall.

Luckily, our room was on the ground floor. I limped up to the window and knocked. There was no response. I knocked harder. Still nothing. I started pounding the glass with my fist.

"Open the fucking window!" I shouted. "It's me, Dallas!"

Finally, the window opened. It was Antonio, looking very sleepy.

"Hey, what are you doing out there?" he asked, reasonably enough.

I didn't bother answering his question. I pushed the window open wider and threw myself over window sill to land inside. Antonio's eyes widened as he looked at me laying there in all my naked glory and with bruises all over my body.

"Shit, man," he exclaimed. "What happened to you?"

"It's a long story. Where the hell is Lonnie?"

"He's not here. He never came back. I went looking for him when it started getting late and found him in the bar. He had made a new friend."

I figured as much. "Was she pretty?"

"It was a man. I didn't like the look of him. Lonnie and he went back to his room. I think they were doing drugs. I haven't seen him since."

Swell. I should have known that it was a bad idea to leave Lonnie by himself with so much time on his hands—and in fucking Mexico of all places. As bad as things had gotten, I guess I was learning not to underestimate the fact that they could still get even worse—especially when Lonnie was involved.

I dragged myself over to my backpack, pulled out a pair of underwear and put them on. Then I pulled myself up to the bed and sprawled on top of it. Now that the excitement was all over, my bruises were really starting to hurt. Antonio looked at me with serious concern.

"Did somebody beat you up?"

"Yeah. Marisol and I fell asleep, and then her father came in and caught us. He wasn't too happy, to put it mildly." I took a deep breath to get through a spasm of pain. "I guess I'll live, though."

Antonio went to the bathroom and came back with a washcloth that had been soaked in warm water. He started wiping my injuries and cleaning away any dirt that was clinging to me. Then he just sat there on the bed, stroking my hair, kind of like my mother might have done when I was younger and had gotten hurt. He seemed to know just what to do. The thought occurred to me that, living on the streets like he had, Antonio had probably gotten beat up a few times himself and probably had friends who got beat up. He was generally such a happy kid that I kept forgetting that he had had a pretty hard life. Definitely harder than Lonnie or I ever had.

I wasn't sure if I really wanted him putting his hand in my hair, but the fact was that it was actually making me feel better. So I didn't tell him to stop. Instead I just closed my eyes and pretended it was my mother doing it. But that was kind of weird too, so then I imagined that it was Marisol doing it. That really started making me feel better.

Maybe it is normal for crazy images to come into your head just after you've had a near-death experience but, as I was laying there and Antonio was cleaning my injuries, my mind flashed on a painting I had seen once in a church. It was of Jesus after he had come down off the cross and Mary Magdalene was there cleaning his wounds, just like Antonio was cleaning mine. Antonio looked so young and innocent and so full of goodness in that moment, I actually started to think he was some kind of saint. Because of the pain, I didn't think that I would be able to sleep. But with Antonio there running his hand down my hair over and over, it wasn't long before I was out like a light.

When I woke up, the sun was up already and the room was full of light. Antonio was over sitting on the other bed, watching me. I looked around.

"What time is it?" I asked. My first attempt to sit up reminded me of all the injuries I had suffered the night before.

"It's nine o'clock."

"Still no sign of Lonnie?"

He shook his head.

"Well, we better go find him. But I need you to do something for me first."

Antonio stood up, ready for action. I found a pen and a piece of paper and wrote my name, address and phone number on it. I folded it in half and handed it to Antonio.

"I need you to take this to room 217. There's a girl there. She's sixteen, but she looks about twenty. Give this to her—and only her. Not to anyone else. And definitely not her father. Under no circumstances give this to her father. Understand?"

Antonio grinned. "Is that Marisol?"

I nodded.

He whistled appreciatively. "Sixteen!"

"Can it," I said. "I'm not in the mood. Just make sure she gets this. I can't go anywhere near her room. If her father sees me, he'll kill me. He's probably already got people out looking for me. I'm never going to be able to leave this room ever again. But I have to get Marisol a way to contact me when she gets the chance. No one will think twice if they see you wandering around over there."

"I'm on the case!" said Antonio, excited to be part of an adventure.

He disappeared out the door. I sat down and looked through Lonnie's things for a pack of cigarettes. I didn't find any. I sat by the window and looked out. In my mind, I ran through everything that happened the night before. It was the most wonderful night of my life. But I felt like an idiot. Why didn't I exchange addresses and phone numbers with Marisol while I had the chance? Why didn't I get out of there before we fell asleep? How bad was she going to be punished? Was she going to be put in a convent for the rest of her life? My head hurt just thinking about it all.

After about fifteen minutes, Antonio returned. He had a serious look on his face. I guessed that he didn't have good news for me. But he did have my jeans and tee-shirt.

"Where did you get those?" I asked hopefully.

"I found them lying on the ground outside. It looked like someone threw them there. Out a window."

I went through the pockets. My wallet was there as well as the money that was in it. Well, at least that was something. Antonio handed my piece of paper back to me.

"She wasn't there. She was gone."

"Where did she go?"

He shrugged. "Home, I guess. I don't think you have to worry about that guy looking for you. The maid was making up the room. She said the whole family had checked out early. They're all gone."

My heart sank. "Did the maid say anything else?"

"Well, she was doing a lot of complaining about how the girl had left the room in a real mess." Antonio couldn't stop from letting out a quick laugh. "And she was *really* unhappy about the sheets!"

As upset as I was, I couldn't help but laugh too. And that's when I learned what that expression means when people say, it only hurts when I laugh. My laughter quickly turned to a groan.

I was quickly becoming depressed. It started sinking in that Marisol was actually gone. I had been so worried that her father was going to come after me when I should have been worrying about her. I guess he was taking his anger out on her instead of me. It didn't seem fair.

The worst thing was that I had no way to get in contact with her or find her. All I had was her name and the fact that she lived in Monterrey. On the one hand, it might not actually be that hard to find her if I went to Monterrey. There could only be so many Carvajals in the Monterrey phone book. On the other hand, what would I do even if I did find her? I could hardly knock on her front door and ask her father to let me resume my relationship with his sixteen-year-old daughter. Could I?

So, what was my alternative? Wait for two years until she was eighteen and then go look for her? She would probably have forgotten me by then. I couldn't imagine that she wouldn't have another boyfriend (or two) by then. Maybe even a fiancé. No, the world was definitely looking very bleak that morning.

Antonio was looking at me sympathetically. "You really liked her, didn't you?"

"Antonio," I said, "I'm in fucking love with her. And I don't know what I'm going to do. I'm probably not ever going to see her again. I don't think I will ever love any woman like I love her. It's impossible."

Antonio laid his hand quietly on my shoulder. He really seemed to get how I was feeling. If it was Lonnie, he would have just made some kind of joke and told me to get on with it and forget about her and go find another woman to fuck.

"So," said Antonio, "will we go look for Lonnie?"

"Yeah," I said, standing up and limping toward my backpack. "Let's go look for Lonnie."

I threw on some clothes, and we headed for the bar. That was always the logical first place to look when you were trying to find Lonnie. Not surprisingly, it was very quiet. And there was no sign of him. I asked the bartender if he had seen my gringo friend. The good thing about asking a bartender, any bartender, if he had seen Lonnie, they always knew right away who you were talking about. He told me that he hadn't been around since the bar had opened that morning.

I was thinking about what our next move should be when I caught some movement out of the corner of my eye. In a shadowy corner, a man was sitting there with a cup of coffee and a newspaper, smoking a cigarette. He was motioning at me and Antonio to come over to him. I went over to see what he wanted.

"You would want to tell your friend to be careful," he said in heavily accented English. "He could find himself in very serious trouble."

Yeah, yeah, he wasn't telling me anything I didn't already know. "Do you know where he is?" I asked.

He looked to one side and then the other. He leaned toward me and spoke a bit softer. "You might look for him in room 103." He paused for just a moment. "It might be for the best if the three of you left Guaymas today."

The guy gave me the creeps. Was he a cop? Could he possibly work for Carvajal? Or maybe he was just a helpful guy giving us some good advice. In the end, it didn't matter. But whoever he was, he had clearly been paying close attention to us for some time.

"*Muchas gracias*," I said. "I think we will."

Antonio and I walked down a hallway until we found room 108. I knocked firmly on the door. There was no response. Why is it, I wondered, no one ever seems to open a door or, for that matter, a window on the first knock? I knocked again, more forcefully.

The door opened. The room was dark inside. A scruffy guy in a dirty white tee-shirt stuck his head out and looked at each of us in turn.

"Yeah?" he said.

"Is Lonnie here?" I asked.

He looked at the two of us again and then called behind him, "Your friends are here."

He disappeared back inside and about a minute later Lonnie appeared. He looked even worse than I probably did. His eyes were only half-open, but that was enough to see that they were bloodshot and bright red. His face was an ashen color. He looked like he hadn't shaved for a few days. His voice was hoarse, like he had been smoking non-stop for a week.

"Oh, hi," he said, like it was a total surprise that he would be seeing us. "What's up?"

"C'mon," I said. "It's time to go. We've been told that it's time to leave Guaymas."

He blinked his eyes and looked a bit confused. "Why? Who said...?"

"We can talk about it in the car," I said. "Now, come on and get your stuff. We're checking out."

"Okay, man. Hold your horses."

Man, he was really out of it. I did not like this one bit. I could hear his new friend saying something to him from inside the room, but I couldn't make out what it was.

"Just minute," he called to me. "I'll be right there. I just have to take care of something first."

The door was closed, and Antonio and I stood there in the hallway, waiting. The two of us looked at each other. I could tell that Antonio really did not have a good feeling about Lonnie's friend or the whole situation. I was feeling the same. Finally, the door opened and Lonnie stepped out.

"Okay," he said. "Let's go."

As we walked back to our own room, he started to get back more to his normal self. He looked me up and down, like he was seeing me for the first time.

"What the fuck happened to you?" he asked.

"I don't want to get into it."

"How did you get on with María whatserface?"

"It was a great night. Until I got beat up."

Lonnie let out a knowing whistle.

"Ouch. Did she have a boyfriend? Or a husband?"

Antonio smirked.

"Worse," I said. "She had a father."

Lonnie looked at me kind of sideways. "Just how old is this chick anyway?"

"Sixteen!" Antonio piped in, helpfully.

Lonnie rolled his eyes with mock disgust and grinned. "You devil!"

"Don't start," I said. "I'll give you the whole story when we get on the road."

We packed up and threw our stuff in the trunk of the car. Lonnie went to reception to settle up our bill. When he came back out, he was looking pretty serious.

"Everything all right?" I asked.

"Yeah," he said, but somehow I got the feeling he would have things to discuss after we got on the road.

We all climbed into the Chevy, and Lonnie said, "So, I guess we'll be heading back up to Hermosillo then."

I turned to look at Antonio in the back seat. His head was down, and he didn't say anything.

"Antonio," I said, "do you still want us to leave you in Hermosillo so you can look for your mother?"

Finally, he answered quietly, "I don't know."

Lonnie was quickly losing patience. "Speak up, kid! That was the plan. You wanted to be left in Hermosillo. Isn't that right?"

Antonio looked up at me. He seemed confused, not his usual cocky self.

"Uh, do you think it would be okay if I just kept going with you guys? I promise I won't be any trouble."

I had to chuckle. Antonio had been absolutely no trouble at all the whole time he was riding with us. Unless maybe you count the time he disappeared on us in Tijuana. I was actually glad he wanted to stay with us. I never felt right about the idea of leaving him on his own in Hermosillo.

"What about your mom?" I asked him gently.

For the first time since I'd known him, he actually looked like he might cry. He turned away and said, "I don't really know if she's in Hermosillo. I didn't like the guy she was with. I had a bad feeling about him. He could have taken her anywhere by now. I don't think he wanted me to find them. If she really wanted to find me, she would have come back to Los Angeles."

My heart was really breaking for the poor kid. It had to be tough to admit to himself, let alone us, that his mother was willing to abandon him for some guy. I felt like I should say or do something to try to make it better for him. But Lonnie spoke first.

"Hey, kid, this wasn't part of the deal. This is just fucking great. So we have to keep looking after your sorry ass and feeding you when we have enough of our own problems to worry about."

I could have killed Lonnie. I knew and accepted that he was an asshole. Like I always joked, it was a key part of his charm. But there was no call for him to be so mean to Antonio. I knew that deep down he didn't mean it. There was something else eating at Lonnie, and he was just taking it out on the kid.

Antonio looked down at his lap and didn't say anything. I felt really bad for him.

"Look, asshole," I said to Lonnie, "if Antonio wants to keep traveling with us, well, he fucking well can, as far as I'm concerned. He was a hell of a lot more help to me last night than you were."

I knew this was liable to piss Lonnie off, but he didn't even seem to be focused on what we were talking about. It was then that I noticed how pale his face was, and his eyes were kind of glassy, like he might pass out or something. At that moment, he pulled the keys out of the ignition and dropped them in my lap.

He opened his door and, and as he stepped out of the car, he told me, "I'm too wasted to drive. You figure out where we're fucking going and who all is going there. And then *you* drive."

Then he opened the back door and told Antonio, "Move, peckerhead. I'm taking over the back seat."

I slid over to behind the steering wheel, while Antonio scrambled over the back of the front seat to the place next to me. He was thrilled to be sitting up front for a change. Me, I was in shock. Lonnie never let me drive his car. He was obviously in worse shape than I realized if he was handing the keys over to me, just like that.

"Well, Antonio, that settles it. Not only are you still part of our outlaw gang, but you've been promoted to the shotgun position. Congratulations."

Antonio's face broke out into a big toothy grin. Just like the first time I ever saw him.

I turned over the engine and took a minute to get familiar with the gearshift. I kept expecting a snide comment from behind me, telling me that I was doing something wrong or that I wasn't treating his pride and joy right. Lonnie was always particular about his cars. At least 'til he crashed them. I glanced at the back seat. Lonnie was dead to the world. He was stretched out the full width of the car, and there was not a peep out of him. I guess I really was in charge now.

"Okay, you're my *número dos* now, kid."

Antonio raised his hand to his eyebrow in salute. "*¡Ay ay, comandante!*" He was really enjoying this.

"So, tell me which way to go, *número dos.*"

"That way, *comandante!*" he pointed. "Just follow the signs to Ciudad Obregón. On *Carretera Quince.*"

"Keen say, eh? That's fifteen, right?"

"Excellent, *comandante.* Your Spanish is getting very good. We'll have you talking like a real Mexican yet."

I knew that wasn't very likely. But I had made up my mind to learn as much Spanish as I could, as long as we were in a country where everybody spoke it. Maybe it was a crazy dream, but I had this picture in my head of finding my way to Marisol's house in Monterrey and knocking on her door. And when she opened the door, I'd be speaking Spanish to her, all fluent like. And she'd be really impressed. And we'd pick up right where we had left off. Yeah, it was a crazy dream all right, but right at that moment it was pretty much all that was keeping me going.

9
The Road South

I DROVE us across the bridge into Empalme and then we joined up with Highway 15, heading south. I kind of hated to leave Guaymas behind and especially the Gulf of California. I really liked being by the sea. We were back to driving straight road though the barren desert, which was kind of boring. It quickly became obvious that this drive was going to be none too exciting. A couple of times, I tried talking to Lonnie, but he was out like a light. That was too bad because we had some stuff to discuss. Like how far we were going to drive that day and where did we want to stop for the night.

I tried the radio, but I could hardly find any stations. The choice was pretty much between mariachi music and some guy jabbering away in Spanish, so I ended up turning it off. To keep from getting totally bored, I figured I would talk some to Antonio. Even though he had been with us for quite a while now, he and I really hadn't talked that much. Usually, it was Lonnie and me doing most of the talking. I really didn't know that much about the kid.

I asked him about the comic books I had seen him reading. Turns out he was a real Marvel fan. His favorites were *Spider-man* and *The Incredible Hulk*. He would read DC comics sometimes, but he didn't like them as much. Superman was kind of silly, he said, and he couldn't take Batman seriously since that TV series a few years ago. And he would be better without Robin or Batgirl. He said *Batman* was best when Neal Adams was drawing the comic book. I had read one or two comic books in my time, but I never paid any attention to who was drawing them. Antonio did.

This led us to talking about all kinds of other stuff. I couldn't get over how much he knew about all kinds of things. Finally, I asked him something I had been wondering about but wasn't sure how to bring up. Because I knew it was probably going to be a sore subject for him.

"So, how long were you living on your own there in L.A. since your mom left?"

"I dunno. I think I was eleven when she left."

"So, you've been on your own for three years?"

He shrugged. "I guess."

"How did you manage by yourself all that time?"

The question obviously annoyed him. "I told you how I managed."

"How long were you staying with Michael?"

He shrugged again. "I dunno. I think it was since February."

"That's only about six months. Where were you before that?"

Antonio was losing patience with all my questions. I guess he felt like I was interrogating him or something. And I guess I was.

"Different places," he answered, a bit testy. "What does it matter? Where were *you* six months ago?"

"Six months ago I was still in high school, looking forward to graduating. I was living with my parents."

"Yeah, well, it must be nice."

"Did you ever go to school?"

"Yeah, I went to school. Why all the questions, *comandante*?"

"I'm just trying to understand you. For a street kid, you seem really smart. I don't just mean street smart. You seem

112

educated. You're always reading comic books, in both English and Spanish. You just seem to know a lot of stuff for..."

"For what?"

"For, you know, a kid who..."

"For a homeless Mexican kid?"

"Well, yeah."

"Before my mom left, I always went to school. I hardly ever missed any days, and I always got good grades too. My teachers always told me that I was going to grow up and get some kind of professional job."

"But you had to stop going to school after your mom left..."

Antonio's face went a little dark. "Yeah. I tried to keep going for a while, but when I got kicked out of the apartment, I had to spend all my time finding a way to buy food."

Antonio didn't say anything else for a while. He just sort of bit his lip and looked out the passenger side window. Finally, he spoke again.

"A few months before I met Michael, I was staying with another guy. For almost a year."

"Was it another guy like Michael?"

"Kind of. He was a professor at UCLA. I met him on the street. Sometimes at night Lawrence would pick me up in his car and... he would give me money..."

It kind of turned my stomach to think about what Antonio had to do for the money. I knew he didn't want to talk about it any more than I wanted to hear about it.

"And you wound up living with him?"

"Yeah. He would always drive around looking for me. Finally, one night he asked if I wanted to go home with him. I said okay. He took me to his apartment in Westwood. After... afterwards, he asked if I had any place to live. I told him I didn't, and he asked me if I would like to stay with him for a while. And I said, yeah."

"Did he... hurt you ever?"

He looked like he didn't quite know how to answer that. Finally, he said, "Mostly, he was real good to me. In a funny way, he was sort of like a dad to me. He looked after me. It's just that... sometimes... he wanted me to..."

"Didn't that... I dunno.. how did you put up with that?"

"I just did what I had to do. I just thought about something else, you know. I mean, it was worth it. I had a safe place to sleep every night and all the food I wanted."

"Yeah, but still..."

Antonio's eyes flashed at me. I hadn't really seen him get mad before. "If you were in the same place as me, I bet you would have done the same thing."

"Hey, I'm not judging you. I just... I feel bad for you, that's all. I wish you didn't have to go through all that."

"Yeah, well, I wish I had grown up my whole life in a nice house with a mom and a dad there all the time. But I got by. I knew kids on the street who got beat up. I knew kids who died. But I wasn't one of them. I figured out how to take care of myself."

He continued, "I didn't like some of the things Lawrence did, but he wasn't really a bad guy. He talked to me all the time. I think he was lonely or something. And he taught me things. A lot of things. It was sort of like having my own private teacher. I guess that's kind of what made it all worth it. I learned a lot of stuff from him."

"How come you stopped living with him?"

"One night one of the other professors came to his apartment. She said the other people on the faculty were aware that I was living with him. She said that he was going to get into trouble, maybe even lose his job if he didn't get rid of me. He gave me a few hundred dollars and said he wished me luck and that he was sorry we couldn't be together anymore. He was really sad about it. I think maybe..."

"Maybe what?"

"I think he was sort of in love with me."

I wasn't having any of it. "Just 'cause he cared about you doesn't make what he did right."

"At the time I wasn't really thinking about what was right or not right. That was just the situation, and I just got through it. The best way I could."

I didn't say anything to this. I just kind of thanked God in my head that I had parents who loved me and I never had to deal with, or even think about, shit like that.

Antonio seemed to be looking for words. "Do you... do you think I'm disgusting? I never really talked to anyone about all this before."

I wasn't sure how to answer this. I took a minute to try to find words for what I was thinking.

"Look, Antonio. I can't shit you and say that some of the stuff you did doesn't make me a little sick. I want to think that, in the same situation, I wouldn't have done what you did. But I'll never know for sure. I guess, in the end, you just did what you had to do. You're a survivor. In spite of everything, I have to respect that. But Jesus..."

I had a question for him, but I didn't know quite how to ask it. "So... because of all the stuff you had to do on the streets... do you... I mean, has it made you, you know, like guys...?"

He answered quick, without even thinking about it. "No. I like girls. I really like girls. I don't like doing it with guys. It's just, you know, sometimes you just do what you got to. You know?"

"Yeah, I know." But the truth was, I didn't know a goddamn thing.

We were both quiet for a few miles. Then I said, "You know, Antonio, you're a pretty amazing guy. I... admire you."

His head was turned down, but he looked up at me with a questioning look, like he wasn't sure if I was being serious or making fun of him.

"No, I mean it," I said. "You're a lot smarter than I was at your age. Hell, you're a lot smarter than I am now. I don't know if I would have come through what you came through in as good a shape. And you can speak two languages. Hell, I can barely talk English halfway right. But you speak it as good as I do, and you know Spanish. That must be cool to do that."

I thought he would be happy to hear me complimenting him, but he stayed very serious.

"It's not easy talking two languages. It gets confusing."

"Confusing? But I never hear you make any mistakes when you talk. Not like I would know anyway if your English was perfect or not. But it sounds right to me."

"It's not that it's hard to talk or get things right. It's just that…"

"It's just what?"

"It's hard to explain. It's like, when I switch from one to the other, I become a different person. I think different. I see things different. It's weird. Sometimes it gives me a headache."

"How d'ya mean? Why would things be different?"

"Like I said, it's hard to explain. But when I speak Spanish, I just see the world in a certain way. Then, when I start speaking English, I see it in a different way. I don't know how to explain any better than that."

"Like what would be different, for example?"

"I dunno. Well, for one thing, the jokes are different. Things that are funny in Spanish aren't always funny in English. And vice versa. Mexicans and Americans just see things in different ways."

"Well, maybe if I learn enough Spanish, I'll understand what you're talking about."

"Hey, I know a joke that you have to know both Spanish and English to get. Want to hear it?"

"Okay."

116

"A fox and a jaguar meet in the jungle. The jaguar says, '*How're ya?*' And the fox says, 'I'm *sorry.*'" He pronounced "how're ya" and "sorry" kind of funny. He grinned like I should be laughing.

"I don't get."

"You see? 'H'wahr' is how you say jaguar in Spanish. *Jaguar.* 'So row' means fox. *Zorro.* You get it now?"

"Kinda. See what I mean, though? You'd have to be smart to get that joke. That just shows you're a lot smarter than me."

I think he appreciated me saying that, but he was getting embarrassed. He obviously thought it was time to change the subject.

"So, what's the story with you and Marisol?"

Hearing her name was like getting punched in the gut again.

"I don't know if I can talk about it," I said. "It's just that... I mean... Damn, now I'm the one finding it hard to put something into words."

"You're really in love with her, aren't you?"

"Yeah, I am in love with her. I know that sounds crazy. I mean, I only met her a couple of days ago. But she's all I can think about. I feel like I'll go stark raving mad if I can't see her again. It's eating me up inside. Damn it, it's driving me insane. I love her. I'll always love her. I'll never love anyone else. I couldn't. Does that sound crazy to you? It has to. But that's how I feel, and I can't imagine it ever changing. I'm fucked."

Antonio smiled at me sympathetically. Just knowing that someone else actually seemed to understand what I was feeling made me feel a bit better.

"That's cool, man," he said. "I think it's neat. I hope I meet someone who makes me feel that way someday. I think Marisol would be lucky to have you for a boyfriend. You definitely have to go find her in Monterrey."

After several minutes of silence, Antonio spoke again.

"Hey, I have another joke. I think you will like this one better."

"Okay. Shoot."

"How come you love the sea and the sun?"

"How come *I* love the sea and the sun?"

"Yeah, you."

The fact is, I always did love the sea. I loved being out of the heat of the San Joaquin Valley and somewhere that wasn't always hot and dry. But how did Antonio know?

"Okay, I'll bite. How come I love the sea and the sun?"

"Because 'sea and sun' in Spanish is *mar y sol*! Get it? Marisol!"

I had to chuckle. Antonio was grinning like a fool. I had to admit, he was definitely clever.

A few more miles went by without either of us saying anything. Then Antonio spoke again.

"You're a good guy, Dallas. Thanks for being my friend."

I actually started to get a lump in my throat. I was really starting to feel close to this kid. But there was no way I was going to get too sappy about it.

"Okay, we're getting way too fucking sentimental around here, *número dos*. Time to shape up!"

"*¡Ay ay, comandante!*"

Within a couple of hours we were past Ciudad Obregón. And the country we were driving through was changing. There was more vegetation, even trees. Things stopped looking so barren. We even started seeing farms. In fact, it was kind of starting to look a bit like home.

All the way, Antonio and I kept talking. I was surprised how much we found to talk about. I mean, we didn't really have that much in common, and he was four years younger than me. But once we got to talking, it was like we knew each other forever. The time flew by, as we passed through Los Mochis and Culiacan.

118

After we passed near a place called La Cruz, we started getting views of the Gulf of California again. It was great to see the sea again.

A few miles further down the road, we passed on old beat-up white sign along the side of the road that said in big black letters, "TROPICO DE CANCER."

"Do people around here get a lot of cancer?" I wondered out loud.

Antonio laughed. "This is the Tropic of Cancer, *comandante*. This is the farthest north the sun comes in the summer."

"Yeah, I knew that," I lied. "So we're officially in the tropics now, huh?"

This new milestone made me feel even further away from home. It was only a few more miles after seeing that sign that we found ourselves coming into Mazatlán. It was getting to be early evening.

I had been watching the gas gauge and figured it was time to fill up. I pulled into a Pemex station and asked for the *lleno*. Then I opened the door to the back seat and started shaking Lonnie.

"Hey!" I yelled at him. "Wake up! I need money for gas."

Lonnie took a while to come to. He was still pretty much out of it.

"Where the fuck are we?" he grunted.

"Mazatlán."

He squinted his eyes like his head hurt. It was probably occurring to him that he didn't have a clue where Mazatlán was.

"How much do you need?" he said, digging a hand into his jeans pocket.

"Fifty pesos should do it."

He pulled some wadded up bills out of his pocket and handed them to me. He shook his head.

"We're, uh, going to have to travel a bit more frugally from now on. No more nice hotels."

"Huh? What about all that money you 'borrowed' from Don? We can't have gone through all of that already."

"Yeah, well, uh, I had some personal expenses."

"What personal expenses?"

I had an idea, but I knew he wasn't going to tell me. "They're personal. That's why they're called personal expenses."

"Hey, if you're spending our money on something, I got a right to know."

"It's not *our* money," he shot back angrily. "I'm the one who brought it. I stole it from my asshole stepfather fair and square. So I don't need to check with you how I spend it, do I?"

He had a point. Although I brought some of my own money, it was mostly the money Lonnie had brought that we were spending.

"So, how much do you have left?"

He got that stubborn look on his face. I knew I wasn't going to get an exact number out of him.

"Look, we should be all right, as long as we don't go crazy with what's left."

"You mean the way you went crazy in Guaymas?"

"Hey, I got a right to have a little fun while we're traveling. I mean, it's sort of like a vacation. And it's not like you were around in the evenings to keep me company."

That crack made me feel a little guilty. For most of our lives, we had had an understanding. Lonnie's job was to get me to do stuff that I knew I shouldn't do. On the other hand, my job was to try to keep Lonnie from doing too many crazy dumb-ass things that he was bound to regret. By leaving him by himself with so much time on his hands in a strange place, I hadn't exactly been holding up my end of the understanding. I was feeling responsible for him going off the deep end in Guaymas. But that was over.

There was no more Marisol to distract me now. It was time to be practical.

"So at least tell me that we've got enough money so that we can afford gas for the drive back home."

"Yeah, yeah, we'll be fine."

"And what about if we have any emergencies? Like if the car breaks down or something?"

"Yeah, well, if that happens, we'll be fucked anyway. I don't know if I trust any Mexican to work on this car."

I always knew in my head that this whole trip was not really the smartest idea. The further we got away from California, the more it seemed like a disaster in the making. I could see us getting stranded God knows where with no way of getting help. But it was Lonnie's car and Lonnie's money, so I knew I didn't have a lot of say. My only choice seemed to be to continue on with him and see what happened. It might not end up pretty, but it was guaranteed to be interesting.

Lonnie pulled his pack of cigarettes out of his pocket and offered me one. He lit both his and mine and then took a long, satisfying drag. He was getting back more to being his normal self. He had a few good puffs without saying anything, and then nodded his head in the direction of Antonio, who was looking at posters on a wall.

"So," said Lonnie, trying to sound uninterested in his own question, "is he your new best friend now?"

That caught me off guard. Even though Lonnie seemed to have been passed out for pretty much the whole day's drive, I wondered how much of the chatter between me and Antonio he heard. It was like he was jealous or something. I found that idea pretty funny, since Lonnie and I had been friends our whole entire lives. Hell, no one knew either of us as well as we knew each other. How did he think anyone else could compete with that?

I laughed at him. "Yeah, the Mexican kid I met just a few days ago is now my best friend in the whole world. Any other questions?"

Lonnie didn't seem to be in a joking mood. "You're really good with him. Kind of reminds me of when Tommy Dowd used to spend time with me when I was about his age. Me, I don't have patience for kids who are a lot younger than me."

I decided it was time to change the subject. "It's getting late, Lon. Where do you want to spend the night?"

He took a look around where we were and said, "Let's drive past Mazatlán and then look for a place to pull over for the night. We'll sleep in the car."

I couldn't stop myself from groaning a little. After a few nights in a hotel, my back was not looking forward at all to trying to sleep in the Chevy again.

After I paid the guy for filling the gas tank, Lonnie bought a couple of quarts of oil and changed the oil in the car. I told him that I would have just had the guy in the gas station change it. But he said he didn't trust any Mexican—or even American, in most cases—gas station jockey to touch his car under the hood. Maybe he was right. Anyway, when it came to his car, Lonnie was going to look after it his own way, no matter what anyone else said.

After he had that job finished and had washed his hands in the restroom, we all climbed back into the car. We were all back in our usual places, with Lonnie in his rightful position behind the wheel.

"Now" he said, without turning his head but directing himself to Antonio behind him, "which way do I go?"

Antonio, consulting his roadmap, directed him through the city of Mazatlán. "Keep following *Carretera Quince*. Follow any signs you see for Tepic or Guadalajara."

Along the way, we stopped at a little store and loaded up on food—some bread and cheese and other stuff—and, of course, Jarritos and Tecate. After we left Mazatlán, Lonnie drove down *Carretera* 15. As it got dark, Lonnie kept on driving. It was like once he got behind the wheel again, he didn't want to stop. After about an hour and a half, we were all getting pretty sleepy. Finally, just as we were getting close to a place called El Rosario,

Lonnie turned down a quiet dirt side road. A mile or two down that road, he pulled over and announced, "I guess this is as good a place as any."

We were all dead tired. Lucky Antonio was able to stretch out in the back seat. Lonnie and I slept sitting up in the front. I was surprised that Lonnie could go to sleep so easy. After all, he had slept all day during the drive down from Guaymas. But, as tired as I was, he was already snoring before I could fall asleep.

It was one of those nights where I felt I didn't sleep at all. But I know I must have because, every time I checked my watch, it was one or two hours later than the last time. I just couldn't get comfortable, and it wasn't exactly natural to be sleeping in a sitting position anyway. The night dragged on for what seemed like forever. It seemed like whole days had gone by when I finally opened my eyes and saw the sky getting brighter behind the hills to the east.

At long last morning had come. And, as far as I was concerned, not a minute too soon.

10
Butterfly Dreams

I STEPPED out of the car and stretched my back and arms and legs in every direction I could. I walked down the road a bit, took a much-needed piss and walked back. Still trying to work the kinks out of my bones, I made a promise to myself that I wasn't going to sleep in the car anymore.

Lonnie and Antonio were still asleep. I reached behind the back seat under the rear window and grabbed Antonio's roadmap. I unfolded it and stood there in the cool morning air trying to read it in the faint light. As far as I could make out, we had driven about a thousand miles since we'd crossed the border into Mexico, maybe a bit more. The scary thing was that this was only about one-third of the length of the country. More than ever, it was sinking in—with me anyway—just how crazy this whole plan was. How crazy? Pretty damn fucking crazy. That's how crazy.

As the morning grew brighter, I studied the map. I measured how far we had driven the day before and then measured the same rough distance to the south. Hell, I thought, if we drove the same distance again today, then we wouldn't be all that far from Mexico City. And something I spotted on the map, about a hundred miles before Mexico City, gave me an idea for a better night's sleep.

I didn't have to wait too long until the other two were awake. Lonnie got out of the car and lit up a cigarette, his morning ritual.

"Morning, fuck face," I greeted him. "I been looking at the map. We should be nearly to Mexico City tonight. If we stop a bit short of there, I see a national park on the map. I think we should camp there tonight. I mean, we have our sleeping bags and we haven't even used them. And sleeping on the ground would have to be easier on my back than another night in your fucking car."

He seemed skeptical at first. "Yeah, and what about tarantulas?"

I hadn't thought of that. He was remembering the humungous spiders we saw in Guaymas, and now so was I. But even that wasn't enough to make me want to sleep in the car another night.

"We won't be in the desert anymore. There probably won't be any tarantulas. Anyway, we can check it out when we get there.

This was a lot of planning for Lonnie to take in before he had his second cigarette and his first cup of coffee.

"Yeah, yeah, whatever you think," he said. "How long before we get out of Mexico?"

"I'd say about three long days of driving, all of them pretty much like what we did yesterday."

He shook his head. "Man, this country just goes on and on. Who knew Mexico was so fucking big?"

"What d'you say to driving into El Rosario and seeing if we can get a decent breakfast? We didn't eat much yesterday."

Lonnie took a drag on his cigarette. "Okay. I could really use a cup of coffee anyway."

So, we got back in the car and headed into the town. But it turned out that it was too early in the morning and nothing was open. Still, it was a nice little place. It had a plaza in the middle, like all Mexican towns seemed to have, and it had a really nice big old church. I wouldn't have minded hanging out there for a while, but we had a long day of driving ahead of us. With our stomachs rumbling, we got back on *Carretera* 15.

We were on the road for nearly three hours before we came to a place where we could find something to eat. That was in a pretty big place called Tepic. It was at the end of ten miles or so of driving up into some mountains. Tepic seemed like a nice place, and there was a very high hill on one end of the town. Antonio, who always had his roadmap in his hand, informed us that it was the capital of the state of Nayarit.

I kind of remembered learning in school that Mexico was divided into states, just like the U.S. is. But I couldn't tell you the name of any of them. I asked Antonio how many states we had been in so far, and he said four. He went over the names of all of them, but I knew I wouldn't remember most of them.

By the time we sat down in the restaurant, we were starving, so we ordered nearly everything that was on the menu. And Lonnie and I kept ordering cups of coffee, even though they were charging us for each and every one. By the time we were finished eating, my mood had improved a lot. I thought I would bring up my idea of camping in the national park again, but before I could, we heard a church bell from a few blocks away.

Antonio stood up. "I think I'll go to Mass, guys. You wait for me here?"

This kind of took me by surprise. I hadn't really thought about whether Antonio would be someone who goes to church. But then why not? Catholics back home always seemed pretty serious about not missing church on a Sunday.

"Fine by me," I said. "I think I'll have another cup of coffee."

Antonio just stood there looking at me a bit hesitantly. Finally, he said what was on his mind. "Why don't you come with me, Dallas?"

"Huh?"

The last thing on my mind was going to church, any church, let alone a Catholic church. Lonnie's and my parents always took us to church every Sunday, but as soon as we got old enough, we just sort of refused to keep going. I figured I had learned everything the preacher had to tell me already, and mostly anymore he was just making me feel guilty about stuff.

"That's all right, Antonio," I said. "You go ahead. We'll wait here for you."

The kid started to get a little smirk on his face. "You should come, Dallas."

"Why," I asked. "Why should I go to church?"

His smirk was turning into a grin. "If you ever want to marry Marisol, you'll have to become a Catholic."

Well, that was something I hadn't thought about. Since meeting Marisol, I had done nothing but think about us "being together," whatever that meant. I suppose, if somehow against all the odds, I did find her and we got together, we might have to at some point talk about religion. But I wasn't nearly ready for looking that far ahead. And I wasn't particularly interested in sitting through a church service that would be in a language I didn't even understand.

Lonnie was looking pretty fucking amused at the whole conversation. He pulled out another cigarette and lit it up. "Go ahead, Dallas. I'll wait here for the two of you. Might do you some good."

"If it does me some good," I answered, "then it would have to really do you a lot *more* good."

Lonnie just laughed. Antonio kept standing there looking at me. I could tell that it would mean a lot to him for me to go with him. Normally, that wouldn't have made any difference, but finally I thought, what the hell, might as well see what church is like in a different country. So I got up and went with him.

He led me to a big church on the plaza. He found a place to sit on one of the pews, and I sat next to him. He knelt down and put his clasped hands on the bench in front of us and started praying. I figured I didn't need to do that. I sat there and had a look around. It was a nice church, bigger and more elaborate than any church I had been to before.

I looked up at the wall and saw a figure of Jesus nailed to a cross. It reminded me of something I heard the pastor in my church, Pastor Travis, say years ago when I was a kid. He said the difference between our church and the Catholics was that our church always had a cross without Jesus because we knew that Jesus had risen. The Catholics, he said, always kept Jesus on the cross.

When the priest came in, everyone stood up, so I did too. I figured I would just watch Antonio and stand up and sit down when he did. There seemed to be a lot more of that than I was used to. Every so often, everyone would kneel, and I wasn't sure if I should or not, but I ended up kneeling too, just so I wouldn't stick out so much.

At one point, the priest led everyone in reciting a prayer.

> *Padre nuestro que estás en los cielos,*
> *Santificado sea tu Nombre...*

Because I knew the word *padre* and because of the rhythm of the words, I immediately recognized it as being the Lord's Prayer. Out of some kind of automatic reaction, I found myself joining in—quietly and in English.

> *Our Father who art in heaven,*
> *hallowed be thy name...*

I hadn't said that prayer in an awful long time. It reminded me of being a small kid, and that made me feel very lonely and far away from home. When it came time for communion, everyone got up and stood in line in the center aisle. Everyone except for me and Antonio.

"You not taking communion?" I whispered to him.

"I can't. I never made my confirmation," he whispered back. "And I haven't been to confession for a long time."

The Catholic religion definitely seemed a lot more complicated than what I was used to. When I went to church with my parents, there would be an excited preacher talking a lot about having a personal relationship with Jesus. The priest here just seemed to be reciting all the same stuff he probably said at every Mass.

If Antonio wasn't in good standing with his church, I wondered, why did he want to bother going to Mass at all? As we were there kneeling, he pulled out the little cross that he wore on a chain around his neck. He held it like something precious in his brown fingers, and then he kissed it. I was hit with an unexpected wave of... I don't know what. Sadness? Longing? It made me remember my night with Marisol and how she had kissed her cross the same way. It brought back that whole night to me and made me miss her even more than I had already been missing her—if that was possible.

For the first time in a very long time, as I was kneeling there, I actually prayed. I asked God to please let me and Marisol be together. There was no particular reason for Him to listen to me, but it was definitely what I was feeling in my heart. I looked over at Antonio. He was praying too. I wondered what he was praying for.

After the Mass was over, we walked back to the restaurant. Lonnie was outside leaning against the Chevy, smoking yet another cigarette. It was obvious he had already spent enough time in Tepic. He was itching to get back on the road.

So off we went, heading south again on *Carretera* 15. We were all pretty quiet that day. I guess we had all spent so much time together that we had kind of run out of things to talk about. Lonnie was back in his usual place in the driver's seat, and he was usually happy to stay silent while he was driving—even on long trips. Antonio was quieter than usual. He seemed to be thinking about something. I had no idea what.

As for me, I was in a funny mood. Being in church had kind of made a lot of things start running through my mind. It made me think about my parents, and that made me think about how worried or mad they must be that I hadn't been in touch with them all this time. It also made me think about what would actually happen if, by some miracle, Marisol and I did happen to get together. My parents wouldn't be too happy that I was with a Catholic girl. The fact that she was from Mexico would only make it worse. I'd definitely be the talk of the town for a while—if I wasn't already.

I was also feeling a bit down about the way this car trip was going. We were covering a lot of miles, but we weren't really seeing much. We kept passing places that seemed interesting and that I wouldn't mind spending some time exploring. As it was, I just got glimpses of life in Mexico. Little villages with adobe houses that seemed to be falling apart. Kids with dirty feet playing ball in the middle of a street. A man in a white shirt herding a couple of cows down the road. An old woman dressed all in black sweeping the dust off her doorstep.

Also, I kept seeing signs for *playas*, which I knew meant beaches. I wouldn't have minded seeing some of them and maybe spending some time swimming or laying out in the sun. Or maybe taking some pictures. I hadn't taken any pictures since that day on the beach in Guaymas with Marisol. But Lonnie was determined to keep going as fast as he could. And I knew from the roadmap that we were now south of the Gulf of California and getting further and further from the Pacific Ocean. We were gaining elevation all the time.

I suppose, on top of everything else, I was just starting to get bored. I mean, we were doing a hell of a lot of driving. And the road just seemed to go on and on. I did enjoy seeing new country that I had never seen before. And seeing the sorts of places where people down here lived and getting an idea of what their life was like. But after enough days of driving all day every day without hardly stopping, well, it was starting to get old.

I wondered if Lonnie was getting bored too. The thing was, as long as he was driving, it kept it interesting for him. It's like he went into a trance when he was driving and the time didn't seem to matter to him. But after about three hours of driving, we came to Guadalajara and he suddenly seemed like he'd had enough.

Guadalajara was a huge city. Mostly what I remember about it was that it had a lot of really large old buildings, including some pretty impressive looking churches. Antonio said the old buildings would all mostly have been built by the Spaniards back in the days when they were in charge of Mexico.

We drove by a huge open air market where people seemed to be selling everything. There were people selling fresh flowers of all colors and also paper flowers. One stall was stacked with cages full of all kinds of different birds, including parrots and parakeets.

Along the street there was an open air meat shop with butchered animals just hanging out in the warm afternoon air, flies buzzing all around. Somehow it didn't make me particularly hungry for a steak or hamburger. There were also lots of different fruits and vegetables for sale, including one stand that had a huge stack of watermelons that looked really good right about then. But Lonnie didn't want to stop. He had something else in mind.

As we were making our way out of Guadalajara, Lonnie spotted a store with a sign that said *Licores* and he pulled over. Without saying anything, he got out of the car, went into the store by himself and then came back with a bottle in a paper bag.

He opened the back door to the car and told Antonio to scoot and told me, "You drive for a while."

We went back to our positions of the day before, with me driving and Antonio riding shotgun. Lonnie stretched out in the back seat with a pint bottle of bourbon. As I pulled back onto the highway, I gave him my dirtiest look in the rearview mirror.

"Starting a bit early, aren't you?" I said with a tone which was meant to let him know that I didn't really approve.

"Hell," he said, "I've done most of the driving on this trip. It's my turn to relax for a while."

"So, are you drinking alone now?"

He held the bottle in my direction. "Want some?"

I had been known to have a beer or two while driving, but not very often. Practically, the only times I ever drank in a car was with Lonnie, and Lonnie was always the one driving. But I knew that drinking whiskey and driving was probably not a good idea.

"Nah, I'll wait until we stop for the night. But thanks for thinking of me, asshole." The idea of Lonnie drinking by himself in the middle of the day didn't seem to me like a very good sign.

Anyway, that was our visit to Guadalajara. We continued heading southeast. We were all pretty quiet for a while. Lonnie drank about half the bottle and then he screwed the cap back on and put the bottle down. He made himself comfortable and then seemed to be having a nap. Apparently, he still wasn't fully recovered from his little party in Guaymas.

For nearly an hour we were driving along the shore of a big lake. It didn't look very deep, but it was definitely long. Seeing all that blue water nearly made the temperature feel cooler than it was. I entertained myself with anything at all interesting that I could see as we wound down the road. A boy on a horse. A man in a straw hat riding a donkey.

After a while, Antonio spoke up.

"So, I been wondering. Just what are you guys doing in Mexico anyway and where exactly are you going?"

I had been asking myself the exact same thing for days now, so I guess it shouldn't have been a surprise that Antonio was wondering too. I hadn't really thought about it from his point of view. He must have thought we were crazy to be making a long trip like this for no obvious reason. He didn't really need to worry about it as long as he was just getting a ride to Hermosillo. But now that he was tagging along for the whole trip, it was only natural that he was curious about where we were going and why.

"It's kind of a long story..." I began. I waited a bit, kind of hoping that Lonnie would jump in and explain, since the whole crazy thing had been his idea. But all we heard from Lonnie was some snoring.

"Well," said Antonio, "I'd say we have plenty of time for a long story, no?"

I couldn't argue with that. "Well, there was this guy back home named Tommy Dowd. And a couple of years ago, he went down to Central America and he was never heard from again. Lonnie has this idea that we might be able to find out what happened to him or maybe even find him."

Antonio's eyes grew big with amazement. "Are you serious? What country was he in?"

It was a logical question. And it made me feel kind of stupid. After all, we had come all this way. I should really have had a good idea of where it was we were going. The truth was, I never expected we would even get this far, so I guess I hadn't worried about it too much.

"I think it was Guatemala. That's in Central America, isn't it?"

Antonio made a pretty darn good effort not to laugh at me. "Yeah, it's right next to Mexico." He took a look at his roadmap. "We're nearly halfway there."

I took a quick glance at the map out of the corner of my eye. "Yeah, I guess we are."

"So what was this Tommy guy doing in Guatemala?"

"Well..." I really wished Lonnie was awake to answer these questions. Me trying to answer them just drove home how stupid this whole thing was. "He went down as some sort of reporter. I think there was a civil war going on or something. I think he wanted to write about it. But he disappeared. No one could find out what happened to him."

"Wow."

To my surprise, Antonio's first reaction wasn't to think that we were completely crazy. He actually seemed impressed.

"What do you think happened to him?"

The truth was, I didn't have a clue. "I dunno. I guess he did something or wrote something that one side or the other didn't like. They might have taken him prisoner. Or killed him."

"Which side do you think it was?"

I had no idea what the sides were in the stupid Guatemala civil war. If it even was a civil war.

"I don't know, Antonio. I guess I don't know enough about it. This is really Lonnie's deal. I don't know exactly what his plan is when we get there. I suppose we'll just ask around and see what we can find out."

I couldn't tell from the look on Antonio's face whether he thought we were the greatest heroes he had ever met or if he thought we were completely insane.

"Lucky you have me along," he said. "You're definitely going to need somebody who can speak Spanish for you."

Well, he was definitely right about that.

"So, what do *you* know about Guatemala?" I asked him. "Can you tell me what the civil war is about?"

Antonio shook his head. "I never been there. I don't know much about it. But I know they speak Spanish. Not everyone, but most of them."

"If they don't speak Spanish, what do they speak?"

He shrugged. "Indian languages. But that would be in really out-of-the-way places. That's true in Mexico too. But most people you'd be meeting would speak Spanish."

"Well, maybe you should start teaching me more Spanish. I got a feeling it could come in handy all right."

So, as we drove along, Antonio would point to things along the way and tell me the Spanish name for them. And I would repeat after him as close as I could. It seemed hopeless that I would actually pick up enough to be able to have a normal conversation in Spanish with anybody, but it helped pass the time. And, in the back of my mind, I kept thinking that, if I could just learn enough to say a few things, it would be a nice surprise for Marisol if... when I saw her again.

A few hours after we left Guadalajara, we came to a big town called Morelia. It was in a valley and had lots of neat old buildings. I was liking this part of Mexico better all the time. We had gained a couple of thousand feet in elevation since we left the coast, and the air was fresher and not as warm. We were in mountains with pine trees, and it kind of reminded me of being in the Sierra Nevada in California. This was another place with a nice plaza in the center with an impressive cathedral. I parked the car, just to have a quick look around, and I noticed a drug store with a sign in the window that said *Fotos de pasaporte*. I told Antonio I'd be right back and I grabbed the camera and went in.

I had used all the film that was in the camera that day I took the pictures of Marisol, and I had been wanting to take more.

In the shop there was a nice old guy with thick round glasses, wearing a white shirt and a tie. He spoke some English, and I bought a few rolls of film from him. I showed him the camera, and he told me what would be the best kind of film for it. He even changed the film in the camera for me. He asked me if I wanted to have the exposed roll developed but, when I asked him how long that would take, he said four or five days. I told him I couldn't wait around that long for it, so he carefully put the exposed roll in a little plastic container and handed it to me.

"Keep it away from the light," he said, "to keep your photos safe."

He didn't have to worry about that. That roll of film contained the only pictures I had of Marisol. I was going to guard it with my life. He told me that I had a very good camera and that I should take very good care of it. I told him I would and said, "*Gracias.*"

After that quick stop, I got back in the car and drove us out of town heading east. As my navigator, Antonio was directing me toward the park I had spotted on the map. He told me to go about 20 miles past Morelia. We came to a little place called El Temazcal, and we stopped for something to drink. Antonio had a Jarritos, and I figured for the hell of it I would try one too. I got the *tutifruti*, the same as Antonio had. It was nice, kind of like Hawaiian Punch. While we were there, we also bought some stuff—bread, cheese, candy bars, more Jarritos and some Tecates, crap like that—for a snack later.

The tiny old woman who ran the shop started jabbering at me in Spanish. I didn't have a clue what she was talking about, so I just said, "*No comprendo*" and pointed her toward Antonio. She started asking Antonio a bunch of questions, and he answered her. Then she began describing something using lots of gestures with her hands. I wondered what they were talking about.

When they got to a lull in their conversation, I asked Antonio, "So what's she saying?"

"She asked me where we were from and what we were doing here. I told her that we're from California and that we're on a vacation. And she said it's a shame that we didn't come in the winter to see the *mariposas.*"

"Mari what?"

"*Mariposas.*" Antonio had to think for a moment to come up with the right word in English. "Butterflies. She said in the winter the forests are full of butterflies. Beautiful orange and black butterflies, she said. They are in the United States right now. They live there in the summer. But for the *Día de los Muertos*, the Day of the Dead, they come back to Michoacán. That's where we are now. In the state of Michoacán. She said she believes the butterflies are really the souls of the dead, returning home. That's why they always come back for the Day of the Dead."

"What's the Day of the Dead?"

"It's a big holiday here in Mexico, right after Halloween. There's big celebrations, but mainly it is to remember and pray for the dead."

"Hmmm. Sounds kind of creepy to me. Ask her to point us to a good camping place."

Antonio talked to her some more, and then he told her, "*Muchas gracias, señora.*" Then he told me, "C'mon. She said to go back the way we came a little ways. There's a side road we should take."

We got back in the car and drove back down the road. Lonnie had not stirred the whole time we were in the little shop. But once the car started moving, he woke up.

"Where the fuck are we?"

"Mitch wha'... Mitch wha'..." I was trying to impress him with my geographic knowledge, but I couldn't quite remember the name of the state we were in.

"*¡Michoacán!*" said Antonio helpfully.

"That's nice," said Lonnie sarcastically, "but where the fuck are we?"

"We're less than 200 miles from Mexico City," I said.

He sat up and quickly found his bottle of bourbon and unscrewed the cap. I gave him a disapproving look, but he ignored me.

"This is a lot of drinking," I said, "even for you."

"God, when did you turn into such an old lady?" he shot back with disgust, as he took a big swig.

Just then Antonio pointed out the dirt road we needed to take, and I made the turn.

"Where are you taking us?" asked Lonnie.

"I'm tired of sleeping in the car," I said. "We're going to camp here in the forest for the night."

Lonnie looked around doubtfully. "What about tarantulas? And snakes? I heard Mexico has lots of poisonous snakes."

I hadn't really thought about that, and very quickly I was starting to have second thoughts. But then I remembered what sleeping in the car did to my back.

"You and me, we camped lots of times up in the mountains back home. I never heard you worry about snakes or spiders those times. Not even after that time you almost stepped on the rattler."

"Yeah, but they got a lot more poisonous things here. Everyone knows that."

"Well, I don't fucking care," I said. "I'll take my chances out here instead of breaking my back in this fucking car another night."

"Don't let me stop you, but I'll be sleeping in the car. It'll be a lot more comfortable having it all to myself anyways."

"Yeah, well, that works out anyway, 'cause we only have two sleeping bags. Antonio can use yours."

It was starting to get dark. We found a place where we could pull over. Lonnie wasn't inclined to get out of the car, so I said, "C'mon, Antonio, help me make a campfire."

Fairly quickly, we had made a circle of rocks and filled it with pieces of wood we had gathered. The pine wood we found was nice and dry and was easy to light. Antonio and I got out the food we had bought and sat down around the fire. When he saw that I had Tecates, Lonnie finally decided to get out of the car and come sit with us.

"You know what we need to get?" I said. "A little metal coffee pot. It would be great to wake up and be able to make a pot of coffee in the morning."

We did a fair amount of bullshitting, as we sat there around the fire. As it got darker, it started to feel like the times I had gone camping in the Sierra Nevada with my dad and my brother or with Lonnie. I could almost pretend I was back in California. After a few beers, Lonnie and I started to tell ghost stories. Without having to say anything to each other, we both knew that it would be fun to scare Antonio. We told all the usual stories, like the one about the guy with the hook for a hand or the one about the hitchhiker that disappeared. But the fact was that Antonio had ghost stories that were a whole lot scarier than ours. He had really creepy stories—about rapists and torturers and murderers. I was finding out that Antonio actually had a pretty dark side to him. And he had a really strange story about a vampire who was chained up inside his coffin for centuries and, when he finally got out, all he could think about was finding woman he loved but who had died hundreds of years before. Even though the night air was warm, I found myself shivering. And I kept looking into the darkness and thinking about the Day of the Dead and all those human souls coming back as butterflies. And I was finding it hard to get the idea of snakes and spiders and maybe scorpions out of my head.

I thought Lonnie would be up all night since he had slept most of the afternoon. But he was the first to turn in. Probably had something to do with the whiskey and the Tecate. He crawled into the car and made sure all the windows and doors were closed.

"We might as well turn in too," I said to Antonio, and I got up and took the sleeping bags out of the trunk. "We'll sleep here close to the fire," I said looking around. "Wild animals won't come too close to a campfire."

I crawled into my sleeping bag and laid there, looking up at the trees above us. Where the trees weren't blocking the view I could see stars. The sky was incredibly clear and not hazy like it had been a lot of the time. From what I could see through the trees, there seemed to be more stars in the sky than I had ever seen before in my life. I was tired from having woke up so early that morning and from all the driving I did. I don't even remember falling asleep. But I do remember the dream.

I usually don't remember my dreams, so it made an impression on me that I remembered this one. And also because of what happened after. I dreamed I was with Marisol. But the dream didn't start out with Marisol. It started out with orange and black butterflies. They were everywhere, flying around in the dark. I was sure they were the souls of the dead—just like the old woman had said. I was sure that two of them were my grandparents. And that another one of them was Kenny Jones, who got killed on his motorcycle when we were sophomores. But then, in that strange way that dreams don't make any sense, the butterflies became candles. Hundreds of candles, flickering in the dark.

I was back in the hotel room in Guaymas. And Marisol was there. She was laying there on the bed, just like she had been in real life, with all the candles around her. I was so happy to see her. I climbed onto the bed and went to kiss her. But she wouldn't let me kiss her. That was strange because, if I knew anything to be true from the short time I was with Marisol, it was that she liked to kiss. A lot. There were times I thought I was going to suffocate because she wouldn't let me pull my mouth away from hers. But in the dream she was teasing me. She was laughing at me and wouldn't let me get my mouth near hers. The longer this went on, the more frustrated I got. I was nearly fighting her, trying to make her hold her head still. I wrestled her, trying to get her to cooperate, but she was surprisingly strong. Before I knew it, she flipped things around and she was on top of me. The more she fought me, the more excited I got. I got to the point where I thought I was going to explode all over myself.

139

About that time, I must have started waking up because I actually realized that I was dreaming. But I didn't care. I didn't want the dream to end because I didn't want Marisol to disappear. So I did everything I could not to wake up, and I just focused on how much I wanted to keep Marisol with me. At some point it dawned on me that it made absolutely no sense that Marisol was there. But I was nowhere near awake enough to think straight about it. The way I was thinking at that moment, through some miracle Marisol was really there with me. It wasn't just a dream. Somehow she was really there. I just refused to think about the fact that it made no sense. All I knew was that, through magic or something, Marisol had managed to find me in a forest in the middle of Micho-ah-what-the-fuck state and she had come to me in the middle of the night.

If it was too good to be true, I didn't want to hear about it. Maybe Catholics had the right religion and maybe by going to a Catholic Mass I had been rewarded with my own personal miracle. The way I felt in that moment, I wasn't going to question how it happened. I was just glad and thankful that it had. I continued to wrestle with Marisol and then, finally, I managed to put my mouth on hers. That's when I became wide awake. And that's when I realized it wasn't Marisol. It was her smell that broke the spell. She didn't have that perfume smell that drove me mad. For days I had been reliving the memory of her perfume's scent, trying not to forget what it smelled like. And there was no trace of that scent now. There was only the smell of a fourteen-year-old boy who seriously needed a bath.

"Antonio! What the fuck! What the hell are you doing?" I was whispering as loud as I could, while trying not to be so loud it would wake Lonnie. The last thing I needed was for him to see what was going on.

Antonio was on top on me, and he was breathing fast. His face looked like a scared rabbit. The weird thing was that, in the dark, he actually did look quite a bit like Marisol.

"Damn it, Antonio! I thought you said you weren't queer!"

"I'm not!" he whispered back. "You were doing so much moving around and talking and crying, I thought something was

140

wrong with you. You... seemed to be in pain. I... I was trying to help."

I gave him a shove and landed him on the ground next to me.

"Yeah, well, you weren't helping. You were taking advantage of the situation. God, it's disgusting. I wouldn't have let you sleep so close to me if I thought you really did like guys."

"But I don't like guys. But you just seemed... I dunno... you seemed to be suffering. I was just trying to help. Really. You were the one who kept trying to kiss me on the lips. I don't like that. I never let any man kiss me on the lips. Ever."

I started to calm down a little. I didn't want to think about it, but maybe he was telling it the way it really was. Maybe it happened mostly because I was the one who went crazy in my sleep. But as far as I was concerned, that didn't make what he did right. The nagging thought that Antonio might have been looking at me ever since he joined up with us and lusting after me, it just made me feel kind of sick.

"Tell me something, Antonio, and I want you to tell me the truth."

He looked at me very seriously and nodded his head slightly.

"Can you swear that you weren't liking the wrestling around we were doing? Swear that you have absolutely no interest in my body."

He hesitated a moment.

"I really like you a lot, Dallas."

Oh, shit.

"But I don't like you like a girl. I didn't get close to you while you were dreaming because it felt good to me. I did it because you are my friend. The thing is, sometimes in the middle of the night Lawrence or Michael would need me to help them and it's just sort of what I did. It was part of the deal. I guess I forgot for a minute that you aren't like them. Whatever it was you needed, there wasn't any way for me to help you. I should have just kept away from you. I definitely will the next time."

"Yeah, well, there's not going to be a fucking next time."

A minute before I had been ready to drive off and leave him there by the side of the road and not care what happened to him. A minute before that, I was seriously considering beating him to a bloody pulp with my fists. Now I felt like shit. I still wasn't happy about what had happened, but I did believe that, whatever he was doing, he was doing it out of friendship and not because he was a pervert. If it turned out wrong, well, it was because of how screwed up his life had been. And that wasn't his fault. I didn't say anything for a few minutes while I tried to get it all straight in my head.

"It's all right, Antonio. It was a fucking confusing situation. I never had a dream like that before. It was so real. And the fact is…"

I wasn't sure if I should tell him this next part, but I decided, what the hell, we had become pretty close friends in a short amount of time. I might as well be honest with him.

"The fact is, in a weird way, you remind me of Marisol. I mean, you're about the right height and weight. And you're both Mexican. So, I guess it comes down to… I was confused. No wonder you would be confused too. I say we forget all about this. Like it never happened."

"Okay, Dallas."

Neither of us said anything for quite a while after that. I thought maybe Antonio had gone back to sleep. But then, quietly in the dark, he spoke again.

"Dallas?"

"Yeah?"

"You know…"

"Yeah?"

"Sometimes? In the middle of the night?"

"Yeah?"

"Sometimes in the middle of the night, I just lay there. And I get really scared. I get so scared, I don't think the night will ever end or the sun will ever come up and that I'll just die. All alone in the dark."

I thought about it for a minute and then said, "Yeah. Believe it or not, that happens to me sometimes too. I think it must happen to everyone."

"Really?"

"Yeah, really. But you know what? The sun always does come up. That feeling always passes. Every time. So don't worry about it."

"Thanks, Dallas."

"Don't sweat it, kid."

Antonio was so smart and usually acted so much older than he was that I kept forgetting how young he was. He was really just a kid. I couldn't really get mad at him and stay mad. He really needed someone to look after him, not to yell at him because he was confused. And I knew just how he felt. And I wasn't lying when I told him I felt the same way sometimes late at night in the dark. More time went by without either of us talking, and I figured he was definitely asleep now. But then I heard his voice one more time.

"*Yo te quiero*, Dallas."

That put a shiver through me because of Marisol having said the same words to me. But it also made me think back to Spanish class. I remembered Miss Daniels once spent a whole afternoon explaining that *quiero* had more than one meaning. I don't know why it stuck in my mind so much, except that we were all really annoyed that she kept going over it until we all got it right. She said that, depending on how you use it, *quiero* could mean "I want" or "I like" or "I love." At the time, I thought Spanish was a really stupid language because it only confused things for a word to have so many different meanings. But now I was thinking that it was kind of cool for a word to have one or more meanings. Maybe he meant to say "I like you" or maybe he meant to say "I love you." Or maybe he meant something in between. In any case, I knew what he meant.

"*Yo te quiero también, Antonio.*" I was proud of myself for remembering how to say *too*.

I could tell by Antonio's breathing that he was definitely asleep now. After a few more minutes, he shifted position and snuggled up right next to me. And it didn't bother me a bit. I pulled out my arm and put it around him. It was the only place I could put it comfortably without waking him up. And that's how we slept. There was nothing sexual about it. We were just two friends, helping each other get through the night.

11
Three Lost Souls

I WOKE up to sunlight coming through the trees and the smell of pine. Sleeping on the ground wasn't as comfortable as sleeping in a bed, but it was a hell lot more comfortable than sleeping in a car.

For once I wasn't the first one to wake up. Lonnie was standing there, leaning against the Chevy, taking a drag on his cigarette. He was smirking at me.

"Well, girls," he said, "I figured you two were lovers, but I didn't expect you to be so obvious about it."

Antonio was still sleeping, and he was practically laying on top of me. I gave him a shove, which pushed him away and woke him up. Lonnie kept going.

"I'm not going to let you fags sit together in the front seat anymore. It'd be too disgusting to watch."

I knew that Lonnie was joking. He and I did this sort of crude teasing back and forth all the time. But I wasn't sure if Antonio knew he was joking. Whether or not he did, he had spent enough time around the two of us to come back at Lonnie with a good line of his own.

"Go stuff it, Lonnie. We all know you wanted to sleep alone in your car so you could play with yourself all night."

Lonnie couldn't help but smile at the kid's quick response. He always enjoyed a good put-down, even when it was aimed at him. I think he had a bit more respect for Antonio after that. Anyway, he changed the subject.

"That idea of yours about a coffee pot is starting to sound good about now," he said. "I'd give anything for a hot cup of coffee."

"Well," I said, "the sooner we get on the road, the sooner we'll find a cup somewhere."

I thought Antonio might be embarrassed about what happened during the night and maybe he would feel weird around me. But he acted like nothing had happened. He was his usual generally happy self. In fact, I started to wonder if the whole thing had been a dream or I had somehow imagined it all. But I knew it had all happened. It's just that things always look different in the daylight than they do in the middle of the night.

I was happy that nothing had really changed between him and me. The fact was that I liked having him around. He seemed to bring out my good side. That made him kind of the opposite of Lonnie, who always seemed to be trying to bring out my bad side.

While Antonio and I studied the map, Lonnie went over the car. He was not happy with its condition. Normally, Lonnie would keep it as clean as a whistle. Back home he washed it at least once a week, sometimes oftener—even during times when we were being told to conserve water. But he hadn't had any chance to wash the car since we left home, and now it was filthy. I could tell that was frustrating for him.

Also, he was meticulous about checking hoses and belts to make sure we didn't have a breakdown. And he religiously checked the water levels in the radiator and the battery. That's one thing I had to give him. If a person was going to go off on a mad adventure like this one, at least Lonnie was a good man to travel with in terms of being able to look after our wheels. But I didn't like the look of concern on his face as he studied everything under the hood. Or when he looked over the outside of the car in general.

"Everything okay with the Chevy?" I asked.

He grunted and didn't say anything for a while. Finally, he decided to answer my question.

"Driving these shit Mexican roads is destroying the body. I don't like it."

"Yeah, but even if it doesn't look as good as it used to, it still runs okay, right?"

He gave a slight nod and grunted again. "We're all right for now, but with all these miles we're putting on her, it's only a matter of time until something goes. A clamp or a belt or something. And when that happens, I don't know where we're going to get parts."

I tried to be logical. "Mexico has to have garages and mechanics. And maybe even auto parts stores. We'll just find one if we need it. I mean, there are plenty of cars on the road. They must have places to get parts and service."

Lonnie wasn't impressed. "Yeah, but every car we have seen here is crap. They're crap cars driving on crap roads. I don't see how most of them keep going."

"Well, let's keep our fingers crossed."

I patted the side of the car like it was a horse.

"This old gal has done right by us so far with no trouble. If you keep looking after her, she'll get us where we're going and home again."

I looked over at Antonio. He was scratching his head as he studied the map. "You got our route figured out, *número dos*?" I asked him.

"Well, we're only a couple of hundred miles from Mexico City. But I don't know if we should head straight for it or try to drive around it."

"Why wouldn't we drive through it? It could be interesting to see what's there."

"Yeah," said Antonio, "but it's a huge city. It's bigger than L.A. But it doesn't have L.A.'s freeways."

I tried to imagine driving through Los Angeles, a city that seemed to go on and on forever, on regular streets instead of on a freeway. I could see Antonio's point. That could easily waste a whole day or even two. As much as I would have liked to see what the capital of Mexico looked like, I had to agree that it was probably smarter to avoid a long drive through a major city.

"So how long will it take to go around it?"

"Well, it looks like the easiest way is to go around to the north. This way."

He drew a curved line with his finger to the north of the city on the map.

"We should be able to get as far as Puebla tonight without too much trouble. That would put us on the road toward Guatemala."

"Looks good to me."

I did a little walking around and took a few pictures with the camera. I was sorry that it was the wrong time of the year for taking pictures of the butterflies. But I tried to find some other interesting things in the woods to shoot.

It was another bright morning. The air smelled fresh and clean. The mountains and forest around us were pretty. And, despite my dreams and my middle-of-the-night conversation with Antonio, I had slept well. The map showed that, against all odds, we were actually making good progress in this crazy quest of ours. And everyone was in a good mood. Things just generally seemed good.

There was no sign that this was the day that everything would start falling apart.

The first thing that happened was that we got lost. Up until my great idea of finding a place to camp, we only had to follow one major road from Santa Ana, Sonora, all the way down to Morelia. But the road we took out of Morelia to find my camping spot was different than the road we needed to take to go around Mexico City. And the road we needed to take didn't seem to have any major towns or cities on it. The one firm thing we knew is that it would take us past a place called Maravatio de Ocampo.

Antonio said we could backtrack into Morelia, about twenty miles or so, and pick up the road there that we needed to be on. But he thought we could save time by continuing straight ahead and finding a road that would cut across to the one we wanted. That seemed reasonable to Lonnie and me, so that was our plan.

So we set off down the road and promptly proceeded to get lost. We must have missed the left turn that should have taken us north to the other road. When it became clear that we had missed the turn, I asked if we should turn around. Lonnie seemed determined not to have to backtrack. When he spotted an old guy walking along the road, Lonnie said to Antonio, "Ask that guy which is the best way to get to the road we want to be on."

Antonio looked doubtful, but when Lonnie slowed down next to the guy, Antonio did what he was told. He leaned out the window, and they exchanged a few words. While he was jabbering away, the old guy pointed in the direction we were traveling.

"What'd he say?" asked Lonnie.

"He said we'd find the road we're looking for about five kilometers further on."

"Cool," said Lonnie. "See, sometimes it pays to ask for directions."

Antonio still looked doubtful. "That's the answer they always give. It's just ahead five more kilometers."

"Huh? Wha'dya mean?"

"I dunno," said Antonio. "It's just something about Mexico. Whenever you ask where something is and they don't know the answer, they never tell you. They just say it's five kilometers down the road."

"You mean, you think he was lying to you?"

"No, not lying exactly. It's just that people don't want to disappoint you. So they come up with an answer, even if they have to make it up."

"That's crazy. If he didn't know where we should go, why wouldn't he just tell us?"

Antonio shrugged.

We drove on another few miles. After a while it became obvious that there was no turn for the road we needed. Lonnie spotted another guy, a younger one this time, walking along the road.

"Ask him where we are," Lonnie instructed Antonio.

Antonio just had a look of resignation on his face. Lonnie pulled over, and Antonio had a chat with this guy through the window. In a weirdly similar way as before, the guy jabbered away as he pointed in the same direction we were traveling. After Antonio told the guy *gracias*, Lonnie interrogated Antonio again.

"So what did this guy say?"

Somehow Antonio managed to answer without cracking a smile. "He said the road we want is five kilometers straight ahead."

Lonnie started to lose it. "Are you shittin' me, peckerhead? You're just messing with me now, aren't you? What did he really say?"

Antonio shrugged again and looked helpless. "I swear. That's what he said."

Lonnie turned forward again and fumed. "Well, if this doesn't beat fuck all..."

I thought maybe it was time for me to jump in. "He's right, you know, Lonnie. I heard both those guys say *cinco kilómetros*."

This only seemed to annoy Lonnie more. "Oh, so now *you're* speaking Spanish too. I'm surrounded by fucking Mexicans. Okay, would the two of you take a look at the map and decide where the fuck we are and if we should keep going down this road."

Antonio and I looked at the map together. We traced the road we had started out on and made our best guess as to where we currently were.

"What I don't understand," I said, "is how we missed the turn. It makes me wonder if we were ever on the road we thought we were."

Antonio was looking more and more uncomfortable. I think he was feeling responsible for getting us lost. He and I talked it over and finally decided that we might as well keep heading down the road we were on. At least until some landmark or other gave us a better idea exactly where we were. From that moment on, the time seemed to drag. Probably because every single minute we were wondering if we were only getting further away from where we wanted to be.

"It'd be nice if they'd bother to put up a fucking road sign once in a while," proclaimed Lonnie.

We were all a bit on edge by this point, so we all nearly jumped out of our skins when the car felt like it lurched to one side and a funny sound came from underneath.

"Shit!" yelled Lonnie. "We got a flat. That's all we need."

He pulled over, and we all got out. Sure enough, the left rear tire was flat as a pancake. Lonnie didn't waste any time. He opened the trunk and got out the jack. He and I had done this enough times before, it wasn't really any big deal. He had the flat tire off and replaced with the spare in no time.

As he threw the flat tire into the trunk, he said, "Well, now we definitely have to find a garage. We have to get this tire patched as soon as we can 'cause, until we do, we're traveling without a spare. And that ain't good. Not on these shit roads."

He and I both looked around. There was no sign that we were anywhere near a town or even a roadside filling station.

"We'll be all right," I said, in my usual role as the one who always looks at the bright side. "We went this far without tire trouble. We'll make it to a garage long before we get another flat."

Lonnie shook his head quietly, as if he wasn't buying it.

"C'mon," I said, "the sooner we get going again, the sooner we can get that tire fixed."

We got back in the car and kept on going down the same road. The countryside was pleasant enough. The road was windy, and we were passing through rolling hills with lots of trees. But we had no idea for sure where we were heading. It was the first time on this whole trip where we really felt like we had no idea exactly where we were. We did have the general sense, though, that we were heading toward Mexico City—the one place we had specifically decided we did not want to go through. It was nearly like Mexico City had a mind of its own and it was pulling us toward it against our will. But we had driven so far by this point, no one was suggesting that we turn around and go back the other way.

Finally, we came across a rundown old filling station. It had a big shed attached to it that looked like it might be a place for working on cars. Lonnie pulled up to the pump, and said, "We had better get gas. And we might as well find out if this guy can patch a tire."

We got out of the car, and Lonnie started filling the tank. An old guy in dirty overalls, who was kind of hunched-over, came walking out of the shed. He was moving none too fast. He had a good look at us and the car as he wiped his hands on a rag that seemed oilier than his hands were. Lonnie told Antonio to ask him if he could fix a flat tire, and Antonio walked up to him and started having a chat. While he was listening to Antonio, the guy kept looking at each of us and then at the car again. We knew that we were in luck when the guy nodded his head and said, "*Sí. Sí.*"

"He says you have to pay for the gas first," said Antonio.

Lonnie grumbled at this, but he got out his wallet and paid him. The guy was looking very carefully at Lonnie's wallet. Then Lonnie opened the trunk and carried the tire into the shed. The guy motioned for Lonnie to put it down on the ground. Then the guy rolled it over to a bench and sat down with the tire between his legs. He started going over it carefully, looking for the leak. Finally, he dug his fingers into a spot and pulled out a nail and held it up for us to see. Then he went about patching the hole.

"Man," said Lonnie. "He hardly has any equipment. And what he does have is really old. How does he manage to fix anything here?"

"Well, he's fixing your tire," said Antonio.

While we waited, we had a look around the place. I was still missing my morning cup of coffee. There wasn't any chance of getting one at this place. There wasn't even a Coke machine. Finally, the guy came out of the shed and said something to Antonio, who then turned to Lonnie and said, a bit nervously, "He says you owe him 400 pesos."

I thought Lonnie's jaw was going to drop to the ground. "The fuck you say...! Tell that asshole that we're not going to be robbed blind. I'll give him..." He looked at me and asked, "What's five dollars in pesos?"

"Uh, sixty-something. I think."

Math was never my best subject.

Antonio obediently translated Lonnie's counter-offer to the guy. The guy crossed his arms and got a very stubborn look on his face. *"No,"* he said with determination. *"Cuatrocientos pesos. No menos."*

Lonnie was quickly losing his temper. "I'm not going to be taken just because I'm an American, damn it. This is fucking highway robbery."

I didn't see how this was going to be resolved. The guy had our tire, and Lonnie was as stubborn as a bull. I didn't want to have to decide what to do if Lonnie decided to try to take the tire by force. So I pulled out my own wallet and paid the guy the 400 pesos myself. But this made Lonnie even madder.

"Damn it, Dallas! You can't just give in to the bastard. You can't let him get away with this."

"I already did. Now grab your tire and let's go."

The guy stood there, counting the money with his oily fingers, while Lonnie stomped into the shed and came out carrying the tire. He was as mad as a hornet as he threw it in the trunk and slammed it shut.

"Let's get the fuck out of here," he growled.

"You had no right to do that," he grunted, as he laid rubber on the road. "We could have taken the tire anyway, and there's nothing he could have done about it. I fucking hate being taken advantage of. And that was money we can't spare."

I knew better than to bother arguing with Lonnie until he had cooled down. But I was thinking of all the ways the situation could have gone wrong. What if the guy had a gun? Or if he had a friend in the local police? Yeah, it was maddening to overpay for something, but not paying could have worked out more expensive in the long run. At least that's what I was telling myself.

After that, we traveled in silence for quite a few miles. I didn't know how long it would take Lonnie to calm down, but I knew from bitter experience not to bother trying to talk to him until he had. The problem was, though, the longer we drove on without talking, the further we were traveling without knowing for sure where we were headed. I was pretty much getting used to the idea that we probably weren't going to make it to Puebla that day. Hell, all I was interested in at that point was a cup of coffee and something to eat.

Finally, after what seemed like an hour or more, Lonnie broke the silence.

"I'm getting fucking tired of Mexico," he said.

I wasn't sure what he was saying exactly. So I asked. "So, are you saying that you want to head back home?"

Lonnie thought about it for a minute.

"Fuck, I don't know what I'm saying. I just know I'm tired of being in the car all day. I'm tired of everyone around me speaking Mexican. I'm tired of people ripping me off. And..." He looked at Antonio and me. "I'm getting tired of the two of you."

I didn't take it personally. The fact was, I was getting tired of Lonnie too. And I was missing home. I was missing my other friends. And I was missing the Foster Freeze and decent hamburgers. I was even missing my parents. But there was one thing new since I had been on this trip. The old me would have been missing Linda, even though that was dumb since she wasn't even my girlfriend. But now I was missing Marisol. And Marisol wasn't back home. She was in this country, in some other part of Mexico.

"So," I asked, "are you ready to turn around then?"

He laughed, and I knew he had gotten over his temper tantrum at the filling station. "Hell, what's the point of turning around when we don't even know which way we're going?"

After a few minutes, he added, "Hell, Dallas. Can I even go home? I mean, I don't even know, do I? There's probably a warrant out for my arrest. Fleeing the scene of a crime and leaving the country only makes it worse."

"It might not be as bad as you think. Michael might not be dead. He might not even have called the cops. I mean, he probably doesn't want anyone to know what happened and why it happened either."

"You've always been fucking Pollyanna. You know that, right?"

"I'm just saying, you won't ever know how bad it really is 'til you go back. Right?"

"Maybe. But the other thing eating at me is the idea that, if I went home, there would be a letter from the Selective Service waiting for me. Telling me to report for a physical. Man, I don't want to go into the army. And I definitely don't want to go to fucking 'Nam."

I didn't have a good answer for that one. But I tried anyway.

"Hell, Lonnie, by the time we get back, we might find out the fucking war's over. I mean, it has to end sometime. It can't go on forever."

"Well, it feels like fucking forever *already*. I don't think it's ever going to end. It's just going to go on and on and on."

Like I said, I didn't have a good answer about the war.

"Well then, maybe you should just stay in Mexico. Until it's over, I mean."

"Mexico? Are you crazy? Can you see me learning Spanish and living down here for the rest of my life. That's not going to happen."

"What about Canada then? I hear lots of guys are going up to Canada."

"Yeah, and everyone says they're cowards. Or traitors. I don't want them to say that about me."

"Well, you're just going to have to decide what it is you want to do. You can't have it both ways. Not unless we get lucky and the war ends before they can ship us out."

"What do you mean 'us,' white man? You're not getting drafted."

"Hey, I know your number is a lot lower than mine, but it could go either way with me. I could be going to 'Nam too. Hell, we could be going over together."

"Well, there's only one thing to do then."

"What's that?"

"When we stop tonight, we're going to buy a bottle of tequila and drink the whole damn thing. Or maybe a bottle of mezcal. We'll do the thing with the worm. Whoever gets the worm has to buy the next bottle."

For once I couldn't argue with one of Lonnie's excuses for getting drunk. I was more than ready to drink that bottle of tequila with him. But, as it turned out, it wouldn't be happening that night.

We continued wandering through the hills until we finally hit a place that had a name that we could match to something on our map.

"Fuck, Lonnie," I said, as I studied the roadmap. "We've really gone off course. Hell, we've been heading south. We're south of Mexico City. We're about halfway between Mexico City and the Pacific Ocean."

"Nice job, peckerhead," Lonnie sneered at Antonio, who kept his head down.

"Leave him alone, Lonnie. He was doing a good job navigating for us until today. It was an honest mistake. He doesn't know this part of the country any better than we do."

"So, what the hell do we do now?"

"We eat. That's what we do. I'm starving."

And we found a little local place and had a big lunch. Antonio and I loaded up on some delicious carnitas and a stack of tortillas. Lonnie had a steak that was too thin for his liking, but he ate it all anyway. I had given up on having coffee, and Lonnie and I were drinking Tecate with our meal. As we were pouring our second round, we looked at the map and tried to make a plan.

We knew that, to get back on the road to Guatemala, we would need to make our way to Oaxaca. But we couldn't for the life of us figure out a reasonable way to get there without first heading back up to Mexico City. There were just too many mountains in the way of a straight shot. It was like Mexico City was still determined to suck us in no matter what we did. After the three of us spent a lot of time talking it over, we decided that we needed to backtrack a few miles and then take a windy road through some mountains that would eventually put us back on our old friend, *Carretera* 15. There was no way we would make it there by dark, so we would have to plan on stopping somewhere before we got to the capital.

We got back in the car and headed out the way we had come in. We all felt much better now that we had food—and in Lonnie's and my case, beer—in our stomachs. At least now we knew where we were and we had a definite plan. Sure, we had lost a day, but it wasn't like we were under any kind of deadline, so that really wasn't a big deal. As for getting ripped off by the guy who patched the tire, well, easy come easy go. Overall, we were in a better frame of mind.

The road we had chosen to go over the mountains to *Carretera* 15 turned out to be in worse condition than we expected—even by Mexican standards. It was very narrow, very steep in places and full of potholes. And we never knew when we'd come across a big rock lying in the middle of the road. At one point, Lonnie and I actually got into an argument over whether it was really a road or just an extra-wide walking trail. More than once I asked whether we should turn around and take a longer way around to where we wanted to go. Lonnie wasn't happy with the condition of the road, but he hated the idea of more wasted time and miles.

"Shit!" he yelled, as a rock or something scraped the bottom of the car. "We should be driving a Jeep instead of a fucking Impala."

My right hand kept a firm grip on the seat beneath me, as Lonnie negotiated the twists and turns while trying to avoid rocks. This was what Lonnie always called "ass chewing" driving because it makes you so tense "your ass is chewing the seat the whole way." I kept thinking what a mess it would be if we got stuck or broke down on this road. We'd be miles from anywhere. Because we had to crawl along so slowly, the drive seemed to go on and on forever.

Finally, we came around a bend and we had a great view below us. We could see a road that looked like it might be the one we were looking for. In any event, it looked a hell of a lot better than the road we were on. And it was all downhill from where we were. There was a sense of relief as Lonnie headed down the mountain. We felt like we had come through the toughest drive of the whole trip.

It took a lot longer than we expected to come down from the mountain and reach the other road. There was still a lot of bending and twisting on that crap road to cover before we got there. But at least our goal was in sight. When we finally reached level ground, Lonnie floored the accelerator, happy to finally get out of second gear. But I noticed a concerned look on his face as he glanced at the dashboard while we approached the junction ahead.

"She's running awful hot," he said. "I don't like it."

"That's not surprising, is it?" I asked. "I mean, it's had to go a long way in low gear doing a lot of uphill, right?"

Lonnie didn't say anything. His attention was focused on the temperature gauge. I reassured myself that Lonnie was just being overly cautious. That car meant a lot to him, and he always tended to fuss over it. As for myself, I was just enjoying the sense of relief as we came up to a decent road. Lonnie made a right turn onto the main road and began accelerating to cruising speed. I was already thinking about where we might stop for the night and get that bottle of tequila.

And then it happened. Suddenly there was a loud sickening thud from underneath the car. It sounded like someone had somehow managed to smash the undercarriage with a sledgehammer. Several red lights came on the dashboard, and the Chevy began coasting to a stop.

"Shit!" yelled Lonnie with a ferocity that scared me more than the noise from underneath the car. "We fucking threw a rod! We fucking threw a rod!"

12
Locked Away

BEFORE THE car had stopped moving completely, Lonnie guided it onto a shoulder. He pulled the key out of the ignition and began violently pounding the door next to him with his left fist.

"Shit! Shit!" he kept yelling.

I sat there in shock, feeling kind of sick. I didn't know as much about cars as Lonnie, but I knew enough to know that throwing a rod was bad. Real bad.

Finally, from the back seat Antonio asked, "What happened?"

"We threw a fucking rod!" Lonnie shouted at the roof of the car.

"What's that mean?"

Antonio's questions were actually helping. They were forcing Lonnie to start dealing with the situation rather than just raging.

"The rod that connects the piston to the crankshaft broke off. It's either jammed in the cylinder head or it's gone through the engine block. Either way, we're fucked. Totally, royally fucked. The engine has to be completely rebuilt. Or replaced. I can't fucking believe this. I can't fucking believe this."

Lonnie pounded the ceiling a few more times. I thought he was going to break his hand or maybe even punch a hole through the roof.

I decided to get out of the car and have a look from the outside. Lonnie immediately followed. There was a drizzle of oil on the road, trailing away from the car.

"That's what happened," said Lonnie when he saw it. "We must have cracked the oil pan on that fucking road. We were leaking oil."

He pounded the side of the car.

"Damn it all to hell! We're screwed. We're completely screwed."

There was no way to talk to him. We were stranded in the middle of Mexico with no transportation. The only way to get going again was to find a garage with a tow truck and pay for a very expensive repair job. I didn't even know how much money we had left. Probably not enough to pay for an engine rebuild. Lonnie was right. There was no way around it. We were screwed.

Understandably, Lonnie was taking it a lot worse than me. He kept kicking whatever he could find on the ground and shouting curses to the sky. That car meant more to him than almost anything. He had to deal with the fact that he might have to leave it here forever. Lonnie's sense of confidence and even his identity was always tied up in his cars. Lonnie without a car was kind of like a bird missing a wing. It was just sad.

I looked into the car to see what Antonio was doing while Lonnie raged. He was looking at the roadmap. He was already trying to figure out where the nearest town was, probably assuming that we would need to start walking to it.

I stuck my head in the window. "You figured out where we are, *número dos?*"

He looked up at me. "I think so."

He didn't look very sure. I think he was still smarting from feeling like he was the one who had gotten us lost in the first place. The fact was, though, we had all looked at the map and decided together which way to go that morning. It wasn't his fault. I wanted to tell him that, but I figured we were better off focusing on the problem at hand.

"So which way do you think we should start walking if we want to find a garage or a mechanic?"

He pointed in the direction we had been driving. "There should be a town a few miles that way. Maybe four or five miles."

"Well, I've walked five miles before," I said. "A person should be able to walk that in less than an hour easy. The only question is, should we all go or just one or two of us?"

Lonnie still wasn't ready to have a rational discussion. He kept stomping around and kicking any rock or bit of roadside litter he could find.

"Maybe you and I should go, *número dos*. I don't mind going, but there's no point going by myself. I'll need you to translate. Lonnie could stay with the car." I was thinking he might need some time alone with it to grieve.

Antonio shrugged. "Okay by me, *comandante*."

I walked over to Lonnie. He was still in no mood for talking, but I figured there was no point wasting time.

"We think there's a town about five miles that way," I said. "Antonio and I can walk to it if you want to stay here with the car."

Lonnie grunted.

"The only thing is," I said, "I need to know how much we can afford to spend on repair work. Unless we want to try phoning your mom or my dad and seeing if they can get some money to us somehow."

Lonnie's face went slightly whiter.

"I can't call my mom. Not after I left there with Don's money. He'll have her turned against me. He'll say that I should just rot down here. That it's what I deserve. There's no way I can call them."

Lonnie went back to kicking things, with even more energy than before.

"Okay," I said. "I can look for a phone and try making a collect call to my dad. He won't be happy, but he might help us out. Unless you think you've got enough money left to pay for the repair ourselves. I mean, things are cheap here. When they're not ripping us off, I mean. Maybe we have enough money to pay for it ourselves."

"I don't fucking know," he said. "I don't fucking know anything anymore."

I couldn't figure out why Lonnie was insisting on being so mysterious about how much money he had left. It was one thing not to tell me when everything was going okay but, now that we were in the middle of a full-blown emergency, it seemed like we should both be putting all our cards on the table.

Just then we noticed a car coming down the road. It slowed down as it got closer. It was going to stop. Well, maybe some good luck at last, I thought. Maybe someone is going to give us some help.

By this time, Antonio had gotten out of the car. I saw his face tighten.

"It's a cop," he said.

The car was so old and beat-up, I thought Antonio was joking. But he wasn't. The door opened and a guy got out. He didn't look like any cop I had ever seen before, but he was wearing a uniform. He had a big beer gut that hung over his belt. He had a big thick mustache and looked like he hadn't shaved for a week. He walked up to us and had a good look at the Chevy, paying particular attention to the California plates on the front and back. He didn't even come close to cracking a smile.

"*Sus papeles.*"

"He wants to see our papers," said Antonio.

"What papers?" asked Lonnie. "We don't have any fucking papers."

That was the problem. We didn't have passports, and we didn't bother to worry about visas when we crossed the border. All we had were our California driver's licenses. I pulled mine out and handed it to him and hoped for the best.

He stared at it for a good minute or two. He gave no clue about what he was thinking. He looked over at Lonnie.

"*Sus papeles.*"

Lonnie was clearly in no mood for dealing with this shit right now. But he reluctantly pulled out his wallet and handed the cop his driver's license. The cop stared at his license for a good minute, just like he'd looked at mine. Then he addressed himself to Antonio. The blood drained from Antonio's face while he listened to him.

"He wants to know if you have visas to be in Mexico."

Showing no patience, Lonnie answered, "You know we fucking don't, Tony. What's he going to do?"

Antonio began talking to the cop. He seemed to be telling him some kind of story. I began silently praying that whatever story Antonio was coming up with would satisfy him and he would just leave us alone. Or maybe even help us, by calling a tow truck or something. But the conversation didn't seem to be going too well. They went back and forth, with the cop getting more agitated and more impatient. I could see from Antonio's face that he was giving up on whatever his strategy was for trying to get us out of trouble.

The cop nodded in Lonnie's and my direction. "*Dígales,*" he ordered Antonio gruffly.

Antonio looked like he was going to be sick. "He says if you don't have visas, he will have to take you to jail."

Fuck, I thought. Just when I thought things couldn't get any worse, they had. It was like a bad dream.

"Isn't there some way to work this out without going to jail?" I pleaded with Antonio.

The cop gave no indication he knew any English, but he seemed to get the gist of what I was saying. He did some more talking to Antonio.

"He says you can buy a temporary tourist visa from him if you want."

Lonnie looked skeptical. "How much?"

"*¿Cuánto vale?*"

"*Mil quinientos pesos. Cada uno.*"

I never thought that Antonio's brown face could actually start looking white, but it actually did.

"He says the visa costs 1,500 pesos. Each."

I thought Lonnie was going to explode. "No way," he snarled. "No fucking way."

I stood closer to him and whispered, just in case the cop could understand English. He eyed the two of us suspiciously. When he wasn't watching the two of us like a hawk, he was eying Antonio up and down.

"I know it's a bribe, but is it worth going to jail not to pay it?" I asked.

As quietly as he could, Lonnie answered, "I've got the money in a hiding place in the car. If I go to get it, he'll be able to see how much we got. He won't be happy with 1,500. He'll want all of it."

I had to agree that Lonnie was probably right. We were at risk of losing every penny we had if we weren't careful. On the other hand, I didn't want to go to jail. Especially not a Mexican jail. I was starting to feel panicky. I tried to think of something fast.

"What if we agree to go to the jail with him and Antonio stays behind, gets the exact amount of money out of your hiding place and brings it down to him afterwards?"

"Are you crazy?" Lonnie hissed. "Do you think, once that kid has his hands on all that money, he will really come spring us out of jail?"

I couldn't believe he was saying that. At this point, I would have trusted Antonio with my life. I don't know why exactly, but I just did. The thought would never have crossed my mind that Antonio might run off with Lonnie's money.

"I trust him, Lonnie. As much as I trust anybody right now. Besides, what choice do we have?"

I could see that the idea of telling Antonio about his hiding place was killing him. I had the nagging feeling that there was something he wasn't telling me. He just stood there, like he was running something over and over through his mind, trying to work it out. The cop was clearly getting impatient with all the talking we were doing between us. Finally, Lonnie spoke.

"Okay. I don't like it, but I guess we don't have a choice."

I was about to walk over to Antonio and tell him our plan, but before I had the chance, the cop starting jabbering away at him first. Antonio looked like he was going to be sick.

"Now he says the price of the visas is 5,000 pesos each."

The asshole either heard what we were saying or figured it out by watching us. Anyway, he obviously decided that there was more money to get out of us. But he was wrong about how much. Lonnie's face had gone white.

"Shit. We don't have that much. We couldn't pay that, even if we wanted to."

I told Antonio that he had to try to talk him back down to the lower price. I could tell that he was giving it his best shot, but that asshole of a cop was insistent. He paid very close attention to Antonio while he was talking, but in the end he wasn't budging an inch.

"You could try giving him what we have," I whispered to Lonnie. "He might be happy with that and let us go."

Lonnie's jaw was set. "Nah. This guy isn't going to be happy with whatever we have. He's not going to let us go no matter how much we give him. He has it figured that we have people back home who will wire however much money he wants. We're screwed. Royally screwed."

I thought I was going to be sick.

"Look," said Lonnie. "This guy is in terrible physical shape. We could outrun him no problem. Why don't we make a run for it?"

Almost as if he knew what Lonnie was saying, the cop pulled out a gun. He opened one of the back doors to his car and motioned for us to get in. I wondered what he would do about Antonio. The answer was nothing. He basically ignored Antonio and left him standing there by the road as he drove off with Lonnie and me in the back of his car.

The inside of the cop car stank. It was like he used it for transporting animals when he wasn't arresting clueless gringos. I did my best to keep any of my exposed skin from coming into contact with the car's interior since I was pretty sure I would get a deadly infection if I did.

During that drive down the road to the jail, I wondered what was going to become of us. But mostly I was thinking about Antonio left there in the middle of nowhere all by himself. What would he do? Where would he go? At the end of it, though, I was pretty sure he would make out better than Lonnie and me.

What a couple of chumps we were. Just a couple of months ago, when we graduated from high school, we thought we were such hot stuff. The world was our oyster. Now I felt like crying for my mother to come take care of me and fix it and make it all better. I felt like pure shit.

Before long we were at the police station. Police station? It was more like one of the shacks where they put up for migrant workers during cotton season. I found myself wondering if this guy was really a cop at all. Maybe he was just a psycho who was pretending to be a cop so he could ambush unsuspecting tourists. But my gut told me that he was really just some slob that the police paid to sit on his ass out here in the middle of nowhere so they could say that they had a cop in the area. What a joke. All I could do was hope that we would get a chance to make a phone call and I could get in touch with my dad and he would deal with the mess I had gotten into. I felt like crying like a little baby.

The police station had two rooms. The first one was an office. The other one, in the back, had a jail cell, and that's where we went. The cell didn't have vertical bars like I had always seen in movies and on television. It was more like a metal cage with both vertical and horizontal bars that made it feel dark and closed-in. The place stank. There was a metal bowl on the floor that was obviously meant for us to pee and shit in, but it looked like it hadn't been emptied in months—if ever. The cop didn't make any effort to communicate with us. He just locked the cell and went to the other room.

"Hey!" Lonnie yelled after him. "I get one phone call! I know my fucking rights, you fucking motherfucker!"

If Lonnie thought this would bring the cop back in, then he was disappointed. As the sound of Lonnie's shouts faded in our ears, we were left standing there in silence.

There we were. Just Lonnie and me. Alone in a cage in the middle of nowhere in the middle of fucking Mexico. And no one knew we were there. For a while we just sat there on the bench in stunned silence. How did we wind up like this? I kept wishing I would wake up and find myself back at home. Or better yet, in bed with Marisol back in Guaymas.

After what seemed like an hour, Lonnie said, "He's going to leave us here just long enough to make us desperate. Then he'll offer us a phone so we'll call somebody to get the money he wants."

I figured Lonnie was right. But another possibility was starting to eat at me. Maybe the cop didn't care. Maybe he was happy just to leave us here and let us rot. Maybe I would never get the chance to call my dad. Maybe I would just stay here until I was dead. I choked on my breath. God, even Viet fucking Nam would be better than this. At least there, if someone was trying to kill me, I could shoot back.

If I was losing it, then at least Lonnie seemed to be keeping it together. On the outside anyway. He had his anger to keep him going. He was angry at every Mexican who, as he saw it, was trying to victimize him. He was angry about his car being left by the side of the road. And I think he was angry at himself for not taking better care of his car and letting it throw a rod in the middle of fucking nowhere.

I was mad at myself too. But my anger was more like, I don't know, sadness. I was mad that I didn't do anything about not letting us get lost. I was mad that I didn't give Marisol my address or get her address from her so that we could get in touch with each other. But most of all, I was mad that I let Antonio down. That I couldn't keep him from being left all by himself in the middle of nowhere. I was afraid of what might happen to him. He had trusted us and stuck with us through all our craziness. He could have stayed in Hermosillo and maybe he would have found his mother and she would have been happy to see him and everything would have worked out for him. But instead he tagged along with us, and he wound up in the middle of fucking nowhere in the middle of fucking Mexico and God knows what was going to happen to him.

I decided not to worry about all the bacteria that the back of my tee-shirt was going to pick up and laid down on the bench. And I quietly starting crying. God, Dallas, I thought to myself, what a pussy you are.

It seemed like we were there for hours. Neither of us was talking. It got dark outside. The time dragged on. Then something happened.

I heard someone come in through the entrance of the police station. I could hear him talking with the cop in the other room. My heart started racing. It sounded like Antonio! I couldn't quite make out what they were saying, not that I would have understood it anyway.

I whispered to Lonnie, "I think Antonio's here. He must be trying to get us out."

Lonnie looked doubtful.

After a while the voices in the other room went quiet. I couldn't figure out what was going on. Was Antonio still there? I couldn't tell. I had just about decided that both of them had left when I heard a low moaning sound. In my head I started going through all the possibilities of what might be happening. Then I heard them talking again. They seemed to be arguing. I thought maybe I was going crazy and imagining things. Then suddenly there was a loud pop.

Lonnie had been stuck in his own thoughts all this time, but the sudden noise caught his attention.

"Fuck," he said. "That sounded like a gun."

We both froze. I tried not to think about all the things that could have possibly happened. The argument in the other room kept going on. Finally the door to our room opened and in walked Antonio. There was a big gash on his cheek, dripping blood. In one hand he had a gun. It was Lonnie's Smith & Wesson. In the other hand he had a set of keys. He unlocked our cell and said, "Let's go. Hurry!"

I was trying not to jump to conclusions, but I really wanted to know exactly what had happened and how Antonio had managed to get us out. When we went out through the other room, the cop wasn't there. Antonio led us out the door onto the road. Lonnie's and my backpacks and sleeping bags were laying there on the ground.

"We got to get out of here," said Antonio urgently. "Where do you want to go?"

"Back to the car," replied Lonnie without hesitation.

"That's not safe," said Antonio. "Anyway, I know about your hiding place, Lonnie, and I have everything that was in it. So we don't need to go back there."

Lonnie looked dumbfounded.

Antonio continued, "So we don't need to go back to the car, right?"

Lonnie had a sour look on his face. "I guess not."

I was feeling very confused. Obviously, there was something I was missing. Anyway, Lonnie and I were pretty much stunned, so we were totally useless for making decisions. Antonio took charge.

"I think we should head into the hills. In case your friend decides to come after us. Come on."

Like I said, I was very confused.

"So he's not dead," I said. "You didn't kill him."

Antonio looked at me like I was crazy.

"You think I would shoot a cop? *Estás loco, comandante.*"

170

Lonnie and I gathered up our gear. I took a quick look in my backpack to make sure the camera and my roll of film were there. Thank God, they were. No matter how bad things got, I felt like I could deal with just about anything—as long as I didn't lose my pictures of Marisol. I couldn't wait for the day when I would finally get the chance to see them.

Antonio led us away from the road and up into the hills behind the police station. I couldn't stop thinking about the gunshot and what Antonio had done to get us out of jail.

"How did you get us out, Antonio? What happened to the cop?"

Antonio wasn't in the mood to deal with my questions.

"I made a deal with him. In exchange for letting you go."

"What deal? What did you exchange with him?"

I went through all the possibilities I could think of—or at least all the ones I wanted to think of. Had he found Lonnie's money and offered it to the cop? If so, how did he get him to take less than he had been asking for? Antonio was grim. Grimmer than I had ever seen him. He seemed a lot older than the 14-year-old kid I thought I knew.

"I don't want to talk about it."

He nodded in Lonnie's direction.

"I'm not going to talk about it in front of him. He won't understand. Hell, *you* won't understand. But you'll understand better than he will. But even you will not understand."

"Did you pay him off with my money?" Lonnie asked him suspiciously.

Antonio untied a cloth bag that had been attached to his waist. He handed the bag to Lonnie.

"Here is all your money. You can count it if you want. It's all there, along with everything else that you had."

Then he reached behind him and pulled the gun out from where it had been tucked just inside his jeans. He handed that to Lonnie too.

"Here. This is yours too." He added, sounding very businesslike. "I owe you one bullet."

Lonnie didn't say anything else. Neither did Antonio. And that was that. Antonio wasn't going to talk about it anymore. At least not for the time being. So Lonnie and I followed him into the night.

For better or worse, it seemed as though our lives were in his hands.

13
Making Plans

THE ROUTE that Antonio led us on had a lot of uphill. For a while adrenaline kept us going. Lonnie and I were so relieved to be out of that hellhole of a jail, we would have been happy to climb Mt. Whitney if it was the only way of being sure we wouldn't have to go back.

But it was late at night and the fact was that we were dead tired from the long rotten day we had had. I wondered if Antonio actually had some idea where he was taking us or if he was just making it up as he went along. At this point, I didn't care. I was ready to follow him right over a cliff if that's where he wanted to go. Fortunately, there was a nice bright moon in the sky, so we had little trouble seeing where we were going.

Finally, Lonnie was the one who said he was getting tired and maybe we should stop for the night. I had to agree, and Antonio didn't seem to mind stopping. We didn't bother trying to make a campfire. We spread out the sleeping bags and realized that we only had two, since Antonio never had one.

"Here's what we'll do," said Lonnie, taking charge.

He unzipped both of them completely and spread one of them out on the ground double-width. Then he spread the other one out on top of it and zipped the two together so that they made one double-size sleeping bag.

"That's how Linda and I used to do it when we went camping in Sequoia," he explained. "It'll be a bit snug with three of us, but Tony's pretty small. He won't take up too much room."

I thought it made sense for Antonio to be in the middle, but Lonnie didn't want to have to be next to him, so I went in the middle. There wasn't much room to move around, but we were dead tired, so it didn't really matter. Even at night in the mountains, that time of year Mexico was pretty warm, so we really didn't need the sleeping bags to keep warm. But they gave us a feeling of security. I thought to myself that at least there wasn't room for a tarantula or a scorpion to crawl in there with us.

I could have gone right off to sleep, but I was dying to get Antonio to explain to me what had happened with the cop. I waited until I could tell by Lonnie's breathing that he was sound asleep.

"Antonio," I whispered, "are you awake?"

After a pause, he answered, "Yeah."

He and I were both laying on our sides, facing in the same direction, away from Lonnie.

"How the hell did you got us out of that jail?"

Antonio took a long time to answer.

"You got out. Can't we just leave it at that?"

"But it doesn't make any sense. How did you get us out if you didn't pay any money? And how did you get that big cut on your face?"

"I really don't want to talk about it."

His voice sounded angry. But it also sounded almost like he might start crying.

"Antonio, we're friends. You can tell me. It's all right. Really."

I really wanted to know what had happened. But part of me was wondering if Antonio was right and maybe I was better off not knowing all the details.

"If I tell you," he said, "you have to promise not to tell Lonnie."

"Why?"

"If you want me to tell you, just promise."

"But I don't understand why."

Antonio sounded even closer to tears.

"Because he will judge me. So will you. But I'm willing to tell you. I'm not willing to tell him."

One rule Lonnie and I always had was that we never kept secrets from each other. I really didn't want to break that rule, but I figured that this might be the time to make an exception.

"Okay, I promise I won't tell him."

"Are you sure he's asleep?"

Lonnie and I had our backs to each other, but I could tell by his breathing that he was deep in sleep. When you know someone as long as I knew Lonnie, you can just tell these things.

"Yeah, he's asleep. So are you going to tell me?"

"Okay, but you're not going to like it."

"You're making too big a deal out of this. Just tell me already."

"Okay. So after I got left there with Lonnie's car, I went to his so-called secret hiding place and got his stuff, including the gun, and then I walked into town."

"What exactly is this secret hiding place you and he keep talking about?"

I would have thought that Lonnie would just have his money in the glove box or under his seat or in the trunk somewhere. I never thought about him having a "secret hiding place."

"He had a metal box attached under the body of the car where it was hard to see. It had a lock on it. I had to break it by pounding it with the lever from the tire jack."

I was blown away. Why would Lonnie have a hiding place like that? What would he need to go to that much trouble to hide?

"But how did you know about the hiding place?"

"I pay attention to things. And I go looking for things when no one's around. It's just a habit I picked up, living on the street. You never know what information is going to come in handy. Anyway, I just watched him without him knowing I was watching him. That's how I learn things."

"Okay, so you got Lonnie's money and his gun, and you went into town. Then what happened?"

"I went to the *policía* and offered a trade."

I wasn't sure if I wanted to know the answer, but I asked anyway.

"What kind of trade?"

"A trade for the only thing I have. The only thing I've ever had my whole life. Myself."

I must have been awful stupid. Or, more like it, I didn't really want to hear what he was telling me.

"What do you mean, yourself?"

"When you live the way I've lived and you get by the way I've gotten by, you learn to read people. Especially men. You get to know what they want or what they will do or won't do. Sometimes I can see it better than they know themselves. I could tell by the way the cop was looking at me that there was something I could do that he would trade for."

I got a sick feeling in the pit of my stomach.

"Are you saying what I think you're saying?"

Antonio's voice became quiet and strained.

"I could tell by the way he was looking at me that he liked boys. I knew that I could give him something he wanted."

"Jesus, Antonio," I gasped, "tell me you didn't..."

"Don't judge me, Dallas. You're not in jail anymore, are you?"

"Antonio, as bad as that pit was, I'd rather still be there than to have you..."

"It's all right. It's the one thing I have to get by. To help my friends get by."

I was starting to feel pretty rotten by this point. I tried to get rid of the picture that was in my head.

"But the gunshot...?"

"Like I said, I can read people. I knew the cop would trade you two for a blow job. But I also knew that he probably wouldn't keep his word. Why should he? Once he got what he wanted, there was no way to make him keep his word. That's why I brought the gun. I had to fire it to convince him that I was serious."

"But if you had the gun, why didn't you just use it to force him to let us go? Instead of... doing that to him first?"

"That's why it's important to be able to read people. I knew that, if I just went in there with a gun and tried to force him to let you go, he would never let us get away. He would try to get the gun away from me. He would make sure we didn't get away. But once I made a deal with him and I kept my end of it, he would know that I was only getting what we had agreed. Because the other thing I could tell about him was, even though he wasn't a man who would keep his word, he was a coward. As long as he got what he wanted, he wasn't going to take chances to try and stop us."

I didn't want to believe what I was hearing. On one hand, it made me sick. On the other hand, I couldn't help but think that Antonio must be some kind of fucking genius to have worked that all out in his head. And it turned out he was right about it all. It worked out the way he figured. But I was sick about what he had had to do save Lonnie's and my sorry asses. There was no way I could ever make it up to him. There's no way I would ever have done something like that for someone else. And I couldn't believe that someone had done it for me.

"Mexico's a fucking perverted country." That's all I could say. But he didn't want to hear that.

"It's not just Mexico, you know," he said. "I had to do the same thing for a cop in Los Angeles. That was the only way I kept from getting arrested on the streets up there."

This was still more stuff that I didn't want to hear. I had my problems from time to time with the cops in my home town, but I always knew they were basically honest men doing their jobs. But obviously, it wasn't like that everywhere. I was starting to realize that there was an awful fucking lot I didn't know about the world.

Antonio spoke again. "You think I'm disgusting, don't you?"

I took a minute to try figuring out exactly what I was feeling.

"I don't think you're disgusting, Antonio. I think what you had to do was disgusting. It's disgusting that you had to do that to get me and Lonnie out of there. But you're not disgusting. Right now I think you just might be my best friend in the whole world."

As miserable as he was, that seemed to make him feel a bit better.

"Even better than Lonnie?"

"Well, it's hard to compare you and Lonnie. I've known Lonnie my whole life. We've always known everything there was to know about each other. Always. I don't think I will ever be able to have a friend as close as that in my whole life. But in some ways, I feel like I'm actually closer to you right now than I am to him. You seem to understand certain things about me better than he ever has. Maybe it's that talent for reading people that you were talking about."

"What do I understand that he wouldn't understand?"

I thought about it for a minute and then I decided to tell Antonio something I had never told a living soul in my whole life.

"Here's something I could never tell him. It's something I've never told anybody ever. You know his girlfriend Linda he talks about sometimes? Michael's sister?"

I swore I could hear a very slight chuckle coming from him.

"You were you in love with her, weren't you?"

"Jesus, you're scary! How did you know that?"

178

"I can see it in your face whenever he talks about her."

"Shit. I've never told anybody that. I was in love with her for more than a year. Lonnie never knew."

I thought I heard another slight chuckle.

"I think he did."

"What?"

"I could see it in his face. I could see by the way he was looking at you while he was talking about her. It looked to me like he knew how you felt about her. Just like I could tell how you felt."

Antonio gave a slight shrug.

"Anyway, none of that matters anymore, right? Because you love Marisol now."

"This is too fucking weird. It's like you're a fucking mind reader or something. Is there any way to keep a secret from you?"

Antonio turned his head toward me and smiled. It was good to see him smile again. I really wanted the old Antonio back. And by that I mean the young Antonio. Not the one who seemed like a grown man who never had a childhood.

I figured what the hell and I gave him a hug. Then I settled in for going to sleep, wedged in between the two of them.

"*Muchas gracias* for saving my life, Antonio. *Yo te quiero mucho.*"

"*De nada, comandante. Yo te quiero mucho también, mi amigo.*"

I was just about asleep when Antonio spoke again.

"Oh *¿y comandante?*"

"*¿Sí?*"

"Please do not dream about Marisol tonight."

179

When I woke up, the sun was rising. It was another nice morning. Every morning we had in Mexico was nice. By that I mean that it was never cold or wet.

I looked around and remembered where I was. I was like the meat in a sandwich, wedged between Antonio and Lonnie. Actually, it was more like being in a burrito, and our double sleeping bag was the tortilla. For one silly moment, I wondered, if I was the filling for a burrito, would I be beef, chicken or beans?

Then everything that happened the day before came back to me. On one hand, I was very happy not to be waking up in that miserable excuse for a jail. On the other hand, I was feeling very discouraged with our situation and not having a clue about what was going to happen today. I squeezed myself out of the sleeping bag and stood there looking at the sun peeking over the top of a hill in the distance, and I thought to myself, man, I could really use some coffee now.

Lonnie was awake and apparently reading my mind. "You know, that idea of yours about a coffee pot gets better every day."

"Tell me about it. Right now I'd just settle for an ordinary glass of water."

He crawled out of the sleeping bag and left Antonio snoozing there on his own. We both had a look around to see where we had wound up the night before. We were high up and had views for a long ways in a couple of different directions. But there wasn't much to see. We couldn't see the little town where the police station was, although it wouldn't have been too awful far away below us. The terrain was rocky, but there were plenty of bushes and trees.

"So, what do you think?" I asked. Couldn't get more general than that.

Lonnie pulled out a cigarette and lit it. He took a couple of puffs and kept looking off into the distance.

"I don't fucking know, Dallas. I just don't fucking know."

I had been doing some thinking about our situation and figured I had narrowed down our possibilities.

"Well, the way I see it, the first thing we have to decide is whether we're going to try to rescue the car. I mean, is there any way we can get it fixed and drive it home? 'Cause if we decide that's not possible, then we have to forget about it and work on getting ourselves to somewhere where we can take a bus or a train home."

I could tell by looking at Lonnie that the idea of abandoning the Chevy was killing him. But it was hard to see any way we could get it fixed. Not the least of our problems was that, as long as we stuck around in the general vicinity where the car was, it was only a matter of time before we would have to deal with that cop again. But I didn't want to be the one saying that we had to forget about the Chevy and leave it to rust by the road and get stripped for parts by Mexicans.

"I know what you're thinking," said Lonnie, staring at the ground. "You think I'm hung up on the car. It's true, I like my cars. But I've totaled enough of them—mainly because of my own bad judgment—to get too sentimental when it's time to walk away from a wreck. It's just that…"

He struggled to explain exactly what he wanted to say.

"It's just that I've never walked away from a car before that was still basically in running condition. Sure, her engine's fucked. But other than that, she's really in pretty good shape."

I figured I needed to talk a little sense into him.

"Lon, the truth is, the car is worthless—unless we can spend the money and the time to get it running again. That's the question. Just how much money and time do we have anyway? I think you're the only one who can answer that."

Lonnie just stood there. I still couldn't for the life of me figure out why he was being so damn mysterious about how much money he had left. I tried again.

"Let's say, for the hell of it, that we could get the car to a mechanic and could get the engine rebuilt for 500 dollars. Could you pay that?"

Lonnie finally seemed resolved to discussing it.

"I don't have that much in cash. But I could get it. I would need to get to a bigger place. Probably to Mexico City."

He wasn't making me any the wiser. But I decided to just go along with him.

"Okay. So, in any case, we have to leave the Chevy where it is long enough for us to get Mexico City, do whatever it is you need to do to get the money and then come back. And how much of the car do you think will still be there when we get back?"

Talking it over with me seemed to be encouraging him.

"Right. But if we could get the car to a mechanic first, he could be rebuilding the engine while we go to Mexico City for the money to pay him. That works out great because it would take several days to do the rebuild anyway. Hell, in Mexico it'll probably take a couple of weeks. That's what we'll do."

"And how are you going to get the mechanic to do the rebuild without paying him something in advance?"

"Well, I could give him a little money as a deposit. But he'd have the car. I could tell him that he could keep the car if I didn't come back. Any car guy would take that deal. Getting that car would be worth more than whatever time and parts he spent on the rebuild."

"And how do you know the price of the rebuild won't shoot up once you come back with the money? Like that tire you got fixed?"

"I don't, do I? But I sure as hell won't be any worse off if that happens. Anyway, I'll burn that bridge when I come to it."

By this time Antonio had woke up. He crawled out of the sleeping bag and wandered off, probably to have a pee in private.

I was determined that I wasn't going to look at him any different than I did before. I had made up my mind that, now that I had my answers as to how Antonio had sprung us from the slammer, I was going to do my best to forget everything he had told me about it. I liked him too much to want him to feel awkward around me. Besides, I had promised not to tell Lonnie any of it, and the best way to keep that promise was to try to forget about it myself. That way I wouldn't be tempted to talk about it. I couldn't imagine what Lonnie's reaction would be if he knew what had happened.

I was kind of surprised that Lonnie wasn't showing much curiosity about what exactly Antonio had done to get us free. He seemed totally focused on finding a way to salvage his car. And that was just as well.

"Okay, so how do we find a mechanic and how do we get the car to him?" I asked, as I watched Antonio walking toward us.

Lonnie flicked his cigarette to the ground, like it was an annoying piece of lint or something. He ground it into the dirt with his foot while he reached into his shirt pocket for another smoke. He put it into mouth and looked with disgust at the empty pack in his hand.

"Fuck," he said, out of the side of his mouth as he lit it up. "This is my last one. I need to get me some more."

I couldn't disagree. I had been around Lonnie before when he ran out of cigarettes, and it wasn't pretty. Let's just say, it didn't do a whole heck of a lot for his disposition.

"What's up, guys?" said Antonio, who had come over to see what we were talking about.

Lonnie took a heavy drag on his cigarette. He was clearly going to make the most what was probably going to be his last smoke for a while.

"Thanks, Tony, for getting us out of that jail yesterday. Whatever you did, that took some balls."

Antonio looked at me, kind of questioning me with his eyes. I gave him a look to reassure him that I hadn't said anything to Lonnie.

"Anyway," Lonnie continued, "we're going to need some more help from you. We need to figure a way to get the Chevy to a mechanic. And we need to find a way to do it without meeting that fucking cop again."

Antonio gave a quiet whistle as he thought about what Lonnie was saying.

"That's not going to be easy, man. The car is right on the road. And the *policía* will probably be keeping an eye on it, just in case we come back. I think you better forget about that car."

"Well, there's no point in *us* going back to the car anyway, Tony," Lonnie said. "We have no way of driving it. The engine is frozen. We need to get someone to tow it out of there."

"And who's going to do that?" Antonio asked.

"I dunno," answered Lonnie. "That's where we need your help. Can you tell by looking at your map how far the nearest garage is likely to be?"

Antonio pulled the roadmap out of his back pocket, unfolded it and then refolded it so he could study the area where we now were. After a minute or two, he looked up.

"The next nearest big town looks like it's about fifteen miles away," he said. "That's a long way to walk."

"Yeah, it is," said Lonnie. He was clearly mulling this information over as he took another drag on his cigarette.

"And we don't even know if that place has a garage," I added.

Antonio spoke up. "There's a little garage in the place just below us. It's just down the street from the police station. I saw it yesterday."

Lonnie and I looked at each other.

"That doesn't do us much good, does it?" said Lonnie. "We're not too likely to get the car fixed there without that fucking cop knowing about it. Hell, it might even be the cop's brother or some other relative of his that owns the garage."

Antonio thought about it for a moment, and then shrugged. "Like I said. I think you better forget about that car."

But Lonnie wasn't ready to give up just yet.

"Look, Tony. I would do this myself if I could. But I can't. I stick out like a sore thumb in this country. And I don't know the lingo."

Lonnie looked at Antonio intently, as he knocked the ash off the end of his cigarette and put it back in his mouth.

"Do you think you could slip into town and check out the situation. Maybe find someone you could ask, what's what. You know, figure out if we can trust the guy at the garage and if he could work on the car without letting the cop know."

It was obvious to me that Lonnie was grasping at straws. I don't think he realized what he was asking. By this time, that cop was probably much more anxious to get his hands on Antonio than he was about finding us. And I didn't even want to think about what the cop would do if he did get his hands on Antonio.

"You can't ask him to do that, Lonnie. It's... it's like a suicide mission or something. If that cop manages to get a hold of Antonio..."

Antonio looked at me uneasily. I had to be careful not to say too much about exactly why the cop would be so interested in him.

"I can try," said Antonio with a dead serious look on his face.

"I won't let you do it, Antonio," I told him. I tried to choose my words carefully. "You know what will happen if that cop spots you. And we won't be able to help you if you get into trouble. I can't let you do it. It's just too risky."

The kid looked at me with a dark smile.

"If I can survive on the streets of Hollywood, with weirdoes and cops everywhere, I think I can manage in a little town like this."

"Yeah, but you can't hide in a crowd like you can in Los Angeles. Everyone here will know each other. They'll know you're not from here. They'll talk to each other about you. Even if you don't run into the cop, word will get back to him pretty damn quick."

Antonio might know more than me about surviving in a big city, but I was pretty sure that I knew more than he did about what goes on in a small town.

"You're not wrong, Dallas," he said. "But I'm just a kid, right? No one pays that much attention to kids. Especially if they're minding their own business, right? And I'm good at not being seen when I don't want to be."

"But that asshole cop will be watching for you…"

"I'll be all right. I promise."

He turned to Lonnie and said matter-of-factly, "Give me some money. I'll get us some food and some water and whatever else you want."

Lonnie was looking pretty darn impressed with him. He pulled out his wallet and handed him a wad of pesos.

"Thanks, Tony," he said. "You've really come through for us, kid. You're all right in my book."

Antonio took the money and scampered down the hill. Within moments he was gone. I had a very bad feeling about this and knew I wouldn't be at ease until I saw Antonio's face again. If anything happened to him, I wouldn't be able to forgive myself.

Lonnie and I stood there for a few minutes, looking in the direction where he had disappeared. Maybe we were watching to see if he changed his mind and came back. But he didn't.

"He's a hell of a kid," said Lonnie. "You were right about him all along. We'd be well and truly fucked if not for him."

Lonnie had his last puff on his last cigarette and then dropped the stub to the ground.

"Shit!" he exclaimed, as he ground it into the dirt. "I forgot to tell him to get cigarettes."

"He's too young to buy them anyway," I said. And, as I said it, I got a sinking feeling in my stomach. I had just reminded myself of exactly how young Antonio was. He wasn't even old enough to buy cigarettes. And we had just sent him into what could be a pretty dangerous situation.

There was nothing for Lonnie and me to do but wait around until Antonio came back. We were both starving and dying for a cup of coffee. And it was hardly any time at all before Lonnie started bitching about needing a cigarette. I found a half-eaten bag of potato chips in my backpack and we shared those, being careful that we divided them evenly.

We sat there awhile, talking shit and telling stories about home and wondering what our friends were up to. Lonnie said he'd like to know how the Dodgers were doing. I would have liked to know too. The previous year, L.A. finished a very distant second in the National League West, behind the Cincinnati Reds, who went on to the World Series. Lonnie and I agreed that L.A. would do better this year and that Dick Allen and Willie Davis were having a great year.

All the while, I couldn't stop thinking about Antonio. I was so worried about him that it was causing a sick feeling in my stomach that wouldn't go away. At least that's what I thought was causing it.

Lonnie took off his shirt and put it over his eyes, so he could try to take a nap. I kept pacing around, wishing the time would go by faster. I found myself feeling hotter and hotter. I just chalked it up to being out in the sun. But then my head started hurting. Then my elbows and my knees started hurting. I felt a spasm in my stomach which, at first, I thought was just hunger. But it got tighter and tighter until I felt like my guts were being tied in a knot.

The pain was terrible. Finally, I got a nasty taste in my mouth, and I knew what was coming. I clenched my teeth and forced myself to breathe slowly. I kept thinking I could stop it from happening if I just tried hard enough. But there was no stopping it.

I fell to my knees and doubled over. I tried to catch my breath but couldn't. For a few seconds, I was filled with terror that I might actually not be able to get my breath and would choke to death. Then I felt the sickening surge of vomit come up through my throat. And I tasted every drop as it shot out my mouth. I didn't think I had much of anything in my stomach, but I managed to keep retching for what seemed like an awfully long time. Just when I thought I was through, more came up. My throat felt hot and raw, and the taste in my mouth was disgusting. But at least the pain in my stomach was relieved a bit.

Lonnie got up and walked over to me. But not too close. He watched me for a few moments with a concerned look on his face.

"Shit, Dallas," he said. "Looks to me like Montezuma's revenge."

14
Meeting the Pérezes

I WAS about as miserable as I could be. My insides were starting to kill me again. My head felt like a balloon that had too much air in it and was close to bursting. The pain made it hard to think straight. I had the unreal feeling of being in a dream. All I could think about was hoping and praying that I didn't have to throw up again.

Well, that wasn't the only thing I was thinking about. I saw Lonnie standing there looking at me, and I hated him. I hated it that I was sick and that Lonnie *wasn't* sick. Why should he be standing there like a normal, healthy person while I was laying on the ground in agony?

Of course, no one likes being sick. But I *really* didn't like it because I normally didn't get sick, so it didn't seem fair that I should be sick now. If I had to be sick, why couldn't it at least happen when I could be at home and in my own bed? I wished that my mother was there to take care of me. I didn't want to be sick outdoors in the middle of nowhere, with no comfort of any kind. This "adventure" just kept getting worse and worse.

I looked up at Lonnie with a bitter glare. "What the hell at you looking at?" I managed to gasp.

Lonnie was never someone good at being sensitive or consoling. But at least he did look truly concerned. Sure, he was in a tough spot, having to figure out what to do about me. But I had no sympathy for him. I would have traded places with him in a minute.

"This is tough, man," he said. "Is there anything I can do for you?"

Yeah, he could be sick instead of me. That was the only thing I could think of that he could do for me.

"Leave me alone," I said. "Keep away. You don't want to get this."

"Damn straight, I don't. But I probably will. The two of us have been eating and drinking all the same stuff. There's no way for you to get this and me not get it."

At that moment, it just sounded to me like Lonnie was just trying to horn in on my sickness. So that it wouldn't all be about me. He was mainly thinking about himself. But deep down I realized that he was right. He was probably going to get sick too. There we were, the two of us, in the middle of nowhere. And not only did we not have a car, but now I was as sick as a dog, and he was probably going to be too. The pain was bad all over my body, especially my stomach, and now it was getting worse. I was actually feeling like I might die, and I wondered what we would do if I got so bad that I needed a doctor or a hospital.

All I could do was try to tell myself that it wouldn't last forever. But I didn't believe it. That's exactly what it felt like—that it was lasting forever and that there was never going to be an end to it.

I completely lost track of time. As I laid there on the ground, every time I started to convince myself that maybe I was beginning to feel a bit better, I just felt worse than ever—even though I hadn't thought that could be possible. Every so often I would feel that terrible tightening in my gut and that sick taste in my throat, and I would crawl a few feet and start puking again. At least I had enough sense and enough strength to manage to throw up a ways from where I was laying.

In between bouts of puking I would just lay there and try to ignore the smell. My head was killing me and it felt like it was burning up. Every time Lonnie tried to come near me, I'd just swear at him and tell him to stay away.

I can't really say much more about the next two days. It just all became a blur, and I lost track of time. I got to the point where I wasn't sure if I had been sick for a day, two days, a week or what. All I knew or could tell myself was that, if I could just hold on, I'd eventually start feeling better. But I got to the point where I didn't really believe it anymore. I became convinced that this was just how things were going to be for the rest of my life—laying there on the ground being miserable forever.

It hurt too much to sleep. Not that I could really tell the difference between being awake and being asleep. I had dreams. At least I guess they were dreams. Maybe they were actually hallucinations or even visions. Anyway, I couldn't tell what was real anymore. Every so often I would hear someone talking, but I couldn't make myself focus on who they were or what they were saying. Sometimes I thought it was my parents. Sometimes I thought it was Lonnie and Antonio. And in a few rare delirious moments, I could swear that Marisol was running her hand over my face and neck and shoulders.

I wasn't sure whether it meant I was getting better or if it meant I was dying when I started to dream of orange butterflies fluttering all around me.

At some point I became aware, for real, of someone wiping my face with a wet towel. That was the moment where my memory became coherent again, and I could start to tell what was actually going on. It was dark, but I was aware of the sun starting to rise over the top of the hills. For a few seconds I actually thought it was my mother with the towel. But then I started coming back to reality.

"*¿Qué tal, comandante? Tú te mejoras, ¿no?*"

It was Antonio.

Except for maybe my mother or our family doctor back home, no face was more welcome than his right at that moment. It started coming back to me where I was and what I was doing there. Antonio kept re-wetting the towel and then wiping my face and my chest. I seemed to be lying there in nothing but my underwear.

My mind flashed back to the morning he did more or less the same thing for me after I got beat up by Marisol's father. The time he reminded me of the painting with Jesus and Mary Magdalene.

I must have been a lot better by this point because it came into my head to make a joke. I opened my mouth to say, "*Número dos*, we have to stop meeting like this." But all that came out was a raspy croak.

My mouth and throat were bone dry. I couldn't swallow because there wasn't a single drop of saliva in my mouth. I kept making noises, trying to talk. Antonio reached over for a bottle of water and poured a few drops onto my lips and into my mouth. I wanted the whole bottle, all at once. But he just kept giving me a few drops at a time.

"*Hombre, por fin tú te despiertas,*" he said, sounding relieved.

I couldn't see Lonnie, but I heard his voice, coming from somewhere.

"Peckerhead here keeps talking to you in Mexican. I think he just does it to bug me. He doesn't want me to know what he's saying to you. What he hasn't figured out yet is, you don't know what he's saying either."

The funny thing was, I actually did know what he was saying. I don't know if it was more stuff coming back to me from Spanish class or the words that Antonio had tried to teach me during our long drive or just being in Mexico with everything in Spanish all around me or maybe some combination of all of those things. But I understood him. It probably just had more to do with the tone of his voice and the look on his face and the fact that we had gotten to know each other pretty well these past couple of weeks. But I knew that he had just said, man, you're finally awake.

I looked around. I seemed to be in more or less the same spot as before. We were still in the hills above that town with the asshole *policía*. I wondered how long I had been laying there. Antonio gave me a few more drops of water.

"You're going to be okay, Dallas," he said. "You're finally getting better now."

"That's not what you were saying last night," said Lonnie, as he puffed on a cigarette. I wondered where he had gotten it. "For a while there, you thought he was going to kick the bucket. Hell, I thought he was done for myself. You were pretty bad there for a while, Dallas."

I tried to talk again. "How... long...?" Talking hurt my throat something awful. And I felt so weak that I wasn't sure I could lift an arm.

"Just take it easy, *comandante*. There will be lots of time to catch up. For now just try to keep getting better."

"Hell, man." Lonnie was taking a different approach than Antonio. "You've been delirious for three and half whole days. For a while there, I thought we were going to lose you for sure. Tony wanted to go for help, but I wouldn't let him. I figured if he ran into that cop, he'd throw all of us, including you, back in jail, sick or not. And that definitely would have been the end of you. No way you would have recovered there."

It was dawning on me that I had missed a big chunk of time. I wanted to know what had happened the last few days. At least Antonio seemed to have gotten into the town and back without being caught by the cop.

Lonnie seemed to be reading my mind.

"You've got a lot to catch up on, Dallas. Tony hasn't left your side ever since he got back from his trip into town. Well, he left once to go back down there and get some more water and other stuff to try to help you. But he's been looking after you like a regular fucking Florence Nightingale the whole time."

Lonnie's cigarette had burnt down to the filter. He tossed it to the ground and, while mashing it into the dirt, lit up another.

"You were right about the kid. We're really lucky we brought him along. I don't know how we would have got through all of this without him."

He savored a drag on his fresh cigarette.

"Hell, he even thought to bring me more cigarettes from town—even though I forgot to tell him to."

Antonio let me take the bottle of water from him and drink from it directly. My throat was starting to feel more normal. I felt like I might be able to talk now.

"How could you buy cigarettes?" I asked. "You're not old enough."

Of all the questions in my mind, that was a funny one to ask first. But I was curious. Antonio smiled.

"Maybe in California I'm not old enough," he laughed. "In Mexico they'll sell cigarettes to anyone tall enough to put the money on the counter. Beer too."

As I drank more water, and my throat bothered me less and less, I became aware that now it was my stomach that was bothering me. I was famished.

"Got anything to eat, *número dos?*"

Antonio pulled out a single saltine cracker and gave it to me.

"Try this for a start. Just to make sure you can keep it down."

I chewed the cracker cautiously, afraid that the sick feeling would come back. I looked over at Lonnie, who was watching me.

"Motherfucker," I said to him. "You didn't get sick at all."

"The hell I didn't. I just didn't get as sick as you. I was lucky. I was only puking for about a day. When I got better and you didn't, I really started to worry."

I looked back at Antonio to verify his story.

"It's true, *comandante*. He was sick as a dog for about 24 hours. I think all the booze in his body helped him fight the germs better."

"And what about you? Did you get sick?"

Antonio shook his head and smiled. "No way. Mexican germs don't bother me. Montezuma don't need to take revenge on me. He only goes after gringos."

It came as a big relief to me that Antonio hadn't gotten the same crud that Lonnie and I had. I would have felt really bad if he had been sick and there was no one to take care of him.

I finished my cracker and waited a while. I felt fine, except that I was starving even more. I had another one. And another one.

"That's enough," said Antonio, sounding like my mother. "Let's not overdo it."

I drank some more water.

"So, tell me what happened when you went down to the town."

I was surprised to see Antonio break into a funny grin.

"I think I have a girlfriend."

"Say what?"

"I met a girl in the town. She's very pretty. And she's about two years older than me. Her name is Graciela."

I shook my head in surprise. A lot seemed to have happened in just a few days.

"Yeah, yeah, you're a regular Casanova," interrupted Lonnie. "The important thing is, I think we have a plan for rescuing the car."

"Whoa, whoa," I said. "I'm having trouble keeping up. Start from the beginning."

I wanted to sit up, but I was still feeling pretty weak. So I just laid there, ready to hear the whole story. But first I had a question.

"Hey, by the way, what happened to my clothes?"

Antonio reached into my backpack and pulled out my jeans and a tee-shirt.

"Sorry. You kept getting puke on them. I finally decided it was easier to just take them off. They're nice and clean now."

"How'd you wash them?"

"Graciela washed them. You can thank her."

"Okay, I guess I better hear this story and get the scoop on this Graciela."

And Antonio began telling the whole story of what had happened after he left us to go down to the town. Lonnie had obviously already heard it all, so he just sat there, smoking his cigarette and watching me.

"So, I went down to the town. It's called San Ramón, by the way. I was very careful not to be seen, in case I ran into that *policía*. Oh, and his name is Alfonso. Alfonso Mendoza. People down there don't like him much."

"Wow," I said, very impressed. "Good job, Antonio. You're a great spy."

Antonio looked pleased, as he flashed a big grin with that mouth full of teeth. He was anxious to keep going with the story.

"So I went down there and I sneaked over to the garage I had seen. There was a man there working on a car. I walked over to him and told him that I had a friend with a car that needed to be fixed. He looked at me and asked why my friend didn't come. I said my friend didn't speak Spanish and that he wanted me to get the information. He still wanted to know why my friend didn't come to ask the questions, even if I had to do the translating. I didn't have a good answer for that, so I just asked if he could, please, just tell me how much he would charge to rebuild an engine. I could tell he didn't trust me, that he thought that I was playing some kind of joke on him. I guess I couldn't blame him. It must have seemed pretty strange to have this kid come in asking about a big car repair job.

"He asked me where the car was. I decided that I might as well tell him, so I said it was the Chevy that was on the side of the road five miles outside of town. This got him really interested. He said he had seen that car and wondered how it got there. About that time a man came into the garage. I got scared and I jumped behind some boxes really fast. I was afraid it was the *policía*. But it was just the man who owned the car that Pancho was working on. Oh yeah, the garage guy's name is Pancho.

"After the guy left, Pancho asked me why I hid and if I was in some kind of trouble. Something about him told me I could trust him. So I just told him the whole story. I mean, all the stuff that he needed to know about how the car got where it was and that the *policía* had it in for us and I didn't want to meet him. Pancho seemed to believe me and he even wanted to help. He said it was about time for *comida* and why didn't I come home with him and eat with him and his family. He could probably tell I was pretty hungry.

"He drove us in his old, beat-up car to his house a few miles outside of town. He lives in a pretty small house on a little farm. I had lunch with his whole family, and they were really nice. His wife Marta had a pozole stew, and it was delicious. That's where I met his son Daniel and his daughters Graciela and Catalina."

"Yeah, yeah" said Lonnie, as he smashed a cigarette butt into the ground with his shoe. "I been hearing about nothing but Graciela ever since the first time he got back from down there."

I could tell Antonio was very happy about meeting these people. Part of me wondered if they could be trusted. But, like Antonio himself said, he was really good at judging people, so they were probably okay.

I have to admit, though, I was a little bit jealous or something hearing him go on and on about Graciela. He and I had become such close friends during the previous couple of weeks that I guess maybe I kind of saw her like competition or something. It was kind of like the way I felt the first time Lonnie got a girlfriend. I was afraid things wouldn't be the same between us anymore. And the truth is they never *were* exactly the same after that—but we still were best friends. Anyway, it wasn't like Antonio was going to stay in San Ramón and move in with this family or anything. The fact was, it was good to see him acting like a normal, lovesick fourteen-year-old boy instead of the streetwise kid who had grown up way too soon and way too hard.

Antonio went on with his story.

"Anyway, Daniel was really interested in our trip through Mexico and he kept asking why we had driven all this way. Finally I told him about your friend Tommy and how you were hoping to find him in Guatemala and he thought that was great. Daniel was a university student in Mexico City until June. He told me about how they killed a lot of students there just a couple of months ago. They were marching in support of the students in Monterrey."

He gave me a look to make sure that I realized that this was same place where Marisol lived.

"The government took away the Nuevo León university's independence, and students all over the country were marching in protest. The government sent in armed thugs to stop the ones in Mexico City. They were called *los Halcones* and they killed 120 people. Daniel barely got out with his life. His parents made him come home after that. They were too scared to let him stay in Mexico City."

"Shit," I said. "I had no idea that was going on down here. I thought things were bad in America, like with Kent State. But that was only four people. I can't believe they killed 120 here."

"My stepdad says those students at Kent State got exactly what they deserved," said Lonnie, as he lit another cigarette. "He says that when the National Guard says to disperse, then you'd better damn well disperse. Pronto. And if you don't, well, then it's your own damn fault what happens to you after that."

"And what do *you* think?" I asked him.

"I think my stepfather's a prick. That's what I think. Hell, what kind of government do they have down here that would kill that many people, just for marching in the street? Anyway, it's not our problem. Go on with your story, peckerhead."

198

"Daniel says that the *Halconazo*—that's what they called the killing in Mexico City—wasn't the first time it happened. Three years ago they killed hundreds in Mexico City.

"Daniel says things are really bad in Guatemala. There are *guerrillas* there that have been fighting against the government, and last year the government declared an *estado de sitio* and death squads have been killing *campesinos* all over the place. That must be what your friend Tommy went down there to write about."

I looked over at Lonnie.

"Still want to go to Guatemala?"

"Hell," he said. "We aren't going anywhere until we get the car taken care of. Go on with the story, Tony."

I could tell that Daniel's stories had a big effect on Antonio. He sounded like he was ready to go fight the death squads himself. Me, I was thinking more and more about going home. I reached for the bottle for another drink of water.

"Anyway after the *comida* Pancho brought me and Graciela back into town and she helped me buy some food and water and"—he looked over at Lonnie—"cigarettes and aspirins and whatever else we could think of.

"I brought the stuff back up here. By that time Lonnie was sick, so I had my hands full for a while. Once I saw that he was getting better, I got the car keys from him and went back down to Pancho's garage. He drove us out to where the Chevy was."

"And you managed to do all this without running into, what's his name, Alfonso the cop?"

"Yeah. Pancho knew pretty much when he would be around and when he wouldn't. He doesn't spend a lot of time working. Like I said, no one likes him much. He's not from around here, and he's not very friendly."

"You can fucking say that again," growled Lonnie under his breath

"Anyway we drove out to the Chevy, but it didn't look very good."

"What do you mean it didn't look very good?" I asked.

"Well, the tires and the side mirrors were gone. And there was a big crack in the front window. There were probably a few other pieces missing too."

I looked over at Lonnie. Of course, he already knew all this, but I could tell from the way he was burning a hole in the ground with his eyes that hearing it again was just as painful as the first time.

"Pancho just shook his head when he saw it, but he didn't seem too surprised. I guess that's just what happens when cars are left by the side of the road around here. Anyway he took a look at the engine. Then he said he'd come back late at night with his tow truck, when he was sure not to run into Alfonso.

"So I hung around at his house until it was time to go get the Chevy. Chela had jobs to do in the house and on the farm, so I helped her."

"Chela?"

"That's short for Graciela. That's what they all call her. She really seemed to like talking to me. We got along really great. She wanted to know what California was like and Los Angeles and everything about *Estados Unidos*. She wanted to know if I had a girlfriend."

"Yeah, yeah, Romeo," said Lonnie. "Nobody cares about any of that. Get on with the story."

"Anyway when the time came, Pancho and Daniel and I went back to the Chevy. Pancho brought four old tires that would fit it, and they put them on. Then he hooked it up to the tow truck and we brought it back to the farm. He put it in a shed that he has there. He said that it was probably better not to have it in the garage in case Alfonso started wondering where the car went. Anyway Pancho says he can fix the engine, but he needs money to get the parts first."

Antonio looked over at Lonnie.

"That's where you come in, *cabrón*."

Lonnie sneered.

"He keeps calling me 'kahbrone,' but he won't tell me what it means."

I had a pretty good idea, but I figured I was better off not saying.

"So," I said, "do you still think you can get the money if we get to Mexico City?"

He didn't look too happy, even though things seemed to be working out a lot better than we could ever have expected.

"Yeah, I can get the money. It just depends on how soon you feel up to taking the bus into the big city."

I made another half-hearted attempt at sitting up. I was better, but I still wasn't a hundred percent.

"Maybe by tomorrow," I said. "But I tell you, after hearing those stories about the... Al Conies?"

"*Los Halcones*," said Antonio. "That's a kind of bird that hunts and kills animals."

"Yeah, after hearing those stories, I don't know how anxious I am to be heading into Mexico City."

"Yeah, well, it can't be any worse than Tijuana," said Lonnie.

Somehow I didn't particularly find that reassuring.

I got better as the day went on and by nightfall I knew I would be fine for riding the bus and anything else we needed to do the next day. Lonnie had a bottle of tequila that he had told Antonio to buy for him. I guess it was true about being able to buy anything in Mexico as long as you were tall enough to put money on the counter. Anyway, Lonnie wanted us to drink the tequila that night. He reminded me that we had promised to drink a whole bottle together five days before, but we never got the chance because of getting lost and getting thrown in jail and getting sick.

I knew that I was in no shape for tequila that night, but I promised him that we would drink it the first chance we got. I knew I was much better off getting a good night's sleep and not poisoning my body with alcohol—at least for one more night.

When I woke up the next morning, I knew I was more or less back to my old self. And I was starving. Antonio was already up and around. When he saw I was awake, he got a big wide grin on his brown face and started rummaging through one of the bags. He pulled out a little can of Sterno and lit it. Then he pulled out a little pot and filled it with water and put it over the can. I watched in amazement as he then pulled out two mugs and a jar of Nescafe. He was making us instant coffee.

"Antonio," I said as he handed me a steaming mug. "You're fucking amazing."

I put it up to my nose and smelled the wonderful smell of coffee. I think that half of my illness might actually have been because of caffeine withdrawal.

"*Amigo,*" I said, "*yo te quiero. ¡Mucho!*"

He handed the other mug to Lonnie. He was absolutely beaming.

Lonnie took the mug gratefully, even while he grumbled, "The peckerhead has had this stuff for days. But he refused to make any coffee until *you* were well enough to drink it. I guess we know who's important around here."

"And don't you forget it... *¡cabrón!*" I laughed. "So, Antonio, where did you get all this stuff?"

"I bought the coffee and the Sterno at the store. The rest of it Graciela let me borrow from her house."

We had a bite to eat with our coffee, and then we packed all our stuff up in our backpacks. Antonio led us down a way that brought us directly to Pancho's house, avoiding the town. The hike took a lot out of me. I had been on longer hikes before, but I still wasn't quite back to full strength after being sick.

It was around midday when we finally got to the house. It was even more humble than I expected. The walls were unpainted wood. The roof was made from faded red tiles. There were chickens running around and clucking everywhere. I couldn't imagine how a family of five could actually fit in it.

Antonio ran up to the door and went straight in without knocking.

"*Buenos, Marta,*" he called. "*Llegan los amigos. ¿Dónde está la Chela?*"

After a few moments, he came running out again and ran around to a shed in back. Then he came back leading a teenage girl by the hand.

"Dallas, Lonnie, this is *señorita* Graciela Pérez Rivera," he announced, bursting with pride.

"*Mucho gusto,*" I said, while Lonnie looked at me like I had two heads.

She barely looked up. She was clearly very shy. After Antonio's enthusiastic descriptions of her, I actually thought she looked kind of plain. But she seemed like a nice girl. She had long straight black hair and thick eyebrows that nearly grew together, on top of huge dark brown eyes.

"How do you do?" she said with a soft giggle, and then she turned to Antonio and whispered, "*¿De veras no hablan nada de español?*"

"*Un poco,*" I said apologetically.

The two of them chatted away for several minutes. It made me feel kind of left out and I wished could understand more. Watching Antonio jabber away in Spanish made me realize that he had a whole other world and language that I didn't understand and couldn't completely share. I mean, he and I could understand each other really well, but the truth was, I had only scratched the surface when it came to really knowing Spanish. It made me think of Marisol and how I hadn't really gotten to know the real her. That I would never really know the real her until I could speak her language. And that seemed like so much work that it would be impossible.

Lonnie and I took off our backpacks and laid them on the ground and waited to see what was going to happen next. About then a guy, a few years older than us, came lumbering out of the house. He looked like he had just woke up. He was a bit on the chubby side and had a scraggly beard. He had a big smile on his face, like he was really glad to see us.

"*¡Hola, amigos!*" he said. "You are well come to May-hee-co. How are you? I am *Daniel*."

"Don Yell?" asked Lonnie, shaking Daniel's extended hand.

"*Daniel*. I think in English you say *Dan* yell."

"Well, at least you sort of speak English. I'm Lonnie. This is Dallas."

"Come, come. You are very well come. I am very interested to hear about your *viaje*. You are going to Guatemala?"

"Well, that was the idea," said Lonnie. "But now I'm not so sure. We hit a pretty rough patch the past few days. I'm thinking we might just call it a day and start heading home once your dad can get my car fixed."

I couldn't tell if Daniel was understanding everything Lonnie was saying. He probably wasn't since even I couldn't understand what Lonnie was saying half the time.

Before long an old beater of car came driving up. An older guy with a pot belly got out. He had a curly head of salt and pepper hair and a moustache. I figured this was Pancho.

"*Caballeros*," he said with a smile, as he bowed his head slightly and extended his hand to us. "Francisco Pérez. *A sus órdenes*."

Pancho seemed like a really nice guy. I could see right away why Antonio trusted him with no problem. He only had a few words of English, so he mainly relied on Antonio to translate back and forth between us. We spent a few minutes asking and answering questions back and forth. It was pretty confusing with Pancho, Daniel and Lonnie all wanting to talk at once and Antonio trying to keep up with the translations. Finally a small round woman appeared in the door of the house. I figured that was Marta.

"*¡A comer!*" she cried. "*Vengan a la mesa.*"

We all dutifully filed into the house. It was pretty snug, and I wasn't sure how we would all fit around the table, but somehow we did. Marta didn't sit down at all and, when the youngest kid appeared, she sat on Daniel's lap. Catalina—they called her Cati—looked like she was about 10 years old and she was as cute as a button. She had a mischievous smile and was not nearly as shy as Graciela.

Marta served us steaming plates of rice with pieces of chicken lying on top. I had the definite feeling that our dinner had actually been alive and running around the yard just an hour or two before. It looked good, and we were starving. Lonnie started to dig in but stopped when I jabbed him with my elbow. Marta made the sign of the cross with her hand and spoke a few words of prayer. Everyone but Lonnie and me made the sign of the cross too and quietly said, "*Amén.*"

The food was plain enough, but it was good. The chicken tasted very fresh and came apart with a touch of the fork. The babble of conversation that had begun in front of the house continued over the table. Lonnie was anxious to find out from Pancho how long the engine rebuild would take and how much it would cost. For his part, Pancho wanted to know more about where we lived and how we made the journey down from California.

Daniel wanted to know what we could tell him about universities in the United States and if there were a lot of protests going on there. Marta was very concerned that Lonnie and I had been sick and that the two of us should be taking care of ourselves better. And, she said, wasn't Antonio a very good boy for taking such good care of us. I felt sorry for poor Antonio. He was so busy translating nearly every word that was being spoken that he barely got a chance to eat anything.

Daniel seemed mainly interested in talking to me, and he was determined to do it, as much as possible, without a translator.

"Antonio he tell you about *el Halconazo?*"

"Yeah," I said. "Sounded pretty bad."

"Yes, very bad. Three friends of mine they die."

"That's tough, man. I'm sorry."

"I have, how you say, *un primo.*"

He looked at Antonio for help, and Antonio said, "A cousin."

"Yes, yes, a cousin. I have a cousin who was in *la Matanza de Tlatelolco.*"

Now I looked to Antonio for help.

"That was the student massacre in 1968."

"After, my cousin Gustavo he must leave México. He go to Chile and cannot come home. In December México get a new *presidente.* Echeverría he let the students in Chile come home. And then there was a bigger *matanza.* In June. More students die. My cousin he wants to go back to Chile. They have a new *presidente.* Salvador Allende. He change Chile. More justice. More freedom. I want to go to Chile."

"I hope you get to go," I said. I didn't know what else to say.

Pretty soon the talk turned to the fact that we needed to go to Mexico City. Antonio explained to Lonnie and me that, after the meal, Pancho would drive us to a place where we could catch a bus that would take us there. He wouldn't bring us to San Ramón in case we'd run into Alfonso. Instead he'd bring us to a place further away where we weren't likely to meet the cop.

When it was time to go, Marta looked at us like she hated to see us go. I thought she was going to cry. And she had only just met us.

"*Muchas gracias, señora,*" I said.

She put out her arms and said, "*Un abrazo, joven.*"

"She's going to give you a hug," said Antonio, helpfully.

Lonnie, Antonio and I all got hugs from Marta, Graciela and Cati—and even from Daniel. Even Lonnie seemed overcome by the affection they were showing us. On an impulse he reached into his backpack and pulled out a bottle of tequila. It must have been the one he bought for him and me to drink together.

"Here," he said, handing it to Marta. "This is for you. Thanks for everything."

This made her even more emotional, and she grabbed Lonnie and squeezed him even tighter. Lonnie looked embarrassed, but I could tell that underneath he was really pleased.

"*Que les vaya bien,*" called Marta as we squeezed into Pancho's car.

Pancho drove us about ten miles to a small place on the main road. Interpreting for Pancho, Antonio explained that a bus would be passing by in less than half an hour, if it was on schedule, which it usually wasn't. He told us how much money to have ready and that, when we got to some other place, we would have to get off and take another bus, and that one would take us to Mexico City. I didn't really pay much attention. I figured Antonio would make sure we did everything we were supposed to.

Pancho waited with us until the bus came by. We climbed on board, and it was pretty crowded. Lonnie and I managed to get seats together, but Antonio had to sit by himself.

As the bus pulled out, I looked out the window and saw Pancho standing there by the side of the road with his hand up. He didn't move for as long as I could see him.

15
A Night at the Plaza

"THOSE WERE really nice people," I said to Lonnie, as the bus bounced and jerked along the road. "We were really lucky that Antonio found them."

"Yeah," said Lonnie. "Almost makes up for all the Mexicans that have tried to rip us off or kill us."

"That was a really nice thing you did, giving them the bottle of tequila."

"Yeah, well, I thought I should give them something, and that's all I had. But I'm going to buy another one. You and I are still going to spend a night drinking a bottle like we talked about. With all the crap that's happened, we've had to put it off way too long."

"Damn straight."

Lonnie was quiet for a while. Then he said, "Man, I really hate buses. Especially this bus."

I had to agree. Sometimes I would take the Orange Belt bus into Bakersfield, and I wasn't particularly impressed with it. But it was like the lap of luxury compared to the rickety old thing we were riding now. At the speed we were going and the number of stops we were making, it looked like we were in for a pretty long ride.

The bus was jammed full of people, and most of them stank. The worst one was an old woman sitting just across the aisle from me. Even though it was warm, she was wearing a heavy poncho. I tried not to stare at her, but I just couldn't believe the smell coming from her. Then I became aware of two beady eyes staring back at me in the vicinity of her midsection. She was carrying some kind of bird—a chicken or a turkey or something—under her poncho. And it was alive and staring at me. Yeah, the Orange Belt was looking pretty good right about now.

"So," I said. "What's the plan? How are you going to get the money to pay for the car?"

"You let me worry about that."

"Lon, I'm getting fucking tired of you not leveling with me. Just tell me what's going on, goddamnit. I think I got a right to know."

He still didn't want to tell me. But he knew it was going to be a damn long bus ride if he didn't.

"Okay, okay, here's the deal. You remember Ed in Guaymas?"

"Is that the guy I found you with the morning we left?"

"Yeah, that's him. I met him in the bar of the hotel and he brought me back to his room for some partying."

"Just the two of you?"

"Nah, there were a couple of girls too. Actually, I think they might have been hookers. Anyway, it was a good night. We were all snorting cocaine."

"You were fucking what?"

"Hey, it's no big deal. I've done it before. It was good stuff."

I was kind of in shock. I knew that Lonnie smoked pot sometimes, but this was the first time I knew that he'd been snorting coke.

"Go on."

"Anyway, he had a few grams to sell at a really good price, so I decided to buy them from him."

"A few grams? How many's a few? Forget it. It wouldn't mean anything to me anyway. Are you fucking crazy, man? So how much money did you give him?"

He didn't really want to say but, now that he had told me this much, he knew that he wasn't going to get away without telling me everything.

"A few hundred dollars. But, hell, it was cheap. I could take it back to California and make a huge profit selling it."

I was really finding this hard to deal with. I had known Lonnie my whole life, and now I find out he's fucking Mr. Big in the drug world. And then it dawned on me that he had been carrying cocaine around with him—with us—ever since Guaymas. I was freaking out over how close we had been all this time to getting arrested for something damn serious or, worse, getting killed by thieves.

"And how were you going to get it back to California? What if you got caught with it? Did you even think about that? And did it ever occur to you that we might actually need that money? Like for car repairs? I can't believe what a fucking idiot you are. I just don't believe it."

I don't think I was ever as mad before in my entire life as I was at that moment. Lonnie had pulled a lot of stupid shit in all the years I had known him. But this really had me scared. I looked around, realizing how loud I was talking and wondering if anyone sitting close to us understood English. Lonnie must have been thinking the same thing because he deliberately lowered his voice when he answered me.

"Okay, okay. I suppose it was a dumb thing to do. But that money I took from Don seemed like a lot. I thought it was way more than we were going to need. I just didn't think we'd miss it. Hell, you know I've never been very good at numbers. Anyway I'll make it right and we'll get the car fixed and we'll head back for home as fast as we can."

"And just what are you planning to do in Mexico City?"

"I'll sell it. Hell, I'll probably make a profit. Then we'll have all the money we need again."

This just got crazier and crazier.

"Are you out of your fucking mind? Who are you going to sell it to?"

"I'll find somebody. Just like Ed found me."

"Fucking Ed fucking found the biggest fucking idiot in fucking Mexico. *You* can't find the biggest fucking idiot in fucking Mexico because you *are* the biggest fucking idiot in fucking Mexico."

"So what do you want me to do? Bring it back to California? Dump it in a trash can? Face it. All our money is in this bag. We can't just dump it. We have to get our money back. We can't just throw it away."

It scared me that Lonnie actually sounded like he was making sense. As scared as I was to be carrying coke around with us, I had to concede that it wasn't exactly smart to just throw away the better part of a thousand dollars. At that moment I really hated Lonnie for getting us into this mess.

"Look," he said. "No one's asking you to be involved in this. When we get to Mexico City, I'll take care of it. By myself. You and Tony don't have to have any part in it."

"And how are you going to manage without someone to translate for you?"

"It'll be fine. I won't be dealing with peasants. The people I'll be looking for will know how to speak English."

So suddenly he was a man of world who had all the answers.

"But what if you get into trouble? What if your customer tries to double-cross you or rob you? You could use some backup."

I don't know why I was saying these things. I wanted no part of any of it. I was scared shitless. But I couldn't stand by and let Lonnie get himself killed because no one had his back.

"I don't want you there," he said firmly. "You've got a terrible poker face. Anyone would take one look at you and know that you're in way over your head. And I don't want Tony there either. He may be smarter than both of us put together, but he's still just a kid. He needs to be kept out of this."

His remark about me being in over my head stung. But deep down I knew he was right about that and right about Tony. I hated it, but I couldn't really argue with him. Just when things seemed like they were going pretty well for us, that sinking sick feeling had come back into my stomach.

We made our transfer to the other bus with no problem. The second bus was a bit nicer than the first bus, but not by a whole lot. Antonio ended up sitting by himself again, but he didn't seem to mind. He seemed happy enough watching the scenery pass by. Me, I had a bad feeling all the way to Mexico City. I felt like Lonnie was heading into a big heap of trouble and there was nothing I could do about it. I kept trying to take our minds off it.

"So, you're resigned to going back and facing the music for whatever happened to Michael?"

"Yeah. I can't run forever. It's time to go back and find out what's what and deal with it. If I have to do time, I guess that's just the way it's got to be." He laughed. "Hell, it might even keep me out of the army."

"And Linda?"

"I miss her. I might not act like it, but I do. She's probably pissed as hell over what happened with her brother and me not calling for all these weeks. But if she still wants me, I'm hers."

I don't know why, but I felt like this was the time to come clean with him. Maybe because we had been through so much and I had been making him give up his secrets, I thought maybe I should give up mine. Maybe I thought that something bad was going to happen in Mexico City and I might not get another chance.

"You know, man," I said. "I... I, uh, I was in love with Linda almost since you first starting going out with her."

He smiled that devilish smile of his. "Yeah, I know."

"You knew?" So Antonio had been right. "Why the hell didn't you ever say anything?"

He shrugged. "I dunno. I guess I figured it wasn't like you were ever going to do anything about it. I mean, you're not that kind of guy. The kind of guy who goes behind his best friend's back. And, I guess, I kind of liked it that you wanted her and I was the one who had her."

I felt like a complete idiot. Here all this time I thought I was guarding this big deep dark secret. And it wasn't any secret at all. Even the Mexican kid I had only known a few days had been able to see it on my face. Anyway, it didn't matter now.

"Yeah, well, you should know that I'm over all that now," I said. "All I can think about these days is María Soledad. When this is all over, I really want to go up to Monterrey and try to find her."

"Yeah, well, I'll let you go off on that adventure on your own. After this little vacation is over, I'm not going anywhere ever again except California. Maybe Tony will go with you. Maybe you and this chick can get married and adopt him." He laughed at his own joke.

It was late when we pulled into the city. And it was a big fucking city. It seemed to go on and on forever. I remembered Antonio saying that it was even bigger than Los Angeles, and he was right. Just when I thought we had finally arrived, the bus just kept going. Finally we got to a bus station right in the middle of it all. Needless to say, we didn't have a clue about where we were or where we should go.

We walked out of the bus station. It was on a big, wide, busy street. There was a line of taxis waiting for customers.

"So now what?" I wondered.

Lonnie walked up to the first taxi and started speaking to the driver. Apparently, he spoke English—or at least enough for Lonnie to be able to communicate him. Lonnie opened the rear door and threw in his backpack.

"Get in," he said. "This guy'll take us where we need to go."

We all piled in, and the car took off. I had no idea where he was taking us, but he turned right down one street and then left down another. Then we were driving down a wide street with a park to our left.

"I think we're getting the scenic tour," said Lonnie, a bit suspiciously.

Antonio was studying his map the whole time. "I think that's *la Bosque de Chapultepec*," he said excitedly. "It's a huge park."

"Cha pool what?" said Lonnie, not sure if he wanted the answer.

We all gripped whatever we could find with our hands, as the taxi sped down the streets at a speed that didn't quite seem safe. The driver weaved around and in front of other cars, frequently honking his horn to let them know to get out of his way. We must have gone more than five miles before he finally pulled up in front of a plaza between a couple of buildings. There were a lot of people milling around. I could hear mariachi music playing close by.

The driver turned around and said to Lonnie, "I get you a girl, okay?"

"I'll get my own girl, thanks. How much?"

Lonnie paid him, but he kept insisting that he would get us all girls. When Lonnie kept refusing, he offered to get us boys.

"I can get you pretty boys," he said enthusiastically.

Lonnie opened the door and we all got out and started walking away.

"What was that about?" I asked him. "How come he thought you wanted a girl?"

"Because that's what I told him I wanted. But I don't want some sleazy whore that he knows. I want to find my own whore."

Antonio was finding the conversation very interesting. I was just confused.

"And why do you want a whore?"

"Why do you think? I'm horny. It seems like forever since I last got laid. I'm in Mexico, and I owe this to myself. I'm going to get serviced by a professional."

"But I thought..."

"Don't worry. This is all part of the plan. This isn't just about getting my rocks off. If I find an experienced hooker, she'll be able to connect me with someone to sell my coke to."

I just shook my head. "How do you know all this? How do you know so much about hookers and connections and everything? When did you become Mr. Big Time Urban Drug Dealer?"

He just shrugged his shoulders. "You pick things up. You hear things. I don't know. Maybe I figured it out from watching TV shows or movies. Anyway, the worst that can happen is that I'll get my brains fucked out."

"But how long will you be? What are Antonio and I supposed to do in the meantime?"

"Look, if I'm going to hire a whore, I'm going to have her the whole night. We'll meet up in the morning."

"Where?"

He looked up and down the street. He settled on a bar down on the next corner. It was called El Águila.

"I'll meet you in front of that bar in the morning. But not too early. Say, ten o'clock."

"Lonnie, I have a really bad feeling about this..."

"Yeah, you and your grandmother. You've always been a bit of a pussy when it comes to these things. Stop your worrying. I'll see you tomorrow, and I'll have a wad of cash to pay for fixing the car and we can go back to living it up in style again. It'll be fine. You'll see. Now beat it, you two. You're cramping my style."

Then, just as I thought he was going, he opened his backpack and pulled out a few things and handed them to me.

"Just in case, I'm only taking enough money to pay the hooker. And the gun. I'll leave the rest of the money and my wallet with you. Just in case there's any funny business."

215

And with that, he hoisted his backpack over his shoulder and, without looking back, walked into the crowd in the plaza, toward where all the mariachi music was playing. As I watched him disappear, I quietly promised myself that he wouldn't just vanish but that he would come back and, if he didn't come back, then I would go find him and kill him with my own two hands.

"I sure hope he knows what he's doing," said Antonio, looking a bit puzzled.

"You and me both, amigo," I replied. "You and me both."

So the two of us were just standing there in the middle of Mexico City in the middle of the night.

"So what you do you want to do now, *número dos?*"

"Let's go hear some mariachi music!"

We wandered into the plaza. I kept an eye out, in case I spotted Lonnie. He wouldn't be too happy if he thought we were trying to follow him. The plaza was full of people. A lot of them were couples. This was obviously the place to come at the end of a date. Everywhere we went musicians came up to me, wanting to play music for me and my friend. It kind of got annoying

"Do they think we're on a date or something?" I asked Antonio.

"They want you to pay them to play their music."

"Well, that's not going to happen. I don't even like mariachi music."

"Maybe someday I'll bring Graciela here. She might like this."

All around the plaza there were restaurants and cantinas, and everyone seemed to be in a party mood. I had to admit that the music did make it festive.

A particularly persistent mariachi tagged after us, having spotted me as an American.

"Have you been to El Tenampa, *señor*? You must go there. It is the heart and soul of this place."

216

"No thanks."

"Then let me play for you. You must hear the real *música*."

"That's okay."

He wasn't going to give up. He was middle-aged but he looked good. His typical mariachi clothes, all black with fancy embroidery, were immaculate and his hair and mustache were perfectly trimmed. A sombrero hung on his back. There was something dignified about him that made it hard for me to be rude to him.

"*Señor*, I am from Jalisco, the home of the real *música, el son jalisciense*. This music, she only come to this city fewer than seventy years ago. You must hear the real *música*. The way it is played in Jalisco."

Finally, I relented and we stood there while he played us a song. It was surprisingly moving. He sang as if his heart was going to break. He sang as if he had all the sorrows of the world on his shoulders. He sang as if it was his last night on earth. I never liked mariachi music before, but I had never heard it like this. It brought up every feeling I ever had about being in love and being sad. I wished Marisol was there with me and, in that moment, we could die in each other's arms, listening to this man sing.

When he had finished, I handed him some money. He was insisting on singing another, but I wasn't sure if my heart (or my wallet) could handle another song.

"*Gracias, señor. Muy bonito*," I said, as I hurried Antonio and myself out of there.

We came back to the spot on the street where the taxi had left us. I was starting to feel kind of tired.

"So what do you want to do now, *número dos*?"

He pointed at the bar where we were supposed to meet Lonnie and started walking in that direction.

"C'mon, *flaco*," he said. "Buy me a drink."

As I followed him, a funny feeling went through my chest. Looking at the back of his head, with his shaggy black hair hanging down to his neck, I could nearly pretend that it was Marisol calling me *flaco* and leading me off to the bar. I wished to God that it was.

"Hey, Antonio, why did you decide to call me *flaco* just now?"

"Huh? Oh, it's nothing bad. It's just what we call skinny guys like you. I didn't mean anything by it."

El Águila was surprisingly quiet for being so close to all the buzz and excitement of the plaza. Maybe it was more of a local place. Inside it was a bit dingy and darkly lit. There was an old jukebox playing in the back. Another funny feeling went through my chest when I recognized the song that was playing.

It was "California Dreamin'." It seemed like it had been forever since I had last heard it. It was on the radio a lot when Lonnie and I were in junior high, and neither one of us never really liked it. We liked listening to the Rolling Stones instead of the Mamas and the Papas. I had pretty much forgotten about "California Dreamin'."

But now, being so far from home and suddenly hearing a song that was so familiar and that reminded me of being younger and being back home, well, it just kind of got to me. I suppose the fact that it was about California had a lot to do with it too. Listening to it put me in a really strange mood. All of a sudden, I was determined to get drunk. What the hell else was there to do?

"What are you drinking, Antonio?"

The way I was feeling, I would have bought him a hard drink if he wanted one. But he just wanted a Jarritos. I ordered myself a margarita. No one batted an eye that a kid as young as Antonio was there. We found a small section toward the back where no one else was sitting. I had to look around to be sure there was no one there because it was pretty dark. We sat at a table in the corner and settled in for the night. More songs from the jukebox could be heard from around the corner.

"So," asked Antonio. "Are you really giving up on finding your friend Tommy?"

He made me feel kind of guilty. I got the feeling that he would have liked to see us go all the way to Guatemala and find him. And that he would have kept going along with us to make sure we didn't get into any trouble.

"I guess it's time to be practical," I said. "We're out of money and the car is broken down. At this point we'll be lucky just to get home. Anyway, we did pretty good to get this far, didn't we?"

"Yeah, I guess."

After a while, he asked, "So how well did you know Tommy anyway?"

"Well, we weren't best friends or anything. He was older than me. He was a couple years older than my brother. I knew him, but I wasn't close to him or anything. I looked up to him. He was really smart. I was always sure that he would do something great with his life."

"How many brothers and sisters do you have?"

"Just one brother. That's all."

"You're lucky to have a brother. I would have liked to have a brother."

"Yeah, well, he can be a pain sometimes, but he's all right. He's away in the Navy, so I don't see him that much. But you know what?"

"What?"

"I always thought it would be neat to have a younger brother. And that's kind of how I think of you. Since we been on this trip together, you're kind of like the little brother I never had."

He smiled. But then he turned more serious.

"What do you think of Graciela?"

"Well, she seems nice. It's kind of hard for me to know what to say about her. I wasn't around her very much. She seems kind of shy."

"Do you think she would like someone like me for a boyfriend?"

"Why wouldn't she? You're a nice guy."

"Yeah, but..."

"But what?"

"It's just that, well, why would *any* girl want me for a boyfriend?"

"What are you talking about? You're a great guy."

The more he talked, the more Antonio looked frustrated.

"Yeah, but I don't have a home. I don't have a family. I don't have anything. What can I give a girl like her? Why would she want me? There's no reason."

I felt bad for him. Usually, he seemed to be full of confidence. I hadn't realized that a lot of it might be for show or to help him survive. He actually had kind of a low opinion of himself. I tried to think of something to say to perk up him as I came back to the table with another margarita. I think it might have been my third one.

"Look, Antonio. You're a really great guy. I don't know if you realize how great you are."

"You think living on the street is great? You think the things I was doing in L.A. and with your friend Michael were great? You think a girl wants a guy like that?"

I was surprised at how bitter he sounded.

"Look. That's all in the past now. You can be something different from now on. Look at all the things you have going for you. You're smart. Even without spending that much time in school, you're smarter than I am. And you're really good looking."

In the dim light, I could barely make out his face. I could nearly imagine that his silhouette was Marisol's.

"I mean it. Really good looking. Hell, if I was queer like Michael, I'd definitely be turned on by you."

Antonio gave me a really confused look, and I really couldn't blame him. That was a really strange thing to say. I tried to fix it.

"What I mean is, if I was girl, well, I'd probably be in love with you. I mean, I would be in love with you. I think any girl would."

That didn't change the confused look on his face at all.

For what happened next, I blame the jukebox. At that moment another song came on. A song that I knew. It was the same song I heard playing the night I was with Marisol. But it was a woman singing it this time, instead of a man. It was "Bésame Mucho."

I can't explain the wave of emotion that came over me when I heard it. Suddenly I was back in Guaymas in that hotel room with Marisol and a million candles all around. I thought of the first time I met her on the beach and how all I could think about afterwards was her. I thought about how good her soft arms felt in my hands and how good her lips tasted on mine. Inside my head I was screaming her name. *¡María Soledad, yo te quiero!* I felt like my love for her had finally driven me insane.

After three (or was it four?) margaritas and sitting there in the dark and looking at that silhouette with the back hair, I somehow convinced myself that maybe, just maybe, just for a moment that it really was Marisol sitting there. That if I wanted it enough, wanted it to be true, then it would be—even if it was just for a second or two. I was positive that, if I wanted something this bad, I could make it happen. I closed my eyes and concentrated on the picture of Marisol in my head and I leaned over. I still can't believe it, but I kissed Antonio on the lips.

Instantly I knew it was a mistake. The minute my lips touched his, I knew it was all wrong, that no amount of imagination could make me believe that he was her. His lips didn't taste the same. And he didn't smell right. He had the same fourteen-year-old boy smell that I remembered from the night we camped near Morelia. It wasn't her smell. It wasn't just that I wasn't smelling her perfume. I knew that her own smell, underneath the perfume, was different than this. And, on top of that, he was starting to get whiskers above his mouth. They scratched. There was no way that I could pretend that his skin was her skin.

But what really made me know it was a mistake was the way Antonio reacted. He jerked his head away. Now, somehow, I could see him more clearly, and his face had a look of complete disgust on it.

"I told you," he hissed. "I never let any man kiss me. Never."

I couldn't blame him for being mad, but I was completely unprepared for how enraged he was. Obviously, I had not been thinking clearly about it, but I guess I had assumed that he would somehow understand. That it would be like the night in the sleeping bags. When he said that he wanted to help, to relieve my pain. Somehow I thought he would get what I was feeling and be sympathetic. But he wasn't.

"You're the same!" he yelled. "You're no different than any of them."

"No, it's not like that," I tried to explain. "I'm sorry. I don't know what got into me. It's just that you've always reminded me so much of Marisol. I was missing her so much. It was driving me crazy. I just thought it might help if I could pretend, just for a second, that you were her."

"I'm not a girl," he said coldly.

"I know that. I can't explain it, Antonio. I guess I'm just tired and I've had too much to drink. And you really do remind me of her. But you're not her. I know that. But I can't help thinking that, if I could find that perfume she wore and put it on you, maybe I could really pretend you were her. Just for a second."

That was definitely the wrong thing to say. I never saw Antonio so angry. "Just because she and I are both Mexican, that doesn't mean we are the same! I told you! I'm not a girl! And I'm definitely not a spoiled, rich girl! Fuck you, Dallas! *¡Mierda!*"

And with that, he stood up and stormed out of the bar. I don't think I had ever heard Antonio swear before. And now I had heard him swear in two different languages.

I wanted to run after him and try to explain better what had happened and why it had happened and that I was sorry and that, if he would just forgive me, it would never happen again. Damn tequila anyway. But I had had enough fights with Lonnie over the years (but never one like this!) that I knew there was no point going after him. I would have to let him have some time by himself and then try to apologize and make it up to him when he had calmed down.

I felt like total shit. I wanted to crawl into a hole and die. Why had I been so stupid? What was I thinking? My heart was sick. For more than a week I had been pining over Marisol, getting depressed over the thought that I might not ever see her again. But this was worse. As bad as it felt to lose what seemed like the only girl I would ever truly love, the thought of also losing Antonio was worse.

I took another sip of my margarita. The ice was mostly melted. Well, I thought to myself, I may have managed to drive off a really good friend, but at least I managed to do it without an audience. It was lucky that we were in a part of the bar where no one could see us. Not that anyone in that bar would know me or ever see me again. But I took some comfort in knowing that my little incident at least had no witnesses.

That's when I noticed a small orange glow off in a particularly dark corner. The glow moved back and forth. It grew brighter, then dimmed again. I knew what it was. It was the tip of cigarette. And then I heard the smoker's voice. It sounded slightly amused. And it didn't sound Mexican.

"Lovers' quarrel?"

16
Vigil at El Águila

THE LAST thing I wanted to do was get into a conversation with some stranger. I just wanted to sit there and ignore the world and keep drinking my margarita. And maybe a few more after that. I would have liked to ignore him, but I had drunk too much tequila for me to do that.

"We were joking around. It was no big deal. We were just having a laugh."

In his dark corner I could see a puff of smoke float up from his cigarette.

"Yeh. When I was his age, there was a priest in the parish with a similar sense of humour like."

I had no idea what his point was. But one thing was for sure. He definitely wasn't Mexican. He didn't sound American either.

"So what are you?" I asked him. "English or something?"

Even though I couldn't quite see him, I could somehow tell that his body had tensed up. He gave another little laugh, but it sounded kind of bitter. He seemed to be tapping his cigarette on his ashtray.

"C'mere, my people did not spend 800 years fighting them bastards just to have some eejit Yank call me English. You might want to learn yerself some geography."

The smell of his cigarette made me want to have one too. It didn't smell like the ones that Lonnie smoked, which were pretty much the same ones that I smoked, since the only cigs I ever seemed to smoke were the ones I bummed off Lonnie. I checked my pocket. There was a pack in there all right, and I pulled it out but then crushed it because it was empty.

The guy in the corner was obviously watching me because he got up, came over, with his pint glass of beer in his hand, and sat in Antonio's chair. He flicked his cigarette pack so that a couple of coffin nails slid out.

"There y' go," he said. "Have one of mine."

No, he definitely wasn't Mexican, but he nearly looked like he could have been. He had a head of thick, curly jet black hair and dark eyebrows. He was wiry and had a couple days' worth of black growth on his face. His skin was kind of like mine: basically pale with freckles but sunburned way too many times. But what I noticed most were his eyes. They were the deepest, coldest blue color I had ever seen.

I took his cigarette and lit it. It was different than what I was used to. It was a darker color. Definitely not menthol like the cigarettes Lonnie liked to smoke.

"Thanks," I said. "So you're not English then?"

"Would you ever feck off with your English shite," he said. "Where are *you* from?"

"I'm an American."

So far he didn't seem very impressed with me. "Well, that much was feckin' obvious. I mean, *where* in the great United States of America are you from?"

"California. From the San Joaquin Valley."

This seemed to interest him.

"Is that so? As it happens, I'll be meeting a countryman of yours here tomorrow evening."

"An American?"

"A Californian."

"Really? What's his name?"

"He's called Peter."

"What part of California is he from?"

"Now, that I cannot tell you exactly. But I think he attended university in Berkeley. So what are you doing in Mexico? On yer holidays?"

"On vacation? Yeah, I guess you could say that. A friend and I drove down in his Chevy. It was just an idea we had."

"He looked a bit young to me for owning a Chevrolet."

"Huh? No, that wasn't him. That's a kid we picked up along the way."

"And what were ye planning to do on this grand tour of Mexico?"

Between the tiredness and the margaritas and who-gives-fuck-all-anyway, I decided not to be cagey with him.

"We had this crazy idea. A friend of ours disappeared in Guatemala a few years back. We got it into our heads that, if we came down here, we might be able to find some information on him. Maybe even find the guy himself. It was a pretty stupid idea."

As I reached for my margarita, I noticed that the guy was giving me a pretty serious stare.

"What is your missing mate's name?"

"Huh? Tommy Dowd. Why?"

For the first time the guy wasn't looking at me like I was someone who was only there for his personal amusement.

"You knew Thomas Dowd?"

"Yeah. He's from my town. He's a few years older than me, but we basically grew up together."

"Well now," he said. "That's very interesting, so it is."

"Why? What do *you* know about him."

He looked down. "Not much really. I mainly just know the name. Peter would know more about him than I would."

It seemed awful fucking strange that, after all this, I had actually just happened to run into someone who had heard of

226

Tommy and seemed to know something about him. I was starting to feel excited about it, and I only wished that Lonnie and Antonio were there too. I couldn't wait to tell them.

"My name's Dallas, by the way. What's yours?"

"Dallas? Like the place in Texas?"

"Yeah, like the place in Texas."

"What kind of name is that?"

"It's the name my mom and dad gave me. I was named after an uncle who died in Korea. So, are you going to tell me your name or not?"

"Sorry. Séamus."

And this guy was giving me shit about *my* name?

"And what kind of name is Shay Muss?"

"Fair play. It's an Irish name. I was named after an uncle too. But he's still alive, along with my eight other uncles."

"Irish, huh? So you ever seen a leprechaun?"

If he was at all amused at this, then he was damn good at hiding it. "Stop right there, Yank. There'll be no talk of leprechauns or fairies or any other of your *Bord Fáilte* shite."

"Bored fall cha what?"

"Forget it. It's *Gaeilge*."

"Gwail guh?"

"The Irish language."

"There's an Irish language? I thought you all spoke English?"

"Yes, there's a feckin' Irish language. What did you *think* we spoke before the English invaded us?"

"I dunno. I guess I never thought about it. Can you teach me a few words?"

With this, he actually became very willing to help.

"Here's a phrase that will come in very handy so," he said. "If you ever meet an Irishman, just say to him, '*Pog ma thon*' and you'll be grand. He'll be very impressed with yeh. He'll surely think yer one of his own."

"Pug mah hone."

"That's it. You've got it. I'd nearly think you were Irish meself if I didn't know better."

I made a point to try to remember that phrase, although I couldn't be sure how much I was going to remember in the morning. Anyway, I was more interested in what this guy knew about Tommy.

"So, is there anything else you can tell me about Tommy? Do you know if he's alive or dead or where he is?"

"I cannot really tell you more than you already know. But it may be that there's a way for you to help him. It's Peter you need to be talking to. If there's any answers to be had, he's yer man."

"And you're meeting him here tomorrow night?"

"I am. Seven or half-seven. There's no doubt he will be interested in meeting you."

It seemed like an amazing stroke of luck that I met this guy. I hoped he wasn't shitting me, but it sure seemed worth it to come back and meet this Peter guy and find out what he knew. And, with any luck, I'd have Lonnie and Antonio with me and they'd see that we might actually have a chance of at least going home with more information about Tommy than we had before.

The Irish guy and I shot the shit for a while longer and then they closed the bar. Séamus said good night and wandered off down the street. I stood there a while on the street, not sure what to do next. I had been hoping that Antonio would come back, but there was no sign of him anywhere. He must still be pretty mad, I thought.

It was awful lonely standing there alone on a dark street in the middle of the night. I was pretty worried about Lonnie and Antonio, but I was actually more worried about Lonnie. Antonio might be just a kid, but I knew that he could take care of himself in a big city. He'd be fine. My only worry with him was that he hated me now and that I'd never see him again. But with Lonnie I was really worried that something bad could be happening to him. For all his talking like a big man who knows it all, he was still pretty naive in a lot of ways. And he was getting involved in some serious shit, with hookers and drugs. I just couldn't shake the bad feeling I had about all of it.

After a while I started to feel silly standing there all by myself on the street, so I started walking. I had no place to go and I didn't want to waste what little money I had on a hotel room since it was only a few more hours 'til morning anyway. So I just walked. I walked up one street and down another and then found another street and walked up and down that one. I saw some strange and interesting things while doing all that walking. Drunks hanging out of doorways. Drunks sleeping in doorways. Couples having fights on the street. Hookers wearing too much makeup asking me if I wanted a date. The night just seemed to drag on. I promised myself that I would sleep in a nice bed in a hotel the next night.

By the time the morning light started appearing behind the buildings, my feet were plenty sore and I was starving. I found a hotel near the plaza where all the mariachis had been, and I waited around until they started serving breakfast. I had something to eat and drank several cups of coffee while I looked at the clock. Only three more hours until it would be time to meet Lonnie in front of El Águila. I prayed that he would be there. And that Antonio would be there too. Being all by myself sucked.

I tried not to think about what I would do if one or the other of them didn't show up. I just refused to consider the possibility. And I hoped to God that Antonio would have gotten over being mad at me. It really hurt to think of never seeing him again. I knew I had gotten attached to him, but I hadn't realized just how much.

After I got tired of sitting there drinking coffee, I did some more walking. When it got to be around nine o'clock, I wandered over to El Águila and just hung out in front of it. I knew I was early, but I figured there was no harm, just in case. I paced up and down the street in front of the bar, as the street filled up with people and cars heading to work. The time really dragged.

When it got to be ten o'clock, I didn't let myself get too excited. I had prepared for this by telling myself there was no reason to worry if either or both of them did not show up on time. Being late was a chronic condition with Lonnie. He never could be on time, even if his life depended on it. In fact it would have been strange if he *had* been on time. As for Antonio, the thought had crossed my mind that he might deliberately show up late—just to make a point, to teach me a lesson. He seemed mad enough that, sure, he just might want to make me squirm a bit before he showed up and told me that he forgave me.

As the time passed, I just kept pacing. I didn't want to wander too far away from the bar and take the chance of missing them. I'm sure there were people who noticed me hanging out for hours there and thought it was pretty strange. But I didn't really care about them. I just wanted to make sure that I didn't miss meeting Lonnie and Antonio.

When it got to be eleven o'clock, I still didn't panic. What's an hour when you're having an adventure in the largest city in North America? When it got to be noon, well, then I did start to panic. I racked my brain, trying to figure out if I somehow got the time or place wrong. Were they waiting for me somewhere else, just as worried as I was? But no matter how many times I ran it through my head, I couldn't escape the fact that this was the very spot that Lonnie told us to meet him and the appointed time was now more than two hours past. I didn't know what to do. I didn't fucking know what to do.

I hung out there for quite a while longer. Even though the bar had been open for business for some time now, I resisted the temptation to go inside and wait with a drink. I didn't want to take any chance of missing them if they showed up. But it was becoming all too clear that neither of them was going to show up. All I could do was hang around, just on the chance that, in spite of whatever was delaying them, they could eventually get to the one spot where we all knew we were supposed to meet. But how long could or should I wait there? Hours? Days? Weeks?

I stopped worrying about Antonio. I knew, wherever he was, he was okay. If he wasn't there, it was his own choice. Maybe he decided to go off on his own. Maybe he decided to go back to San Ramón by himself. Whatever he decided to do, I was sure he was fine.

Lonnie was a different case. I had no doubt that he was in trouble. And I didn't know how to find him or help him. I thought about looking for a police station and reporting him missing. But our experience with the cop in San Ramón discouraged me from doing that. I was afraid that, if he was in jail, I might get thrown in jail too. And the time I spent in the San Ramón jail had put the fear of God in me of even the slightest risk of going into another Mexican jail. Besides, I told myself, how far would I get anyway without Antonio to translate for me?

Finally, I got so tired and depressed that I just sank to the ground and sat there with my back against the wall and my head on top of my knees. I noticed that one of the knees in my jeans had worn a hole in it. I closed my eyes and prayed for it all to be a bad dream. Or that Lonnie and Antonio would come walking down the street, laughing about how they had freaked me out. But they didn't. I just sat there, losing track of time.

After I had sat there so long that I couldn't stand it anymore, I stood up and went into the bar and ordered myself a Tecate. As I sat there at the bar, I looked at the clock. It was after three o'clock. Time to come up with a plan. But as hard as I tried to come up with one, all I could think of was to just keep waiting and hope that one of them would eventually show up. What else was there to do? Call my parents? Ask my dad to fly down and help me look for Lonnie? Or worse, call Lonnie's mom and tell her that he was missing in Mexico City? That was a phone call I was not ready to make.

I looked in the back section where I had had my fight with Antonio, the last place I saw him. For just a moment I thought, wouldn't it be funny if he had gone back there, to the very same table where we had sat last night and was there waiting for me? But he wasn't. There was no one there.

Then I remembered the Irish guy and the fact that he was going to be there in just a few hours with that Peter guy. It wasn't really much of a plan, but it was something. I would meet with them at seven or "half-seven." What was "half-seven" anyway? Six-thirty? Seven-thirty? Three and a half? It didn't matter. I would be there at six. I would meet with those guys, and maybe they might even have some ideas about where I might look for Lonnie. It wasn't much of a plan, but it was the only plan I had.

Having officially given up on waiting in front of El Águila anymore, I left and found a taquería that looked like it might not give me dysentery and scarfed a couple of chicken tacos. Then I had myself a little walking tour of that part of the city. I came across a big fancy building that seemed to be some sort of museum with a big golden dome on top. According to a sign, it was called *Bellas Artes*. Not too far from there was a palace that was covered in colorful tiles called the *Casa de los Azulejos*. I didn't completely understand what they were all about, but they were interesting to look at and I took some nice pictures.

As I was walking around the city, I kept hoping that by some incredible stroke of luck I would just happen to run into Lonnie or Antonio or maybe even the two of them together. But I didn't. When it got to be close to six o'clock, I wandered back to El Águila, got myself another Tecate, sat myself down in the same chair I had been in the night before, and I waited.

After I had slowly sipped three more Tecates, it got to be about a quarter to eight. I was starting to think that I could add Séamus to the list of people who were going to disappear on me in Mexico City, but then there he was.

"How're y' keeping, Yank?" he said when he saw me.

I struggled to remember the phrase he had taught me. "Pug mah hone," I said proudly.

His face brightened up. "Well done there, Dallas. Well done indeed. We'll have y' talking like a right Gael yet."

"So where's Peter?"

He had a look around the bar. "He's not here yet. No worries, we won't be long waiting for him. What're y' drinking?"

Actually, we waited nearly an hour for him. I wasn't sure I should be drinking much more beer, but it seemed important to Séamus that we both get fresh drinks at the same time, so I traded off buying rounds with him.

It was nearly nine o'clock by the time Peter showed up. He didn't look at all like I expected. Since he was from Berkeley, I was kind of thinking he might be a hippie with long shaggy hair and a beard. But Peter had a short crew cut and was wearing a sport shirt and slacks. He had thick round glasses and his face looked a teenager, even though he was probably in his twenties.

"Howzit going there, Peter?" said Séamus, not bothering to introduce me.

"Hello, Séamus," said Peter. "Sorry I'm late."

Peter had a kind of high-pitched voice. He looked at me curiously. Obviously, he didn't know anything about me and hadn't expected me to be there.

"Hi. I'm Dallas."

Peter cautiously shook my hand while he looked at Séamus for an explanation.

"Dallas is from California, Peter. He was friends with Thomas Dowd."

Peter looked surprised and impressed. "Is that right?"

"Yeah, he and I grew up in the same town. He was a few years older than me. But we were friends. Actually, he was better friends with Lonnie. He's the guy I came down to Mexico with. But I've kind of lost track of him since yesterday."

He studied me. It was like he was trying to decide if he could trust me. If I was really what I seemed to be. He looked to Séamus, who gave him a slight nod, as if to say that he had sized me up and I seemed okay to him.

"And are you familiar with Tom's work in Guatemala?"

"I know he went down there. As some kind of reporter or something. And then he disappeared. His parents were never able to find out exactly what happened to him. Lonnie and I had this crazy idea that we might be able to find out something about it if we went down here. Maybe even find him... if we got really lucky."

"But do you know what it was he was doing in Guatemala?"

I shrugged. "I guess not really. Writing about stuff, I guess."

"Yes, that's what took him down there initially. He wanted to write about the state of siege imposed by Guatemalan president Carlos Arana, about the death squads that oppress the Guatemalan people. And about how the U.S. government has been training them and supporting them."

Peter's eyes had become very intense while he was talking. Almost like a crazy man.

"Sit in, Peter," said Séamus, standing up. "What'll y' have?"

Peter took a seat at our table, and Séamus quickly brought three more beers.

"So you know Tommy?" I said. "When was the last time you saw him?"

"I only met him once." Peter lowered his voice. "It was at a camp in the western highlands. You see, Tom came to a realization that it wasn't enough to merely write about the situation in Guatemala. It was important to help the people directly."

"So what are you saying? That he took sides and became some kind of soldier?"

"Yes, that is essentially what he did. He realized that the forces of oppression are helped when good people do nothing but stand back and observe. He didn't want to restrict himself to being nothing more than a chronicler of a people being suppressed."

"So do you know what happened to him? Do you know where he is?"

Peter's face turned dark. Even though he didn't seem be an emotional guy, I got the feeling that he was feeling very upset deep inside.

"I only heard about what happened second-hand. I don't know how accurate the account is. But what seems to have happened is that Tom was moving with some of the resistance when they happened on some members of *la Mano Blanca*."

He pronounced the Spanish words just like a Mexican.

"Only a couple of the *guerrilleros* escaped. They couldn't say for sure what happened to Tom, but since a body was never found, it was presumed that he had been captured."

It seemed amazing to me that I was finally hearing something about Tommy from someone who actually seemed to know what he was talking about. Up 'til then I had pictured Tommy being arrested by a cop, kind of like what happened to Lonnie and me in San Ramón. But the truth was turning out that he was really some kind of hero, like in a movie. It was exciting. I only wished Lonnie was there to hear the story with me.

"And nobody knows any more about what happened to him after that?"

Peter shook his head. "A lot of people disappear in Guatemala. Nobody knows for sure what happens to them."

"Damn. Just when I thought maybe I was going to get some answers."

"If it makes you feel any better, your friend is a hero in Guatemala. To the Guatemalan people, I mean. Their struggle doesn't get much attention outside of Central America. They feel very alone in their fight for liberty."

"Yeah, I've never heard any of this before. It's weird to think that all of this is going on down here, and we don't hear anything about it in America."

"The fight for justice begins with breaking free of the brainwashing you've received your whole life."

"Huh? You think I've been brainwashed?"

"Well, you refer to the United States as 'America.' You were taught that in your school and in your community. All of the western hemisphere is *América*."

He said the name like a Spanish word, not an English one.

"*América* is not just the United States. By expropriating the name for the U.S. government, you are being conditioned to see all of North and South America as belonging to the U.S."

I wasn't sure if I was liking the way this guy was talking. There was something about the way he talked that was familiar to me. After a while it dawned on me. He was lecturing me just like Pastor Travis used to do at the church I went to every Sunday most of my life. Anyway, I thought, brainwashing is something that happened in the Soviet Union, not in America—I mean, in the United States. After all, we have freedom of speech and freedom of the press. We get to hear all sides, not just one side. Right? Or was it possible we were all brainwashed too? I didn't really want to think about it just then, and I didn't want to get in an argument with Peter, so I just changed the subject.

"So you're from Berkeley?"

"I got my bachelor's at Cal. I was there for four years, but I'm not from there."

"So where did you grow up?"

He looked a little uncomfortable telling me. "I grew up in Los Angeles. In Brentwood actually."

"You're kidding. Hey, I was in Brentwood just a little over two weeks ago. Now, isn't that a coincidence? Say, do you happen to know a girl named Kathy? I didn't exactly catch her last name. She has a brother named Kevin. You wouldn't know her, would you?"

He seemed just the smallest bit amused. "It's a pretty big place. And I haven't lived there for several years. Those names don't ring a bell. Sorry."

"You have an eye for the ladies, Dallas?" asked Séamus with a grin.

"Well, I have met a couple of nice girls since we started this trip. I met a really nice one in Guaymas."

"A local girl?"

"Not exactly. She was from Monterrey. The one in Mexico, I mean, not the one in California. She was gorgeous. Her name was Marisol."

"Marisol?"

"Yeah. María Soledad Carvajal."

Séamus and Peter gave each other a funny look.

"I wonder if that would be Eduardo Carvajal's daughter," said Peter, almost more to himself than either Séamus or me.

"Who's Eduardo Carvajal?"

Wouldn't it be something, I thought, if this guy from Brentwood didn't know Kathy but he could put me in touch with Marisol?

"He's a very wealthy and powerful man," said Peter. "He's from one of several right-wing families that run everything in northern Mexico."

"Cool," I said. "So that means she's really rich."

Peter looked disappointed. "That means she's part of a power structure that keeps this country in poverty and suppresses democracy. If she's even his daughter, which we don't actually know for certain."

"What's he look like?" I asked. "I, uh, sort of met him once."

"I couldn't really tell you. Anyway, it doesn't really matter. Or are you planning to see her again?"

"Yeah, I don't know how likely that is. But I can tell you one thing about him. He throws a mean right hook."

Remembering that night in Guaymas made me feel the pain in my ribs again. I decided it was time to steer the conversation back on course.

"So anyway, is that all you can tell me about Tommy? I mean, it's not much, but at least it's still a hell of a lot more than I knew before. Somehow I sure as hell never pictured him picking up a gun and becoming a soldier."

I had known guys who were actually anxious to go to 'Nam and fight, but Tommy was never one of them. And he never really had to worry about the draft because, during the time he was in college, Nixon hadn't done away with student deferments yet. So it was funny to think that he had actually *chosen* to go fight in a war—and one that wasn't even for his own country.

Just then something popped into my head.

"Hey, Séamus, last night you said something about maybe there was something I could do to help Tommy. What exactly did you mean by that?"

Séamus and Peter gave each other a look, and then Peter gave him a slight nod.

"The thing is, Dallas, we have no way of knowing if Thomas is dead or alive. But if he were alive, his only hope of being freed would be if Guatemala got a new government. And, even if he's not alive, a new government for Guatemala is what he would want. If he's dead, then the best thing any of us could do for him would be to do whatever we can to realize his dream for the Guatemalan people. You understand what I'm saying?"

"I think so. But what the hell can you or I do about the government in Guatemala?"

Séamus took a long drag on his cigarette and smiled.

"You or me alone? Not a feckin' thing. But there's more than just you and me in it. This is a struggle that concerns more than just Guatemala or any other one country. It's a struggle that is going on in many countries. And there are many of us in many countries who are doing our bit to help where we can. Because the people in countries like Guatemala are poor and cannot stand up to thugs with guns by themselves. Do y' cop on to what I'm saying?"

"So what can I do? I mean, if I wanted to help those people?"

At this point Peter took over.

"Séamus and I are part of a group that is providing support to an organization involved in the fight against the Arana government. It's not anything dangerous. We just help get certain items to them that are hard for them get by any other means."

"Like what kind of items?"

"Sometimes it's humanitarian support. Like food or medicine. Sometimes it's technical items. Like short wave radios or walkie-talkies or something as simple as binoculars. Things like that. Things that are relatively easy for us to get but are hard for them to acquire within Guatemala."

"Well, that doesn't sound like so much to do for a good cause. So are you going back down there soon?"

"Well, that's just it, Dallas," said Séamus. "We have a small delivery to make, but the problem is that, by this time, the lads on the border have seen Peter's and my ol' pusses a few times too often. And it's fierce important that this one get through. It would be better if it was brought through by someone they've never seen before. Someone who is clearly just a tourist with absolutely no connection to the region. Do you follow me?"

I didn't like where this was going. "Are you saying you want *me* to take it?"

"Steady. There's absolutely no danger in it. You have my word on that. You wouldn't be carrying any contraband or anything like that. We just need you to get a letter through. That's all."

"A letter? To who? Where would I have to bring it to?"

"Not far beyond the border. You would simply walk across and meet the lad and hand it over to him. That's all. That would be the end of it, as far as you're concerned. No bother at all."

I had a bad feeling about this. I wished I hadn't been drinking beer all evening so I could think about it more clearly.

Peter piped up. "I can tell you for certain that it's what your friend Tom would want. In a small way, you would be

239

carrying on his work. Thanks to you his work would not have been in vain."

I started looking for reason why I shouldn't or couldn't do it. I just had a nagging feeling that it wouldn't be exactly as easy as they were trying to make it sound. Then it hit me.

"I'd really like to help you guys, but there's one small problem. I can't go crossing any borders. I don't have a passport."

Peter looked confused. "How is it you don't have a passport? How did you get here without a passport?"

"Well, it's kind of a long story. Lonnie and I just drove across the border at Tijuana. And we just kept driving. Until our car died in a place called San Ramón. And then we got here on a bus."

The two of them just shook their heads. Peter looked like he couldn't believe what idiots Lonnie and I were, but Séamus was laughing like he hadn't heard anything so funny in ages.

"You're one hell of a chancer, Dallas, that's for sure," chuckled Séamus. "But as it happens, you won't be needing a passport anyways. You'll be walking across the border in a place that isn't patrolled."

"Not patrolled?"

"Well, not regularly. The odds of meeting any border guards are small. I'll be driving you to a national park where you can just walk across. There'll be a lad waiting for you about a mile in on the other side. You look fit enough to walk a couple of miles with no bother. You'll get your fresh air and exercise and be back to us healthier than you were before."

"But if there's no border guards, why can't *you* take it in?"

"Because there's always a chance you could run into one of them. And if it was myself, they'd know me. But if it's yourself, they won't know you. You're just a clueless gringo tourist who's wandering around lost. They'll just point you back the way you came and send you on your way. No bother at all. Trust me."

He made it all sound so simple and easy. So why did I have such a bad feeling about it? I tried to think of any other reason why I shouldn't do it. But Séamus wasn't finished. It was like he could read my mind and knew what would convince me. "C'mere, when you get back, we might be able to help put you in touch with that Carvajal girl that you seem to fancy so much."

"You could do that? Even though she's oppressing people?"

"Just because her father's a capitalist pig doesn't mean that she's not all right. Many of the strongest fighters against oppression are the oppressors' own children. Like your friend Tom. He joined the right side, even though he grew up in a family that was part of the power structure that oppressed migrant farm workers in the San Joaquin Valley."

My head was starting to hurt. He was basically calling my own family oppressors too. But I didn't want to focus on that right then. I was trying to keep my focus on what was really important.

"But I can't take off for Guatemala now. My friend Lonnie is missing. I've got to find him first. Maybe after I find him, the two of us can take your letter down there."

"Trust me. Lonnie's off having the time of his life. I'd say he's plastered and four sheets to the wind about this time, not giving you a thought. You don't need to be worrying about ol' Lonnie, that's for sure."

Even though Séamus didn't have a clue about Lonnie, I wasn't actually sure he wasn't right. But I couldn't take that chance.

"No, something's wrong. He was supposed to meet me this morning and he didn't show up. Lonnie may not be the most responsible guy in the world, but he wouldn't disappear for this long unless he was in trouble."

"Fair enough. But you'll only be a couple of days traveling down to the border and back. When you return, Peter and I will help you find Lonnie. We're well familiar with D.F. by now. We'll know all the places to look for your mate. We'll have him located for you in no time."

I was running out of reasons not to do what they were asking me. After all, it did sound easy enough. And once I'd done it, they'd not only help me find Lonnie but maybe even Marisol too. It really seemed too good to be true. And it seemed too good a deal to pass up. The only thing that would make it perfect is if they could find Antonio for me as well.

"Okay, I'll deliver your letter for you. But I'm going to hold you to all your promises."

"Sound, Dallas," said Séamus with a satisfied smile, as he took a gulp of his beer. "Sound."

17
Dead End Trail

BY THE time we left El Águila that night, I was pretty wasted. Séamus asked me where I was staying and I told him that I didn't really have a place. They brought me back to the hotel where they were staying. It wasn't anything fancy, but it definitely beat walking the streets for another night. They had a small room with two beds. They let me sleep on the floor, and I didn't mind a bit. Even though the floor was hard, I slept like a log.

In the morning we had breakfast in their hotel. Peter and Séamus were more interested in talking to each other than to me. While we were eating, they had a big discussion about how soon the capitalist system would collapse completely. Séamus thought it would all fall apart by the end of the century. Peter was certain that it would happen a lot sooner. He couldn't wait because he knew that the people would insist on replacing all the governments in the world with a socialist system that would be fair to everybody—and not just benefiting a lucky few.

After breakfast, I walked with the two of them to a parking garage. Séamus, it turned out, had an actual Jeep. It was dirty and beat-up, but it looked sturdy as hell. This is definitely what Lonnie and I should have been driving, I thought to myself.

As I was about to climb in, Peter handed me the famous letter that there was so much fuss about. He gave a look that was as serious as a heart attack.

"I cannot emphasize enough how important it is that this letter be delivered," he said. "And only to the man that Séamus and I have described to you. Do you understand?"

"Yeah, yeah. I'm not a moron, Peter. I get it."

"There's something else."

"Yeah?"

He handed me a small cardboard box. It was wrapped up with a lot of brown tape.

"Give him this as well."

"What is it?"

"You don't need to know that. In fact, it's better if you don't."

"Now, wait a minute. It's one thing to just bring a letter across the border, but this is a different. What if I get caught with it, whatever it is? That would be a lot more serious. I don't like it."

"Look, everything will be fine. You won't be stopped. Just do this and everything will be fine. Understand? It's too late to back out. You have to do this."

I took the box and sat into the Jeep. I was not one bit happy.

"Let's go, Séamus," I said. "Let's get this over as soon as possible."

And so Séamus and I headed out of the city to the southeast. It was a long drive that lasted until late into the night. We passed through Puebla, Córdoba and Villahermosa.

The two of us did a hell of a lot of talking, since Séamus apparently couldn't stand for it to be quiet—even for just a few minutes. But for all the talking he did, I didn't really feel like I got to know him all that well. But I did learn that he was from a place called Galway and that his family owned a pub and that both his parents were school teachers and that his father was also a councillor, which seemed to be some sort of politician. That seemed to me like a lot of jobs for one person to have, but Séamus seemed to think it was normal.

I also learned that he had four brothers and three sisters and that he went to school at Trinity College in Dublin for a year and then dropped out and went traveling. For the past three or four years he had been in lots of different countries around the world, including Australia and South America.

I had thought that Lonnie smoked a lot, but even he couldn't hold a candle to Séamus. That Irishman smoked non-stop. And like Lonnie, he had no trouble stopping every once in a while and having a beer—sometimes when we stopped for gas and sometimes when we stopped just because he was thirsty.

I can't remember everything we talked about during that long drive, but a lot of it was about politics. I asked him what he could tell me about the *Halconazo* and if it was as bad as Antonio had heard.

"The Corpus Christi Massacre?"

"No, the one in Mexico City."

"Yeh, that's the one. It happened on Corpus Christi day."

"But Corpus Christi is in Texas."

"Yeh, and Dallas is supposed to be in Texas. But you're here in Mexico. And the Corpus Christi Massacre was in Mexico. Y' know, yer awful thick."

Séamus said that, if anything, the *Halconazo* was a lot worse than I had heard. He said he was there when it happened and that the *Halcones* had started out by attacking the students with bamboo sticks but, when that didn't stop them, they started shooting at them with high-caliber rifles. Not only were 120 killed but the *Halcones* actually followed the injured ones to the hospital. Séamus made a point of emphasizing that the *Halcones* got their training in the United States from the CIA.

He said things were no better in his own country, that British soldiers were rounding up people in "the North," for no better reason than that they were suspected of being supporters of the Irish Republican Army. He said that attacks on Catholics by paramilitary groups had been going on for years and that the police weren't doing anything about it.

As for the United States, he said he thought that President Nixon was a war criminal for waging war in Southeast Asia. I didn't say anything back to him about this, since I really didn't want to get into an argument. I always thought that, when your own country gets in a fight, you have to support your country. On the other hand, I had never really figured out exactly why we were fighting in Vietnam in the first place. I just wished the war would hurry up and be over.

Séamus said the one bright spot in the world was Chile. He said the year before they had elected a Socialist guy named Salvador Allende as president. According to Séamus, he was in the process of taking back the country for the Chilean people by nationalizing the country's copper mines, giving workers more rights and giving land to poor people. Séamus had been in Chile when Allende was elected and he said that there was a really optimistic mood in the country. He predicted that Chile would eventually lead all of Latin America to a bright socialist future full of liberty and justice for everyone in the country, not just for the rich and privileged. Listening to him, I couldn't help think that it did sound pretty good, at least the way he described it. As I saw it, people should get whatever kind of government they want to vote for.

"The world is changing, Dallas," he said. "I can feel it. I think Chile might well be the beginning of it."

"You think what happened in Chile could really happen in Mexico?" I asked him. "I mean, how can things change when anytime students try to march they send in the *Halcones* and just mow them down? From what I heard, the same one political party has been running things in this country forever. How do you change that?"

Séamus smiled. "It won't always be that way. Maximilian and Carlotta are dead, y' know."

"Who?"

"Ah, y' need to learn yer history. You know that big Mexican holiday, Cinco de Mayo? The fifth of May is the date Mexico won its independence, and do you know who they won it from?"

"Spain?"

"That was the first time. But after Mexico had been independent awhile, Napoleon III of France invaded them. He imposed an emperor and empress on them. An Austrian emperor and a Belgian empress. You see, the imperial powers in Europe just couldn't let Mexico go. But Mexican republicans drove out the French and they executed Maximilian. In the end, the people will always fight back against imperialism."

I was learning a lot from Séamus, that was for sure. Mexican history was a lot more complicated than I ever realized.

As the hours dragged out and it got later and later, I found myself getting more and more worried that Séamus was going to fall asleep at the wheel. Especially after all the stops we had made for beers. After our last stop for gas and beer, he looked half-drunk when he climbed back into the driver's seat. When he pulled back onto the road, I got scared when I noticed he was driving on the wrong side of the road. I kept waiting for him to shift the car to the right, but he kept on driving through the dark on the left side. Before long I saw headlights in the distance. Oh shit, I thought.

"Uh, are you going to get in your own lane, Séamus?"

"Jayzus!" he shouted as he swerved suddenly to the right. "I feckin' forgot where I was there for a moment."

I was wide awake after that, and I made a point to keep a close eye on his driving until we stopped for the night. Now I was the one who was doing everything to make sure the conversation kept going.

"So what happened to Carlotta?"

"Wha'?"

"Carlotta. Did they execute her too?"

"Oh. No, she had already gone back to Europe. She was trying to get various European powers to come rescue Maximilian. She ended up going insane."

"I guess it's not easy being an empress either?"

"Wha'?"

"I mean, I know it's no picnic being a peasant. But I don't think that it's that easy being a king or an emperor sometimes either."

"Feck off with that shite. There's much bigger problems in the world than worrying about how easy things are for people on the top of the class structure. They deserve every bad thing that happens to 'em, that's what I say."

"But in the end, like you said, Maximilian and Carlotta are dead. Isn't that what it all comes down to? It doesn't matter if you're an emperor or a peasant. In the end you're just as dead either way."

"Jeez, Dallas," he said. "I hadn't taken you fer a feckin' nihilist."

I didn't say anything more after that—mainly because I didn't want to have to admit that I didn't have any idea what a nihilist was.

It must have been around midnight when we left the main road and he drove us up an unpaved side road for a couple of miles. He pulled over at a wide spot in the road.

"We'll stop here for the night," he said. "I don't mind telling you, I'm feckin' knackered. You'll want to get plenty of rest so you're fit for your walk in the morning."

And with that, he nestled next to his door and promptly went to sleep.

As for me, it took a while before I managed to doze off. A lot of things were going through my head. Mostly, I was thinking about Lonnie. Wherever he was, I was only getting further and further away from him. And I thought about Antonio. I wished he was there with me. Nothing had been right since he had stormed out of El Águila two nights before. I wished I could tell him how bad I felt about what I did and how I would do anything to make it up to him.

Then I started thinking about the next day and wondering exactly how it was going to go. It would be like some kind of crazy cruel joke if, after coming all this way to try to find out what happened to Tommy Dowd, more or less the same thing wound up happening to me that happened to him. And, if it did, the thing that would bother me the most would be never finding out what happened to Lonnie and Antonio.

After all that had gone through my mind, then I started thinking about all the political stuff Séamus had talked about all day. About how he and Peter said they were working for the good guys and that my country's government were the bad guys. Could I have been seeing things so wrong all my life? Was I really brainwashed? How come I had to be the one who was brainwashed. Maybe it was Peter and Séamus who were brainwashed. I mean, if you always have to be wondering if you're brainwashed, how can you ever believe in anything? Before I could think much more about it, though, I was asleep.

I woke up to the sound of water running. I opened my eyes and looked around. It was Séamus peeing against a tree, not too far from the Jeep. When he noticed I was awake, he threw me a candy bar.

"Breaky!" he called cheerfully.

It was early enough that the morning air felt a little cooler than it was going to later. I had a look around, while we sat there in the Jeep chewing on our candy bars. For a park, there weren't all that many trees. But the bushes were thick and green. In fact, everything around us was really green.

"So is this what Ireland is like?"

He laughed. "Not exactly. We wouldn't have them palm trees, for one thing. And it would be a hell of lot colder. But yeh, I suppose it's not that different in the grand scheme of things."

"Plus there's no leprechauns," I said, waiting for his reaction.

"Feck off with yer feckin' leprechauns!"

Séamus kept making small talk, as he checked his watch every so often. Finally, he stepped out of the Jeep.

"It's time for your ramble, Dallas."

I gathered up the letter and the cardboard box and followed him. He led me over to a spot by some bushes and pulled one back and pointed.

"There's a trail of sorts through here. Look for notches on the trees every so often—like this one—if you're not sure which way it goes. You won't even know when you've crossed the border. Just keep walking until you meet yer man. He'll be wearing a white shirt and he'll have a mustache. He'll be wearing a watch on his right hand wrist. Not the left but the right. That's important. Don't forget. On his right wrist."

He put his hand on my right wrist, just to make sure that I knew which one was the right one.

"It'll be about three miles all together before you meet him," he said.

He looked me straight in the face with those ice cold blue eyes of his.

"You'll be all right, Dallas. You'll be grand. Don't worry about a thing. You'll be back in no time, and I'll be right here waiting for you."

I started walking. Every so often I looked back. The first few times I could see Séamus standing there, watching me. Then I couldn't see him anymore. The trail wasn't hard to follow, but I kept watching for the notches just to make sure that I hadn't gone wrong. My heart was racing. What the hell had I gotten myself into?

It's funny the things that come into your head sometimes. For one thing, the thought struck me that I had now traveled the entire length of Mexico. Any minute I would be crossing the southern border of Mexico, after having traveled all the way down from its northern border. And I was completely on my own. Along the way I had managed to lose the two friends I had started out

250

with. No matter how long I live, I don't think I'll ever feel as alone as I did on that walk.

The idea also came into my head that, somehow, I had become some sort of spy. I thought of the James Bond movies I had seen, but they were nothing like this. There was nothing exciting or glamorous about walking down this trail. It was boring and scary at the same time.

I walked for what seemed like forever. I started to think about all the things that could go wrong. What if the guy wasn't there? What if I met a border guard? What if everything went like it was supposed to but, when I walked back to where I started, Séamus wasn't there? What if he just abandoned me once he got me to do what he needed? Finally, I decided I was doing too much thinking.

I looked around at all the trees and bushes around me and thought, who would ever have thought that I would wind up here? I'm seeing a place that probably no one I know has ever seen. And I'm here by myself. I stopped and took out the camera and shot some pictures. Then I started walking again.

The air was warm and humid, and I was sweating. It's funny how a distance seems so much longer when you're walking in a place for the first time. It seemed like I had been walking that trail forever. I must surely be in Guatemala by now, I thought to myself. Then I laughed. Here I am, I said to myself, in my second foreign country, and I still have never had a passport.

The more I sweated, the more my tee-shirt stuck to my skin. My hair was feeling even greasier than usual. I promised myself a nice bath the next time I got the chance.

Then I thought I heard something. I stopped to listen, but it was hard to hear anything over the sound of my own breathing. I hadn't realized how hard I was breathing with all the walking and the humidity. I closed my mouth and forced myself to breath slowly. Then I heard it again.

It sounded like a footstep in the grass. I was actually happy to hear it. I figured it must be the guy I was supposed to meet. They hadn't even told me his name, but he was supposed to have a mustache and be wearing a white shirt and a watch on his right wrist. I stared ahead of me, hoping to see him. The thought crossed my mind that, if this was a James Bond movie, this would almost definitely be some sort of trap.

I kept walking forward, expecting at any moment to see the guy I was looking for. But when the trail brought me in a half-circle around a tree, what I saw made my heart freeze. About fifty yards ahead of me was a man in a uniform. And he had a machine gun.

I started to back up, but he had seen me.

"*¡Alto!*" he yelled.

I stood as still as a statue. He was walking toward me, and I just stood there waiting for him. I nearly shit a brick. This is it, I thought. This is how I die.

He kept his gun pointed at me, and I raised my arms. The cardboard box dropped to the ground. The guy looked young. Really young. He looked like he might even be younger than me. And he looked scared. Really scared. And that scared me because the last thing you want is for someone really scared to be pointing a powerful gun at you.

I kept trying to look as innocent as I could so that he wouldn't panic and do something stupid—like mow me down in a hail of bullets.

"*¿Qué hace usted aquí?*"

I figured my best chance was to play as dumb as possible, like Peter had said. I spoke to him in an extra loud voice.

"Sorry there, amigo. I don't speak any Spanish. I was just out for a walk in this beautiful country. Did I do something wrong?"

He approached me cautiously. When he was close enough, he used one hand to feel all over my body while he kept a firm hold of the gun with his other arm. He was obviously checking to see if I had any kind of weapon. He relaxed a bit when he didn't find any, but just a little bit. He picked up my backpack and slung it over his shoulder. He also knelt down to pick up the cardboard box.

"*¿Usted no habla español?*"

"No comprendo," I answered, sounding as American as I could.

He walked around me until he was behind me. He indicated with the barrel of his gun that he wanted me to keep walking in the same direction I had been headed.

"*¡Adelante!*" he barked.

So I continued my walk, but now with a machine gun pointed at my back. I kept trying not to panic, but I couldn't get rid of the thought that I was going to be killed or locked up for the rest of my life and people back home would always be wondering what happened to me—just like they always wondered what happened to Tommy Dowd.

We walked a long distance. I wondered if we were going to run into the guy I was supposed to meet, but I guessed, probably not. If he had been anywhere around, he would have definitely made himself scarce at the first sign of a guy with a machine gun.

We finally came to a road. There was a car parked there with another guy in a uniform sitting in the driver's seat. My guy motioned me to get into the backseat.

The three of us drove down the road, probably about ten miles. Finally we came to some sort of military or police compound. It was surrounded by barbed wire and there were uniformed men with guns everywhere. I wondered if Séamus and Peter knew that this place was here—so close to where I was walking—when they sent me off on this little errand. I was starting to feel like a real sucker.

They parked the car and brought me inside a building. It wasn't much, but it was a damn sight better than what passed for a police station in San Ramón.

"Does anybody here speak English?" I called out generally to everyone inside. "I think there's been some kind of mistake."

No one answered me. They put me in a small room with a table and a couple of chairs and then closed the door and locked it. I sat there for about twenty minutes, waiting to see what was going to happen next. Finally, a heavyset guy in the same uniform everyone else was wearing came into the room and sat down across the table from me.

"Yore name?"

"Great, you speak English. My name is Dallas Green. There's been some kind of mistake. I was just out for a walk. You know, visiting this beautiful country. I didn't know I was doing anything wrong."

He was filling out some kind of form. I couldn't tell how well he understood me. His English didn't seem to be great.

"See ten sehn ship."

"Citizenship? I'm an American. I mean, I'm from the United States. *Estados Unidos*."

He kept writing.

"Pasa port?"

"Uh, I must have left it at the hotel when I went out for my walk. My driver's license is in my backpack. Did you see that?"

I figured he had. I figured they had gone through my backpack and pulled everything out of it—including that letter that was so damned important. In fact, I know they did because, at that moment, he pulled out the letter and showed it to me.

"Ware did yoo get thees?"

"That's a funny story. I just found it on the ground while I was out on my walk. I thought it might belong to somebody and I just picked it up and put it in my backpack. I didn't even look at it or anything."

The guy kept writing. Listening to my own bullshit, even I had to cringe at how stupid it sounded. The only question in my mind was why I hadn't already been taken out and shot.

"Hoo gave yoo the letter?"

"Like I said, I just found it. It was just laying there on the ground. Why? What is it? Is it something important? I just wanted to get it back to whoever lost it. You know, my good deed for the day. I was actually a Boy Scout once for a few months."

Okay, now I was starting to ramble on like an idiot. That wasn't good. I told myself to shut up.

He wrote a few more things on his form and then got up and left. I sat there alone for probably a good hour or more. All the time I was fighting the urge to panic. But what was the point? Whatever was going to happen was going to happen. Antonio wouldn't be rescuing me this time. One thing was for sure. I was in a heap of trouble. My only comfort was knowing that, no matter what happened from this point on, at least I wasn't going to die a virgin.

Finally, the door opened again. A different guy walked in. He wasn't wearing a uniform. And he didn't look Mexican or Guatemalan. He was wearing black slacks and a white shirt opened at the collar. His long sleeves were rolled up. He was mostly bald with pale blue eyes. His big forehead was sweaty and creased with lines. He looked like someone who was overworked. Like someone who had been awake all night. He sat down in front of me and pulled out a file folder with lots of papers in it. He started reading them.

"Dallas... Green?"

"Yeah! That's me! You're American?"

He didn't answer me. He just kept reading through the papers in front of him while he asked me another question.

"What are you doing on the Mexico-Guatemala border, Dallas?"

I wanted to feel relieved that an American guy was now involved in this. I wanted to feel like this meant that everything was going to be okay. But the truth is, I didn't know what it meant.

"A friend and I came down from California. Just a little vacation. Just wanted to see what Mexico was like."

He kept looking at the papers, never looking up. And he kept taking something out of his shirt pocket and putting it into his mouth and chewing on it. I think it might have been sunflower seeds.

"What is your friend's name?"

"Lonnie McKay, sir."

"And where is he?"

"Well, that's kind of a long story. I had to leave him in Mexico City. We kind of got separated."

For the first time he looked up at me.

"So why did you come down to the Guatemala border by yourself?"

The way I saw it, I had just a second or two to decide whether to stick to the dumb-tourist-on-a-walk story or to just tell this guy the truth. My gut told me that he would see right through any bullshit in no time flat.

"I, uh, met these two guys in Mexico City. They asked me to deliver a letter for them. They said it would be no big deal. They said it would easy. I didn't think I was doing anything wrong. I was just doing them a favor. I didn't think it would cause all this trouble. Am I in trouble, sir?"

The guy went back to reading through his papers. "And these two gave you the box as well?"

"Uh, yeah, they did. They kind of slipped that in at the last minute. I didn't even know what was in it. I still don't. And I don't know what was in that letter. I actually don't know what any of this is about. I guess I was just being stupid."

"What were their names, Dallas?"

"Their names?"

"The two who gave you the letter and box. What were their names?"

I felt like I was between a rock and hard place. I was already feeling like a coward for telling this guy everything I knew. If I believed that Séamus and Peter were the good guys, then I should be refusing to give any information about what I was doing.

256

But the fact was that I didn't have a clue what I was taking into Guatemala or why, and right then my top priority was saving my own skin. I needed to get out of this mess the best way I could so I could go back to Mexico City and find Lonnie. Still, giving him Séamus and Peter's names seemed like ratting on them. I might be a lot of things, but I had never been a snitch. In the end, though, I decided I didn't have a choice. Besides, I had a strange feeling that he already knew their names.

"Their names were Peter and Séamus. They never told me their last names. Peter was American, and Séamus was Irish."

I watched him to see if he recognized their names. But his face never changed. And he hardly ever looked at me directly.

Until now. Now he was staring at me like an interrogation lamp.

"Dallas, what can you tell me about the Guerrilla Army of the Poor? The E.G.P.?"

"The what?"

"The Guatemalan Labor Party? The Organization of People in Arms? ORPA? The Rebel Armed Forces? FAR?"

"I really don't know what those are, sir."

He kept studying me for any reaction that I had to any of those names. I don't know exactly what he was looking for, but since I didn't recognize any of them and they were all so much gobbledygook to me, I hoped that he could see that in my face. Whatever he thought he was learning from me, though, I was learning absolutely nothing from him. His face never changed.

"You never met this Peter and Séamus before a couple of days ago?"

"That's right. I just happened to meet Séamus in a bar. He introduced me to Peter. I never met them before that. All I was interested in was finding my friend Lonnie and going home."

It was kind of like what I imagined it would be like to take a lie detector test. Between whatever information he had on those sheets of paper in front of him and my answers and whatever my face was doing, he seemed to come to the conclusion I was telling the truth. He relaxed a little bit.

"Dallas, I'm afraid you've gotten yourself mixed up with some very bad people."

"They didn't seem like bad people. They just talked about wanting to help the poor and stuff like that."

"Their motives may be sincere, but I can tell you that they are misguided. The governments in this part of the world may be authoritarian but they are also anti-communist. Trust me, if your friends were to get their way, the governments that would replace them would be no better and, in fact, they would be far worse. On top of that, they would be anti-American, Soviet puppets. All their talk about freedom and justice are lies."

Now this guy was starting to remind me of Pastor Travis too. He never told me his name, but in my own head I started calling him Frank because, for some strange reason, he reminded me of Frank Sinatra.

"I understand, sir. I was just stupid. I don't know why I agreed to help them. They just kept insisting. And they said they would help me find Lonnie."

"Dallas, you are going to be driven to the Mexican border. On the other side you will be able to get a bus there back to Mexico City. I advise you to return to the United States as quickly as you can. And I advise you not to get involved with these sorts of people again."

"Thank you, sir. Thank you very much. And I'm very sorry. I'll never do anything stupid like this again."

He started writing something on one of his papers. I couldn't believe my luck. I was actually going to get out of this. Part of me just wanted to get out of there as fast as I could. But another part of me thought that this might be my one chance to get a couple of questions answered.

"So, uh, who exactly are you?" I smiled like I was making a joke. "Are you CIA or something?"

He didn't look up and his face didn't change. And he didn't answer. It was like I hadn't said anything.

"Uh, can I ask you something?"

He looked up at me. His face seemed to say that it had already been a long day for him and he didn't really need any stupid questions from a clueless kid.

"There was a guy in my hometown. His name was Thomas Dowd. He came down to Guatemala a few years ago and then disappeared. Nobody ever found out what happened to him. It's been killing his mom and dad not to know what happened to him. You wouldn't know anything about him, would you?"

"There's nothing I can tell you about that," he said matter-of-factly.

"Okay, well, thanks anyway."

I was disappointed. But at least I had given it a shot. Then a look came across Frank's face that said that maybe he actually did care a little bit after all.

"Look, if it's any help to his family, you can tell them that they will not be seeing him again. I can't tell you any more than that."

Well, that was something. I felt like I was on a roll now.

"Oh, and my friend Lonnie disappeared on me in Mexico City. Do you possibly have any way of finding out where he is?"

Frank shook his head and almost smiled. I think he was starting to be amused by me.

"No," he said. "I'm afraid you're on your own with that one."

He stood up, as if he was going to leave.

"And what about Chile?"

"What?"

"Séamus said that Chile was the start of a whole new change in South America. That it is going to be some sort of socialist paradise. Do you think that's true?"

He shook his head. "That country is in absolute chaos. Economy activity has stalled. The education system is in a shambles. Middle-class people—people like you and your family—are cowering in their homes right now because they don't feel safe. That country is going to hell in a hand basket—and fast."

He was totally convinced—and convincing—in what he was saying.

"Trust me. The government there will not last. In a couple of years no one is going to remember the name Salvador Allende."

He looked at his watch.

"It's time for you to go now."

"Uh, there's one more thing, sir."

He was clearly starting to lose patience.

"Uh, my friend and I came down here without passports. Will we have any trouble crossing the border when we go home?"

I wondered if I had pushed my luck too far. I wondered if he would change his mind about me and just let the Guatemalans throw me in a pit for the rest of my life. But he sat down and pulled out a piece of paper, signed his name on it and handed it to me.

"Show them this at the border. You shouldn't have any trouble."

"And can I have one for Lonnie too?"

He looked exasperated.

"Who's Lonnie again?"

"He's my friend. The one I came down with. You have his driver's license. It was in my backpack."

Frank pulled out another sheet of paper and signed it. I was encouraged enough that I decided to try taking it one more step.

"And we have another friend with us. His name's Antonio. Can he get a letter too?"

I had clearly gone a step too far.

260

"Goodbye, Dallas."

He stood up again.

"And, Dallas, I strongly advise you to forget about all this utopian nonsense and just go back to driving your tractor or whatever it is you do there in..." He pulled out one the sheets in his folder and glanced at it. "...Kern County."

"Yes, sir."

"Now, I'm serious about this. If you and your friend don't cross back into the U.S. within the next several days, I will know about it. And, if you don't, I cannot guarantee you the protection of the U.S. government. Do you understand what I'm saying?"

"Yes, sir."

Then he walked out of the room without saying another word.

18
Return to D.F.

I WAS left sitting there by myself for a good half-hour or more. I wanted to relax and enjoy the fact that I wasn't going to wind up in a jail or get shot in the head. But I couldn't let myself believe that I was going to get out of this situation okay until I was finally back somewhere that I felt safe. I couldn't get rid of the nagging idea that Frank might have been lying to me or that, once he was gone, the Guatemalan soldiers would just do whatever they wanted with me—like use me for target practice.

Finally, a couple of soldiers walked into the room and indicated that I should go with them. If they were there to set me free, I didn't want to take a chance on messing anything up, so I didn't say a word to them. They didn't talk to me either. They only mumbled to each other once in a while in Spanish. They didn't seem too happy that they were having to bother with me.

They put me in a car. It looked just like the one I was brought there in. Hell, it probably was the same one. They drove off down a road—not the same one we had driven before. I crossed my fingers and looked out the window and hoped that they were bringing me wherever they were supposed to and not to some isolated place where they could shoot me and leave me by the side of road. As soon as that thought came into my head, I immediately did my best to get it out of mind. I tried to think of anything except that. Next thing I knew I was whistling quietly. The soldier in the front passenger seat turned around and gave me a dirty look.

We must have been driving down that road more than a half-hour. The longer the drive went on, the more nervous I got. I was seriously wishing that I hadn't been afraid to ask to go to the bathroom before we left. I squeezed my thighs together as tight as I could and tried not to think about taking a piss. No way was I going to try asking them to stop the car.

Finally we pulled up to a checkpoint and I started to feel less nervous. There was a barrier across the road and soldiers on the other side with different uniforms than what my guys were wearing. That and the flags on the buildings made it pretty clear that this was the crossing into Mexico. The guy who had given me the dirty look got out of the car and had a little talk with one of the Mexican soldiers. They talked for about five minutes or so and the Guatemalan guy showed him a piece of paper. The Mexican guy didn't look particularly happy, but he didn't make a fuss. Finally, the Guatemalan guy motioned to me to get out of the car and to come toward him. Meanwhile, the driver had gotten out of the car and opened the trunk of the car. He pulled out my backpack and handed it to me.

The barrier was opened, and the Mexican guy indicated that I should walk to the other side. I finally felt that I was safe. They were really letting me cross back into Mexico. I slung the backpack over my shoulder and wasted no time going to the other side. I just kept walking and didn't look back. I went on down the road until I was pretty sure that I was out of their sight. Then I stopped and looked around to make sure no one was following me or watching me. I couldn't see anybody. I was standing there all alone.

The first thing I did was drop my backpack and run a few yards off the road to take a desperately needed piss. I needed to go so bad that I thought I was going to wet myself before I could unzip my jeans. I never ever enjoyed a piss so much before in my whole life, and I couldn't believe how long it went on. It felt like I was emptying the whole damn Pacific Ocean there on the ground.

When I finally finished, I went back to have a look inside my backpack. To my surprise, everything seemed to be there—even the camera and the rolls of film. It seemed like some sort of miracle that they hadn't taken them and kept them, but I guess it was pretty obvious that I meant no harm and was just a stupid kid who didn't know what he was doing. I wasn't even important enough for them to worry about.

I had a good look around. I guess I was kind of thinking that Séamus might be there, that he might have figured out what happened and would have come to this border crossing to wait for me. But there was no sign of him. I wondered if he had even bothered waiting around for me at the other place. Or did he expect all along that I was probably going to get picked up when I crossed the border? Did he take off back to Mexico City as soon as I was out of sight? Anyway, I felt pretty sure he was long gone. He probably didn't want to be there for me to give him hell for the trouble he had gotten me into. And that was fine with me. I didn't want to have to tell him that I had given his name to the fucking CIA. I didn't think he and Peter would have taken that too well.

I had no idea where I was, but there was only one road and only one direction to go. No way was I going back to where I had been. I started walking. After about twenty minutes I came to a small store. There was a guy sitting there on the ground in front. He was reading a book and taking occasional sips from a bottle of water. He had long shaggy hair and a beard and wore round glasses. He looked like he was in his late twenties. A large backpack with a sleeping bag was laying next to him. The title of the book was *Ringworld*. I had no idea who he was or what he was doing there, but I was sure glad to see him.

"You American?" I asked him.

He looked me up and down. "Yeah."

"You have any idea where I could get a bus to Mexico City?"

"There's a bus that stops here that will take you to D.F. But there won't be another one until tomorrow morning."

I remembered that Séamus had called Mexico City "D.F.," so that was good news.

"Cool. So are you taking it too?"

"Yeah."

"So why do people call Mexico City 'D.F.' anyway?"

"It's *Distrito Federal.* Kind of like the 'D.C.' in Washington D.C."

I looked around.

"Is there a place to spend the night around here?"

He shrugged. "I was just going to roll out my bag around here somewhere."

"Do you mind if I camp next to you?"

"Be my guest."

I went into the shop and bought myself a Tecate and some potato chips. The American guy seemed more interested in reading his book than talking to me, so I left him alone. I just sat there for a while, sipping on my beer and thinking about how my day had gone and how lucky I was to have gotten out of Guatemala in one piece. And I thought about Tommy and what I had learned about him and how excited Lonnie would be when I told him about it—assuming I ever saw Lonnie again. Before I knew it, it was dark and I was ready for some shuteye.

The next thing I remember was the guy shaking me gently. It was still dark.

"The bus is coming."

I sat up. "Thanks, man."

There were a few other people waiting for the bus too. As we all got on board, I asked him, "Do you mind if I sit next to you?"

He just shrugged his shoulders. I took that to mean that he didn't mind.

As we sat down, I said, "My name's Dallas, by the way."

"Hello, Dallas. I'm Barry."

"So, you just traveling around down here?"

"I'm on my way home. To Colorado."

"Where you coming from?"

"Chile."

I thought maybe he was joking. After all, even I knew Chile was an awful long way away. And why, I wondered, did people keep mentioning the name of that country to me?

"Really? How come you're on a bus and not on a plane?"

He shrugged. "You don't see very much in a plane."

"So you've been traveling all this way from Chile by land?"

"Yeah." He said it like he couldn't understand why I would think it was strange.

"I didn't even know that was possible."

"Yeah, you can drive all the way from Alaska down to southern Chile or to Buenos Aires by road. It's called the Pan-American Highway. There's just a section between Panama and Colombia that was never built. You have to take a boat around that part. I met a Canadian one time where I was living in southern Chile. He was driving a Jeep with British Columbia plates, and I asked him if he had really driven it all the way down. He said, 'Yeah, but I wouldn't recommend it.'"

"Wow. What were you doing in southern Chile?"

"I work for the Peace Corps. I was living among the Mapuche Indians."

"This is amazing. Yesterday I spent the day driving with an Irish guy and he was telling me that Chile was going to be the beginning of a whole new socialist future in Latin America."

Barry raised an eyebrow but didn't say anything.

"He said things were really improving there, that this Allende guy was really helping the people. But then later I was talking to this American guy. I think he was working for the government or something. Anyway, he said that Chile was in chaos, that everything was terrible."

Barry looked interested but still didn't say anything.

"So how long were you there?"

"Seven years."

"And..."

He just looked at me.

"You were there before Allende got elected, and you were there after he got elected. So what's the truth? Are things better there now than before or are they worse?"

Barry shrugged. "It's all true."

"Huh?"

"It's all true."

"What's all true?"

"Everything."

"What do you mean, everything?"

"Everything you've heard is true."

"How can everything be true? How can it be true that things are better and worse at the same time?"

He shrugged. "It's just all true."

"Come on. You're not making any sense."

He looked like he was trying to find the right words to explain it to me, kind of like he was trying to figure out a way to explain something really complicated to a small child.

"Latin America is different than North America. Logic doesn't always work here. Paradoxes co-exist all the time. It's a place where people believe in magic, and nobody thinks there's anything strange about that. It's just a different world. Things aren't black and white like people try to make them in the Anglo-Saxon world. I don't know how to explain it any better than that."

"So you're not going to tell me whether you think Chile is better off now than it was before."

He shrugged his shoulders again. "It's all true."

It was a long ride back to Mexico City. I spent some more time talking with Barry, but I could tell that he was really more interested in reading his book, so after a while I left him alone. I just sat there and watched the scenery pass by and continued to think about all the strange things that had happened to me in the previous couple of days.

Finally, the bus pulled into the bus station in Mexico City. It was a different station than the one where we had arrived four days before. As we were getting ready to get off the bus, I decided that I needed to ask Barry for help.

"I first got to Mexico City a few days ago with a couple of friends," I told him. "One of them went off by himself the first night, and I'm afraid that he might have gotten himself into some kind of trouble. I hardly speak any Spanish and I don't have any idea how to try to find him. Do you think you could help me find him?"

I was afraid that he was going to give me another talk about how logic doesn't work in Latin America. But instead he asked me a few questions about Lonnie, his full name and what he had been planning to do, and I answered them. He didn't express any opinion about how stupid Lonnie was. He didn't even look like he thought that any of this was even very strange. He just led me to a stop for city buses and then had us get on one that was heading downtown. Barry seemed to know his way around Mexico City pretty well. I was guessing he had been there before.

We got off near a big official looking building. I could tell it was a police station. He led me in, and I watched as he went up to a policeman sitting at a desk and proceeded to have a long conversation with him in Spanish. I was amazed at how well Barry could talk in Spanish. I wished I could talk like that. It would have made a few things a hell of a lot easier.

Finally, Barry came over to me and asked, "Do you have six-hundred pesos?"

I dug into my pocket. That was nearly all the money I had left. I handed it to him. He walked back over to the policeman and gave it to him. Then Barry passed by me as he walked out of the building.

"Your friend will be out in a few minutes," he said.

And then Barry was gone. No goodbye or anything. I never saw him again. Looking back on it, I should have thanked him. He was a real help when I really needed it. But I was completely focused on what was going to happen next.

I stood there for several minutes, wondering if Lonnie was really going to come out or if I had just handed away all the money I had left for nothing. Finally, after what seemed like an hour, there he was. There was Lonnie.

I was never so happy to see anybody in my life. As easy as that, Lonnie was standing there in front of me, and it suddenly hit me how scared I had been that I would never see him again. He had a few bruises on his face, but otherwise he didn't look too worse for wear. I thought he might be grateful to be out of jail. But he wasn't. In fact, he was totally pissed off, and he was looking at me like I had just shot his dog or something.

"Where the hell *you* been?"

If he only knew. "It's a *really* long story. I don't even know where to begin. I'm just glad to see you. Sorry I didn't get you out sooner."

He started to calm down. "Well, at least it wasn't as bad as that shit hole in San Ramón. But it wasn't any picnic either. I was starting to think that I was never going to get out of there."

I looked around nervously. I was afraid if we hung around there too long, one of the cops would decide to arrest both of us for loitering or something. The past couple of weeks had made me really afraid of men in uniforms.

"C'mon. Let's get going."

We walked out onto the street and kept going. We didn't pay any attention to where we were headed. We just kept walking while we talked.

"So what happened?" I asked him. "Did you get arrested?"

Lonnie started to get mad all over again. "Yeah. That fucking whore set me up. She got someone to buy my coke, but after they got there, they took it off me. And the gun too. They beat me up and left me there. I was so fucking mad. I tried to go after them, but they were long gone. I did find the whore, though. I gave her a punch in the face. I'm not proud of it, but I did. That's when the cops got me, and they threw my ass in jail. I'm betting that was part of the setup."

"Fuck, man. I'm sorry. I had no idea where you were. And I didn't know where to begin looking. I was afraid to go to the cops after what happened in San Ramón. And to top it off, Antonio's gone. We sort of had a fight and he left. I still don't know where he is. And then I met this Irish guy. But that's a long story. What are we going to do now? I'm out of money."

"We should be okay. I just have to find a Western Union."

We stopped a few people on the street until we found someone who could understand us and direct us to the Western Union office. And then we started walking again.

"They let me have one phone call," Lonnie said. "I used it to call my mom collect. Thank God she answered and not Don. She was mad as hell, but at least she didn't hang up on me. She said that Don was really pissed about me taking the money and the gun. But I told her that I needed money to get the car fixed and come home, and she said she'd wire it. It should be there by now. She wasn't going to tell Don about it. She said he was mad enough as it is. Man, she really chewed my ass out. She said that, when I get home, I'm going to have to work until I pay Don back and then I have to keep working until I pay her back too."

"I'll pay half of what you owe," I said. "It's the least I can do. After all, I've basically been living off of you for the past few weeks."

He put his hand on my shoulder and said, "Thanks. The money has been waiting at Western Union for days. I just wasn't able to get out of jail to go get it."

As we walked down the street, I kept wishing that I could track down Antonio as easy as it turned out to be to find Lonnie. I was really worried about the kid. I saw a taxi speeding by and it made me remember the night we first arrived in Mexico City and that taxi driver told us he could get us some "pretty boys." I hoped to God that Antonio hadn't gone back to selling himself on the street.

We found the Western Union place, and after some paperwork, Lonnie got his money. He held a wad of it up in the air to admire it.

"Fuck damn!" he grinned. "We're rich again!"

I looked around nervously and told him to not be stupid and to put the money away. There was no way to tell who was watching us.

As we walked back out onto the street, he said, "It's time to celebrate. We're going to stay in a nice hotel tonight."

"Hey, don't go spending it all so we don't have enough left to pay Pancho for the car," I said.

"Don't worry," he replied with a wink. "I padded the amount I told my mom I needed. There's enough here for having a good time during our last few days in Mexico. And I'm going to buy a bottle of tequila. We're long overdue for that night of tequila drinking we promised ourselves."

So Lonnie got his bottle of tequila, and then we walked around until we found a hotel we liked, and we checked in. We had a nice dinner in the restaurant, and it seemed like the best meal I had ever had. I hadn't eaten right in days, and I was starved. Then we went up to the room and opened the bottle. We didn't completely finish it, but we came pretty close. We didn't even use glasses. We just passed the bottle back and forth and took turns taking sips. And we talked most of the night.

I asked him, "So what did your mom say about Michael? Were the police looking for you?"

"She didn't say anything about it. She just said that Linda was really mad at me because she hadn't heard from me. That's all. So I guess I didn't kill him after all."

"Was she talking to my mom?"

"She didn't say. We really didn't get into it. She didn't want to keep me on the phone too long in case Don would come in and find out who she was talking to."

"So no other news from home?"

"Nope. I can't wait to get back. As soon as I can get the money together, I'm going to buy me a new car. Even if the Chevy makes it back with us, it will have been all the way to hell and back. Time for some new wheels."

"So do you want to hear what I was up to the past few days?"

"What's to hear? While I was sitting in jail, you were out wandering around not getting me out of jail until today. You were probably having a great time. Good for you."

"It wasn't like that, man. I was doing my best to find you. I just didn't know where to start. I tried to get help. I met this American guy and this Irish guy, and I thought maybe they could help. But the Irish guy ended up bringing me all the way down to Guatemala. And wait 'til you hear..."

"Hear what? That you were having a great time traveling around while my ass was stuck in jail?"

"No, listen. I'm trying to tell you. I found out something about Tommy. You're not going to believe this. After coming all this way and after all we've been through, I actually found people who knew about him."

"The fuck you say."

Lonnie finally seemed interested in what I had to say.

"Yeah. The American guy and the Irish guy knew who he was. Tommy actually went to Guatemala to fight with the guerillas. It's like he's famous or something. And then, when I went to Guatemala, I got arrested and I met this other guy. I think he was CIA or something."

"*You* got arrested?"

"Yeah, that's what I've been trying to tell you. It wasn't any picnic for me while you were in jail. I thought maybe I was going to be locked up for good or even killed while I was down there."

I thought Lonnie would be impressed. But he only seemed to be getting mad again.

"Well, that was pretty fucking stupid. What would have happened to me if you hadn't gotten out of there?"

"But it worked out. We both got out. But I'm trying to tell you about Tommy."

"Fuck Tommy."

"What?"

"I said, fuck Tommy. I mean, did you actually find him?"

"No, I didn't. The CIA guy said no one would ever see him again."

"So, he's dead, right? We knew he was dead, didn't we? Even before we left home, we knew he was dead."

I couldn't believe Lonnie was talking like this.

"I didn't know he was dead. I was always hoping he was still alive. I thought we might even be the ones to find him alive."

"You didn't even want to come on this trip. I was the one who had to talk you into it."

"Yeah, I thought it was a crazy idea. But once we decided to do it, I was hoping we would find Tommy. Weren't you?"

"I always figured he was dead. Everyone did. It was only an excuse to get you to come on this trip. You'd never do anything fun or interesting if I didn't give you an excuse. You'd never have come if I didn't talk you into it."

I was feeling pretty stupid right about then. And kind of mad.

"Doesn't it mean anything to you to find out for sure that he's dead?"

"Everybody fucking dies. All the guys in Vietnam are dying. You and I are going to die. It's just a matter of when."

"Jesus, Lonnie," I said. "I never knew you were such a fucking nihilist."

"A what?"

I meant to make him feel stupid for not knowing what the word meant. But the fact was that I still wasn't so sure myself what it meant. So then I started laughing. Lonnie just stared at me for a minute like I was crazy. And then he started laughing too.

"It doesn't matter," I said when I could finally stop laughing. "We obviously need to drink lots more tequila."

"Yep," he agreed. "That's definitely the answer to everything."

We talked about all kinds of shit as the night went on. I wouldn't have thought we could find so much to talk about, since we had already spent so much time together driving the whole length of Mexico. Lonnie wasn't interested in hearing any more about my past couple of days. He wanted to talk about himself, and I decided to mostly just listen to him. And he told me some things that surprised me.

For one thing, he told that the previous summer, when he had that big fight with Don and left town for a couple of weeks, he had gone up to Placer County and found his dad. I hadn't even known that he knew where his dad lived. It turned out that his dad was up there living in a trailer and panning for gold. Lonnie had this idea that he was going to live with him and forget about school and just pan gold with him. But it turned out his dad didn't really want him there. I could tell that really hurt him. It amazed me that all that had happened and he hadn't even told me about it before.

I told him I was sorry about being in love with Linda but that I was over all that now. It didn't seem to bother him a bit.

"Hell," he said. "If it was the other way around, I would have fucked your girlfriend if I got the chance and I wouldn't even think twice about it."

And I knew he was telling the truth.

I knew that, after that night, I wasn't ever going to look at Lonnie exactly the same way again. I had always been kind of jealous of him for being better looking than me and for having better luck with girls than me and for not being as afraid of things as me. But now I kind of felt sorry for him. Underneath all that self-confidence I could see now that in some ways he was even more scared than I was.

Late in the night when the bottle had gotten nearly empty and I was feeling pretty drunk, I told him about Antonio.

"He's gone, Lonnie. I don't think I'm going to see him again. I really miss him. It kills me to think he hates me now."

"I can't believe you had a fight with him. You two were really close. What was it about?"

"It was stupid. It was fucking stupid. I got really drunk and I was missing Marisol and I don't know how to explain it but I guess I just went crazy and for a minute I thought he *was* Marisol and, well, I kissed him. And he blew his stack and he stormed out of the place. I can't believe I did that. It was the stupidest thing I ever did."

I didn't really mean to tell Lonnie all of that, but I was so wasted that I couldn't really stop myself. Besides, it had been eating at me inside for days, and I guess I just needed to tell someone. I prepared myself for Lonnie being totally disgusted with me and to call me a queer or a fag and to make me feel even worse. But that's when he really surprised me.

"Hell," he said. "You're not responsible for anything you do when you're drunk. Hell, that's the whole point of getting drunk in the first place. Not being responsible. Besides, that Tony's a cute kid. If I was completely drunk out of my mind, I might even have kissed him myself."

I seriously couldn't believe I was hearing this. But then he quickly added, "'Course by the time I would've got *that* drunk, I'd have passed out already."

"You know the worst thing?" I said.

"What?"

275

"It wasn't even that good. I didn't enjoy it a bit."

And that made us both break out laughing like we were fucking crazy.

And then I started feeling sad. "I sure do miss him though."

Lonnie must have figured he needed to try to cheer me up because then he started pretending that he was all insulted, and he said, "Hey, what about me? How come you never kiss *me* when you get drunk?"

And it worked. I started laughing, and I said back to him, "'Cause by the time I would've got *that* drunk, I'd have passed out already!"

This made the two of us laugh like maniacs. Not too long after that, we *both* passed out. But not before he put his arm around me and said, "I love you, man," and I said, "Yeah, I love you too, fuck face."

We woke up the next morning with serious headaches. It was the maid who woke us up when she came in to clean the room. Fortunately, we were both used to hangovers, so that didn't slow us down much. We went down to the restaurant and had a good breakfast and then made our way to the bus station.

"I can't wait to get the fuck out of D.F.," I said.

"Out of what?"

"D.F. *Distrito Federal*. You know, Mexico City."

I said it like I'd been calling it that all my life. Lonnie just shook his head like he didn't know who I was anymore.

We were somehow able to remember enough about how we had gotten to Mexico City from San Ramón that we didn't have too much trouble going back the way we came. We even managed to get off in the right place and change to the right local bus to get back there. It made me appreciate how much easier things were when we had Antonio along. He always looked after stuff like that for us.

We figured we had no choice but to get off the bus right in the middle of San Ramón. We could have gotten off in the same place where Pancho had brought us to catch the bus in the first place, but that would have meant a hell of a long walk back to Pancho's garage. As we stepped down off the bus, we were both looking over our shoulders, afraid that we might get spotted by that fat asshole cop Alfonso. We were lucky that he didn't seem to be around.

We quickly made our way over to Pancho's garage. Pancho was there by himself, working under the hood of some old beat-up junker.

"*¡Hola, Pancho!*" I called. "We're back!"

He pulled his big greasy face out from under the hood and gave us a big grin.

"*¡Hola, muchachos!*" he said. "*Su auto ya está listo.*"

He immediately closed up his garage and drove us back to his house. By the way he was smiling and talking, I figured he had finished the engine rebuild with no problem. I wanted to ask him about Antonio and if he had come back by himself. But there didn't seem any point, given my piss poor knowledge of Spanish. It was easier just to wait until we got to his house and see for myself.

As Pancho got out of the car, he called out, "*¡Marta! ¡Hijos! ¡Regresan los muchachos!*"

Chela and Cati came running out of the door, followed by Marta. They all had big smiles on their faces. I couldn't believe how glad they were to see us. It was like we were famous celebrities or something. They were all chattering at us, all of them talking at once, and I couldn't understand a word of any of it. Then I noticed someone stepping out of the shed and looked to see who it was. At first I couldn't be sure I could trust my eyes. Then I felt a huge relief.

It was Antonio.

I just stood there looking at him, for what seemed like minutes. I wasn't sure what to do or to say. All I could do was just stand there and keep looking at him and be glad that he was all right. Finally, he came running over to me and put his arms around me. He squeezed me until I thought I wasn't going to be able to catch my breath and that I was going to pass out.

"I'm sorry, Dallas," he said quietly. "I'm sorry."

I hugged him back. "What the hell are *you* sorry about, Antonio? I'm the one who's sorry. You were completely right to get mad at me. I wasn't thinking straight at all. I was just thinking about myself and feeling sorry for myself and I wasn't thinking about you at all. And you're practically the best friend I ever had. You had every right to be mad."

"It wasn't even about you," he said. "It just made me remember a lot of stuff I didn't want to remember. And…"

"And what?"

"I think I got jealous of Marisol. Sometimes I think you only like me because I remind you of Marisol."

"Amigo, the truth is that, when it comes down to it, the reason I like Marisol so much is because she reminds me of you."

By this time I noticed that Antonio and I had been hugging for so long that Lonnie was giving me kind of a strange look. And Marta, Chela and Cati were giggling and giving us that look that girls have when they see guys doing something they think is really cute.

"Come on, amigo," I said. "Let's go for a walk. We've got a few days to catch up on."

I told him about all the shit that happened with Séamus and Peter and my little visit down to the Guatemala border. He told me that, after he left me at El Águila, he didn't calm down until the next day. By that time he was back on the bus to San Ramón. He said he was worried about us, but he figured we'd eventually show up to get the car.

"So how's your romance going?" I teased him, nodding my head toward Chela, who was busy trying to communicate with Lonnie.

His face turned dark. "She doesn't like me as much as I thought," he said very seriously. "I found out she has a boyfriend. She was just being friends with me."

My heart broke for him. I knew exactly how he felt. I put my arm around his shoulder and said, "Amigo, I know it doesn't feel like it right now, but trust me, you're going to be breaking a lot of hearts in the next few years. You're going to be fighting women off with a stick."

He smiled. I could tell that he already felt a little better because of having someone to talk to about it.

"Listen, Antonio," I said. "I been doing a lot of thinking riding the bus back here from Mexico City. When we get back to California, I want you to come home with me and live with us, in my parents' house. We can get you enrolled in school. You're so smart, you'll make up for all the time you missed with no problem. We'll get you a high school diploma in no time."

I had it all figured out in my head. The only thing I hadn't figured out was exactly how we were going to get Antonio back into California. But there were so many Mexicans crossing the border illegally all the time and with no apparent problem that I figured it couldn't be that big a deal to get him in.

As Antonio looked at me, I thought he was going to cry.

"You would really do that for me?"

"Of course, I would. Hell, we've been through too much together. We're practically like brothers now. Fact is I'm closer to you than I am to my own brother. And he's moved out, so there's an extra room in the house. I'm sure my parents won't mind. I mean, after I talk to them and explain everything."

He just kept staring at me with his big brown glistening eyes. I figured the matter was pretty much settled.

"I can't tell you how much that means to me, Dallas," he said. "But I'm not going back with you."

"What?"

"I mean, it sounds really nice. Really nice. But I'm not going back. I'm staying here. In San Ramón."

"Why? Don't you understand what I'm saying? I'm not talking about you going back to L.A. You'd be living with my parents and me. You'd have a family. We'd take care of you. We'd give you all the help you need."

I could tell that this was really hard for him.

"I don't understand. Why would you want to stay here when things didn't work out the way you wanted with Chela? And that asshole *policía* Alfonso is around?"

"I would only be staying here for a little while."

"And then where would you be going?"

"You remember Daniel talking about his cousin Gustavo? The one who was in Chile? Well, he's going back there. He's tired of Mexico. He wants to go back to the new *paraíso socialista*, the new socialist paradise. Daniel is going with him. I told them that I wanted to see the socialist paradise too, and they said I could go with them."

This was like a bolt from the blue. No matter where I went I kept hearing about Chile.

"But how do you know what it will really be like? That American guy I was talking to in Guatemala said that it was all chaos there, that it wasn't as great as people were saying."

"But how will I know if I don't see it for myself? I just know this is something I want to do, to experience. Do you understand?"

"I suppose."

I didn't really. I couldn't understand why someone would want to go off to a country where he'd never been before instead of living in a nice home like my parents' in America.

"But how can you go to Chile? You'll need a passport, won't you? How are you going to get that?"

By this time Daniel had come out of the shed and walked over to hear what we were talking about.

"Daniel has a way to get me a passport. Don't you, Daniel? He has it all figured out."

Daniel had a big smile on his face as he explained. "I have a brother. Same age Antonio. He die. When he is a baby. But we have his... *certificado de nacimiento.*"

"His birth certificate," Antonio translated.

"His birth certificate. We use that to get Antonio *pasaporte.*"

Antonio was beaming. "My new name is going to be Miguel Pérez Rivera," he said proudly.

This was a lot to take in. It made me sad to think that I would soon be saying goodbye to Antonio and I might never see him again. I put a hand on Daniel's shoulder.

"Listen. You better take care of him, Daniel. If anything happens to him down there, you'll have to answer to me. You hear?"

"No worry, no worry," he answered with a smile. "No worry."

19
Partings

WE SPENT the night there. The house was so small that there really wasn't room for us, even on the floor. So Lonnie and I slept outside in our sleeping bags. We woke up bright and early thanks to a noisy rooster.

Marta gave us a breakfast and then we loaded our backpacks into the Chevy. Lonnie started her up and revved the engine as loud as he could. He looked impressed.

"Really nice job, Pancho," he said. "She sounds great. You have any trouble getting parts?"

Antonio translated for Pancho. "He says he has lots of friends. They got him the parts he needed really fast."

Lonnie got out his wad of cash and paid Pancho. After he counted out the amount Pancho asked for, Lonnie gave him some extra.

"Gracias, amigo," Lonnie said. "You really got us out of a jam. If you ever get to California, I'll take you out for a few drinks."

Pancho grinned. The whole family was there to see us off. It was touching how sad they all seemed that we were going.

I decided to try some of my high school Spanish on Marta. "¿Papel? ¿Lápiz? ¿Por favor?"

She understood me perfectly. She disappeared into the house and came back with a little stub of a pencil and a scrap of paper. I jotted down my address and phone number in California and then handed it to Antonio.

"Promise me that you will write me after you get to Chile. I want to keep in touch with you. I'm going to really miss you."

He held it in his hand and smiled, like I'd given him a hundred-dollar bill. "Sure thing," he said. "But you're going to have to learn more Spanish because I'm not writing you in English!"

Marta looked like she was about to burst into tears. She said something to Antonio while she was looking at me.

"Marta wants to know, can't you stay a few more days?"

"That's really nice of her," I said. "But we need to get back as soon as possible. If we don't cross the border pretty quick, we could be in trouble. We can't really take a chance on delaying."

Not only was I surprised at how sad the whole family was that we were going, but I was also surprised at how sad I was. We didn't really know them all that well, but they had been very nice to us and took us in like we were family or something. I was going to miss them. I wished there was a way to stay a bit longer. But I knew I wouldn't feel safe until I was back in the U.S. And I just needed to get home. We had already been away three weeks, and it seemed like a lot longer than that.

"Hold on," I said.

I got the camera out of my backpack and indicated with my hands that I wanted the whole family, including Antonio, to pose for a picture. They obediently organized themselves as a group and put on big smiles. I got a few shots and then told Lonnie to go stand there with them while I took some more.

I was putting the camera back in my pack when Daniel came over and pointed to it.

"I take you," he said. "I take you the three."

He pointed to me and Lonnie and Antonio. The three of us stood together, with me in the middle, with our arms on each other's shoulders. It made me sad to think that this would the last time the three of us were together.

After the pictures were taken, everyone in the family had to get a big hug from Lonnie and me.

"*Buen camino, joven,*" said Pancho, as he squeezed the life out of me.

"*Que les vaya bien,*" said Marta with tears in her eyes, as she got her turn.

Antonio and I left each other for last. I just looked at him and hoped I would get through it without breaking down like a baby.

"*Abrazo fuerte, amigo,*" I said to him. "*Yo te quiero mucho.*"

Tears were actually coming out of his eyes. "*Yo te quiero muchísimo. Yo te quiero para siempre.*"

And with that Lonnie and I got into the Chevy and took off. I looked back through the rear window. They were all standing there in a group waving at us energetically. They kept on waving until I couldn't see them anymore.

"I can't believe that I'm not going to see him again," I said.

Lonnie was immune to emotional goodbyes.

"Hell, you'll probably see him again someday. He'll probably decide that he doesn't like it wherever he's going and he'll come looking you up in California. Or maybe you'll go visit him down there. Hell, you like traveling. You'll probably go down there someday. Not me though. Not anymore. This trip has gotten it all out of my system. I don't think I'll go traveling anywhere again."

Since we didn't have Antonio with us, I had to be the navigator now. But Antonio had marked the roads we needed to take very clearly on our roadmap. The first thing we had to do was drive right through San Ramón. I was feeling pretty nervous and couldn't wait to get a few miles down the road so we didn't have to worry about running into our friend Alfonso.

We headed out of the town until we were nearly to the spot where the car had broken down nearly two weeks before. I noticed that there was a car parked in pretty much that same spot. As we got closer I got a sick feeling that the rusting hunk of junk I was seeing looked a little too familiar. Sure enough, it was Alfonso.

"Shit, Lonnie! It's that fucking cop!"

"I see him."

Alfonso obviously had seen us too because his junker of a car pulled off the shoulder and onto the road until it was blocking our way. He opened his car door and got out, standing there with his arm extended, telling us to stop.

"Fuck," I cried. "And we were so close to getting out of here. I can't fucking believe this."

I expected Lonnie to slow down, but he didn't. He sped up. In fact, he floored the accelerator. I really couldn't fucking believe it.

"Better move, asshole!" he said with gritted teeth.

As the Chevy went faster and faster, I was convinced that Lonnie had gone insane, that we were going to die. After all this, we were finally going to die. When Alfonso realized that Lonnie wasn't going to stop, he ran in a panic off to the right shoulder of the road. I didn't think his fat ass could move so fast.

Lonnie kept accelerating and steered the car as far to the left as he could. There wasn't much of a shoulder on the left, but Lonnie used as much of it as he could. I braced myself for the impact. We hit the front end of the cop's car and it spun around. By some miracle, the Chevy kept going and Lonnie steered us back onto the road. I was too scared to relax, even a little bit. I just kept gripping the seat and gritting my teeth, as Lonnie leaned his head out of his window and screamed at the top of his lungs like a fucking crazy madman.

"Remember the Alamo! You goddamn fucking mother-fucker!"

I wanted to turn around to see the look on Alfonso's face. But I was petrified. I just sat there in my seat as the car sped down the highway. I kept waiting for the engine to stop or some part of the car to fall off—or at least for one or more of the tires to go flat. But we kept going. We must have both been in shock or something because neither of us said anything for quite a while.

After we had driven enough miles, Lonnie must have figured that it was safe to stop and he pulled over to have a look at the car. There was a big dent where it had hit Alfonso's car, but amazingly nothing more serious than that.

"That's American workmanship," said Lonnie with satisfaction. "Detroit builds cars to survive a collision. U.S. cars don't crumple and fall apart like those sissy little Japanese and European cars."

And then we got back on the road. It was a long old drive back, mostly on the same roads we had driven down on. But we were plenty used to long drives by this point. We didn't stop for long in any one place, but I did take the chance to stop and get photos in some of the places where I hadn't got them the first time.

Lonnie and I still found lots of stuff to talk about. I told him all the different things I had heard from different people about Chile. I told him that it really bothered me not to know what it was really like—especially when everyone's story was completely different. He just said it didn't matter to him because he wasn't planning to go there anyway.

We decided to cross back into California at Mexicali instead of Tijuana. It just got us out of Mexico a little sooner. We had absolutely no trouble getting across the border. The border guard looked impressed when I showed him the letters Frank had given me. He raised an eyebrow and took a good look at us. He asked to see our driver's licenses and he had a good look at them. But that was all. He just waved us through. He didn't have a look inside the car or the trunk. Damn, I thought to myself, we could have snuck Antonio in the trunk with no problem.

As we drove up through the Imperial Valley, I was surprised how much it looked like home. Lonnie said the first thing he wanted to do now that we were back in civilization was to find a Denny's, or maybe a Sambo's. And, sure enough, we stopped at the first Denny's we came across.

It seemed so strange to be sitting in an American restaurant again, where they bring you a nice tall glass of water with ice—without even asking—and you can actually drink the water. And the waitress speaks English and calls you "hon" and you can talk with her and joke with her and she doesn't look at you like you're from Mars.

"It's good to be back," said Lonnie happily, as he lifted his giant burger to his mouth.

From there we drove up along the Salton Sea, mainly because I had always wanted to see it. It was kind of weird seeing a big body of water like that in the middle of the desert. It just seemed to go on and on.

We avoided L.A. by going through San Bernardino, Victorville and Mojave. It was night time when we crossed over the Tehachapis and into the San Joaquin Valley. I remembered looking down at the valley nearly four weeks before when we were driving up the Grapevine and thinking I hated it. Now that big flat valley, with its dots of light in the dark, was the best thing I had ever seen. There's nothing like coming back to the one place you know better than any other place in the world.

When we got back to town, I got a kind of weird feeling. Nothing had changed. It looked just like it always had. But, at the same time, it looked different too. After being in Mexico, the streets in my own town seemed impossibly wide and quiet. The houses also seemed very quiet and very dark. Only the occasional glow of a television bled through the curtains in a picture window to disturb the darkness.

Lonnie dropped me off at my house. I just sort of looked at him before he drove off. We had been through a lot the last several weeks. It's the kind of thing that binds you to someone forever. I sure didn't envy him going back to his house and having to deal with his stepfather.

As for me, I had it pretty easy. My mother was so happy to see me, I felt like I'd done her a big favor by coming home. My father was all right too. After Mom was finished making a fuss over me, though, Dad took me aside and gave me his little speech. He said he had been young once and he understand that there comes a time when young men need to go out and "sow their wild oats." But then he said that he expected me to be more responsible from now on. And then he added the kicker.

"Your mother was very upset when you left without saying anything and she didn't hear anything for weeks," he said. "It would have been nice if she had at least gotten a phone call."

That made me feel like shit—which was how I deserved to feel.

A few days later, I took all the rolls of film I shot down to the Rexall to get them developed. A week after that they came back. I was surprised how many pictures there were. The time we had spent in Mexico had started to feel like a dream—like it never really happened. But now it all began to feel real again, as I looked at all the color pictures of everything from Malibu down to the Guatemala border. There were photos of beaches and farms and men with donkeys on the side of the road and lots of other things I had nearly forgotten about. Like the pictures of Kathy that I took in Michael's bedroom. It was strange to think that, minutes after taking them, I had left her there and would never see her again.

And then there were the pictures of Marisol. Photo after photo showed her leaning back against that palm tree on that beach, throwing her head back, laughing at me and smiling that smile that made me fall in love with her. But now I was seeing something I hadn't seen before. Something like a trace of sadness underneath the laughter. I had seemed to strike a chord when, in my ignorance, I translated her name as Mary Loneliness. Just when I had started to think that the whole business with her had been some sort of temporary insanity, here she was back and making me fall in love with her all over again. My common sense told me to forget about her, but my heart said that someday I was going to pay a visit to Monterrey, Nueva León. Just for the hell of it. Just to see what happens.

But as much as I was enjoying looking at all the pictures of Marisol, my eyes kept going back to one particular photo. The one that Daniel took of the three of us in front of Pancho's house in San Ramón. There we were, three comrades in arms with our arms around each other's shoulders, looking like we had just returned triumphant from the wars and nothing could stop us. There was me, the skinny freckly one in the middle. Lonnie on the left with his messy blond hair and muscles bulging under his tee-shirt, looking better than he had a right to—with a look on his face that said that there wasn't anything he couldn't do. And there was Antonio, small and dark with a big smile full of teeth. Looking like he never had a care in his whole life.

It made me smile. But it also made me sad. A thought passed through my head. Was it possible that the best times I was ever going to have in my entire life were already over?

That's right. In spite of the long boring stretches of driving, in spite of getting thrown into a rotten hell hole of a Mexican jail, in spite of getting so sick that I honestly thought I was going to die, that trip to Mexico was the best time I had ever had in my whole fucking life.

A couple of weeks later, Michael came up from L.A. to visit his family. I was nervous about seeing him, but I knew that I had to. I called his mother and asked if she could send him over to our house. He came over pretty quickly. I don't know what I expected, but when he walked through the door, he just looked like the same old Michael. Suddenly, the things I had learned about him and that had disgusted me didn't seem quite so important.

I told him that I was sorry that Lonnie had whacked him on the head and I hoped that he hadn't been hurt too bad. And I told him that I was sorry that I went off with his camera. I gave it back to him and told him that I thought it was still in pretty good shape despite being carried the entire length of Mexico and back.

He didn't seem too bothered by any of it, but he was glad to get the camera back. He asked if I had taken any photos with it, so I got them out and let him have a look. He seemed pretty impressed.

"God, Dallas," he said. "These are really good. You have a really good eye for composition. You should take a photography course."

His face froze when he got to the photo of the three of us in San Ramón. He actually let out a small gasp.

"Antonio," he said softly.

He stared at it a long time.

"So he *did* go off with the two of you. I was really worried about him. Is he okay?"

"Yeah," I said. "We left him down there with his family."

I figured he didn't need to know any more than that. He kept staring at the photo.

"Do you think I could get a copy of this?"

The question made me uncomfortable. He seemed to like looking at that photo of the three of us just a little too much.

"I don't know if that's such a good idea, Michael."

He gave a nod and didn't push it any further. I felt like I needed to say something else to him.

"Look, Michael, I really don't care what you do in private. I mean, as long as I don't have to see it, you know. But you really need to leave underage kids alone."

"It's not like you think," he said quietly. "I really did care about him."

"Yeah, right."

Nothing he could say would ever convince me that he wasn't wrong but, all the same, I couldn't judge him too hard either. After all, didn't I more or less fall in love with Antonio myself?

In the end I wound up taking Michael's advice about the photography course. I went back to working for Walt and spent the next year saving up money. After I kept my word to Lonnie and paid him half of what he owed to Don and his mother, I kept saving up until I could afford to buy a nice camera of my own. After that, I put everything I earned into the bank.

At the end of the year, I got myself an apartment in Bakersfield, enrolled at the new state university there and signed up for some classes, including photography and Spanish. I was lucky to get a part-time job in a photography shop. Mr. Thomas, the owner, took a liking to me and was always giving me lots of practical tips that I didn't get in class. He also let me use the darkroom for developing my own photographs. Later on I also got a job stringing for the Bakersfield newspaper and regularly got my photos published.

I really missed Antonio and I thought about him a lot. I only heard from him one time after I got home. One day months later, out of the blue, I got a postcard. It was from Santiago, Chile. The picture was of the entrance to a big park. It looked kind of like a castle or something, with lots of trees around it, right in the middle of a city. The caption read, *"Parque Cerro Santa Lucía."*

On the back of the postcard there were some lines scribbled by Antonio. They were in Spanish, but I was pleased with myself that I could read them without having to use a dictionary too much. He wrote that he and Daniel and Gustavo had gotten to Chile okay and that it was a beautiful country and that he knew I would like it there because it was a lot like California. He said that the people there were very friendly and that it was an exciting time to be there. At the bottom he signed it "Miguel Pérez Rivera."

After that, I kept an eye out for anything I could find about Chile in newspapers and magazines. There wasn't very much. Every so often there would be a column on the editorial page of the Bakersfield paper saying that Allende was a Communist and that he was ruining the country.

Then, about two years after our adventure in Mexico, there was quite a bit of news about Chile. There was a military takeover and Allende died. A lot of other people died as well, and a lot of people were arrested and tortured. Under the military government a lot of people disappeared and weren't heard from again.

I worried a lot about Antonio and Daniel. The hardest part was not being able to get any information about them. I didn't have an address to write them and had no way to get in touch. But I knew that Antonio was a survivor and that he knew how to keep his head down. I had to believe that he was a still as good at looking out for himself as he had always been, when he was living on the streets of Los Angeles. Anyway, I prayed that he was.

And when I say I prayed, I really mean that. The Sunday after I read about the coup, I went to Mass at a Catholic church near where I was living in Bakersfield. While I was there kneeling, I prayed to God that he would look out for Antonio and Daniel and keep them safe.

I should have prayed for Lonnie too.

In the end, my number was high enough that I didn't get drafted, but they got Lonnie all right. He was lucky though. By the time he went into the army, Nixon had begun pulling American troops out of Vietnam. He had decided to make the Vietnamese do more of the fighting instead. So Lonnie ended up going to West Germany.

Lonnie was never much of a letter writer, but every so often I would get a short letter from him. He hated boot camp and he was really glad when that part was over. He was glad to be going to West Germany instead of Vietnam, but pretty soon I got letters telling me how he was bored as hell over there and that the time was really dragging and that he couldn't wait to come home. He said he was spending all his off-duty time smoking dope because there was nothing else to do. I wrote back that he should stop complaining and just be glad he wasn't in fucking 'Nam.

But I didn't really have to tell him that. He knew how lucky he was. We both did. So that made it seem like a really bad joke when he ended up coming home in a box anyway.

About a month before he was due to get discharged, he was riding in the back of a military truck on the autobahn. It was involved in some kind of accident and he was one of two soldiers killed.

They shipped his body home and he got a military funeral with an honor guard and everything. There was an American flag on his coffin and at the graveside, they folded it up and handed it to his mother. Lonnie would have had a good laugh over him getting a big hero's funeral just for being in a traffic accident. Not only that but a traffic accident where he wasn't even driving. He would have laughed his fucking ass off over that.

I hated being at that funeral. I hated seeing his mother sobbing through the whole thing. And I hated thinking about the fact that I was never going to see him again. I kept waiting for someone to stand up in the middle of it and say that there had been some sort of mistake and that it wasn't Lonnie in the coffin after all. But, of course, no one did.

At the graveside, though, the strangest thing happened. A single orange butterfly came fluttering out of nowhere and landed right on top of the coffin.

"That's a monarch butterfly," whispered Walt, who was standing next to me. He sounded surprised and impressed. "I wonder what it's doing around here this time of year."

Linda took Lonnie's death pretty hard. She was a complete basket case for about six weeks. Then she started coping by dating Wayne Jefferies and then by getting engaged to him and then by marrying him.

Sometimes, when Wayne would go off on one of his weekend fishing trips, Linda would come into Bakersfield and see me. By this time we had both turned twenty-one, so she and I would meet in a bar at a Mexican restaurant near where I was living and get a little drunk talking about Lonnie.

One time, when I had a bit more to drink than usual, I told her, "You know, sometimes when I'm by myself late at night, I pour myself a glass or two or three of tequila. And while I'm sitting there all alone in the dark, Lonnie comes and visits me. I know it sounds weird, but I really believe his ghost comes and talks to me."

She didn't seem to find this strange at all. But then why would she? She was, after all, the same girl who once believed that candy bars grew on trees.

"And what do you and Lonnie talk about?" she wanted to know.

I laughed. "Just the same old crap we always talked about. Making the same old jokes. Talking the same old shit."

She smiled a sad little smile.

I went on. "One night he told me to be sure and tell you that he misses you and that he's sorry he didn't come back. But he also said you were probably better off the way things worked out."

She laughed. "Yeah, that sounds like him all right."

She took her drink in her hand and studied it.

"And what do *you* tell *him?*"

My mouth was feeling dry. I took another sip of my drink.

"You know what I tell him? I tell him... Hey, Lon, it's time for another adventure. I tell him listen, buddy, we need to get the old Chevy running again. And we have to be sure it's in really good condition this time. Because this time we need to drive it all the way down the Pan-American Highway. All the way down to fucking South America.

"I tell him... Hey, Lon, we need to go find Antonio."

About the Author

Scott R. Larson was born and grew up in California's San Joaquin Valley. He has also lived in France, Chile and for many years in and around Seattle, Washington. He currently lives in the West of Ireland where he writes one of the internet's longest running film blogs.

Lightning Source UK Ltd.
Milton Keynes UK
UKOW02f0743050914

238074UK00002B/27/P